MASON DIXON, MONSTER HUNTER

MASON DIXON, MONSTER HUNTER

SEASON ONE

ERIC R. ASHER

Charlotte, NC

FALSTAFF
BOOKS
WWW.FALSTAFFBOOKS.COM

I

MASON DIXON, MONSTER HUNTER

C hrist Mason," Dylan said, interrupting his own muttered curses. "I haven't had this much mud in my boots since the flood."

"Which one?" I asked, glancing back at him. Missouri wasn't exactly what you'd refer to as a dry state.

Dylan tugged at his leg a few times before it came loose with a sucking pop. He wiped away the short mop of soaking wet blond hair that had fallen into his eyes.

"Just try to keep the tent out of the mud this time," I said. "Yeah?"

A string of curses exploded from Dylan that would've made my grandma blush, and that's no small thing.

"One time," he said. "It happened one damn time when we were still in *college*. Will you ever let that go?"

"Wasn't so long ago."

"Why are we out here in the rain?" Dylan said. "This is a mess, Mason."

"You want to go stay in town?" I asked, stepping quickly around another mud hole. "It seems like a pretty warm and inviting place. Pretty sure every street corner is haunted, but other than that it's great."

"Shut up. Louisiana, Missouri was creepy as hell."

I grinned and pulled myself up higher on the hill. The underbrush and canopy kept the ground drier here in most areas, and I was relieved when we didn't get stuck so easily. We walked for another thirty minutes before we heard the scream the locals had told us about. It started low and rose into a high-pitched screech, raising goosebumps on my arm as it broke into a stuttering series of barks.

"Did you catch it?" I asked.

Dylan nodded quickly. "Say something. We can edit it later."

"Mason Dixon here," I said softly, looking down at the camera and gesturing to the forest around us. "We're in the woods. We haven't traveled more than a few miles into the trees outside Louisiana, Missouri. You could almost mistake that cry for a big cat, but I tell you now it's not a cat. Oh no, it's bigger and harder to find than any mountain lion, cougar, or panther the locals talk about."

Something cracked deep in the woods, and I tilted my head to focus on the sound. When nothing else followed it, I turned back to the camera.

"Want to know what I think? It's Momo. Yes, I think that cry is, in fact, the Missouri Monster. Now, some folks think it's a sasquatch with a pumpkin-shaped skull, but me?" I shook my head. "I think it's something else. It's a rare sasquatch to reach nine feet tall, and we've spoken to witnesses that put Momo closer to ten feet tall!"

Dylan made a gesture in an effort to quiet me down a bit. Sometimes the excitement got to me.

"Follow me," I said, "and let's see what's really out there."

"That was great!" Dylan said. "This is going to be our best episode of *Cryptid Hunter* yet. I think you should play it up more. Talk with your hands, you know?"

I gave him a smile. "You bet. We almost hit fifty views on the last one, and that was our best yet."

"I'm telling you, that video of the kingdoodle should've gone viral."

"It was a *big* lizard," I said. "No doubt there. But who names these things?"

"Please," Dylan said. "If you're hunting cryptids in Missouri, you better be used to stupid names. But the kingdoodle ... that was *amazing*, Mason. I'm telling you, special effects are ruining our profession."

I grinned at Dylan. "Well, look at how many hoaxes are out there. You can kind of understand people not believing they're looking at a three-foot-tall lizard some eight feet in length. We could have screwed with the perspective without needing special effects."

Dylan sighed. "I know, I know. Let's just find out what's here and stop worrying about all the hoaxers."

Lightning flashed in the distance, enough to cast jagged shadows through the woods and make every shifting branch look like a deadly threat. Thunder crashed a moment later, and the grating cries echoed around us again.

"Let's turn the lights up," Dylan said. "I can't see shit."

"We're close," I said. "I don't want to scare it off."

A brighter, wider beam of light ignited behind me, and I froze. Dylan bumped into me with the camera and cursed. Rain trickled through the canopy of falling leaves, creating a cacophony of sound that would mask a great many things.

"What is it?" Dylan asked.

I pointed at the soggy earth as he stepped up beside me. "Tracks."

Three toes and what looked like a fourth arching out from the side of the print branched from the deep indentation. I crouched down and pulled off the leaves covering part of it.

"Bear?" Dylan asked.

I shook my head. "It's far too long to be a bear." I frowned, trying to tell if there was any hair or fur, but it was hopeless in what light we had.

"Take a few steps back," Dylan said, "so we can record you finding it."

I pursed my lips and then stood up, following our own short trail backwards through the underbrush.

"Holy hell," Dylan said. "Do you smell that?"

Dylan pointed the camera at me again, and I slipped easily into the personality of the host for the show. It may have been my sudden need to escape the awful stench setting my nostrils on fire.

"We're so close now we can smell it!" I said, shaking my head quickly as I spoke. "And it smells terrible. Like a … like a skunk run straight through a tire fire." I shivered in over-animated disgust before gesturing for the viewers to follow. "Come on."

Thunder and lightning crashed again, and I could have sworn the trunk of a tree moved. All I had with me was my grandfather's tranquilizer gun he used to shoot bobcats with. He never wanted to kill them, even when they came for his chickens. I left the gun in its holster, but my eyes stayed locked on the shadows for another few seconds.

"Go on Mason," Dylan said, prodding me to get back to work.

"Look there!" I said, almost prancing around the footprint I knew to be just ahead of us. I pulled out a butterfly knife that unfolded into a wicked-looking sawblade with a ruler along the back. I carefully used it to move some leaves away from the print before holding the ruler up and leaning back.

"Look at that now. Ten inches on my knife here from tip to base, and that foot's at least twice as long." I put my finger at the end of the blade and then shifted it over to make my point. "We have three toes, and that's a lot like other bigfoot sightings, but look at the toe coming off the side. Don't think I've seen that before, except on Missouri Monster sightings. And we all know there haven't been many of those."

"What's that?" I said, cocking my head to the side. "Some of you haven't heard of Momo? Short for the Missouri Monster?" I went through a quick spiel about the earliest sightings of our very own sasquatch in Missouri. Of course, some folks—including me—thought it was something else, something darker with a pumpkin-shaped head that liked to eat dogs. And possibly kids.

Dylan's eyes widened behind the camera. "Something behind you," he hissed. Lightning flashed, and whatever had been behind me was no longer my concern. A giant's silhouette loomed behind Dylan, easily mistaken for a tree but for the way it slowly closed the distance.

"Run!" I shouted, but it was too late for a warning. The shadow behind Dylan snapped forward, pulling him backwards briefly before hurling him away. Dylan crashed to the earth, tumbling deeper into the woods with a cry. I fumbled at the snap to my holster and finally managed to raise the tranquilizer gun.

Something wide and furry and thick as a log smacked down across my arms, sending me into the mud. I heard Dylan scrabbling nearby as heavy footsteps rushed toward us, squelching in the soaked earth and leaves before a horrible, hollow thump echoed through the woods. But those footsteps had sounded behind me. Then what the hell had been in front of …

A flash. Only a glimpse showed me the soiled flesh before it struck out at me. I thought I was dead, but again that furry log pushed me to the ground, and then it roared. The bellowing sound threatened to burst my eardrums, and the sheer bass of it vibrated my body.

The light mounted on the camera rolled across the muddy path, and I fell backwards staring up at the shaggy fur-covered head. It had to be seven feet tall if it was an inch, carrying a smaller furry form under its arm. The creature held its hand out to me, as if it was telling me to stay put. Then it gave chase, pursuing the thing with fur so black it seemed to be eating every bit of light.

It leapt over Dylan, and I could have sworn it was chasing a shadow, something that had no right to be lithe. It moved like the crack of a whip.

"Dylan! Dylan! Did you see that!" I said, running over to him. My racing heart stammered when my eyes locked onto Dylan's. He stared blankly at the forest canopy, his blood-coated face and grotesquely twisted neck lit by the cold white light.

The sickening hollow crack on the tree. It had been Dylan. I didn't need to feel the displaced vertebrae in his neck or the lack of pulse beneath my shaking bloody fingers to know, but I checked anyway.

Dylan Jane was gone.

And the monsters' howls tore through the night.

2

_____

F ive years," I said, swirling a bit of bourbon I'd found in the old cabin. I wouldn't have been surprised if it was far older than five years itself. I slammed the rest of it and set the glass on the coffee table.

"Since we lost Dylan?" Emma asked, wiping a speck of dust off the camera with a microfiber cloth. She squinted at the lens, turning it in the dim light. Satisfied, she finally laid it back in its case. Emma brushed a hand through her short brown hair and glanced at me.

I nodded when I met her eyes. "Yeah, since Dylan."

"Well," she said, "I imagine he'd be right happy to hear you were still making crazy videos in the woods that no one watches."

"You're probably right about that."

"Of course I am," she said with a smile.

I exhaled slowly and checked the buckles on my holster. You couldn't be too careful in Missouri. If you didn't run into some meth heads in the middle of nowhere looking for a quick score while rebuilding the lab they just torched or some good old boys running moonshine, you might just run into a bear.

Emma checked the CO_2 tranquilizer pistol on her hip, an odd-looking contraption that took a CO2 cartridge up front and accepted gel collar darts at the back.

"You bring some 3.0 CC darts for that thing?" I asked.

She nodded. "What did you bring for the rifle?" She toed the case on the floor between us. It held what looked like a bastardized M4, but was in fact a CO2 cartridge rifle.

"Five-point-oh and ten-point-oh."

"Ten-point-oh CC? Are you planning on bringing down a sasquatch?" She slowly raised an eyebrow.

I laid two barrels for a Magnum Research Desert Eagle into the case in front of me, one .44 and one .50 caliber. I preferred to shoot the .44 rounds, as the recoil was far less likely to break my wrists, but sometimes we needed a bigger boom. Tranquilizers were preferred, but we weren't going out unprepared. I kicked the case closed and threw the latches, meeting Emma's hazel eyes.

"You haven't seen one," Emma said.

"Maybe," I said, remembering that lumbering shadow and the sickening crack of Dylan's skull bouncing off an oak tree. Remembering the shocked look in his dead eyes ... "Maybe not. But there *are* bad things out there."

I rolled my neck, grabbed the handle of the gun case, and stood up. "Let's go see if old man Raleigh is as crazy as his wife thinks."

"You want to record this one for the show?"

I glanced at the schoolhouse clock on the wall, as if it might give me an answer. "Sure."

"You feel like being 'on' for this?"

I turned to look over my shoulder as I led the way out the front door. "An actor's work is never done."

Emma rolled her eyes and followed me out to the old three-wheel ATVs. Once we had everything strapped down, and buttoned our jackets up against the cold, we started downhill. It was easy to find the path the old man had told us about; it looked like an archway set in the wall of trees bordering the holler.

In my experience, folks in the Missouri backwoods liked to refer to most any clearing with a cabin in it as a holler. I took a deep breath, hit the button on the camera mounted on the ATV's handlebars, and flipped the switch on in my head, too.

"We've got a good one for you this week," I said, raising my voice half an octave and injecting a level of excitement I hadn't felt in a damn long time. "Who out there knows what a gowrow is?" I paused, raising an eyebrow. "No one? Well, that's what we're out chasing today.

"Now, you might think a lizard the size of a small car would be easy to find, but just look at some of the gators they've got down in Florida." I bounced heavily in the seat as the ATV hit a dip. The cheap stabilizer on the camera did its job, and I knew we'd still end up with a decent shot. "And those are just the ones we've *found*."

Emma cursed behind me. I slowed and spared a glance back. She'd slammed into the same rut I had and nearly lost the load on the back of her ATV.

"What was that?" I asked, making sure she hadn't said something else I'd missed.

She slowed and came up beside me. "What the hell was that old man doing up here? I mean, most folks I know his age would be broken into half a dozen pieces on a path this rough."

"Don't underestimate the country folk, Emma. My grandpa used to say the locals were made from hearty stock. You don't know the half of it."

Emma shook her head and revved the engine. "Alright, let's just get up to the bluffs."

"Raleigh's wife said it wasn't really a bluff. More of an overhang. We'll see soon enough.

"Nancy," Emma said. "She has a name for God's sake."

"I'm sure she does," I said. "It's a shame we don't know what it is."

I wasn't sure if Emma or the ATV engines growled louder. My finger brushed the edge of the trigger for the ATV's horn, and I slid it off quickly. We'd installed what amounted to a train horn in the chassis. It was great for scaring things away. Bear mace? Oh no, *train horn*.

We spent another fifteen minutes bouncing down one hill and up the next until the relatively clear path became something far closer to a deer track. It was narrow, winding, and not much of a path at all.

I pulled some goggles over my face and waited for Emma to do the same before we plunged down the next hill. The narrow path didn't give us much resistance on the ground, but branches cracked us across the face and arms and headlights every few feet.

About the time I was ready to curse vehemently at the next tree that dared to hit me, the path broke wide at the base of a hill. We crossed a shallow creek that was currently dry, but likely roared when the rains came.

"Jesus," Emma said, pulling to a stop beside me.

"Emma Lucille Rainwater," I said. "Such language." I followed her gaze and whistled. "That's maybe not natural." I pulled the goggles off and hung them on the ATV's handlebars.

Emma started unpacking the good camera while I took in the odd structure in front of us. "I can see why the old man called it a bluff," she said.

I nodded slowly. It was a sheer cliff, but what made it? There was no water here other than a shallow creek, and no signs there had been anything more significant than that, and the formation was perhaps three hundred feet long from end to end where it tapered down into the earth.

"It almost looks like one of those amphitheaters built to look like a shell."

Emma frowned. "Maybe a little bit. But what do you think it's made out of? Looks like limestone."

"I think it is," I said, "but it also kind of looks like a wave carved from stone."

"Shh," she hissed.

Boom.

"The hell was that?" I whispered back.

Boom.

"Guns out."

Boom.

It was loud and closer than I would have liked without knowing

11

what the hell it was. The booms sounded again, echoing around the clearing and sending a small flock of birds screaming up into the sky.

The booms came closer together, like the ever-quickening beat of a deep drum. I raised the tranquilizer rifle to my shoulder and waited. If there was one thing my father had taught me, it was how to let the prey come to you. If there was one thing Dylan's death had taught me, it was don't be afraid to shoot first and apologize later. I didn't like shooting things, especially endangered things, but I didn't like dying either.

Another series of booms sounded, and I could feel it in my feet. *Boom. Boom. Boom. Boom.*

And then silence reigned. We waited, guns raised, for almost a solid minute. When nothing made a sound, I broke the silence.

"You still recording?" I asked.

Emma nodded.

"Right then," I said, in a voice just above a whisper. "You all heard that, and now we're going in for a closer look. So, don't get too close to the screen. I wouldn't want you to get any goo splattered on you."

"Goo?" Emma said, one eyebrow crawling up into her hairline.

"Emma, our noble cameraman, agrees!"

Boom.

My gaze snapped back to the shadows of the limestone. "Stay behind me," I said. "I don't know what's down there, but I'm pretty sure the old man is in his right mind at this point."

The next thing I saw was the tracks leading down a wide earthen slope that vanished into the darkness of the overhang. I flipped out my butterfly knife and unfolded it so I could get at the ruler. The tracks were huge, and they were deep enough that I knew damn well no bear had made them.

"Well," I said, looking up at the camera, "I think we have a big one here."

The glint of white in the afternoon sun as it broke through the clouds caught my eye. I cursed. "Shut the camera off, Emma."

"Why? This is great stuff."

I didn't respond, but I heard the click of the screen folding back against the body of the camera.

"Bones," I said, pointing to a pile worthy of a mass grave. The more I studied it, the more worried I became. Leave it to Father Noah to give us an assignment chasing down a depraved cryptid. Some bones were easily recognizable, like the deer and half of the skull of a large hawk. Others were just ribs or shattered lengths of white bone, splinters that would never be recognizable.

"One gowrow could have done all that?" Emma asked, though we both knew the answer.

"Not likely. We need to see if there are human bones in there. Look for something obvious, like a skull or ribcage. Maybe a femur. And keep your tranq locked and loaded."

"Look how deep those tracks are," Emma said, crouching done next to me. "You think it's a maneater?"

"If it *is* a gowrow, and a maneater, there's no coming back from that. We have to put it down."

"How the hell did we end up here?" she asked with a sigh.

I wasn't sure if she meant that in an existential way, or if she just meant how we'd ended up chasing down a gowrow in the hills of southern Missouri, but I was pretty sure the answer was the same either way.

Noah.

"What's the catch, Father? Why do you want to hire me to hunt cryptids? I already do that, for free."

The priest had a kind face and spoke with a soft confidence that made you want to instantly trust him, so of course, I didn't trust him an inch.

"There is no catch," Noah said. "The Church has noticed your activities and penchant for tracking down beasts that would do harm to our parishioners."

"I thought y'all just cared about demons and what have you."

ERIC R. ASHER

"We do not care for demons, unless you speak of men who can still be saved."

Gag me with knife. "Why me?"

"Your web series."

"Are you kidding?" I said. "Half those shows end in us finding an unidentifiable tuft of fur or badly faked footprints. Sometimes you can still see the logo from the damn shoe we used. We don't air conclusive footage."

Noah smiled. "You include details no one could know without encountering the beasts themselves. Just small things. The description of Momo's smell, the sounds of some of the … larger creatures, and how those cryptids can use almost anything, even stone, as camouflage. Most telling perhaps was the story of the birds that appeared to you as oversized eagles."

"We never released the footage of Momo," I said quietly, clenching my hand into a fist while I ignored his clumsy hints. Dylan had died recording that. I never would have turned that into an episode.

"I have a higher calling," Noah said. "And for that calling, we are granted resources. I believe we can help each other."

"You hacked me," I said, rolling over the security of our network in my mind. It wasn't great. I wasn't exactly preparing to defend my videos of our adventures from intruders. Even if someone got their hands on them. They'd do what? Sell it to a tabloid?

Noah ran a hand over his chin, smoothing his close-cropped beard. "We employ resources that are gifted with accessing data that we need."

I narrowed my eyes. "Not very Christian of you, is it?"

Noah crossed his arms. "What do you have to lose? We have a rogue cryptid outside Columbia, Missouri, and we are willing to pay you to go after it. Even should we fail to fulfill our end of the bargain, *you* will still have footage to produce another episode of *Cryptid Hunter*."

I let out a short laugh. "It sounds kind of stupid when you say it like that."

It galled me, but he was right. I didn't have anything to lose. I'd

14

already lost my best friend, and I'd been ignoring most everyone else since then. Emma, one of our childhood friends, had tagged along for a few episodes, and maybe she'd like to help out with whatever the Church had going. I shrugged. "Alright, Father. Sign me up. Let's see what you have to offer."

3

I patted the butt of the tranquilizer rifle slung over my shoulder. Noah had kept his word so far, but Church folks still made me nervous. Even when they paid on time. Maybe especially then.

"You remember that first trip to Columbia?" I asked as we approached the lip of the leaf-obscured pit full of bones.

"Was that the mutant boar?"

I let out a short laugh. "No, that was Moberly, I think. Columbia was the college."

Emma didn't respond.

I glanced back and found her gaze ready to cut me in half.

"Yes, Mason, I'm aware of the *college* in Columbia. I *attended* college in Columbia. At Mizzou in fact, which isn't even the only college there."

"No disrespect meant."

"Then don't be disrespectful."

I stepped down into the bones, silently praying I wouldn't sink into a pit of rot, but hoping our conversation would die before it broke into another argument. A bone cracked beneath my heel, loud enough to be a gunshot.

"Smooth," Emma said, walking along the outer edge of the bone pit.

"Looks like a few deer," I said, "and a lot of smaller varmints."

"Varmints?" Emma said with a small snort.

I wasn't going to be living that college comment down anytime soon. I kicked a few bones away with the toe of my boot. They rattled across a cleaned deer skeleton like the morbid snap of a snare drum. I didn't see anything out of the ordinary, other than the lack of flesh on any of the bones, which accounted for the near absence of stench I'd have expected from a pile of dead things.

"Shit," Emma said, the biting sarcasm flowing away in an instant. She stepped down into the pit and picked a broken branch up from the leaves. She leaned forward with it, poked at something a few times, and then raised what was quite clearly a human skull.

"Out," I said. "Get out of the pit. Safeties off." I raised the stock to my shoulder and swept the area around us again.

Emma slipped and crashed into the pit, sending a cascade of stained white bones over the edge to clatter down into the limestone depression. We waited, and I could hear my own heartbeat pounding in my ears.

Boom.

We both froze. I don't care how many times you've encountered something in the wild, you still freeze for a split second.

Boom.

"*Move!*" I hissed, backpedaling while keeping my tranquilizer aimed around Emma. She was almost out. We could get back on the ATVs and come back with bigger guns. 10cc darts? I should have brought the 50cc cannon. This was a mistake. The old man wasn't crazy at all.

Boom. Boom. Boom. BoomBoomBoom.

The gowrow erupted from its lair like it had been spit forth by an angry god. Its stubby, bulbous body might have been humorous paired with its long scaly neck if not for the tusks fit for a mammoth gleaming in the dying sun. It would take that creature zero effort to kill us in one charge.

17

Its movements seemed awkward, but its attacks were practiced. The gowrow swiped at Emma with a four-toed webbed foot, a lethal claw extending from each digit. She fell backwards and rolled away, barely avoiding the attack.

Any doubt this gowrow was a maneater fled in a heartbeat.

I cranked the air pressure as high as it would go on the tranquilizer gun and fired. The dart rose slightly in a wind disturbance created by the massive creature and pinged harmlessly off the field of spiky scales lining its back. I cursed, flipped the butt of the rifle open, and loaded another dart.

Emma wasted no time, firing into the gowrow's underbelly with her own tranquilizer. The dart stuck, but the animal didn't so much as flinch. The darts Emma was firing didn't have enough punch to knock out something so large. The best we could hope for was to make it groggy.

I sprinted back to the ATV and slammed the button down on the horn. To call it deafening would be a gross understatement. The train horn thundered through the holler, drowning out the roar of the gowrow.

Any hope of the sound scaring the gowrow back into its lair faded when the beast trundled toward me at an alarming pace. Emma slipped into the woods beside the bone pit. The gowrow lowered its head, leveling its tusks to a height that would run me and the ATV through like a kebab.

I raised the tranquilizer, aimed ahead of the beast, and fired. The 10cc dart launched with a pop and lodged inside the gowrow's sizable nostril. The creature reared back, the momentum of its massive form causing it to slide forward as it tipped over and rolled past us, uncomfortably close to the ATV.

"That got its attention," I said, throwing the case on the back of the bike open.

"Where'd you hit it?" Emma asked, pulling a .454 Taurus revolver out of the case.

"Nose," I said, dropping a clip of .44 ammo into the case before crushing the release on the side of the gun and flipping the .44 caliber barrel off. I scooped up the .50 caliber barrel and slid it home before jamming the lone clip into the reassembled hand cannon. Nine rounds. Christ, I should have brought more.

"Shoot to kill," Emma said. "Don't get all noble on me now."

I grimaced. I didn't want to kill the thing, it was a gowrow for God's sake. How many were left? Was I going to kill the last one? I despised poachers and rare game hunters. I'd rather see *their* heads mounted on a bloody wall. But a maneater was a maneater, and that wouldn't change. That took the decision out of my hands. If I let it live and some unsuspecting hunter got eaten up? Or a backpacking family?

The gowrow righted itself. I watched in confusion as its tail curled up and lashed out like a bull whip, the ends separating as if it were a flail. Emma tackled me just before the gowrow tore the fender off the ATV.

She yelped, aimed awkwardly from the ground, and fired her hand cannon. The gun barked twice, staggering the gowrow before Emma curled up onto herself. "It got me, Mason. Jesus, it burns."

Blood spread across the camouflage on her back left shoulder, seeping through the fabric at a rate that told me we needed to get it closed up, and fast.

I pulled myself up onto a knee and rested the pistol on the seat of the ATV. The gowrow was up again, but moving slow. Emma had clipped it, disorienting the beast. I'd been shooting guns as long as I could remember. My grandfather skipped right past teaching me how to shoot a BB gun and moved straight onto .22 rifles. Shooting a fixed target is nothing like shooting at an angry stubby dragon that just flayed your friend, but practice makes things a hell of a lot easier.

Three shots rang out, and the gowrow shook them off again. I dropped the clip and slid a new one home. Breathe, I reminded myself. Just breathe. Even pressure. Lead the head just enough ...

The gowrow opened its jaws and roared, its upper and lower tusks scything apart like a goddamned guillotine. I exhaled, and fire burst from the pistol's barrel one last time. The gowrow stumbled and collapsed a few feet from the bone pit, its tusks scarring the earth under the weight of the creature's head.

"Emma," I said, turning away from the gowrow's death rattle.

"I'm alright," she said. "Might need a stitch or two."

"Get your Kevlar off. Let me see."

"Lame, Mason." She winced and dropped the vest to the ground. "Always trying to find a way to get my shirt off."

"Since the seventh grade," I said flatly, gently helping her peel the bloody undershirt off. "Wow, that's not deep at all."

"You never were a very deep kid," Emma said with a small laugh.

I frowned at the wound on her shoulder. "Funny. It's bleeding like mad, but it's not too deep, and the cuts are clean."

"That thing's tail must have had a toxin in it, or at least an anticoagulant to keep the blood thin."

I slid a small first aid kit out of the gun case while Emma talked. It took only a minute to flush the cuts with peroxide and tape them shut with a few butterfly bandages. It still bled faster than I liked, so we doubled up with a gauze bandage.

"You know a lot of cultures harvest cryptids for medicinal uses," I said. "I wonder if anyone has ever ground up gowrow tusks, or used the venom in that tail for anything."

I tightened the gauze bandage.

"You're pretty terrible at distracting your patient," Emma said.

"That obvious, huh?" I asked, setting the gauze in place with some tape. "Well, I think you're good. It's not bleeding through yet."

"Do you think it was the only one here?" she asked.

"I haven't heard anything else," I said, handing her shirt over. "But we need to check it out. I can't imagine one gowrow creating a pile of bones that large. Not without decades of nesting here. And if it had been here for decades, I suspect there would have been more rumors about it."

"That makes sense." Emma flinched as she adjusted her Kevlar over the bloodied top. "This isn't cut out for stopping claws. I'm going to need a new vest."

"I'll cover it. Don't worry."

"The show will cover it," Emma said. "Now that you're a sensation."

"Sensation?" I said, raising an eyebrow.

"Yes," she said. "At the moment, the sensation is nausea."

I gave her a flat look. Our views *had* increased a bit over the past several months, and that was always cause for a little celebration.

"So? Are we going to check the bluffs before we go or what?"

"We can come back tomorrow," I said. "We should get your shoulder looked at."

"It's good enough to walk." Emma raised the .454, aimed, and fired without warning. She flinched a little, much like my eardrums, and gave a small half shrug. "I can shoot. I'm happy with that. Besides, I'm not liking the idea of riding on that ATV while this is still burning."

"So be it. We'll sweep the bluff, give the painkillers time to soften you up, and then head out for the night."

She eyed the gowrow. "I don't think we should put *that* on the show," she said.

"Probably not. Although we might be able to make it look fake enough."

Emma rubbed the back of her neck. "Alright, let's get this over with."

4

N oah," the father said when he picked up after the twelfth ring.

"Bad time?" I asked, unable to keep the impatience from bleeding through in my words.

"There is never a bad time for righteous work. Are you ready for your next assignment?"

"You have another one already?" I asked, somewhat surprised. Cryptid cases didn't seem to pop up too terribly often. I reined in my curiosity. "We have a dead gowrow that needs cleanup."

"Where?"

"Aisle six," I said. "Track the transmitter."

"What transmitter?" Noah asked, sounding genuinely perplexed.

"Noah wants to know which transmitter," I said to Emma.

"Tell him to use the GPS signal on the ATVs we rented. And maybe tell him he's going to have to pay for some body work on those ATVs."

I glanced back at the bikes, namely the bike missing its rear fender. "Yeah, ATVs took a bit of damage. Emma said you can track the GPS units on those. So have them do that."

"Who told Emma about that?" Noah asked, dropping the façade of confusion.

"Who told you about the GPS?" I shouted back to Emma as she prodded at the gowrow's tusk.

"A little bird," Emma said.

A slow smile stretched the corners of my mouth. "That would be a bird ... sir."

"Himari was *not* authorized to disclose that."

"That you're tracking us?" I asked, somewhat amused. "We just assumed you were, really. Himari's got tabs on everyone's cell.Why even bother with the GPS on an ATV?"

"She what?" Noah asked.

I brought up my contacts and texted Himari. *Where's Noah?*

"Explain yourself," Noah said. "I did not ask her to track your phone."

"It's not just ours," I said as Himari's message came back. "I see you're at that Irish pub downtown again."

Silence greeting my words. I wasn't sure if Noah had muted his phone or was just spending a good deal of effort coming up with an excuse.

"Cleanup will be there tonight," Noah grumbled. "Now go annoy someone else."

The line went dead.

I texted a thank you back to Himari, who responded only with an emoji of a cat.

As much as the kid had annoyed me when we first met, or maybe I should say when she first hacked into my network, she could be damn useful.

"There's a ramp down into the fissure," Emma said.

I snapped a flashlight onto the barrel of my tranquilizer rifle and brought one over for Emma, too. She shined it down the rocky slope.

"I only see fifty or sixty ankle breakers," I muttered. "Let's get this done."

What had seemed a narrow path was, in actuality, quite wide. It made sense, considering the girth of the awkwardly shaped gowrow. Some of the larger stones in the path were driven into the dirt. I suspected a stampeding gowrow exerted a great deal of force when it stomped around. It wasn't long before the limestone bluff eclipsed the light above us, and all that lit the shadows below were our flashlights.

We stopped at the bottom of the ramp, an eerie quiet enveloping us as the smaller stones rolling beneath our steps ceased their movement, and the hard-packed soil muted any sound above us. I shined a light down the left path and swept it to the right.

"You got the camera on you?" I asked.

Emma hesitated. "Yeah?"

"Let's do a quick shot here. I really don't want to be out in the middle of nowhere next weekend to film an entirely new show."

"I thought the middle of nowhere was the only place you liked to be." Emma had the camera up and pointed at me before I even had a chance to respond.

I ignored her comment and jumped into my onscreen personality, albeit a bit quieter than normal. "We found the lair!" I gestured at the expanse of shadowy limestone and dirt around us. "The gowrow might be down one of these very paths. Just look at the dirt, clearly compacted by something heavy. I don't see any good tracks, but maybe as we get deeper. Follow me."

The gowrow had attacked from somewhere to the right of the bone pit, so we took the right path. I guessed that it would turn, following the curve of the limestone wall above us, and the fissure didn't disappoint.

"Kill it," I said.

Emma lowered the camera. "You see something?"

"Yeah, more bones."

She stepped up beside me and cursed. "Human."

I nodded. "Three skulls at a glance, completely stripped of flesh. They're either very old, or …" I crouched down to get a better look at the bones. Each was marred with chisel-like slashes and cracked wide open. A pair of shattered femurs came close to forming a grisly skull and crossbones. "Marrow's gone from the large bones."

"Is there another gowrow down here?" Emma asked.

"I don't know," I said, answering honestly.

"Then lie to me, Mason," she hissed.

Emma could almost always tell when I was lying. She'd known me too damn long. It had led me to generally not lie to her, which was sometimes good, and sometimes not.

We followed the curve of the fissure, past the bones, and a wide cavern opened before us. It went on and on, and the ceiling swept upwards, leaving what had to be a tenuous stretch of earth supporting the cave.

"What in the hell?" I said. "This looks like an entrance to the bloody Meramec Caverns, and I've never even *heard* of this place."

"Without the gift shop I guess I can see it," Emma said.

I raised an eyebrow. "Sarcasm? At a time like this?" I took it as a good sign that her injuries weren't too bad.

"Christ," Emma said, her eyes widening as she pointed behind me.

I spun, tranquilizer raised, as I faced down ... a very dead gowrow. Long dead from what I could tell. Its bones had been broken in places, its flesh long since rotted or eaten away. The age showed in moldered yellow hues of bone.

"You could have told me it was dead." I bent down to pick up one of the beast's claws. It had a fairly terrifying resemblance to a raptor claw, which I was quite glad I hadn't known before facing down the very alive gowrow, which was now also very dead.

"Want to do a scene?" Emma asked.

I nodded. "Don't get the whole skeleton in though. Let's focus on the claw. People will think we mistook a dinosaur bone for a gowrow."

"Do we have that many dinosaur bones in Missouri? I thought it was mastodons mostly, right?"

"Just one dinosaur I'm aware of," I said. "It's actually the state dinosaur."

"Of course," Emma said, "because why wouldn't we have a state dinosaur?"

"Maybe the gowrow descended from it."

"I like that," Emma said. "Let's use it in the clip."

So we did. I spent a few minutes jabbering about the *Hypsibema missouriensis,* and how the gowrow may have descended from it. A few dramatic "did you hear that's" while Emma tossed rocks in the background, and comparisons to a raptor claw, and we wrapped an engaging, if not completely full of bullshit, segment.

I was making one last run through the cavern when I heard the tapping.

5

W hat the hell is making that sound?" Emma asked.
"Something big," I said, the tapping firing up again.
"Define big?" Emma hissed.
"Not as big as the gowrow," I said, hoping that might help dissuade any flights of common sense.

Three taps, a pause, and then three more taps. It echoed around us. I tried to angle my head to pick out exactly which path it was coming from, but it was nearly impossible with the acoustics of the cavern.

"It's deeper inside the cave," I said, walking back into the deepest part of the shadows. The flashlight showed a relatively smooth floor, and now that I was really looking, I could see the indentation where the gowrow had likely slept.

We followed the curve of the indentation and found another around the corner. I stepped into the small dip in the stone, and the taps grew louder.

"Where is it?" Emma asked, close behind me, sidling up to one of the smaller limestone boulders in the cavern. The taps sounded again, followed by a guttural chirp, and Emma hopped backward. "It was right next to me. Mason, I don't think these are rocks."

"What?" I said, shining the light onto the limestone boulders.

"It's coming from that keg-sized stone. I'm telling you."

I gave her a doubtful look and touched the stone. Three taps sounded again, and something pushed against my palm. "Holy shit, those are eggs."

"Those? Plural?"

"Hell yes," I said, pushing one of the eggs to see how heavy it was. "It's a little soft, but I'm pretty sure we can carry it without too much trouble."

"Are you *insane?* Have you already forgotten mommy dearest that tried to eat our faces off? I haven't. I haven't forgotten that, Mason."

"It's soft. And the gowrow's already pushing on the shell."

Emma cursed behind me. "At least record something for the show," she muttered.

I gave her a beaming smile.

She started recording and pointed at me to start talking.

"You won't believe what we found in the gowrow's cave," I said with enough enthusiasm that any sane person would probably question my sobriety. I turned and gestured wildly to the boulders. "Eggs! It's an unbelievable find, it is. Two intact gowrow eggs. Now, I'm leaving them here so they can hatch and grow up in the woods like they were meant to, so don't you come looking for them."

Emma raised an eyebrow.

"In a few months, two new gowrow will be born. If the locals are right, there hasn't been a baby gowrow in southern Missouri going on a hundred years now." I pressed gently on the shell. "See how soft that is? It's no stone, that's for sure. Now, I have to sneak out of the cavern before their momma comes back. Won't be able to make another show if I'm dead." I gave the camera a huge smile. "Remember, just because they're scary monsters, that doesn't necessarily mean they want to eat you."

Emma shut the viewer and tucked the camera back into its carrying case. "You said you're leaving the eggs here."

"Yes."

"Which means you're not, are you?"

"Correct." The large egg, the one that had been so conversational, wasn't really as big as a keg. I managed to get my arms around it and pick it up without too much trouble, careful not to crack the soft shell. It was still probably fifty pounds, which was pretty awkward in the shape of an egg. "Grab the little one, will you?"

"You tell your viewers to stay safe. You tell me to pick up the egg with the face-eating gowrow." Emma frowned and adjusted her holster, but she carefully picked up the second egg. "What are we doing with these, Mason? I know you're not going to make omelets out of them."

"Right you are," I said, taking slow steps to the front of the cavern and patiently leading the way back up the ramp. I kicked a few of the larger stones that were still loose out of the path, feeling my way where I couldn't see around the egg. "Noah sent us here to kill a man-eating gowrow, and we did."

"Mason."

I didn't look back at her. "I'm not leaving these eggs here for them to destroy, Emma."

"What the hell are we doing with them then?"

"Taking them someplace safe. Gowrows aren't dangerous if they aren't provoked, and to call them endangered would be a fairly generous understatement."

I stubbed my toe on a rock and grunted. The egg tapped against my chest in three quick successions.

"I think my egg is whistling," Emma said.

"Sounds right. They'll be hatching soon enough, and I'd really like to have them relocated before that happens. Spiky little dragon babies are hell on a truck's interior."

We reached the top of the slope and waddled back to the ATVs before we heard it. A low hum that wouldn't be noticeable if you hadn't been around the Department of ExtraDimensional, Mystical, and Occult Nuisances' black helicopters before. That's DEMON for short. And did Noah seriously contact DEMON about this? I cursed and scanned the horizon. I didn't see any movement yet, but they'd be here soon enough.

"Hurry," I said, setting the egg onto the back of my ATV. I wrapped a coat around it for padding before feeding a couple ratchet straps around the bundle and tightening it very carefully.

Emma did the same.

"We can't get caught with these," I said. "Come on. There has to be another path back through the woods. We'll take the long cut."

"Sure," Emma said, "that always ends well."

I ignored her jab and said, "Since when does DEMON come out for clean ups?"

"I'm leaving the fender," Emma said.

My first instinct was that was a bad idea. But Noah already knew our position, which meant DEMON likely knew what we had for breakfast. I nodded and fired up the ATV, pulling onto an overgrown trail near the edge of the limestone bluff.

It took us deeper into the woods at first, and we caught glimpses of headlights traveling a good hundred feet above us. Even if they figured out it was us—hell, even if they wanted to bother to talk to us —it was unlikely they'd make it down the slope. But DEMON was here, and they'd proven themselves very resourceful. I had little doubt they'd have FLIR cameras and God knows what else documenting every fingernail at the scene.

Himari, however, had proven herself adept at spoofing our GPS signals. I hoped Noah wouldn't decide to tip the feds off to our little tricks one day. In the meantime, Himari remained our ghost in the machine.

We spent an hour creatively pathfinding in the woods. By the time we made it back to the cabin, it was well and truly dark. The egg on the back of my ATV tapped again.

"That's the third time since we got here," Emma said.

I nodded. "We need to get out to the Ozarks."

"What?"

"Plenty of caves for them to grow up in. Plenty of fish to eat, and quite a few clusters of apple trees. And I know a guy."

"Do I even want to ask?" Emma said, unhooking the ratchet belts and gently placing her egg into the back seat of the old black and gray Ford Bronco.

"Gowrows are *crazy* for apples," I said. "If a gowrow was ever a maneater, it's probably because some idiot came between the gowrow and an apple."

"Are you serious … of course you are," Emma said. "Never mind."

"I wish we could sleep here," I said, "but too many people know we were here. We need to leave. We can stop at a hotel if we get too exhausted."

Emma nodded. "Then let's get on the road." She slid the camera bag and gun cases into the back with a cooler.

"We'll leave the ATVs. Noah can pay for the damage, and we'll be able to call this a job well done. And an episode that just needs a little editing."

"A lot of editing," Emma grumbled as she opened the car door. I hopped into the driver's seat, started the engine, and turned on the heater. One of the eggs hummed in time with the rumble of the engine, and the other started tapping rapidly.

"They just need to make it until morning. Then we can get them to Larry's."

6

How long a drive is this?" Emma asked after we left a gas station and hit the road again.

"We were close to Taum Sauk, so I'm guessing about three hours altogether. But we're already to Highway 68. We just have to hit forty-two and take it straight through Brumley into Osage Beach."

"Wake me up when we're there." Emma shifted in her seat, resting her head on the window.

The tapping from the eggs grew more regular, and I could scarcely comprehend how Emma was going to sleep when there was a gowrow on the way.

We crossed through one of dozens of passes along the highway where they'd drilled and blasted the road out of the very hills. The trees would be mostly bare now, but I couldn't see much of anything outside the line of our headlights.

A few deer flashed by, thankfully staying on the side of the road instead of committing vehicular suicide. I glanced down at the map on my phone. The dot moved slowly toward our destination.

The rest of the drive passed by in shadows and the occasional headlight.

I checked in to the Golden Door Motel, careful to let Emma sleep as long as I could. Once the car was parked outside our first-floor room, I dragged the sack of apples I'd picked up at the gas station into the motel.

"Emma," I said, gently nudging her awake. "We're here."

She blinked and looked around slowly. "Home?"

"No, Osage Beach. Already got the motel room. Now we just need to get everything inside."

Emma yawned and nodded, unbuckling her seatbelt and following me to the back of the truck.

I tucked my arms under the larger egg and slid it out. It distended and cracked as I carried it. "Emma," I hissed. "Emma, it's trying to hatch."

"Well put it down and hope it doesn't hatch," she said back, but her suddenly wide awake eyes told me she wasn't as calm as she sounded.

"This wasn't the plan," I said. "I didn't think they'd hatch for another week. Or they could at least wait until morning."

"Maybe they will?"

I blew out a breath and carried the egg to the bed closest to the heater. "If we keep them warm, they might not hatch yet."

Emma kicked the door closed behind her and sat her egg next to mine. "What are we going to do?"

"Take shifts," I said. "We need sleep. We'll leave for the bridges an hour before daybreak. If we're lucky, they won't hatch before then."

"I already got a couple hours in the car," Emma said, exasperation clear in her voice. "I'll do a little editing and take the first watch."

I nodded and flopped onto the bed. A memory flickered through my mind about the last time I'd bent the rules, and Noah had threatened to feed me to the agents of DEMON if I disobeyed again.

A small smile lifted the corners of my mouth before I fell asleep to the tapping of a gowrow egg.

W ake up!"
        I bolted upright at Emma's shout, my mind trapped halfway between sleep and some semblance of consciousness. Someone pounded at the door, and it sounded like the wood was coming away in splinters.

It took my mind a moment to remember where we were. Golden Door Motel. Brumley. No, Osage Beach. Big tears in the gowrow eggs.

No one was pounding at the door.

"Apples!" I said. "Grab the apples!"

The larger egg sounded like a muffled woodpecker. Non-stop tapping, until the tapping became a long tear and a narrow green head popped out of the now-deflating shell.

"It hatched," Emma said, slamming the apples against my chest hard enough to bruise.

I tore a hole in the bag and handed Emma an apple before grabbing one of my own.

"Take a bite of it," I said, "then give the gowrow the bigger half." I crunched into the apple. It was sweet with a little bitterness to the skin. I held the larger chunk out to the gowrow. It tilted its head back and forth for a bit before leaning forward and crashing face-first onto the bed, its hind quarters still stuck in the egg.

I shook the apple, and the gowrow kept its eyes locked on it. It shook its body a few times, and the shell tore, finally exposing the slightly gory form within. Gowrow eggs apparently had some seriously messy innards. Slimy goo and blood trailed the gowrow across the comforter while it pumped its stubby, and wholly unbalanced, legs.

It tripped again, and I gingerly petted its snout before holding out the apple. The apple vanished in one quick chomp. I wiggled my fingers, happy to see them all still attached.

We watched it chew, bobbing its head up and down before it swallowed and turned to Emma. She held the apple out with a smile that said, "Please don't eat my hand."

The gowrow snatched it, overbalancing and nearly tumbling off the bed before it caught itself. It rocked back and forth before turning to its unhatched sibling, kicking off the last of its shell and stalking over to the other egg.

"What's it doing?" Emma asked.

"Just wait."

"It's going to eat the other one, isn't it?"

"I doubt that very much."

The gowrow bit into the egg and ripped a section away. A whip-like tail popped out of the hole, and the egg rocked back and forth. The first gowrow growled, which wasn't much more threatening than the squeak of a large mouse, and slapped his clawed foot down on the egg.

His target immobilized, the gowrow ripped away the rest of the shell, flinging bits of goo and blood all over the wall, some of it dripping slowly like one of those octopus wall crawlers we all had as kids.

"That's disgusting," Emma said.

"Maybe Himari can help us," I said. "Bury it in the expenses so Noah will unknowingly pay for it?" As though that somehow addressed the increasingly gross display. I handed Emma another apple.

Emma frowned at the mess, and the pair of gowrows splashing in said mess.

"Give her your apple."

"Her?"

I nodded. "See the two vertical ridges on her forehead? Those will be horns one day. As long as the tusks, but only the females grow horns."

Emma crept forward, tentatively holding out the apple. The smaller gowrow flared her nostrils and led a wobbly charge. She left her brother behind, but had trouble figuring out how to stop.

"Mason. Mason!"

The gowrow charged off the end of the bed, snatching the apple out of Emma's hand even as the long-necked reptilian soccer ball bowled her over. Emma and the gowrow crashed onto the floor, each covered in muck from the egg.

The gowrow squeaked happily and started wobbling around the room, sniffing at everything she saw.

"Right then," I said, looking around at the mess. "This did not go quite as stealthily as I'd hoped."

I snapped up the bag of apples and made my way into the bathroom. It had a tub shower combo that I figured would work just fine. The water burst to life at the turn of the faucet, and I waited for it to warm up.

Emma yelped from the other room, and a moment later two muck-covered gowrows poked their heads into the doorway.

"Come on," I said, smacking the warm water with my hand.

The brother charged forward, crashing into the edge of the tub and rolling over onto his back. His sister was somewhat smarter, using her brother as a stepping stool before splashing into the shallow water. The gowrow in the tub purred, sending a ripple of soundwaves through the water.

"She's clearly the smart one," I said. Once the other regained his feet, I scooped him up and tossed him into the tub. "Which means you must be Pinky, and your sister's Brain."

"Are you serious?" Emma said, folding her arms in the doorway. "Should I get the camera?"

"Oh hell no. I don't think we could write this one off as a prank."

"We can send it to Himari though," Emma said. "You know how much she loves to see the clean footage of cryptids."

Emma knelt down by the tub and pulled an apple out of the bag. The smaller gowrow, now and forever known as Brain, extended her neck over her brother and slurped the entire apple up, crunching the slightly-too-large fruit with exaggerated, fang-bearing bites.

"They're kind of cute," Emma said, watching the scaly soccer balls bite at each other before they grew bored and started blowing bubbles in the rather nasty water instead.

I switched the water flow to the showerhead and rinsed the rest of the muck off. Some of it remained trapped in between the spikes on their backs, but they didn't seem to mind as I blew the worst of it out with the water.

"How are we going to get you out of there now?" I said, eyeing the dripping wet reptiles.

Emma held up and apple, and Brain bounded off Pinky's head, smacked into the tile floor face first, rolled twice, and scarfed the apple down. She started nosing at Emma, and I had little doubt we were going to need more apples.

"That works," I said, holding an apple out to Pinky. He scratched at the tub a bit, trying to reach the top edge with his stubby legs, before flopping down into the enamel tub with a huff.

I picked up the exhausted gowrow and led him back to the front room. His sister followed us with Emma. The comforters were a total loss, so I threw them onto the floor, not really thinking. The gowrows immediately sank their teeth into the fabric, shredding it and nesting in the remains of their slaughtered comforters.

"We're not getting them into the car tonight, are we?" Emma asked.

"It's a truck," I said. "A Ford Bronco is not a car."

"It's an SUV," Emma said, clearly not wanting to engage in our tried and true car-truck-SUV argument. It was like rock, paper, scissors, but far less fun.

"No," I said, watching the gowrows flop onto each other until their necks were very nearly a pretzel. "Let's get some sleep. We'll leave early."

"What if they run away?"

I shook my head and dumped the bag of apples into the end table drawer. "Trust me. They aren't running anywhere as long as we have apples."

Emma arched an eyebrow. "Whatever you say, boss."

I sat down on the edge of the bed and smiled. Tomorrow would be an interesting day.

7

My phone buzzed incessantly twenty minutes before we were supposed to get up. I stared at the screen, bleary eyed but still able to make out the Totoro poster in Himari's office.

A low whistle sounded at the end of my bed. The gowrows had dragged their nest up onto the mattress and were now snoring like miniature freight trains.

The phone buzzed again. I groaned and answered the call.

"It's a little early for a video chat," I said.

"Why weren't you at the lair?" Himari asked, her face lit ominously by a cluster of monitors while her fingers buzzed across a bizarre upright keyboard. "Noah is looking for you."

"He hasn't tried calling," I said, "but I may have pissed him off during our last chat."

Himari leaned back from the camera. "Mason, did you tell him that I tracked him?"

"Not on purpose."

"Ugh," she groaned and smacked her head with the palm of her hand. "No wonder he was such an ass last night. Just because he was at that pub again doesn't mean he was drinking, Mason. Have you *tried* their fish and chips?"

"Kid, don't even worry about it. You could burn that man's house down, and you'd still be his favorite. Now, why are you calling me at five o'clock in the damn morning?"

"Noah's looking for you. DEMON told him some insane theory about the gowrow having hatchlings."

"That *is* insane," I said.

Himari grimaced, most likely detecting the lie. "Why are you in Osage Beach, Mason?"

"It's a beautiful vacation spot."

"Mason."

"There's nothing for you to worry about, okay? Just let it go."

"I have to tell them where you're at. So, if for some reason you're not actually taking an unscheduled impromptu vacation, lose your phone, tear the GPS unit out from under the rear left wheel well, and get the hell out of there."

I sat up straighter. "You already told them, didn't you?"

Himari nodded. "Noah was *here*. In my home! He is seriously pissed at you. He left right before I called."

Himari was just outside Columbia, which meant we had less than an hour. If they were airborne, a lot less than an hour.

"Can I see it?" Himari asked.

As much as I wanted to drop everything and run, I figured one extra minute wouldn't hurt. "Emma, wake up. We're leaving." I flipped the light on and reversed the camera, focusing in on the tangled nest with two green heads flopped out at awkward angles.

"Oh my God, they're adorable!" Himari's squeal woke them up, and the two heads rose in unison.

"Well, get your screen shot," I said.

"Already done."

"Good, I expect to see those two next to Totoro next time you call me."

"Oh, you will, but you still owe me more footage. And you two be careful. Get moving." Himari ended the video call.

Emma and I hurried as much as one could with two baby gowrows underfoot, which involved a lot of tripping, cursing, and swaddling scaly soccer balls in motel towels to slow them down.

We took the equipment out first. Trying to wrestle gowrows, cameras, and guns at the same time just sounded like a particularly bad idea. Once all the gear was loaded in and strapped down, we went back for Pinky and Brain.

"What if someone sees us?" Emma asked.

"Anyone that sees us at this hour is probably out fishing or drunk, and no one's going to be taking a story from either of them seriously."

"That's … actually a good point."

Emma wrestled Brain into a motel towel and scooped her up. The gowrow snorted and snuffled and finally gave up, flopping her head onto Emma's shoulder.

I wish I could say Pinky had been as cooperative. He careened back into the bathroom, smashing into the tub hard enough to crack it, then zipping back out between my legs. Only, he was a bit too wide to fit between my legs without the spikes on his back catching my jeans. The sudden pull threw me off balance, sending me crashing to the floor.

Emma snorted a laugh as the gowrow circled her and then charged back at me. I managed to get a towel over his head, and he froze. He tried to look from side to side, flinging the towel up and down to no avail.

"Good boy," I muttered, wincing as I climbed back to my feet. I lifted the larger gowrow into my arms. The towel fell off his head, but he'd apparently worn himself out, as he didn't try to run again.

The parking lot was thankfully empty, and we had the gowrows tucked into the back seat in no time. Emma was already in the car by the time I started to worry about how much time we'd wasted chasing the critters. Well, how much time *I'd* wasted if I was being honest.

I was almost in the driver's seat when I remembered the GPS. I dashed around the back, felt up underneath the wheel well, and found a low-profile black box. The magnets didn't want to let go, and it took a minute to work the damn thing off. Relief washed over me when it finally came loose. I left it where it fell, resisting the urge to stomp it into pieces. If it was destroyed, they'd know we were on to them.

I hopped back into the car as a black form crossed the face of the moon. DEMON's helicopter slid across the sky, vanishing once it cleared the moon's disc.

"Shit."

"Go!" Emma said.

I started the engine, and we crawled out the parking lot, careful not to use headlights or even tap the brakes until we'd made it back onto Highway 42. If they had a FLIR camera up, which wouldn't have surprised me at all, they may have seen our departure. I prayed they didn't.

"We just need to make it to the swinging bridges," I said. "They won't look past that."

"Why?" Emma asked.

There were things I knew that Noah didn't want me to know. Things about the more intelligent cryptids in the Midwest, and especially Missouri, but some things that could be dangerous to know. I wasn't sure if Emma would want to be in on that knowledge or not, but she was already in deep.

"Just tell me," Emma said, as if she'd read my mind.

"DEMON has an agreement with some of the local sasquatches. They don't set foot on sasquatch land, and the 'squatches police themselves."

"You're saying that in plural."

"Yes I am."

"We're heading for sasquatch land? But I thought Momo was a sasquatch. The thing that killed Dylan?"

I shook my head. "Sasquatches aren't typically violent, although I did hear about a violent pack of squatches down south and some crazy talk about them being werewolves. Sasquatch werewolves," I said with another quick shake of my head.

"Shit," Emma said, squinting and pointing out the window. "Chopper. They're onto us."

"What?" I said. "How? Shit. Do you still have your phone?"

41

"Yes, why?"

"They have to be tracking it. I thought they'd only be tracking mine, and Himari didn't say anything about yours. Shit."

"Mason, I'd really rather not go to lockup tonight."

The gowrows squawked agreeably from the back seat.

"Put your harness on," I said.

"Mason?" Emma asked hesitantly as she pulled the racing harness over her shoulders.

I did the same, awkwardly buckling the crotch piece with one hand. "Drop a couple apples on the floor board. I want the gowrows as low as they can get."

She pulled two out of the glove box and tossed them into the back. My seat bounced forward when the first gowrow dove for the nearest apple.

"Alright kid, let's see what you got me." I pushed the power button on the radio and held it down. Three seconds later, a panel slid out with a series of very much not factory approved features.

"What the hell are we doing?" Emma asked.

I floored the accelerator. We hit sixty pretty fast, at which point I said, "Nitrous," and hit the big blue button. The engine screamed as the injection hit and rocketed us up to 110 miles per hour, which is a really stupid thing to do on a country highway.

"Oh shit oh shit oh shit," Emma said as the force of the acceleration smashed us into our seats. The gowrows squealed in the back, their necks stretched over the seat, and jaws widened like they were screaming. I ground my teeth together. It felt like we were leaving the earth as we crested the small hills, and the tires screamed around gentle turns that were barely turns at all.

In the end, it would only buy us a few seconds against the helicopter, but that might be enough. We soared through another two miles, and I crushed the brakes when I saw the turn off for Swinging Bridges Road in the distance. Smoke and screeches and the squeals of the gowrows filled the early morning air.

I wrenched the wheel and bounced off the highway as fast as I dared in the old truck.

"Gravel!" Emma shouted. "Why are there still gravel roads out here!"

"Wait until you see the bridge."

8

T o say the bridge looked rickety would be a grave insult to the rickety bridges of the world. The ancient suspension bridge protested with the creak of old wood and cries of rusted iron when the truck reached the edge.

The shadow of the helicopter behind us veered off as we bounced up onto the old bridge. There are few things I do behind the wheel of any vehicle that would result in me white-knuckling it on the steering wheel, but between the nitrous and the old bridge, I was going to need a pry bar to let go.

"Is this really going to hold us?" Emma said, looking out the window at the shallow creek. It wouldn't be a long fall if the bridge gave out, but it would be cold, and we likely wouldn't come out of it unscathed.

"It'll hold."

The bridge answered with a disturbingly loud crack. The rusted metal and cables supporting us looked like something out of an apocalyptic pulp movie, all discolored and twisted around each other. It wasn't like anything you saw in the city. It was aged and worn, with only enough maintenance done to keep it from falling down. Of course, that said nothing for the ancient timbers supporting the truck.

Rubber tires bounced on the gravel as we exited the bridge, and I'd be lying my ass off if I said I didn't feel a sense of relief. It wasn't thirty seconds of being off that bridge before Emma's phone rang.

"It's Noah," she said. "How does he have this number? It's a brand new phone for God's sake."

"Put it on speaker."

As soon as she answered the call, Noah's voice filled the truck.

"Mason."

I almost smirked at the irritated tone in his voice. "Yes, Father?"

"We sent you to investigate the claims of the man-eating gowrow and *slay* it."

"I did both of those things." I had, no two ways about it. The man-eating gowrow was real. And it was real dead.

"And what about the hatchlings?" Noah asked. "Our mission is to protect people from these creatures. The Church does not pay you to shelter them."

"Newborn gowrows aren't a mystical nuisance. Call DEMON off."

Noah growled at me. Honest to goodness growled at me. "I will not take that bait, hunter. Deliver them to the DEMON agents."

"You already bugged Emma's new phone?" I asked.

"No."

I frowned at Noah. "If it wasn't her phone ... you bugged the *camera?*"

His lack of response told me I'd nailed it.

"Are you fucking kidding me?" Emma said. "That camera is an *antique!* Do you know how hard it is to keep it working? To find *parts?* If these shots turn out like crap, I'm making you comb Craigslist for a new one. Unbelievable."

I nodded my head to Emma's rant. "And without Himari knowing it was bugged?" I asked. "Interesting, and that was faster than last time. Emma's gonna have some stern words for you, Father. And Emma can make nuns with yardsticks look like a ticker tape parade."

Emma frowned at me. "I don't know what to say to that."

Noah's voice was perfectly balanced when he spoke again. "You do good work for the Church, Mason. See that your misguided efforts do not result in it failing to continue."

I hung up on him. I don't take well to threats. Idle or not. Noah was a good man, I knew that, and he knew he was *completely* out of his depth when it came to "monsters that ought not exist."

"What an ass."

Brain wedged herself in between the seats. She snorted and rolled over when we hit a bump. Her jaw cracked open enough to let her tongue flop out over her face.

"Dylan would have liked you two," I said, scratching at the gowrow's belly. "That he would have."

The sun was higher by the time we crossed the second bridge.

"Is this a dead end?" Emma asked, leaning toward the dashboard.

"Only if you don't know what you're looking for."

I followed the overgrown road to what appeared to be its end and then veered off to the right. We didn't need four-wheel drive while the ground was dry, but if it rained, it would be the only way through. The sparse gravel led us through a rough path in the woods until it broke free from cover again, skirting the shore of what was known as the Grandglaize arm of the Lake of the Ozarks.

Clear water lapped at the rocky beach, a short glimpse of a beautiful landscape before the road turned us into the shadow of the woods once more. Branches and saplings crashed against the truck until we burst out of the forest, into a small clearing with a large hand-painted sign, much like you'd expect to see at an Old West ranch.

I pulled up beside the gate, which displayed a truly impressive array of No Trespassing signs, many of which threatened unique and creative ways you were about to die.

"That's new," I said, reading the *Are you bulletproof or just stupid?* sign.

Emma chuckled. "Trespassers will be shot. Survivors will be shot again. Man, you just don't get warm welcomes like that in the city."

The gowrows perked up, raising their heads like periscopes when the car fell silent and I opened the door. The engine hissed, and I was glad to see the hood hadn't melted into slag from the nitrous. Not that it would actually melt, but the old truck wasn't really built for that kind of trouble. Emma followed me out and stared up at the hand-painted sign.

"Larry's Orchard Extravaganza?" Emma asked, raising a skeptical eyebrow. "That's a lot of death threats for an orchard."

"No better place to hide a gowrow." I ushered the larger gowrow into a duffel bag and hefted him up onto my shoulder. His sister backed up farther into the truck.

"That you, Mason?" someone said from the shadows behind the orchard sign, their voice carrying a thin German accent. "You need to announce yourself proper like, son. I nearly took your head off."

"Larry," I said, taking a few steps toward the voice and extending a hand as the silver-haired man walked toward us. Wrinkles and laugh lines formed a history on his face, and he had a rifle on his shoulder that looked like it would have *zero* problems taking my head off from about a quarter mile out. "How are your gowrows?"

"Plural?" Emma asked, staring at Larry wide-eyed. "You have more than one?"

"A few," Larry said. "And they're mighty fine, thank you."

"Can you spare the space for two more?" I asked.

Larry ran his thumb over the butt of his rifle and feigned disinterest. He failed miserably, leaning forward as his eyes widened. "Guess that depends how big they are. You bring me a beast like Old Willie, and I'll have to find some new caves under this here ranch." He stomped on the grass for emphasis. "Course, Dolly's getting long in the tooth, so she may not be with us more than another season or two."

I pulled the duffel bag off my shoulder and held it open. A tuskless gowrow popped his head up and chuffed at the old man.

"Sakes alive, Mason. Where'd you find a baby?"

Emma leaned into the truck and coaxed Brain into a bundle of motel towels. Emma picked Brain up and turned around, revealing the second, even smaller misfit.

"*Two* babes. But how?"

"I had to put their mother down," I said.

Larry looked wounded. "Why would you do that, Mason?"

Pinky, now free of his duffel bag, promptly threw up all over Larry's boots.

"She was a maneater," I said.

Emma nodded her agreement. "And her mate had been dead long enough to be little more than a skeleton."

"That's a damned shame." Larry reached out toward Brain. She sniffed at him a few times, likely smelled apple cider on the man, and then struggled to leap into his arms. Emma handed her over faster than I could blink. "Troublesome little footballs, aren't they?" he said.

"Ha!" I said. "I thought they looked quite like a scaly soccer ball myself."

"Why you Americans call a football a soccer ball ..." Larry shook his head.

"Hey, you're an American too," I said. "Second generation? Third?"

Larry gave me a smile and patted the gowrow on the snout. "Yes, born and raised in Hermann, but my father would rise from the grave to slap me for calling a football a soccer ball. He played what you all would call league ball."

"And now you have an apple orchard?" Emma asked. "And raise gowrows?"

"Yes, ma'am. That I do."

"Before you take them in," I said, "I want you to know, DEMON was after us. The Church wanted us to turn them over, but these two hadn't even been born yet."

"Did you see them hatch?" Larry asked, his lips curling into a smile. "I've never seen one born."

"It's disgusting," Emma said. "Eggs full of blood and mucus and ..." She shivered. "Nasty."

"It wouldn't have been so bad if they hadn't liked you so much," I said, keeping my voice flat and even.

Larry flashed Emma a grin. "I've heard told you've been working with Mason for almost five years now. I'd think you'd be used to the dirtier parts of the job."

"Seriously?" Emma said flatly.

Larry laughed and held an apple out to each of the gowrows. "Come along. I'll show you the ranch, and let you see where the hatchlings will be living." He looked up at me. "And don't worry about DEMON. I have a good friend who happens to have excellent connections with the local sasquatches."

"Of course you do," Emma muttered.

I grabbed two tranquilizer pistols, locked the car, and patted Emma on the back, careful to avoid her injury, though she was moving very well. We followed Larry and the two scaly soccer balls into the ranch.

9

H ow do you keep this place hidden from outsiders?" Emma asked.

Larry glanced back at her. "Other than the gravel road, the barbed wire fence, and the no trespassing signs? Haven't really had a need. Most folk, if they're out to raid an orchard, stick to the outer trees anyway."

"Sure," I said, "but you have gowrows here too. How do you keep them out of sight?"

"They stay in the caves most days," Larry said. "Now, mind you, when it floods, it can get a bit interesting since those caves fill up like a jug of shine. But, as I figure, people like to assume they didn't see what they actually saw when it doesn't fit into some notion their minds can handle."

I nodded, remembering some of the odd stories I'd encountered when hunting cryptids. Elephants in the woods, tall hairy men, big lizards, shadows that looked like dragons, and tarantulas the size of dinner plates had all become phrases I'd learned to translate into what might actually be waiting in the forests.

Larry led us around a bend in the path and then cut straight down a series of switchbacks. Once we left the trail, I would've been completely lost without a compass, map, or preferably, GPS.

Parts of the trail were slick with leaves, but others were relatively bare. Each time we caught the gravelly dirt of the switchbacks, I had a much better footing, until we started into the underbrush yet again.

"Look how big those apples are," Emma said as we crossed into the actual orchard part of the orchard.

"You won't find a better fertilizer than gowrow shit, ma'am."

Emma wrinkled her nose, and a small smile lifted the corner of my mouth.

"Now, you each grab one of them apples. Make it a big one." Larry paused thoughtfully. "Grab two as a matter of fact."

He pulled two down big enough to pass for a small melon and handed them to the brother and sister bouncing around his ankles. Brain sank her teeth into it, and promptly got her jaw stuck, the apple too wide to bite through. She didn't seem to mind though, bouncing along the trail beside Larry.

"This was definitely the right place to come," Emma said, flashing me a smile.

I nodded.

"Here we are," Larry said. "Now then, keep those apples ready."

I didn't see anything other than the hill rising back the way we came and the orchard flanking us, very nearly surrounding us. Most of the trees still had an abundance of apples, but it was easy to see where the gowrows had gotten into a few of them.

Boom.

"Oh my," Emma said, staring at something behind me.

BoomBoomBoomBoom.

I turned slowly to find a gowrow that dwarfed the maneater. Two massive horns swept back in a gentle curve from the gowrow's forehead, mirroring the enormous tusks that jutted forward. Huge yellow eyes stared down at me, blinking slowly.

The gowrow leaned down, sniffed me once, hard enough I thought she might suck the shirt right off my back, and then held out her tongue. Literally, a giant dragon-sized lizard sat there patiently holding her tongue out.

"I'd give her that apple if I was you," Larry said. "She can get a little feisty if she has to wait."

I reached out, placing the apple on the tongue that rested on teeth as long as my palm was wide. The gowrow's tongue slurped up the apple, and the beast chewed for what seemed quite a long time for just eating a small piece of fruit. She shuffled sideways and did the same to Emma.

The two little gowrows stared up at the behemoth.

"Now you've met Dolly," Larry said. "Let's see if Old Willie is up and about. Why don't you show the kids around the cave?" Larry said to Dolly, as if the gowrow could understand him.

Dolly stretched her neck out and sniffed the brother and sister. She then used a claw to delicately usher them closer. The larger gowrow pulled a pouch open on her belly, and the little ones happily climbed in like some kind of scaly soccer ball kangaroo.

"Whoa," I said. "I've never seen that."

Dolly pushed her nose into the ground and lifted a hatch I hadn't noticed. Half the hill opened up, and the gowrows vanished into it. I raised an eyebrow and turned to Larry.

"Are you kidding?"

"What?" Larry said.

"You have a gowrow bunker," Emma said. "And you trained them to open it."

"They're smart buggers, but I'm surprised Dolly took the hatchlings in so quick. Usually they won't be so friendly to other gowrows' offspring unless there's an immediate threat."

"Dolly probably recognized Mason for what he is," Emma said.

Larry laughed and grinned at Emma. "Come on you two," he said, pulling open what looked like a somewhat rotted cellar door set at an angle in the ground. "I'll introduce you to Old Willie before you go."

We followed Larry through, down the narrow stairs behind the door. It led to a landing, took a sharp turn to the right that threatened to send us tumbling down a second, even narrower set of stairs, and then banked back to the left and out into a damp cave.

"Larry," I said. "This is *much* larger than last time I visited."

"Yep," Larry said, looking up at the ceiling some twenty feet above us. "Reckon Old Willie enjoys his digging."

"It's a bloody cavern down here," Emma said, taking in the distant walls and shadowy paths that led deeper into the bunker. Claw marks were clear in the stone walls, but there were still a few spots, several in fact, that showed stalactites dripping from the ceiling.

"Most of the cavern's still natural," Larry said. "Reckon the hatchlings will have plenty of room to run around and irritate the old gowrows." He punched a button on the wall and a dim light rose along the edges of the stone room. "Come on now, Willie's right back ..."

Larry stopped talking and jogged toward a large, scaly shadow that wasn't moving. The old man cursed, and then cursed *much* louder. Larry sprinted into the cavern, and Emma and I exchanged a look.

"What's wrong?" she asked.

"I don't know," I said, walking closer to what had to be Old Willie. The huge form expanded as it took a ragged breath. Light glinted on the blood running down the base of the gowrow's neck.

"What the hell?" I said.

"Did the other gowrow do that?" Emma asked.

"No." I leaned in and barely touched Old Willie. He growled, and it was deep, rumbling, and full of violent promise.

"Stop it, you," I said, smacking the gowrow higher on his neck where he wasn't injured. "You know me."

The gowrow growled again, but I was mostly sure he wasn't about to kill me. I flipped out the survival knife I carried and measured the four slashes, and they proved to be nearly parallel from top to bottom.

"Gowrow strikes taper down. And these claw marks aren't wide enough to be from a full-grown adult."

"Damn straight," Larry said, rushing back into the cave with an armful of bandages and two spray bottles. "Goddamned howler done that."

"What?" I said.

"Ozark Howler," Larry said, tossing Old Willie an apple before spraying down the wounds with one of the bottles. "Don't tell me some big cryptid hunter like yourself doesn't know what a howler is."

"There hasn't been a sighting in a century. *More* than a century."

Larry snorted. "Don't give me that damn fool speak. You hear talk of panthers in the Ozarks?" His accent turned "panthers" into "painters," and the thought sent my mind reeling. Panthers were a common legend around Missouri, maybe the most common I encountered. Stories of massive cougars and panthers stalking the hills at night.

"Are you sure?" I said, asking a question I was starting to think I already had an answer to. I'd learned to look for the truth inside the story, but how had I missed that with the big cats? Stupid.

"You measured those claw marks yourself, didn't you?" Larry said.

"Couldn't a bear have done that?" Emma asked. "You have black bears down here."

"Yeah," Larry said. "We have bears alright, but I never seen a bear try to take on a full-grown gowrow. Shit." He pressed and plied gently around the cuts on the gowrow, revealing another bad series of claw marks higher on the gowrow's neck. "Old Willie needs stitches. These bandages aren't gonna hold him together."

"There's no way we can take a gowrow to a vet," Emma said. "What do you usually do when they get hurt?"

"Stitch them up when I can," Larry said, "but this is worse, a lot worse, than anything I've had to handle."

"I might know someone who can help," I said. "He specializes in animals with … unusual anatomy."

"Are you talking about some whacko cryptid vet?" Larry asked. "There aren't enough cryptids in the world for any vet to specialize in them, boy."

"You'd be surprised," I said under my breath as I scrolled through my contacts. I made it down to "Doc" and hit dial.

Two rings and a deep groggy voice with a British accent answered. "Emergency line. Someone better be about to die. Six in the bloody morning." He grumbled out another string of grumpy curses before I cut him off.

"Doc, it's Mason."

Silence.

"Mason from the *Cryptid Hunter* show?" I repeated.

"Oh, I'm well aware of that fact. I'm just debating on hanging up on you or seeing what kind of madness you have today."

"I wouldn't have left you in the swamp if—"

"Yes," he said, drawing out the word. "I've heard that story before, and yet the fact remains that you *did* leave me in a swamp, surrounded by a group of swamp monsters."

"They were perfectly friendly sasquatches," I said, somewhat taken aback. "And I had an emergency."

Doc sighed. "What do you want, Mason?"

"We have a gowrow that's been attacked by an Ozark Howler. Four parallel slashes on its neck, and the wound is reopening every time it moves."

Doc was scribbling notes, his phone sensitive enough to pick up the scratch of his pencil. "Where are you?"

"That's ... that might get a little complicated."

"Why?" Doc asked, and Larry echoed the question.

"We're in the Ozarks, on the far side of the Brumley Swinging Bridges."

Doc cursed.

"Not exactly friendly territory for an agent of DEMON," I said.

"Mason," Doc said. "I'll be breaking treaty clauses if I set foot in that territory for any reason other than helping the sasquatches."

"Figure something out," I said, "and I'll owe you. Otherwise this gowrow is going to die."

"Dammit, Mason."

"You live an hour from here, man. Book it."

Doc cursed and hung up.

"That really *the* Doc?" Larry asked, looking between me and the wounded gowrow.

I nodded and grimaced. "We have a history. He's helped me out before with some … unusual creatures."

"After you tried to put them down?" Larry asked.

I pinched the bridge of my nose. "No, Larry. I don't put anything down that doesn't need it. And I sure as hell don't put anything down without proof it's a maneater."

Larry turned back to the gowrow, flushing the beast's wounds and wrapping its neck in gauze bandages as best he could. Emma helped when Larry's arms wouldn't reach around the mass of scales and muscle.

"One hour," I said. "Old Willie can make it an hour." I fed the gowrow another apple and patted its snout. Old Willie rested his head on the ground and exhaled violently. *Hurry Doc* was the only thought in my head.

10

Get out of here," Larry said. "I can watch after Old Willie and the others." He patted the monster rifle laying at his feet. "Just find that howler and take it down."

"I don't like killing things," I said.

"Well get yourself over it," Larry said. "Howlers have been breeding like rabbits the past few years. Taking out one or two aggressive bastards isn't going to hurt anything."

Larry was stressed, and I knew it, so I didn't push the topic any further. It was interesting how he'd clearly been upset about the death of a gowrow, but now he wanted us to put down an Ozark Howler. But how many of those old panther legends were actually howlers?

"Leave the door unlocked when you go," Larry said.

I chewed on more lower lip for a moment and then nodded. "Come on, Emma."

"Back to the truck?"

"Yeah. Let's see if we can pick up a trail. Look for bear tracks. Fresh ones, and it'll probably be a howler."

Emma led the way up the narrow staircase. She threw open the cellar door, and I thought I might go blind from the sudden blast of sunlight. I left one side of the door open so there was no way it would lock.

"You think Doc can get in and out of here without being noticed?" I asked as we cut through the switchbacks and headed back to the truck.

"I don't know," Emma said. "You said the 'squatches don't watch Larry too closely, right?"

I nodded. "They don't have much interest in gowrows, as long as the overgrown soccer balls keep to themselves."

"Well, it's right across the river." Emma glanced behind us. "And once you're more than a few feet into the woods, nothing is going to see you from a distance. Except Dolly of course."

"Sasquatches might be able to, too," I said. "Especially trackers. They might be more civilized than you'd expect, but they have senses that will outperform a human any day of the week."

We reached the truck and folded the rear hatch down. I lifted the floorboard out, revealing a touchpad safe. Six digits and the little red light flashed green.

Emma lifted the top of the safe. "Mason."

"What?"

She eyed the ammunition inside. "I see three types of rounds here that are almost as legal as setting up a moonshine business in the middle of Saint Louis."

I tilted my head to the side and nodded. "Sounds about right."

"We run into any conservation agents and you'll be in deep shit."

"I'm more worried about running into a big cat with horns that disembowels me before I can put it down."

Emma blinked. "I thought these things were like bobcats. Big bobcats, sure, but still just big cats."

I grimaced. "If they're anything like the stories, they're going to be a hell of a lot faster than that gowrow we put down. And don't think of them as bobcats. They're more like a bear."

"Christ," Emma muttered, eyeing the rows of clips. "Steel core?"

"Custom made," I said.

"Copper jacket?"

I nodded.

Emma blew out a breath and popped the cylinder out of her .454. She dumped the rounds and picked up a speed loader, sliding it home and releasing it before slamming the cylinder closed.

I tossed her a backpack and grabbed another, loading it with clips for my Desert Eagle. We locked the safe up when we were done, and I frowned at the tranquilizers laying on top of it. I scooped up one of the pistols and slid it into the holster at my belt.

Emma eyed me for a moment and did the same. "10 CC?"

I nodded.

"If that thing comes after us, we're killing it dead, Mason. The slashes on that gowrow's neck were deep enough to take a man's head off."

"I know," I said. "I'd try to save the howler if it wasn't trying to kill the gowrows, but I can't risk a gowrow, Emma. There are too few left."

Emma nodded. "I'd also like to not die."

I smiled at her and locked the truck. We headed into the woods, hunting a beast that could shred the scaly armor of a gowrow.

"Here," Emma said, calling me over to the lakeshore. Her theory was simple. The mud would be the perfect spot to find a track, and maybe give us some more information on what we were tracking.

I cursed when I saw the prints, deep in the mud, as wide as my foot was long. I shouldn't have been surprised after seeing the wounds on Old Willie's neck, but there it was.

"If this was any other time," Emma said, "I would have bet my life on those being bear tracks."

I shook my head. "Look at the claw marks. All parallel. If it was a bear, it would have to have its paw flexed, and no bear is going to flex all four paws at once. Even if it did, it wouldn't leave such a clean print. The weight would have been on at least two paws, and that would've smeared the print when it flexed."

Emma frowned at the print and eyed the surrounding area. "Looks like it spent some time by the lake."

"This won't be a stealth hunt," I said, looking into the woods around us and the orchard at our backs.

"Why's that?" Emma asked. "Are howlers confrontational?"

"That's what the stories say," I said as I nodded. "You'll never see a howler if you aren't making noise. They're silent, big, and deadly. And if they're bold enough to attack a gowrow, we'll be lucky if they haven't killed any humans yet."

"I don't like that all you seem to know about them comes from stories, Mason."

"Neither do I."

We spent two hours traipsing through the forest with nothing to show for it but ticks and a dead copperhead.

"You could probably use a snake load next time," I said, picking another piece of exploded snake off my pants. "Or just let me move the poor thing like I asked."

Emma blew out a breath. "I said I was sorry, okay? I hate snakes. Especially poisonous snakes. It's like you and centipedes."

"It's nothing like me and centipedes," I muttered. "And I'd appreciate it if you didn't bring that up again."

"How can you be okay with bears and copperheads and black widows but run screaming at the sight of a centipede."

I stood up a little straighter. "I did *not* run screaming."

"If that was just you walking, you should probably run competitively. I've never seen a man walk that fast."

I blew out a breath. "It's a phobia, alright? I'm quite sure I'm allowed one phobia. And that was *years* ago."

"We'll go by the Insectarium next time we're at the zoo in Saint Louis. Test that out."

"Fine," I said, rolling my eyes. "Shoot giant holes in the snakes. I won't complain."

"Thank you."

I couldn't help but laugh slightly at Emma's response.

"Mason?"

"Yeah?"

"Stop. Look around. There are rub signs on almost every tree in this clearing."

It wasn't unusual to see most of the bark rubbed off a tree. Bucks tended to polish the trunks pretty well when their antlers were coming in. But this was different.

"What in the world?" I said, crouching down beside one of the skinned trees. "Look how low this is." The bark had been shredded into ribbons. It would have made a fine mulch.

Emma reached out and patted the tree above me. "They aren't all low."

"I would have thought that those scratches were made by a cougar."

"Cougar with a paw the size of a bear?" Emma said skeptically. "I don't think so."

"I know, and the fresher marks are all parallel. Two howlers marking this as their territory."

"We're still on Larry's land," Emma said. "The gowrow could have come this far without much trouble. Look!"

She pointed past the trees, a little deeper into the woods where a few larger trees had been broken over, like a tornado had dropped right into the forest, and then dissipated without causing further harm.

I drew the Desert Eagle and flipped the safety off, keeping my index finger loosely on the trigger guard. Emma kept her hand resting on the .454, but she didn't draw it.

"It's an ambush hunter," I said. "Stay alert, and if something moves, kill it. Unless it's Larry saying, 'Don't shoot, it's Larry,' right?"

Emma let out a nervous laugh and slid her pistol out of its holster.

"We move side by side, do *not* split up. Let's get a closer look at those broken trees. I stepped on a downed branch, and it cracked like a gunshot. I held my hand out for Emma to stop, and we both froze.

Deeper in the woods, a series of clicks sounded, as though they were made by something much larger than a man, or something with a voice much deeper. Four clicks, a pause, and another four.

"What the hell is that?"

"I don't know," I said. "Stay alert."

We moved in closer to the damaged trees, and I started to come to an understanding of just how violent the fight with the gowrow had been. The oaks must have been fifty years old, thicker than I could put my arms around, and they'd been snapped off like saplings. A walnut tree leaned precariously on the far side of the battered oaks, its roots lifted slightly and torn from the ground. Black earth and red clay mingled in the carnage.

"Look at the walnuts," Emma said. "Some of them have been crushed where they aren't driven into the ground."

I nodded. "And it's not like they were chiseled open by squirrels. Some are split like they were hit by an axe."

"Claws?"

"Probably," I said, stopping to look at a pool of blood and the ragged stump of a pine tree. "I'd say it ended here. Old Willie didn't go down without a fight."

Emma leaned close to me and cursed. She reached out with her left hand and hesitated. "It's not poison or something is it?"

"If it is, I've never heard of it."

She picked up the bloody curved bone that wasn't really a bone at all. "Mason, this looks like a goddamned sabretooth tiger fossil. Like one of the huge ones."

"No, it doesn't. It's still colored like a healthy tooth."

"Smartass."

"Never said I wasn't." I looked around the tossed underbrush at the smeared tracks and winced at the gowrow scales scattered across the pine needles. It was when I studied the blackberry briar that my skin started to crawl, and the hairs on the back of my neck stood up.

Emma felt it too, or she noticed a change in my demeanor, as she went rigid beside me.

A series of clicks echoed around the clearing again, and a shadow moved behind the briars. The clicks stopped, and a howl rose up, the unnatural blend of an elk's bugle and the howl of a wolf.

Emma shivered at the unholy sound. The crack of wood echoed behind us, far closer than I would have preferred, not knowing what it was.

I kept a bead on the shadow in front of us as best I could. Shooting it through the briars might just scare it off, or make it very, very angry. I wanted a clean shot. I wanted to see what the hell it was.

"Watch our backs," I said. "I've got the front."

Emma turned, sweeping the forest behind us.

There was the vague form of a cat, lithe and graceful as it cleared the briar, but the bulk of the creature was muscled like a bear. It was stocky, thick, and moved with a predatory grace that was entirely wrong.

I cursed and kept the Desert Eagle trained on its head.

11

I tried not to tense up too much. The last thing I wanted was to give the howler a reason to attack before I could fully assess the situation. It took almost a minute for me to realize what was wrong.

"Emma," I hissed. "It's not the same one."

"What do you mean."

"Look."

She turned around and saw what had entered the clearing. "Holy shit. Mason. Shoot it!"

She raised her arm to put a slug in the howler's forehead, and I slammed her hands down. It was a stupid thing to do. I could've set her gun off, she could have pulled the trigger and torched my arm, or shot her own foot.

"Why?"

"It has both fangs," I said. "Look at its front leg."

Four parallel claw marks had torn angry red lines in the black fur of the howler. It turned its head, tilting it slowly from one side to the other, displaying the thick horns that rose from either side of its skull, curling back like great ridged ram horns.

"Stay behind me. Back against a tree that isn't marked."

I stepped forward slowly, careful to keep my mouth shut. Exposed teeth, to most animals, were a call to arms. I didn't want the howler to see anything as a sign of aggression, and hopefully it wasn't experienced enough with humans to recognize the guns.

Just in case, I tapped the butt of the Desert Eagle, beating out a slow rhythm that may have been similar to the clicks echoing out from its throat. Time in the wilderness of Missouri had taught me a few things about predators, and wild animals in general. Approach them from an angle. And don't smile.

Smiling was the equivalent of baring your teeth, much like the howler was doing now. Even as it sank lower in its stance, I couldn't help but marvel at the pitch-black coat, so dark it eclipsed the shadows around it.

I took two more steps toward the howler, and it stopped pacing. The rhythmic tapping in its throat became something more like a purr. A purr that promised to disembowel you, but a purr nonetheless.

The howler flattened itself against the ground, and I lowered myself to the leaf-covered earth as well. The creature licked its paw and blew a breath out through its nose, disturbing the leaves piled near its snout. I bit my lips and holstered the Desert Eagle. It hung from the holster across my shoulder, but I kept nothing in my hands, leaving them palms up.

"Mason," Emma whispered.

I shook my head, slowly moving it from one side to the other, not risking a glance back at Emma.

The howler reached a paw toward me, extending claws that could gut bison. It smacked the ground in three quick strikes and pulled its leg back faster than I could follow. The snarl on its face faded, and its teeth disappeared into its mouth, all except for the wicked fangs curling down below its jaw.

It stretched, raising its hindquarters up into the air, and then plodded toward me, weaving back and forth until I could smell the thick musk and sour breath. I could see every scratch and chip on the howler's fangs, and every line in its huge yellow eyes.

I don't know if I've ever tested my ability to sit still under duress quite like the moment the howler flopped onto the ground next to me, sniffing my palms before resting one of the enormous horns on its own paw.

"*Mason*," Emma hissed.

"Why did you not shoot him?" a booming voice asked from behind me, and a frisson of fear shot down my spine.

The howler tensed, raised its head, and then flopped onto its side. Whatever had spoken wasn't human, but it didn't seem to concern the howler.

I turned slowly, both surprised and not surprised, to find the hunched hairy form of a sasquatch beside a dried-out briar.

"Well?" he asked, standing up until he had to be approaching nine feet tall. "You could at least rub his belly."

Emma stared up at the mountain of hair. "Hi."

The sasquatch raised its brow. "Greetings, little one. I am sorry to inform you this is protected land, and you must leave now."

"We're hunting an Ozark Howler."

"If you hurt my beloved Fang," the sasquatch said, "I am afraid you will not leave this place alive."

"Not a pacifist, is he?" I said to the suddenly fluffy-looking howler. I reached a hand out and patted the giant black furry belly. The howler purred like a house cat and then rolled over on top of my legs. I smiled at the howler and its rather terrifying fangs sticking straight up in the air.

It bent its neck to eyeball me when I stopped petting it, so I resumed a vigorous scratching, even as the feeling started to leave my legs.

The sasquatch stared at me. "You … are not a normal man."

"Friends of Larry's," I said. "We brought him two gowrow hatchlings today."

"I'd appreciate it if you didn't eat us," Emma said.

The sasquatch cracked a broad smile. "Do not worry. Humans taste quite awful. I would prefer a skunk."

I frowned at the sasquatch's words. It sounded like he'd eaten people before, but it also sounded like he didn't enjoy it, so I thought we were probably in pretty decent shape.

"Do you have a name?" Emma asked.

The sasquatch nodded once, shifting the long hair along his head. "I am Sonny."

"What?" Emma said.

"My name. It is Sonny."

I slowed the belly scratching, and the howler smacked my arm with his paw. The realization of what an angry howler might do when I stop scratching him had me questioning my decision to scratch him in the first place.

"Good Fang," I said.

"I am familiar with the one called Larry," Sonny said. "I believe the howler that attacked Old Willie is the same that struck Fang."

"Is that an old wound?" I asked, trying to get a better look at the howler's leg while it twitched in the air.

"Only a day. They are fast healers. Nearly as fast as they kill." Sonny gave me a smile I wanted to believe was meant to be reassuring, but in reality was terrifying. "A great many howlers have descended on our land this year. They are most often solitary creatures, but I believe this is one of the decades they mate."

"You know their mating habits?" I asked, genuinely curious.

Sonny nodded. "A life in the shadows can lead to the study of many unusual things. One of my obscure indulgences," Sonny said, his gaze flicking between us, "is actually the show, *Cryptid Hunter*."

I gawked at the sasquatch. Fang batted at my hand when his belly scratches slowed.

"No way," Emma said.

Sonny nodded. "Regardless, finding you here was a surprise. Most humans would have run far away by now, at the sight of myself and Fang."

"Well, I'm not going to stop petting him until you say he won't eat my face."

Sonny frowned and glanced at Emma. "You may need to. I am afraid your companion has gone quite white. From shock perhaps?

Human physiology is somewhat lost on—" He titled his head to the side, and his expression took on a deep frown. Sonny turned his head and shouted, "Howler!"

I barely registered what had happened when a black blur hurtled out of the tree line. Sonny's head snapped toward the bounding form a moment before the ram horns lowered and a second Ozark Howler smashed into him at a full sprint.

Sonny bellowed, and the sound shook the very earth around us. A human would have been crushed by a blow like the howler had delivered, but the sasquatch rolled with the inertia and came up in a guarded stance.

Fang rolled off my legs and leapt up from the ground, charging the newcomer. I was left with horrible pins and needles in my legs while I tried to drag myself closer to Emma. The new howler whipped around to face Fang, and their horns collided with crack fit for a gunshot. A flurry of paws and barking howls followed until Sonny managed to grab the offending howler by the hindquarters and hurl it into the briar patch.

It released a strangled, screeching howl as it pulled itself free of the thorns. When it settled onto the earth, panting, the broken saber-like tooth was plain to see. The howler opened its jaw to release a nails-on-the-chalkboard worthy screech, and I was both amazed and mortified to see how wide that mouth went. It made sense; how else could the thing stab something repeatedly with those fangs? I stared in awe, realizing too late that had been my chance.

The howlers crashed together again, the ball of fury and fur tumbling ever closer. I dove at Emma as the feeling in my legs returned to normal, pushing her out of the way moments before the pair snapped the tree she'd been standing in front of. The sapling slammed against the earth, narrowly missing Sonny.

"When I get them apart," Sonny said, "shoot it."

"Tranquilizer?" I asked.

The sasquatch hesitated, and a look crossed his face that I didn't recognize. His voice, however, carried an obvious sadness. "No, shoot to kill."

I raised the Desert Eagle, keeping the sights locked on the snarling ball of black fur.

One of the howlers screeched again, and the sound broke into the hissing of an angry cat.

"No!" Sonny said, diving into the fray. He pushed one of the howlers away, revealing a bloody gash in Fang's side, only the presence of both curved fangs revealing his identity to me. But if that was Fang...

I swept the Desert Eagle toward the other howler, but Emma beat me to the shot. The .454 thundered out three rounds before the Desert Eagle joined it, barking fire and smoke and sending a hail of steel core rounds into the howler. It whimpered twice and collapsed, leaving me with a sick feeling in the pit of my stomach.

Blood spewed onto the earth. The howler's legs twitched for a short time, and it fell still.

"He's hurt bad," Sonny said, his voice losing some of its formality.

"We have a vet coming for the gowrow," I said. "Can you carry him to Larry's?"

Sonny nodded and scooped Fang up. The howler whimpered, even as Sonny was careful not to touch the bloody wound in its side. "Will they be able to help? We must hurry."

Sonny led the way, crashing through underbrush and clearing a direct path toward the caves.

I figured it was best just to lay all the cards on the table and let Sonny decide, rather than surprising the sasquatch with potentially unpleasant company. "It's a vet from DEMON."

"DEMON?" Sonny said, his voice rising, but his pace remaining constant. He looked down at the howler in his arms. "If they could save Fang, I would welcome the Momos."

"Plural?" I said between ragged breaths. Keeping up with Sonny was becoming a sprint. "Not just one Momo?"

"Never just one," Sonny said. "They are boogeymen to the sasquatches. A Momo is bigger, crueler, and more violent than any of us prefer to be."

"Mason," Emma said. "Something else is here."

I wasn't sure what she was talking about, until a moment later when something cracked and rustled in the woods to our left. Forms darker than the shadows sucked the light from the woods, scurrying between trees and briars alike.

"Do not fear them," Sonny said. "They have come to protect their brother."

We burst into the clearing that led to the cellar door and the cave, and three bulky Ozark Howlers exploded from the tree line on the other side of the clearing. They raised their noses to the air and released that odd bugling cry we'd heard before, but they didn't come closer.

Emma pulled the cellar door open, and Sonny frowned at the narrow steps below.

"Sit down and slide," Emma said, ushering the sasquatch into the doorway.

"I'll go first," I said, hopping down in front of Sonny. "I don't want anyone shooting anyone else. Or tearing their arms off. No tearing off of the arms."

I heard Emma say to the sasquatch, "No, I'm pretty sure he was talking about you," as I slipped into the shadows of the cave.

12

Larry?" I said, raising my voice a little, but not enough to startle a gowrow. Or so I hoped.

"That you, Mason?"

"Yeah. You have visitors. So don't shoot them. Did Doc make it in?"

Something metal clattered to the ground as Doc stepped around the corner, staring at something behind me. Probably the sasquatch carrying the Ozark Howler.

"Help him, please," Sonny said, hurrying around me with Fang in his arms.

Doc shook his head in disbelief. "Of ... of course. What ... what happened?"

"A male rival, the same one that attacked Old Willie. It invaded the howler's territory just to the southwest of here."

"Follow me," Doc said, jogging back into the larger cavern. Old Willie snored in the corner on top of a huge tarp. The gashes in his neck were covered by enormous strips of gauze and some kind of medical tape.

"Put him on the edge of the tarp."

Sonny set the howler down, rubbing small circles between Fang's horns. "It calms them. If you need to calm them."

Doc gave the sasquatch a sideways smile as he loaded a syringe. "I prefer the artificial method."

"Of course," Sonny said, staying at Fang's side until the drugs took hold.

Doc immediately pulled the fur back, studying the wounds in Fang's side. "It doesn't look too terrible. The slashes over his ribcage are bleeding the most, which is probably a lucky thing. You don't want a wound like that in soft tissue. I'm going to have to shave him a bit to stitch him up." He glanced up at Sonny, silently requesting permission.

Sonny nodded. "Whatever you need to do. I am in your debt."

"Well, you can pay your debt by never telling anyone I was here. Boss would have my ass if she found out I was in a red zone." Doc moved with a swiftness that I could scarcely follow, a battery-powered razor buzzing in his hand, leaving an ever-growing pile of bloodied black fur on the tarp beneath the howler.

Old Willie cracked an eye open when the razor caught in some matted fur and Doc cursed.

Larry moved to block the gowrow's view of Fang. Instead of lashing out or attacking the howler, Old Willie gently ushered Larry to the side with a clawed foot, and then laid his scaly head down beside Fang, closing his eyes once more.

Doc hesitated for only a moment before continuing.

The rest of us just stared. Including Sonny.

"I have never seen that in all my years spent here, amidst the Ozarks. Howlers do not befriend other species."

"He befriended you," Emma said.

"I ..." Sonny frowned and rubbed his chin. "You see me as an animal? A specimen no different from an ancient howler who cannot vocalize the syllables of the humans who have invaded their lands?"

"That's not what I meant," Emma said quickly.

"It's kind of what she meant," I said, drawing a scowl from Emma, "but I don't think she intended it as an insult."

Sonny considered that for a moment. "That is a reasonable assumption, I suppose. Most of us do not wear clothing as you do. You would not be aware that some of us are technologically proficient."

"Really?" I asked.

"Yes," he said. "There are enough of us that we need to be aware of how to avoid many means of detection. Most annoyingly, those game cameras you people post all throughout the woods."

I looked down at Doc and winced. He was covered in bloody and matted fur, but Fang's wounds had been cleaned with an antiseptic that was burning my nostrils at a distance, and Doc was getting the injury stitched up.

"Sonny," Larry said, drawing everyone's attention away from Doc. "Are you okay? Are the other howlers here too?"

"I am, thank you. Some of the howlers were with us. I am not comfortable with them all being together here. The likelihood of being spotted increases significantly."

"You're welcome to stay on the orchard," Larry said. "Old Willie is clearly fond of Fang, and I always enjoy our talks."

"Thank you," Sonny said, inclining his head to Larry.

"Would you like me to patch up his leg?" Doc asked, glancing up at the sasquatch.

"Does it need attention?"

Doc combed through the fur and pursed his lips. "You know, it seems to be healing well enough, and I don't see any signs of infection. At least it isn't presenting the way I'd expect to see an infection in a bear, or cougar." Doc looked at the curled horns. "Or a ram."

Sonny smiled and sank onto the floor beside Doc, Fang, and Old Willie. "Ozark Howlers have an impressive recovery time. I believe you may leave Fang's leg as it is. I will tend to it if it worsens." Sonny hesitated for a moment. "Or perhaps I could contact you?"

Doc raised an eyebrow. "I'll probably regret this, but do you have email?"

A slow smile lifted the fur on Sonny's face. "Indeed."

Doc nodded to himself a few times. "Alright, don't leave without getting a card from me. I need to wash up before I go fishing around for my wallet."

"You're a bad influence," Emma said, leaning into me.

"Don't I know it. But this is totally not my fault."

"Really?" Larry asked. "If I recall correctly, you brought the two small gowrows and a howler into the orchard."

"And involved an agent of DEMON," Emma said.

I sighed and flopped down to lean on the wall beside Sonny.

"Have anything to eat?" Emma asked.

"Apples?" Larry said.

Emma huffed out a short laugh. "Sure."

Larry nodded. "I'll be right back."

"Can you point me to a sink?" Doc asked. "Fang is all stitched up. Do you think he'll need a cone of shame?"

"A cone of shame?" Emma said. "On an Ozark Howler?"

"I suspect I can keep him from abusing the wound," Sonny said, apparently grasping the reference. "Thank you for your efforts. It is appreciated more than you know."

Doc nodded. "Anytime I can treat something I haven't treated before is a good day."

"Come on," Larry said.

Doc followed, his bloody gloves and arms held up in the air like a doctor on a low-budget television drama. Only he was covered with the blood of beasts that most folks wouldn't believe existed.

"Do you have a lot of trouble out this way?" Emma asked, her gaze moving from Doc's exit back to Sonny.

"Usually not," Sonny said. "We have had a lone sasquatch disturb the peace on occasion, but my family keeps to themselves most days. It is the out-of-town visitors you need to worry about most."

"You mean the fishermen and the families?" I asked.

Sonny shook his head. "No, no. I am still referring to the sasquatches. Much as you might avoid a lone vampire, it is best to stay well away from the isolated ones. They are often short-tempered and prone to violence."

"Sounds like most people," Emma said.

The sasquatch chuckled, and the sound vibrated the rock around me. "The irony is not lost on me, little one."

I'd never thought of Emma as little. Hell, she was only four inches shorter than me at most. Maybe that was just a term of endearment from Sonny. Emma didn't seem to mind.

"Have you ever seen a jimplicute?" Emma asked.

"A … what?" Sonny said, his brow furrowing and sending sprigs of hair in several random directions.

"It's like a giant dinosaur ghost," Emma said, "but it lives on blood."

"Those aren't real," I said.

"Oh please," Emma said. "Some of the shit we've seen? You're just going to write off jimplicutes?"

"Honestly, I'd just rather they weren't real. Incorporeal blood-sucking dinosaurs? Leave it in the B-movies please."

"What's your favorite movie?" Emma asked, sitting down cross-legged between me and Sonny.

"Anything that is showing on Halloween," Sonny said.

"What?" I asked. "Why's that? Big fan of the horror stuff?"

"Oh, some of the horror films are not bad, but on Halloween, we can visit the local theaters and no one looks twice, other than to comment on our height and shoddy costumes."

I blinked. "You go out? In public?"

If I didn't know better, I would have sworn Sonny was wearing a smirk under all that fur. "It is refreshing, after hiding for so much of the year."

"Well," Emma said, "now I'm wondering how many of those costumes I've seen over the years were actually cryptids completely *not* in disguise."

"Crazy," I said, and exchanged a smile with the sasquatch.

13

I t wasn't ten minutes before Larry returned with a tray of apples, a jar of peanut butter, and Doc following behind him with two Ball jars of something that looked suspiciously viscous. And possibly vicious.

"Now," Larry said, "you two haven't had any of my special recipe before, so take it easy. Unless you'd like to sleep in the cave, then feel free to drink as much as you'd like."

I unscrewed the lid after Larry passed it to me and took a deep whiff, promptly coughing in mild horror. "What in the seven hells is that?"

Emma snatched the jar from me and took a deep breath. "Oh, that's moonshine." She inhaled over the jar again. "And it has a good yeasty smell."

"I'm glad one of you has some sense when it comes to shine," Larry said. "Sonny?"

The sasquatch held out his massive hand, and Larry tossed him a jar. He spun the lid off using his thumb and index finger. The motion was effortless, practiced, and it made me wonder how many times Sonny had split a jar of moonshine with the locals.

Emma started to take a drink, but Larry held up his hand.

"Wait a minute. We need a proper toast."

"For the peanut butter you brought?" Emma asked.

Larry glanced at Emma.

"She's always like that," I said. "Go on."

"To friends," Larry said. "Both new and old, and unique."

Sonny raised his moonshine to that and took a sip. Emma did the same before passing it to me.

"When in Brumley," I muttered. The moonshine was cold on my tongue, but that was immediately replaced by fire in my mouth that I felt crawl its way down my throat and settle into my stomach. "That's smooth," I wheezed out.

"You bet it is," Larry said. "You won't find any of that half-assed shine on this orchard. Although I do have some cinnamon apple cider on occasion."

"How long have you been distilling here?" I asked.

"My family was just a bunch of moonshiners before I was born," Larry said. "Never got caught, although when I was older I learned that was because they gifted a crate of shine to the local police. Every third batch as a matter of fact."

By the time Emma passed the jar back to me for the second time, and Larry regaled us with tales of his father's moonshine business, I realized I may have underestimated the potency of Larry's drink. It didn't burn as it went down anymore. In fact, it felt pleasant and warm, and not unlike settling in next to a fireplace.

"Oh, he's feeling it alright," Emma said.

"But who puts peanut butter on apples?" I asked, for what was probably not the first time. "*Apples*. It's brilliant. You're brilliant, Larry."

"He's ignoring you," Emma said, prying the jar of moonshine out of my hand.

"I can't say that I care too much at the moment," I said, watching Doc and Larry speaking animatedly about the anatomy and care of old gowrows.

"How are you?" I asked, turning to Sonny.

The sasquatch stared into his jar of moonshine. "I believe Larry may have increased the potency of this moonshine."

"Oh my God," Emma said. "We are hanging out with a drunk sasquatch."

Sonny raised his eyebrows. "I have only have, uh, had, half of this fine beverage, and … yes. I should likely not operate heavy machinery."

I laughed at that, a bit more than I should have. I switched topics immediately, sensing a vulnerability, or at least a chance to ask a question without judgement. "Have you ever seen a snawfus?"

Sonny sipped his moonshine and smiled, the expression strange on his hairy face. "Now you speak of a creature that is a mere myth even to my people."

"It's one of my favorite stories," Emma said. "I always thought it sounded like it was straight out of an anime, or an old Japanese story."

"That's because anything that's related to a forest spirit reminds you of anime."

"*Princess Mononoke* is one of the greatest movies in history, Mason. Don't even make me have this conversation with you." She took another slug of moonshine.

"It is an excellent film," Sonny said.

I blinked at the sasquatch. "Okay, okay. Tell me this. What's the strangest thing you've run into this year?"

"Other than you?" Sonny asked. He held up the Ball jar of moonshine. "And this?"

Emma laughed. "He has better jokes than you do, Mason."

"Yes, hilarious," I said, turning my attention back to Sonny. "So?"

Sonny frowned and took another drink. "That would probably be a bingbuffer."

"No way," I said.

"Now that is a creature with no sense of stealth, but you will only find it in the deepest woods, where there are no people, and only the spirits of the forest keep you company."

"Like the snawfus?" Emma asked.

Sonny shook his head. "You play games, Miss Emma. It is entertaining to see the frustration on your partner's face."

"Oh, God no," Emma said. "Mason isn't my partner. He's my employer."

"What?" I said. "We've been friends for like fifteen years!"

"Yeah?" Emma said. "But that's not what he meant by *partner*."

"I'm afraid she's right," Doc said, cutting into our conversation. "Sasquatches refer to their mates as partners."

"Oh," I said. "But really no snawfus? That makes me sad. One day I hope to find a snawfus. Do you think it will have flowers for antlers? I hope it's one like that, breathing out the blue haze of summer all across the Ozarks."

"He's quite poetical when he's drunk," Larry said.

I grinned at him and turned back to Sonny, leaning past Emma and placing a hand on the sasquatch's forearm. "Okay, no snawfus. Can you tell me anything about Momo?" My tone sobered. I didn't think the question was lighthearted for any of us.

Sonny hesitated and took another sip of moonshine before answering. "Why would you wish to know about our nightmares?"

"I think one of them killed my best friend." I flinched at my own words.

Sonny raised his bushy eyebrows, showing off the bright brown eyes beneath. "Where?"

"Outside Louisiana, Missouri." Flashes of Dylan's last moments echoed through my mind. The scream, the smell, the death. I took another drink.

Sonny frowned, and the expression was mildly terrifying on the sasquatch's broad face. "How long ago?"

"About five years now."

Sonny made an odd expression I thought might be a grimace. "I had heard of an attack," he said, "though most of my people have written the event off as a rogue sasquatch attack."

"It wasn't a sasquatch," I said quietly. "I have … I have the attack on film if you'd like to see it."

Sometimes it was hard to read Sonny's expressions, but eventually he nodded. "I may be able to identify it, or at the least confirm what you actually saw."

The skepticism in Sonny's voice was so sure, so concrete, that I almost dreaded showing him what I'd seen. There was enough of it on that video to know it wasn't a sasquatch, or if it was, it had been grossly deformed.

"I'll email it to you," I said. "Or I'll have Himari email it to you."

"What is a Himari?" Sonny asked.

Emma grinned. "You mean *who* is Himari. She works with the Church sometimes. She's ... very gifted with computers."

"A hacker?" Sonny asked.

Emma nodded.

"A really good hacker," I said. I frowned at the jar of moonshine. "Don't think I'm going to a hotel tonight."

Emma snatched the drink away and took another sip before passing it to Doc.

"I met an old boy once that seen a snawfus," Larry said. "At least, he swore he did. You know how the hill folk like their tales. I figure he saw a deer with some flowers screwed up in its antlers."

Doc sipped and winced at the moonshine. "Alright, Sonny. What's the scariest thing you've seen in the woods?"

The sasquatch considered.

"Would've been a jimplicute if he'd been looking," Emma said. "Nothing creepier than blood-sucking ghost dinosaurs."

Sonny shook his head. "I believe it would have to be the giant centipedes."

"Giant *what?*" I squawked, mortified at the mere *thought* of a giant centipede.

"Oh yes," Sonny said. "They dig deep burrows, always growing, always hunting. You never want to be trapped in a cave with one of those. Though if you need shelter from the ice, or even a tornado, their burrows are a fine place to hide."

Emma snorted a laugh. "Mason's going to have nightmares for a week."

"Shut up," I said. "Three days tops. Centipedes ..." I shivered.

We passed the moonshine around a while longer, until we all lost track of time, and eventually consciousness.

14

The next morning was rough. And I mean, sunlight prying my eyes open with a hot poker rough. But after a moment, I realized the sunlight was just a tiny crack near the cave entrance that shouldn't have been blinding at all. I cursed at the kink in my neck, wondering why in the hell my pillow was hard as a cave floor.

I blinked a few times and then frowned at the scaly green comforter. "What the..."

"He lives."

I squinted up at Emma.

"Where are we?"

"*You* are still curled up on the floor with the gowrows. The rest of us slept on the tarp like civilized folk."

I squinted at the pillow again, and it opened its eyes. Brain made her strange chirping bark and licked my cheek, which pretty much felt like warm wet sandpaper. "Jesus. No more moonshine. Ever. Never ever. I'm gonna be sick."

"Don't you worry," Larry said, coming into the cave like a spritely man half his age. "I have all the bacon, eggs, and pancakes you can eat. It'll fix y'all right up."

Something grunted in the corner, and Sonny slowly pulled himself up into a sitting position. "I have been known to make better decisions," he said, patting the rear leg of Fang beside him.

The howler, for all his size and rather intimidating fangs, just raised his head and chuffed at Sonny before laying his head back down with a thump.

"Where's Old Willie?" I asked, realizing the huge gowrow was no longer in the cave with us.

"Out in the orchard with Dolly," Larry said. "Seems like Doc got him fixed right up." Larry held out a card to Sonny. "Doc left his contact info, just like he said. I scribbled Mason's email on there for you too."

I vaguely remembered that conversation. Something about sending him the Momo video.

"Thank you," Sonny said, studying the card. He stood up and tucked the card into the fur at his waist.

"Do you have pockets in all that fur?" Emma said, bluntly asking the question I'd thought may be considered rude.

Sonny nodded and lifted what looked like a low-profile fanny pack made out of fur. "We knit them from our own hair. Most anything the sasquatches of Missouri wear is stitched from sasquatch fur. It blends in with our coats."

"So even when you're wearing something, you're naked."

Sonny tilted his head to the side. "I suppose so, in a way. Though we rarely wear anything more than a satchel. Missouri summers are much too warm for anything else."

"Now come on you three," Larry said before Emma could take the questioning to further awkward heights. "Let's get some breakfast in you before I give you the bad news."

I exchanged a look with Emma. Being hungover in a cave with gowrows, a howler, and a sasquatch didn't sound like a great time for bad news.

L arry had to take a phone call before he finished passing out stacks of the fluffiest damn pancakes I'd ever seen. He let us finish half our plates before he said more. "Here's the thing. DEMON is saying you violated the pact of this place by bringing unlicensed gowrows into the orchard."

"*Unlicensed* gowrows?" I said, stuffing a chunk of pancake into my mouth.

Larry nodded. "Like an unlicensed exotic pet that you yourself weren't licensed to transport. Because of that, they're saying they have the right to come onto the sasquatches' land."

"Bullshit," Emma muttered. "That's ridiculous. Even if *we* broke some stupid agreement, the sasquatches sure as hell didn't."

"I know," Larry said. "Look, I tried to argue it, I really did. They have some division I've never heard of that's like the Missouri Conservation Department. Only ..." Larry shook his head.

"What?" I said, in awe at the gall of such an accusation. Where would you even *get* a license for cryptids?

"Here's the thing," Larry said. "They know you two are here. And they know you're behind the *Cryptid Hunter* shows."

"And where are our guns?" I asked.

"On the cooler by the door," Emma said, pointing her thumb toward a deep freeze with nothing on top of it.

I turned back to Larry. "Really?"

"I don't want no shootout in my home, Mason. I'm sorry, but you need to use your words."

I pinched the bridge of my nose and laughed, the sound entirely without humor.

"You do not need your weapons so long as I am here," Sonny said. "I am well versed in the treaty that defines this land."

Larry hesitated, then vanished back into the kitchen.

"This should be interesting," Emma said, rubbing her thumbnail.

"Yes it should," I said.

"Too late to run?" Emma asked.

I nodded. "Let's just enjoy some pancakes before whatever happens, happens."

"It is good not to fight on an empty stomach," Sonny said, "though I do not wish to fight if it is not necessary."

"Of all the sasquatches in the world," I said, "we meet the pacifist."

"He wasn't a pacifist in the woods yesterday," Emma said.

Sonny smiled and stuffed a pancake into his mouth. He didn't bother cutting it up. The pancake folded neatly in half as he scarfed it down. As well-mannered as he was when speaking, he was an eating machine.

Larry returned a minute later, before we'd finished our breakfast. I still didn't feel what I'd call "fantastic," but I didn't feel like I needed to hibernate for the next six months.

"This is Stewart," Larry said, pointing to the suit that walked up near the table. "I didn't catch your name."

A tall blonde didn't look up from her phone. Her fingers flew over the screen, and then she tucked it into a pocket in her vest.

"We're with the CCD," the suit said, adjusting his tie. He looked like a strong breeze might send him into the air, though I suspected the gel in his dark hair might be heavy enough to keep him anchored. "My name is Stewart, and this is—"

"The what?" I asked.

"The Cryptid Conservation Division," the blond agent beside Stewart muttered, one hand on her forehead.

"Oh come on," Emma said. "You're just making that up to get your DEMON agents onto sasquatch land."

"How dare you," Stewart said, straightening his narrow shoulders.

"No," the tall blonde beside him said, cutting him off. "The CCD is just ... new. Call me Amy, and I'm not with him. But I *am* one of those DEMON agents you're talking about."

"It is our understanding," Stewart said, "that you transported two gowrows across county lines without a permit."

"Did they do something wrong?" Emma asked. "Is there a law against eating half a motel room?"

"Probably yes," I said under my breath.

"That is inconsequential," Stewart said. "Without a proper license for the handling of cryptids, we cannot be sure you will not endanger the lives of civilians."

"And where might I acquire such a license?" Sonny asked. He blinked slowly, all of the attention in the room focusing on him. "I am quite good at handling *cryptids* as you call them. Some might say over-protective. If anyone were to attempt to take Fang from these protected lands, as a theoretical example, I would tear their arms off."

Sonny took a delicate bite of bacon and chewed slowly.

"Not helping," I hissed.

Sonny smiled.

Stewart looked flabbergasted for a moment until his expression tightened, and I was pretty positive he was trying not to run. But there was a crack in Agent Amy's demeanor. She wore a thin smile, and I was fairly sure she was somewhat amused at the sasquatch's not-so-veiled threat.

"Look," Agent Amy said, "new rules say you have to have a license to transport cryptids across county lines. Come down to the CCD office and—"

"Stop now," Stewart said. "You are trying to give them a loophole when we clearly have cause and evidence to arrest them." He pointed at Sonny.

Sonny raised an eyebrow. "I am here of my own free will and arrived here under my own power, Stewart. It is *you* who has arrived on a technicality, leveling threats against my host. And that is before we consider the legal ramifications of your trespass onto undisputed sasquatch territory."

Stewart took half a step back.

Sonny smiled, only it didn't feel like a smile. It felt like a wild animal baring its teeth right before it tears your throat out. "If anyone has cause in this situation, it is me."

"Sonny," Emma said. "Larry has our guns."

"I do not need guns," the sasquatch said.

ERIC R. ASHER

"Just keep your mouth shut, Stewart," Agent Amy said. "We're going to need to have a talk about your decorum in the field."

"Amy!" someone shouted from the kitchen, his voice the basso baritone of a man I imagined liked his guns as much as his beer. "Agent Amy!"

The blond agent tensed.

"I swear to God I will call you Agent Hot Pants in front of these fine people if you do not get yourself in here right now."

Emma snorted a laugh. "Who's that?"

"Backup," Agent Amy muttered, turning toward the door. "Bubba! What in the hell are you ..."

She trailed off when a man walked, well, *ducked* through the door-way. He had to be some six-and-a-half feet tall with tattoos running the length of his arms and a baby gowrow cradled against his chest.

"Look at this thing, will you? It's like a scaly puppy dog." The mountain of a man had Brain in his arms, and she was emphatically licking his beard. "It likes me!"

"What did you spill in your beard, Bubba?" Agent Amy asked.

"Nothing."

She raised an eyebrow, and I got the distinct impression there was something more than a strictly professional relationship between the two.

"Maybe, and I say *maybe* there may have been a little mishap with a pancake."

Sonny stood up, and Bubba frowned.

"Are you wearing pants?" Bubba asked.

"No," Sonny said. "It is only a loincloth braided from my own fur. I am surprised you noticed."

"They don't wear pants in the South ..." Bubba said. "So, uh, yeah, I noticed."

"Enough of this," Stewart said. "You're clearly in violation of CCD section four point nine, illegal transport of a cryptid across county lines. And from its nest no less! I am calling the other agents in to place you under arrest."

"Oh no," Bubba said, "look at that giant angry gowrow!"

Stewart looked where Bubba was pointing, and Bubba cracked him in the back of the head, sending the CCD agent to sprawl out across the cave floor.

Bubba winced and tapped his ear. "Shut up, Skeeter. He's fine. Just a little nap." Bubba gave in and picked the gowrow clawing at his shins back up. "He might be bleeding a bit. You still out there, Doc?"

Doc poked his head out of the kitchen and slunk back into the room. "Glad to see none of you shot each other."

"You're welcome to borrow one of our tranquilizer guns," Emma said, indicating Stewart's limp form.

Bubba turned to Agent Amy, and she silenced him with a look before he could utter a word. "No, of course not," Bubba said. "But Doc, could you stitch Stewart up if he needs it? That gowrow got him good."

Emma grinned.

"Look," Agent Amy said, "everyone needs to make themselves scarce. All of you. Get to the CCD office in Columbia. Go to the Blue Note on 9th Street. Ask for Chuck. He'll get this straightened out."

"Why are you helping us?"

"Mostly because I don't like Stewart," Bubba said. "And my friend Skeeter loves your show."

"How did you even know we were here?" Emma asked. "And with gowrows?"

"Noah," Bubba said. "He may have spent a little too much time blabbing to Uncle Father Joe."

"Who?" I asked.

Agent Amy waved her hands in dismissal. "It's not important. Just go see Chuck. Take the test. Get your license, and you won't have to worry about DEMON coming after you on a technicality."

Bubba sat Brain down, and the scaly soccer ball yipped and ran around the group on her stubby legs. "Look, y'all have a live and let live thing going with that show, and I hope that's how you really are. I dig it. I like it."

87

"You are the monster hunter in the South," Sonny said. "The one who fought the werewolves." He didn't say it as a question.

"And the were-squatches," Bubba said.

Sonny rubbed the back of his hand. "Barry was an acquaintance of mine. One might call him a friend, though I had not seen him in quite some time."

"I liked Barry," Bubba said. "He didn't wear pants. Of any kind. Just left it all out there, you know?"

Agent Amy slowly turned to Bubba, looked like she was about to say something, and then gave up on it before responding.

Bubba pressed at his ear again, and this time I noticed the small headset. "Skeeter, no. Would you— But—" He sighed and turned to me. "Would you mind signing something for Skeeter? He might like that show more than I realized."

"Uh, sure," I said, still feeling way off balance from the entire conversation. So far I'd met a sasquatch that liked *Cryptid Hunter*, and apparently Bubba's friend, or the voice in his ear, was a fan, too.

Bubba held out the leathery white shell of a gowrow egg.

"Where in the world did you get that?" I asked. "The motel?"

"Yeah, you left quite a mess back there. That was our first stop before coming here. I did have to laugh at the bloody paw prints on the window though."

Emma pulled out a marker that she always kept in her pocket, and I signed my first autograph, which just happened to be on the outer eggshell of a cryptid. I blew on it a bit and handed it back to Bubba.

"Thanks, Mason."

A groan sounded from the vicinity of Stewart's flattened form.

"Go," Agent Amy said. "Get yourselves to Columbia."

"Thank you," Emma said, exchanging a handshake with the agent. "If you ever need any help with cryptids, you know where to find us."

"Even if we don't," Bubba said, "Uncle Father Joe can ask Noah."

"Thank you," I said, shaking Bubba's hand and marveling at how mine sort of disappeared into his massive palm. "Larry, can we get our guns back?"

"Done and done," Larry said.

"Sonny," I said, "we'll talk more later."

"I await your message."

I nodded to the sasquatch and followed Emma out the cellar door. I looked back once, taking in the sleeping gowrow and Fang nestled up beside him. The last thing I heard was Bubba saying, "Now tell me about that moonshine you have there."

15

W
e're pretty low on ammo," I said as we neared the bridge in downtown Jefferson City. I was trying to inventory everything in my head of what was left of the clips and tranquilizers in the back of the truck.

"There's a store outside Columbia," Emma said. "We can stop there after we get licensed."

"So you think the CCD will be as strict as Missouri's Conservation Department's rangers?" I asked.

Emma blew out a breath. "I don't know about that. But I do kind of wish we'd stopped at that Perkin's to get some food."

"Giant pancake breakfast not pulling its weight for you?"

"A bit more than its weight," Emma said with a grimace.

I smiled and moved to pass a slow trailer.

The rhythm of the road changed when our tires hit the bridge, and the river opened up to either side of us, flanked by trees showing the last vestiges of color for the year. We passed the airport and caught Highway 63. That would take us the rest of the way to Columbia.

"We won't be seeing much outside of the winter brown and gray soon," Emma said.

"I know. But once winter passes, we hit prime cryptid hunting season."

"You know 'Cryptid Hunter' is a terrible name for the show."

"Why's that?" I asked.

"Because you don't actually hunt them. You track them, rescue them, and only put them down if there's no other choice."

I smiled and set the cruise at precisely five miles per hour over the speed limit. "It works. Don't worry about that. I have at least one fan out there after all. And what more do we need?"

I could have sworn she muttered something about needing money for more food than ramen noodles, but I let it go.

We spent most of the drive in relative silence, pondering the insanity of the past day, and possibly what the rest of the year would bring.

I squinted at the road signs as we approached Columbia. "I don't usually come into the city from this direction. Was that our exit back there?"

"You could have used the GPS."

"Really?" I said. "Think about that for minute."

"Right, government agency tracking us down. Never mind. Then just get off at Broadway."

"That's the plan, but where's the exit for Broadway?"

"You're driving by it."

I cursed, checked my mirrors, and swerved across the solid white line into the left-hand turn lane for Broadway. Lots of folks ignore the solid white lines in Missouri on a daily basis. Those folks tend to run into things.

"It's not really an exit though," Emma said as we made the turn. "Being a stoplight and all."

"Yeah, yeah. You know there's a great comic book store around here," I said. "Rock Bottom Comics."

"Since when do you know anything about comics?" Emma asked.

"Dylan was into them. He taught me a little bit."

Emma was quiet for a time, maybe remembering some old conversation about Dylan's favorite comic book shops. The kid was crazy about them, and I spent more than a few afternoons with him, hunting for hole-in-the-wall storefronts with undiscovered treasures.

"I miss him," Emma said.

"Me too."

"That Jimmy John's!" Emma said, pointing to one of the brick shops with a wide black banner.

"Yeah?"

"I went on a terrible date there once. I ditched the guy and went over to Gunther's Games back when it was still around."

Emma had always been a gamer, and I had more than one fond memory of her kicking the local pros up and down the arcade floor, and more than once making some excellent money off some very illegal gambling.

"There's 9th Street," she said.

I turned onto the street and drove about a block before parking across the way from the Blue Note.

"We should have picked up Himari," I said. "She's not far from here."

"And put her where? In the mud and blood in the back seat?" She laughed and looked up at the Blue Note. "I haven't been here since I was twenty-one," Emma said. "Maybe twenty-two."

"How's your memory of the layout?" I asked.

"Fuzzy. At best."

The building looked more like I'd expect a bank to look than a music venue, two stories of pale brick and tall rectangular windows, and a strange half story on the top with eleven arched windows.

"This building makes my OCD go crazy," Emma muttered. "Eleven windows. Who does that? And the brick in the alley doesn't come close to matching the façade."

"It has character," I said. "You have to give it that."

Emma grumbled a bit as we waited for a few cars to pass before crossing the street. The front door was unlocked. We ducked inside and headed to the left, and within a dozen steps into the club, I wouldn't have known it was daylight outside.

"Not open," said a twenty-something bartender with enough tattoos to rival Bubba. She didn't look up from the counter as she wiped it down, her reflection lit by the golden bulbs around the mirrored bar back.

"Is Chuck in?" Emma asked.

The bartender paused and glanced at us before dropping her towel and briefly fingering a piercing in her eyebrow. "He's in the back. Take the stairs to the left and head backstage. He's in the green room."

"Thanks," Emma said, leading me toward the old stage.

Ten years ago, The Blue Note was the kind of club I lived for. Seeing some of the local bands make good, opening for national touring acts was an exciting time. It was rewarding, and there was nothing quite like being happy for the success of your friends. Now though the club felt hollow. Maybe it was just the absence of bodies and deafening quiet of the floor space, or maybe I was further from who I used to be than even I realized.

"Mason?" Emma said, stopping and looking back at me.

I shook my head and glanced back at the balcony that loomed above us. "Right. Lead on."

Our footsteps echoed on the wood floors until we started up the dim staircase that led to the back, vanishing behind the arch that framed the stage. Emma stopped at a staircase that led down beneath the wooden floor.

"Is that it?" I asked.

"I think so."

"Chuck?" I shouted.

"Yeah," a slightly nasally, high-pitched voice came back. "Come on down."

We made our way down a creaky staircase and into a room plastered with old stickers, layers of posters, and signatures that had been written over so many times you'd need and excavator to reach the wood underneath.

"Chuck?" I said.

"Over here."

I turned toward the voice, and in the back corner of the room, a sliver of light opened into a full-sized door. A man stood there in silhouette as he adjusted his glasses.

"You have a secret office behind a basement green room?" I asked.

"Oh, yes indeed," Chuck said, gesturing for us to follow him in. "We don't want anyone to find us, unless they're already in the know."

Once we were in the room with Chuck, and I got over the slightly mind-bending experiencing of walking from a club's backroom into a small office that could have passed for the DMV, I focused on our host.

Chuck rifled through a stack of papers, occasionally pausing to brush his shoulder-length brown hair out of his grayish blue eyes. A short sleeve button down revealed forearms that I'd guess belonged to a drummer.

"Oh right," Chuck said, shaking his head and squinting through a pair of thick black glasses. "I already pulled the forms when Amy contacted me."

Chuck studied the two papers before crossing his arms and handing us each one. "Now, if you two will both sign, you'll be all set for transporting cryptids across county lines."

"No test?" Emma asked.

"Not yet," Chuck said. "I'd like to put a test together. Maybe like the Tri-Wizard Cup? Wrangle some cryptids before they can eat you?" Chuck laughed in one of the most ear-stabbing sounds I'd ever heard, like a goose getting smacked by a semi while they were both honking. At least he seemed thoroughly amused with himself.

I skimmed the application and scribbled my name at the bottom. Emma did the same.

Chuck pulled a carbon copy off the back and handed it to each of us. "Now, your cards give you a license to transport and capture cryptids as you see fit. You only answer to the CCD, which in central Missouri is pretty much just me for now. We'll have more agents in the field soon enough." He followed up the paperwork with a very nice metal card. CCD was embossed in the corner. Mine said M. Dixon Agent Four.

"E. Rainwater Agent Five," Emma said, frowning at the card. "These are awfully nice."

"There's a little talk about getting some cheaper material, but I'm going to fight it."

"I guess you have to pick your battles," Emma said. "Something Mason could stand to learn."

"Hey now," I said.

"You two are great," Chuck said. "A hell of a lot more interesting than some of the stodgy suits that have shown up so far. And you would not believe how much some of them complain about having to come into a sweet club."

"Thanks," I said, tucking the card into my wallet. "Anything interesting come through the office yet?"

Chuck didn't hesitate. "Chawgreen. Without a doubt."

"In Columbia?" Emma asked. "They're usually a bit more rural."

"Used to be rural here," Chuck said. "One of the gas stations up off 63 built too close to the chawgreen's home. The chawgreen raids their tobacco almost every night. Funniest damn thing I've ever seen."

Emma and I exchanged a look.

"And how late does that usually happen?" Emma asked.

Chuck grinned. "Couple hours from now. Look for the Break Time right at 70 and 63. Can't miss it."

"The owner hasn't done anything about it?" Emma asked.

Chuck shook his head. "Oh no. Chaw's practically a tourist attraction in himself."

"Gives us just enough time to hit the depot and be back for the show," Emma said.

I drummed my fingers on the counter and nodded. "Thanks Chuck."

"You two be safe out there!" he said as we made our way out of the CCD department's office.

16

How far out is that gun shop you were talking about?" I asked as we passed what felt like the fifteenth exit. I glanced at the clock. "I don't want to miss the chawgreen."

"Not much farther," Emma said. "Next exit, and I don't want to miss the chawgreen either."

The next exit ended up being two miles down the highway, flanked by a very large billboard. "Oh my."

Emma leaned forward and grinned. "Yep. It's run by some good old boys."

The billboard by the exit read simply BEER, BAIT, & BULLETS. I followed the ramp, and near the top we were greeted by another remarkably subtle sign the size of a house indicating the direction of said beer, bait, and bullets.

"Gee," I said. "I wish this place wasn't so hard to find." I pulled into what I think may have been an asphalt parking lot at one time, but weather and time had turned it back into a mostly-gravel lot.

A gaudy neon open sign flickered on the side of what I'm pretty sure used to be an old gas station, and had possibly been converted into one of those many "World's Largest Adult Video Store" attractions, until it finally achieved its final form.

Emma and I got out of the truck and walked inside.

"Oh, and they added a snack bar," Emma said, the uncertainty in her voice an amusing counterpoint to her earlier confidence in the shop.

"I don't mind if you have those guns in the shop," a young woman in cutoff jeans and a white tank said from behind the counter, "but make sure the safety's on, yeah? I don't need another one of *those* this week." She pointed up to what looked suspiciously like a shotgun blast in the ceiling. "The local police don't much like it when I have to call them in."

"Sally?" Emma asked.

"Yeah?" Sally brushed a lock of dirty blond hair behind her ear.

"My God, girl, how old are you?" Emma didn't wait a response before she said, "Aren't you freezing your ass off in those shorts? Damn. Is Gil around?"

"You know my dad?" Sally asked, her freckled face perking up a bit. She tugged the frayed edge of her cutoffs down a fraction of an inch. "I'm pretty new here, but how did you know my name?"

"I've known Gil for years," Emma said. "He used to go hunting with my dad. You all still sell tranquilizer darts?"

"We have RDDs," Sally said. "Is that what you're looking for?"

I pulled the rifle out to show her what we were using. She barely glimpsed it before she said, "Oh yeah, we have loads of those. What size?"

"10 CC if you have them."

"Done and done. Dad's been sick for a few months. It looks like he's going to pull through, but it's been rough."

"I'm sorry to hear that. Tell him Emma said hi next time you talk to him. I bet he remembers me."

"I will," Sally said. "Who's your friend?"

"This is Mason Dixon," Emma said, "the world-famous Cryptid Hunter."

Sally arched a very skeptical eyebrow and set a handful of RDDs on the counter. "Anything else?"

Emma rattled off some heavy-duty rounds that I *never* would have expected to find in a retail storefront. Sally put a couple boxes of ammo on the counter and then walked into the back.

She returned with a small wooden crate. "But your name is really Mason Dixon?"

I took a deep breath and leaned forward onto the glass countertop, resting my chin on my knuckles. This was a question I'd grown used to. Folks never seemed to believe that my parents would have named their kid Mason Dixon.

Sally smirked and threw a rug to the side on the floor. I raised my eyebrows when she started pulling out boxes of ammo from the hidden stash in a floor safe.

"Well?" she asked.

"Yeah," I said, figuring it wouldn't hurt to entertain the kid a bit. "That's why no one should ever gamble away their right to name their kid."

"You serious?"

"As a sasquatch," I said, nodding.

"I think that's it," she said, dropping the last three boxes of iron shot onto the counter. "You must know Gil. You're both always making weird references."

"Not as weird as seeing them face-to-face," Emma muttered.

Sally paused, one hand on the register. "What?"

"How about ringing me out so I can get back to filming?" I asked.

She narrowed her eyes but started tallying up the ammo regardless. "Emma said you have a show. Trying to get into prime time?"

I offered a thin smile and shook my head. "*Cryptid Hunter* will never be prime time, Sally."

She pointed to the total on the handwritten receipt.

I dropped a small stack of bills onto the counter and gathered the ammo up into a camouflaged tactical duffel bag that was apparently complimentary when you spent unholy amounts of money.

"Be careful with those flashbangs. We had a bad batch that had a bit more pop to them than they should have."

"Thanks for the warning," Emma said.

"You know anything about the chawgreen around here?" I asked.

Sally rolled her eyes. "Oh, lots of folks talk about it."

I nodded at Sally and headed toward the door with Emma. I had one foot out when she stopped me with a shout.

"Mason! At least tell me what station you're on."

"YouTube."

She tried to cover up a laugh.

"That's why I didn't tell you," I said.

Emma grinned and patted my shoulder. "Tell Gil we said hi. It was good to see you, Sally."

"I will!"

We made our way back to the old Ford truck that looked to be constructed from mud as much as it was from metal.

"Hard to believe that's a gorgeous two-tone paint job hiding beneath that mess."

"It's black and gray," Emma said flatly. "Not exactly what I'd call gorgeous. And your SUV needs a bath."

"My truck isn't the only thing that needs a bath."

"You don't need to tell me."

I nodded sagely. "It's a glamorous life."

We pulled back onto the highway and headed toward the gas station.

Y es," Emma said, literally putting her foot down in the parking lot. "We are absolutely making an episode out of this."

I groaned and leaned on the truck, and then cursed when I realized I'd just gotten more mud smeared across my jeans. "I am filthy, grumpy, and generally done with people right now, Emma. And I'm not positive, but I think I might still be hungover from Larry's special jars of 'you're gonna wish you're dead in the morning.'"

"Oh come on. It's perfect." She flipped the camera open. "You look like you've been in the field for forty-eight hours straight."

"Because I *have* been in the field for forty-eight hours straight."

She grinned, and I blew out a breath.

"Come on now," Emma said. "Just turn that Cryptid Hunter charm on for ten minutes. Ten little minutes and I won't complain about the smell."

I shook my head and smiled. "Fine, but we're taking a vacation after this. Somewhere without cryptids. And without DEMON. And most assuredly without moonshine."

"Uh huh. And we're filming."

I closed my eyes and took three deep breaths before taking two low-to-the-ground strides and spinning to face the camera. "We're just outside a gas station in Columbia, Missouri, where it's rumored a real live chawgreen visits *every* night! If we're lucky, maybe we'll catch sight of this elusive beast. Come on now," I gestured for the camera to follow me, "we're going to get set up for the best view."

I paused and glanced back at the camera. "I haven't seen a chaw-green myself either, but those who know their Missouri history will tell you it's like a bear, with a tail styled like a barber pole." I paused dramatically. "And *apparently* chawgreens have quite an affinity for chewing tobacco, which is where they get their name." I inclined my head to the side and laughed. "I guess we'll see!"

Emma lowered the camera. "Perfect. Now let's see if this thing actually shows up."

Worn out, feeling like hell, and surprisingly hungry is not the best time to visit a gas station. We walked out with drinks, chocolate, a surprisingly good gas station donut, and more bags of chips than we were likely to eat in the next week.

I was halfway through a super-sized slushy when something moved at the edge of the field beside the station. I didn't think much of it until the shadow swayed from side to side a bit, growing larger as it closed in on us.

"Emma," I hissed, pointing toward the lumbering form.

She snapped the camera up, and I watched, slack-jawed as a bear-shaped *thing* with a bushy, striped barber pole for a tail waddled its way up to the door. It smashed its face into the glass, grunting a bit, until the door finally slid open.

"Do we follow it?" Emma asked.

"I don't want to scare it," I said.

"Scare Old Chaw off?" an older woman at the pump nearby said. "Nothing'll keep Old Chaw out of the station. He'll let you pet him some nights, if he's not grumpy." She climbed into her car like nothing particularly unusual was happening, started her car, and drove off.

"Go," Emma said. "Let's go in."

We crossed into the fluorescent lights of the gas station. I opened the door for Emma, letting it close behind us.

"Oh my God, it's adorable," Emma said.

"Shh," the clerk said. He was an older man, standing off to the side while Old Chaw hooked a paw onto one of the shelves.

"Look how easily he grabs the shelves," I whispered, marveling at the dexterity in its paws. Old Chaw pulled himself up to the third shelf and slid a can of chewing tobacco off the shelf. He dropped back down to the floor and broke the can open with quick squeeze of his paws.

"Are you kidding?" Emma said.

The chawgreen shoveled the contents into its mouth and sauntered back towards the door, right at us. It had a broad face that reminded me a bit of a sloth with a permanent smile plastered across it. Old Chaw raised his bushy tail as he came closer, and I stayed as still as I could when the critter brushed up against my leg. He did the same to Emma, and she couldn't resist scratching him behind the ears.

Old Chaw rubbed on her leg a bit more, raising his tail straight up. Emma grinned at me until Old Chaw spit a wad of chewing tobacco out on her shoe, and then made his way back outside. She kept the camera on him while he passed out of the station lights and vanished into the shadows across the parking lot.

"Eww," she said, looking down at her shoe.

"Oh, he liked you, miss. That's rare for Old Chaw to share his loot."

"Have you ever followed him?" I asked.

"Oh sure," the clerk said. He lives in a little hole not too far off the parking lot. "You know, I hear there are other chawgreens around Missouri, but I've never heard of one so comfortable around people."

"Other than the mess," Emma said, "he'd make an awesome pet."

"Oh no, miss. That he would not." The old man lifted his hat slightly and scratched at his sparse hairline. "You saw Old Chaw on a good day. Reckon when he's grumpy, those claws could tear you up something fierce."

"Let's follow him a bit," I said.

Emma nodded and said goodbye to the clerk. We passed another local getting gas, who either hadn't seen the chawgreen walk by or who didn't consider the presence of an incredibly rare cryptid to be anything out of the ordinary.

We caught up to Old Chaw out into the field, though "field" is a generous term for the patch of land between highways. He sauntered down into the drainage ditch, and then he was gone, his tail the last thing to disappear into the shadows.

"I got it," Emma said.

I glanced back at her and saw her grinning at the screen on the camera.

"Okay," she said, "now we need an outro."

She turned the camera on me, and I hesitated for a moment. I turned back toward the shadow where Old Chaw had vanished. When I turned to look at the camera over my shoulder, I was back in character.

"Did you see that? Can you believe it! That big bushy tail was quite a sight, and now you can all say you've seen a chawgreen. Stay safe out there, viewers. This is Mason Dixon, Cryptid Hunter, and I'll see *you* next time."

Emma chuckled and closed the view screen on the camera. "Perfect. We'll have two episodes out of this trip easily."

"And don't forget our fancy new CCD licenses," I said, patting the wallet in my pocket. "You want to drive all the way home tonight?"

Emma glanced at her phone. "Oh hell no. That's almost two hours."

I nodded. "Maybe more."

"Let's just get a hotel."

"Noah will cover it."

"Are you sure?" Emma said, leading the way back to the truck.

"Noah's already going to have to cover that room the gowrows destroyed."

"And he'll have to cover tonight, too. I'm sure Himari will help us convince him if we need to."

"Oh yes she will," Emma said, perking up. "She'd be happy to do that in exchange for some pristine chawgreen footage, wouldn't she?"

"Why I do believe you have some insight into our technologically gifted friend."

I climbed into the driver's seat and took a deep breath, relief flooding me with the knowledge our insane day was coming to a close.

"Let's just go get some sleep," Emma said a moment before she yawned.

17

I sat at the old pressed wood desk in my tiny studio office above the butcher shop, the screen capture thumbnails from Dylan's video filling the window on my laptop. I'd drafted the email to Sonny twice already, until I finally just sent it without reading it for the fiftieth time.

That done, I had an urgent request from Noah to call him. I tapped his contact info and waited for the line to pick up.

"Thanks for the footage," Himari said when she intercepted the call.

I smiled. "Thanks for helping get my reimbursement pushed through."

"Mason," she said, "if you send me video of adorable monsters that shouldn't exist, I will get you the keys to the kingdom."

"I appreciate it, Himari. And I owe you."

"Maybe a little. Hold on, I'll patch you through."

Static buzzed in my ear for a moment before I heard Noah saying "Hello" repeatedly.

"I'm here. Sorry about that. Must have been some kind of interference."

Silence ruled the phone line for a brief minute. "Look, Mason. You've done good things, but the expense is too high. I can't have you destroying hotel rooms like you're some kind of mid-life crisis rock star on a bender."

I remembered the destruction of the motel room quite differently, with two bloody and recently-hatched scaly soccer balls causing a world of trouble, cracking a bathtub, shredding the bedding, and generally wreaking absolute havoc.

"Those gowrow eggs were meant to be sold off for research."

Irritation bled into my words. "They were *babies*, Noah. Offspring of some of the rarest creatures on this planet. And I'm sure whoever you were slated to auction them off to got plenty of use out of their dead parents."

Noah exhaled in a puff of static. "Yes, Mason, but the Church could have done more good with the windfall from the live gowrows."

"If someone tries to kidnap those gowrows, they're going to die," I said.

"Are you *threatening* me, Mason?"

"No."

"Oh really?" he said, hostility raw in his voice.

"That orchard is guarded by a pack of very grumpy Ozark Howlers. For some reason, and I don't fully understand why, the gowrows under Larry's care are friendly with most of the howlers. You send someone in there, those howlers will tear them apart. Guaranteed."

"That won't happen," Noah said.

"The dying? Or the sending people in to die?"

"Dammit Mason, I'm not sending anyone onto Larry's orchard. Somehow you and Emma have been certified by the CCD, even though no one is supposed to know that branch of DEMON even *exists* yet."

Something slammed on the other end of the line, and I suspected it was Noah's hand on top of whatever hard furniture he had handy.

"Mason," he said. "We're getting off track. You've been reimbursed, and I fully intend to keep working with you for now. The Church has sanctioned your little web series because they think it will distract people from the truth."

"Ironic," I said. "That show is full of truth. We just use fuzzy footage to save the viewers' sanity."

Noah released a humorless laugh.

"I hear you know some friends of ours," I said.

"What are you talking about, Mason?"

"Uncle Father Joe?"

Noah was silent for a time. "How do you know Father Joe?"

"We had breakfast with his nephew, Bubba."

"Are you serious? DEMON sent Bubba in to apprehend you?"

"No," I said. "I'm pretty sure they sent Agent Amy in to apprehend us, but luckily things worked out."

"You're going to be the death of me, Mason," Noah grumbled. "Keep your phone on. We've had some sightings I may need you to look into, and I don't want to have to send Himari out hunting you down again."

"Of course."

"Of course he says," Noah said as he slammed his phone down.

My phone rang a moment later with an unknown number. I figured it was either a sales call or Himari. "Hello?"

"Just remember I always know where you are," Himari said brightly.

"You creep me out, kid. I just want you to know that."

"Noted. Now, when do I get my next cryptid fix?"

"I have a few more minutes of chawgreen footage," I said.

"Send it!" she said, clapping her hands in the background. "Send it now. That is the most adorable thing I've ever seen. Except when it spit on Emma's shoe. That ... was gross."

"You'll have it today," I said. "And thanks again for helping us straighten this out."

"Pay me in cryptids, Mason, not in gratitude."

I smiled slightly. "Will do." I hung up and stared at the computer screen, wondering what Noah would be getting us tangled up with next.

***

I t was almost a week later when I finally heard back from Sonny. He sent me a link to some convoluted secure email system and insisted that I sent him the video over that. I cannot fully express my irritation at a sasquatch requiring more email security than our own personal hacker. Regardless, I attached the video and sent it with no further explanation.

Sonny's email had also informed me that Larry had named the gowrows.

"What did he name them?" Emma asked when I relayed the story to her the next day while we were out investigating some suspicious tracks near the bootheel.

I finished pouring plaster into a muddy footprint and said, "Sid and Nancy."

"No way."

I nodded. "I know."

"I thought for sure it was going to be more old country references. Or even a Branson reference!"

I smiled at Emma, and we sat back to wait for the plaster to dry. "I still think Pinky and Brain were much better names."

"If Larry's going to be taking care of those two," Emma said, "he should get to name them. That's only fair. We should take Sid and Nancy back to meet the Raleighs."

"Good God, Emma," I said. "Why would you want to give those two a heart attack?"

"Oh come on. Hearty stock, Mason. You said it yourself, the folks around these parts are from hearty stock."

I t was two days before I heard from Sonny again. His message contained only three short sentences. "That is not a sasquatch. We need to talk. Contact me."

I stared at the message, and the phone number left below it, as I ran my index finger along the edge of my keyboard.

"Well, shit."

THE END...FOR NOW

II

MASON DIXON & THE
WAMPUS OF REED SPRINGS

1

E asy pop-up tree stand my ass." I kicked the last support as it finally settled into place, the large rounded stone under my boot giving way, causing me to flail to catch my balance.

Emma unhooked the winch—it took a damn winch to lift the thing —from the ATV without comment and glanced down at her watch. "Three hours I'll never get back." She brushed away a lock of dirty blond hair from her face.

I took a deep breath and listened to the relative silence of the woods around us. The air smelled clean here, and after a weekend in Saint Louis doing paperwork with Noah, clean air was a noticeable improvement. "If that bingbuffer is out here, I doubt very much we'll be seeing it today. We've been the loudest thing out here for hours."

"Don't care," Emma said, snatching up a rifle case in one hand and slinging a soft cooler over her shoulder. "Let's eat."

I followed her up the ladder and settled into the camouflaged swivel seat mounted in the grated platform. A platform that gave me a rather unpleasant glimpse of where I could fall to my crunchy death.

"Nice view," Emma said without inflection. "Where are we moving to next?"

I narrowed my eyes and unzipped the cooler when she handed it to me. "It wasn't that bad. This is only the third location we've moved to."

Emma raised an eyebrow.

"The bingbuffer has been moving around more than I expected. We'll camp here for a while. We've seen a lot more raccoons in the area, and that's their favorite food source. Or so Larry says, and I tend to believe the old man."

"It's been a long day, Mason."

I hesitated. "Two days ..."

"Right."

"There's only one more spot to check after this. We can break down the tree stand and haul it to the other side of the river."

"I'm pretty sure we could have built a tree stand out of two by fours at each stop faster than it takes to set this thing up. We should have just bought the nice collapsible ladder stand and been done with it."

I handed her a somewhat smashed hoagie roll piled high with roast beef before digging my own out of the bottom of the cooler. "Look," I said, gesturing with my floppy sandwich, "we could be stuck up here for two or three days hunting this thing. You want to trust a rickety ladder stand for days?"

"Yes," she said with a vigorous nod. She took an impressively angry bite of her sandwich.

We didn't speak for a time, just watched the slow curve of the James River pass by in the distance. The water lapped against the shore, which, in turn, gave way to what amounted to a field of river stones.

I hadn't picked the rocky clearing out of an intentional desire to make assembling the tree stand an unholy nightmare. I picked it because the deposits of old rounded river stones were exactly the sort of place a hinge-tailed bingbuffer would come to reload on rocks.

Emma sighed and scarfed down the last bite of her sandwich. "Good idea stopping by the orchard on the way down." She lifted the small jar of moonshine and shook it. "Larry's certainly generous in his old age."

"I was just happy to see the gowrows were adjusting to their new home."

Emma nodded. "Hasn't been much more than a month, right? They looked a little bigger."

"It'll take them quite a while to get as big as Old Willie."

A kayak passed by in the distance, the motion of the paddle barely visible in the dying sun. I squinted, trying to see if I could make out the ripples in the water, but it was a bit too far.

Emma cracked her neck and started raising the fabric around the perimeter of the tree stand. The camouflage wasn't a perfect match, but I hoped it would be enough to keep anything interesting from noticing us. I pulled up the edge closest to me and wrapped a Velcro tie around the rail to hold it up.

I checked the small case of tranquilizers at my feet. We had a good supply of darts and quite the selection of gauges to choose from depending on what came our way. I opened the butt of my tranquilizer rifle, swiveling it to the side and inserting a dart before locking it up again. I removed the old CO_2 cartridge and snapped a fresh one on as well.

"Didn't you just open that cartridge yesterday?" Emma asked, eyeing the discarded cylinder.

"Yeah, but I really don't want to get surprised by something and not have the juice to knock it out. You remember how those darts bounced off that man-eating gowrow?"

"No, Mason, I totally forgot about the giant gowrow that almost killed us."

I smacked my lips and leaned forward against the gun rest, and waited.

Nightfall in the country isn't like city living. Even small towns have a lot more light pollution than you'd think. But out here, a reasonable distance from much of anything, it was mesmerizing. No matter how many times I saw those faint lights grow into a brilliant blanket of stars, it didn't get old.

"Orion's up," I said.

"There are constellations besides Orion," Emma said.

Even without a telescope or binoculars, the Orion nebula was clear to see. It was one of the first things my grandmother had taught me to find in the night sky, and it brought some measure of comfort, no matter how old I'd gotten, or how long she'd been gone.

Emma squinted at the stars. "Look at the Pleiades," she said. "You can see the dust from here. Now that's my favorite. Except for those spiral galaxies, but you can't see them without a telescope."

"Not very well at least," I said before something cracked in the distance, followed by a tremendous splash.

Emma grinned and pulled the camera out of its case. The light came on, and so did my persona. Emma kept the camera low, keeping the light beneath the edge of the fabric that concealed us in the tree stand.

"Ready," she said.

I leaned forward, raising my head a little to peek out into the moonlit clearing before snapping my gaze to the camera.

"You'll be surprised to hear we're out in the woods again, I'm sure. You'll never believe what we have for you today. We're on the trail of the elusive hinge-tailed bingbuffer."

I shook my hands at the camera. "Now I know, you're thinking that's one heck of a ridiculous name, but believe me, it's not a ridiculous cryptid. The locals say it's the size of two adult elephants in one massive creature, and it can hurl a twenty-pound stone faster than a major-league pitcher. With its tail!" I paused and blinked. "Well, maybe that's a little ridiculous, but it's no doubt dangerous, and it would make a *terrible* house pet. It's going to be a great episode."

Emma turned the camera to infrared, and I waited for my night vision to come back. Even with the light as dim as it had been, I had flashers in my vision. Emma pointed the lens out toward the river.

And we waited.

Close to an hour had passed when something low and deep

rumbled through the night like the explosion of a distant fog horn. We both froze. Emma panned the camera across the river. No river here was big enough to warrant needing a fog horn of that volume.

"Was that it, Mason?"

"Don't know yet," I said, but it was only a moment before it blared again, fracturing into a bleating chortle. It was a hell of a lot closer this time.

Something cracked below us, and a nearby oak tree shook with the force of it. I leaned back in my chair, peering through a slit in the tree stand's fabric that passed for a window.

"Holy shit."

Below us, but not as far below us as I would have preferred, was a towering creature, a shadowy form that lumbered out of the woods, trailing the thick branch it had broken off in passing.

"Mason," Emma hissed. "That thing could practically step on us!"

Water rolled off the back of what could easily be mistaken for a hippopotamus, only twice as tall as a hippo and as wide as an elephant. Moonlight glinted in the puddles of water the hinge-tailed bingbuffer left behind, its gray flesh slowly drying in the night air. A ponderous gait brought it ever closer to what now felt like our incredibly flimsy tree stand.

Something crunched below us, a brief scream of metal and what sounded very much like an exploding tire. The bingbuffer raised its foot and blinked its huge black eyes slowly at the pancake of metal and oil that had been an ATV a moment before.

"Seriously?" Emma snapped.

The wide round eyes below us swiveled up, and we ducked back into the tree stand. Emma held her hand over her mouth, and we waited. It was about then I remembered the floor was only a grate. The bingbuffer snorted and stuck his head behind the supports below us, looking up at us with some interest.

"Point the camera at him," I said.

"How do you know it's a him?" Emma whispered, angling the camera down at the grated floor.

The hinge-tailed bingbuffer made a sound like the rising whine of

115

distant train a moment before something slammed into the side of the tree stand.

Emma cursed and dropped the camera, opting for a death grip on the railing instead. I did the same, glancing out the back of the stand to see what had hit us. What greeted me looked like the flattened trunk of an elephant, only about three times as long.

I stared at the thing and watched as the bingbuffer lowered its tail, and the hinged bones in its backside retracted, letting the tail curl up into a manageable tangle of gray flesh.

The creature snorted at us again and pulled his head out of the tangle of tree stand supports. He barely bumped the cross bar, but Emma and I both squealed when the tree stand leaned precariously away from the river, the anchors pulling easily out of the rocky mud. I didn't breathe again until the legs crashed down onto the river rocks and the stand rattled back into a somewhat stable position.

"How big is he?" I asked, watching in awe as the massive form trundled away.

"Bigger than that Clydesdale that made your mom blush at Grant's Farm."

I blinked. "Did you just?"

Emma grinned at me. "It's kind of hard to miss when he's walking around with a fifth leg down there, Mason."

"Touché."

The hinge-tailed bingbuffer lived up to his name, unfurling his massive tail and flexing the hinge-like structure on his rump. He turned in a slow circle, sniffing at the rocks until he found one that seemed particularly interesting.

His tail snaked forward and wrapped around the stone, scooping it up and splashing the stone in the river a few times. The bingbuffer studied the dripping wet rock, smacked it into the water a few more times, and then turned toward us.

"Oh shit," I said. "If it starts to throw that at us ..."

"What?" Emma asked. "Run?"

The bingbuffer shifted his jaw back and forth as though he was grinding his teeth. His tail raised the stone again and slipped it into a fleshy pouch just below his jaw. The stone distended his cheek, making the bingbuffer look like he'd had half his face inflated. The creature repeated the process until he looked like a cross between a hippo and a hamster, and then he slipped into the river. This time I could see the wake in the water as he roared toward the opposite shore.

I looked at Emma. "Did that just happen? Did we seriously just watch a hinge-tailed bingbuffer load up on river stones?"

"River stones?" Emma asked. "Some of those were boulders, Mason. Look." She pointed out to the river. The bingbuffer sat low in the shallows. He'd be easily mistaken for a large outcropping of rock on the shore. No wonder people hadn't seen one of these things in decades.

"We're staying as long as he stays," Emma said, checking the stats on the camera. "Plenty of space to keep recording."

Half an hour passed. The constellations shifted above us, but the bingbuffer remained motionless. I leaned on the tree stand's frame and stared at nothing, until a shadow caught my eye.

I tapped Emma's leg and pointed at the far side of the clearing. Something was moving. It was large and low to the ground, hurrying around like it was on a mission.

"What is it?" I asked.

Emma shook her head and squinted into the night.

The shadow skittered into the moonlight, and my jaw dropped open. "It's a raccoon, and it's huge!" The massive furry form started flipping rocks over at the edge of the river, devouring whatever unfortunate creatures waited beneath.

"How big is that?" Emma asked. "It has to be almost two feet high at the shoulder—"

The bingbuffer's tail snapped forward like a sling. The old stories said they could throw a stone with the force of a rifle shot. After watching the raccoon explode on impact, I was pretty sure a rifle shot was a gross understatement of the power in that tail. The stone cracked like thunder against a nearby boulder.

Waves surged across the river as the bingbuffer sprinted, well, lumbered onto the shore. It released what I suspected was a satisfied chortle when it reached the mess of what remained of the raccoon. The bingbuffer scooped up the chunks of its prey and happily scarfed them down.

"Rest in peace, Rocket."

The horrified look on Emma's face made me want to laugh. Watching the bingbuffer eat made me want to puke. It wasn't long before all signs of the raccoon were gone, and the bingbuffer had even licked the splatter from the rocks and trees. The giant creature looked back at us, tilted its head a couple times, and then vanished into the James River.

Emma cursed a few times and turned the camera on me. "Just sign off, Mason. We are getting the hell out of here."

I shook my head, tossing my hair around a bit before staring at the camera. "Wow! Can you believe that? We just saw a hinge-tailed bingbuffer turn a raccoon into dinner. Now, I know you might be worried about Missouri losing a *very* large raccoon, but they're as common as pigeons compared to the bingbuffer. And remember, they might be monsters, but that doesn't necessarily mean they want to eat you."

Emma closed the camera and took a deep breath.

Something whistled in the distance.

2

Noah's going to be pissed," Emma said, eyeing the metal pancake of what used to be one of our ATVs.

"He should be used to it by now," I said, tying off the last surviving gun case to the back of Emma's ATV. I was just impressed the hinge-tailed bingbuffer had been able to flatten the ATV so thoroughly, and without apparent injury. There were a lot of sharp parts on those bikes, and he'd seemed fairly indifferent about the whole thing.

"Let's just get back to the hotel and get some sleep," Emma said. "Where you riding? Handlebars?"

"I take it you won't be letting me drive us back to the truck?"

"A Bronco is not a truck," Emma muttered under her breath as she pulled a helmet on. She threw a leg over the ATV's seat and patted the narrow stretch of vinyl behind her.

I climbed on, wrapping my arms around her waist. "Don't drive too crazy. I don't have a helmet, and that's a stupid way to die."

"Of all the stupid ways you've almost died, *that's* the one you're complaining about?"

She ... may have had a point.

The ATV rumbled to life, and we rode the tooth-rattling trail away from the clearing, bouncing back to the truck. It wasn't another thirty minutes before we had the ATV on the trailer, the cooler and gun cases loaded into the back, and were making our last preparations to leave.

"When is Noah going to start putting us up in some nicer hotels?" Emma asked, tightening the last of the camouflaged ratchet straps before we closed the tailgate.

"Nothing wrong with that little motel were staying at."

Emma pursed her lips. "Well, the pizza place with all the cameras sure is good. I won't complain about that."

My stomach rumbled at the thought. "I wish we had some leftovers. That pepperoni did not suck."

"Maybe we can stop by one of the abandoned gas stations on the way back into town."

I cocked my head to the side. "If I didn't know better, I'd say you weren't the biggest fan of Reeds Spring."

Emma narrowed her eyes before hopping into the Bronco and slamming the truck's door.

I laughed and hopped into the driver's seat, rolling down the window for the short drive back. We followed 413 until it turned into Main Street, passing one of Emma's aforementioned abandoned gas stations.

A small white building that looked like an old home more than anything else bore the letters "Reeds Spring City Hall" off to our right. A larger building rose beside it, an eerie mix of pale clean stone and aged, stained rock. I wasn't sure if it was a school or another government building.

The road curved, and the small red sign that designated the motel popped into view. I slowed and turned onto the street, passing Pop's Dari Dell. I had no idea what a dari dell was, but I suspected we'd find out before our stay was over.

"Let's go back to the pizza place for breakfast," Emma said. "Seriously. It's just past the abandoned Amoco station down the street."

I laughed and pulled into a parking spot. "I get it." Maybe we wouldn't find out what a dari dell was if we kept going back for pizza.

We unloaded the essentials and dragged them into the motel room. It wasn't a resort by any means, but it was clean, and the staff was friendly. Emma pulled the comforter down and flopped onto her bed as I locked the door.

My phone rang, the number from somewhere near Columbia, MO. I answered it.

"Hello?"

"That was amazing!" Himari said. "Did you think it was going to squash you like an annoying beetle? I did. But I hoped it didn't. But sometimes you're not very nice and I think bad things."

I blinked slowly. "How did you see the feed?"

"Emma's camera has Wi-Fi. I connected it to your hotspot last time you were on Noah's network."

I rubbed my forehead and sighed. Sometimes it was the best thing in the world to have a teenage hacker obsessed with Hello Kitty on your side. Sometimes it was just annoying.

"Don't hack my camera," Emma muttered into her pillow.

"Why is she so grumpy? She's alive! That bingbuffer could have vaporized you like it did that raccoon. Oh, that poor raccoon. It was so cute, and then it was ... yuck."

Emma groaned.

"Dinner," I said with a small laugh. "What do you need, kid?"

"Kid," she said with a huff. "The GPS on one of the ATVs died. I can't find it."

"The bingbuffer stepped on it," I said.

"It crushed the GPS?" Himari asked. "Are you sure? I didn't see that. I would have liked to see that. Noah's not going to like it if there's a big repair bill. Did it crush the fender?"

"No," I said, wincing a bit at the thought, "it flattened the ATV. It's like a metal pancake out by the river."

Himari giggled, most helpfully, before falling silent, her keyboard clacking in the background. "You're in Reeds Spring," she said. "Flattened metal by the river is going to get all the UFO whackos coming after you."

"I don't think they're whackos," I said.

"Really? Why?"

"Jesus," Emma grumbled. "What do you need, Himari?"

"An all expenses paid trip to the Ghibli Museum in Japan."

"Tonight!" Emma said, exasperation clear in her louder-than-necessary response. "What do you need *tonight?*"

"Noah's looking for you. He's probably been getting a busy signal for the last few minutes, but he has a new and exciting mission for you. Actually it's pretty awful, so good luck with that."

The line went dead.

I looked at Emma and blinked. "That doesn't sound good."

My phone lit up again a moment later. I answered and put it on speaker, sitting the phone on the end table between me and Emma.

"Noah," I said.

"Mason. Emma with you?"

"Yeah, so try to watch the language this time."

Emma snorted a laugh.

"What do you need, Father?" I asked.

"Have you made any progress locating the wampus?"

I exchanged a look with Emma before scratching the back of my head. "Not exactly, but we did locate the hinge-tailed bingbuffer. Whoever your source is down here, they weren't lying."

Noah sighed. "I should not have told you about that sighting."

"The bingbuffer was feeding on a raccoon. And you should have seen the size of that thing."

"I have no interest in those creatures, Mason. Not unless you tell me they pose a threat to the locals."

"No danger at all," I said, figuring this wouldn't be the best time to explain how a hinge-tailed bingbuffer flattened our ATV in one careless step, as that in itself probably marked the lumbering giant as a threat.

Emma raised an eyebrow but didn't say a word to the contrary.

"Follow up on the wampus," Noah said. "Something's killing the repairmen near that pipeline, and it's for damn sure not a panther. Find it."

Noah ended the call.

"I guess we need to hunt that wampus down."

"What's a gally-wampus doing in these parts anyway?" Emma asked. "I know they used to nest nearby, but that's what, a century ago?"

I nodded. "Yeah, and if they're killing locals, why?"

"I don't think the why matters so much about the killing," Emma said. "We just need to stop it."

"We will."

The sun's reflection off the glass front of an old alarm clock finally convinced me it was time to get up. Emma was still snoring on the other bed, and I stared in confusion at my phone.

"11:00?" I blinked a few times. "11:00 in the morning? Shit." I flipped the coffee maker on. "Emma. Emma! We're late!"

A pillow greeted my face, thrown with impressive accuracy considering I didn't think Emma was really awake yet. She rolled over and cursed at me, mumbling something into the remaining pillow she hadn't thrown.

"What?" I asked.

"I don't have coffee," she snapped, raising her head slightly.

"They'll have coffee at the pizza place. Breakfast of champions."

"Fine. I need to shower."

"No time."

She threw her legs over the edge of the bed and slowly pulled herself up. "No time for showers? No time for coffee? Why in the hell did I agree to help you with these shows, Mason? Why, in the hell?"

"The glamor, Emma." I grinned at her as I swapped my flannel pajamas out for jeans and a camouflage T-shirt.

The scowl on her face could have flayed the skin off someone who wasn't prepared for it. She grunted and fumbled for her shoes, leaving the same jeans on she'd slept in overnight. Emma pulled her hair back in a sloppy ponytail, grabbed the nearest gun case, and walked to the front door.

"Let's get this over with, Mason."

I smiled and held out a coffee. The last of the brew hissed on the warmer.

"I hate you a little less now," she said as she pulled the door open and walked over to the Bronco. She was already buckled into the passenger seat by the time I finished slipping on my boots and climbed into the truck.

Emma sipped at her coffee and eyed me. "Sure you don't want to mention why we're really down here to the viewers?"

I shook my head and started the truck. "We've had people go out to places the show has gone, Emma. We don't need some curious fan getting himself clawed in half by a wampus."

"You know, that bingbuffer was a lot bigger than Larry told us."

"Another damn good reason for having Himari strip every identifiable bit of GPS coding off the videos," I said.

Emma focused on her coffee and watched the scenery roll by outside the windows.

We passed the old Amoco station and reached a stretch of storefronts not unlike most small towns in Missouri. A quaint Main Street with all the essentials: bars, antiques, post office, and pizza. An old museum sat beside a thrift shop, long closed, but one of the locals told us it used to be a museum of the unexplained. Apparently, there used to be some serious UFO buffs in rural Missouri.

I pulled into the parking lot at Reeds Spring Pizza Co., steering the Bronco into a spot near an aged wooden fence.

"Not sure the trailer really fits," I said.

"Don't care," Emma said, looking out the passenger window. "There's enough space for people to drive around it, and there's more coffee inside. Let's go."

I turned the engine off and followed her through the front door.

"Who are we meeting, anyway?" Emma asked.

"Not sure. Larry said we'd recognize him."

"No way," Emma said at the same time I recognized the man who had to be our contact.

3

C huck, agent of CCD—the Cryptid Conservation Division—raised his hand and waved at us, looking a bit more excited than someone ought to be who's keeping a low profile.

"Hey guys! Come on, I already ordered an Athens. Hope you like olives."

"Gross," Emma muttered as we slid into two empty chairs at the small table. A wall of display cases filled with antique cameras loomed behind us, and as irritated as Emma was, I still caught her ogling the menagerie of old lenses and bodies.

"No olives?" Chuck asked. "They're super healthy for you though."

"How've you been, Chuck?" I asked while Emma ordered a pepperoni pizza.

"Not as good as those two gowrows you left with Larry."

"Pinky and Brain?" Emma asked. "They're good?"

"Like a kid in a candy store," Chuck said. He paused. "Well, if the candy store was full of apples and actually good for you."

"Larry renamed them though, right?" I asked.

Chuck laughed and shook his head. "He tried. They'll only answer to Pinky and Brain."

I relaxed into the banquet chair a bit. It was good to hear the two gowrows were doing well. I'd been worried when we saved the eggs and took them to Larry. Some cryptids don't do well in captivity, not unlike a lot of animals, actually. Of course, Larry's sprawling orchard, his extravaganza as he called it, wasn't what most people would think of as captivity. It felt much more like a free range gowrow farm guarded by sasquatches. And Ozark howlers.

"So what are you doing down here?" Emma asked. "I thought you'd be running the CCD from your super-secret office under Columbia's *premier* music club."

Chuck dipped his head slightly and drummed his fingers on his glass of water, suddenly finding the black veneer of the table fascinating. "We've had three deaths this week, Mason." He glanced between me and Emma, and then returned his focus to his fingers as he spoke. "We're not sure what it is. We just know it whistles, and men die. Do you think it could be the thing that killed your friend?"

I crossed my arms and blinked at Chuck, somewhat taken aback that he knew the story of what had happened to Dylan. Unless he was asking about someone else, but I doubted that. The CCD was involved with DEMON to some degree, so maybe I shouldn't have been surprised at all.

Our server dropped off two coffees and refilled Chuck's water. When she'd left, I shook my head. "Momo killed Dylan," I said. "It didn't whistle. It just grunted, and killed, and howled, and it stank like a tire fire."

Chuck nodded. "I didn't think so. It was only a theory. I don't like the idea of cryptids killing folks. Kind of hoped it might be the same one."

I took a deep breath and rubbed the stubble on my chin. It wasn't really stubble anymore. I'd been lazy enough about shaving that I already had a beard again.

Emma finished a long swig of coffee, sighed, and set the mug down. "Tell us what you know."

"Not much," Chuck said. "A few of the men working on the pipeline claim they saw a gally-wampus. Not too unusual in itself, as there are more of them in Reeds Spring than the rest of the world."

"Still? I thought they'd been pretty sparse for the better part of a century."

Chuck shook his head.

I tapped on the tabletop. "But they avoid people, Chuck. They aren't hostile to humans by nature, and they wouldn't be swimming around a construction site."

"I didn't tell you they were swimming." Chuck narrowed his eyes. "Do you know something, Mason?"

I frowned at Chuck. "Seriously boy scout? And here I was about to braid you a friendship bracelet out of hemp."

"Mason," Emma said. "Rude."

"Sorry. Look, my patience has gone to hell in my old age."

"You're like thirty," Chuck said.

"Like I said, old age. My back hurts, my left knee hurts, my wrists ache. I'm falling apart over here."

"Is that a Leica?" Emma asked, leaning toward the nearest display case. "Oh wow, that's gotta be from the forties or fifties."

"Some of us just have old souls," I said with a nod toward Emma.

"What?" she said.

Chuck smiled. "I didn't mean to offend you, Mason. It'll be like the Lord Howe Island stick-insects. You know how folks are down here." He shifted closer to the table and lowered his voice. "If the locals think something's out there killing folks, they'll hunt it down like the rats devoured those stick insects. Maybe there are forty or fifty gally-wampuses left. After that? None. Hasn't been a panther in these parts in a hundred years. Not since the locals hunted them down and the gally-wampuses settled in, as a matter of fact."

"Panthers are one thing," I said. "We don't know what's killing those men. Unless they cornered it, a gally-wampus wouldn't so much as raise a paw against them."

Emma turned back to the table. "It's a whistling-wampus."

I blinked.

Chuck stared at her.

"They hunt in cedar thickets," I said.

The server returned with two pizzas, one looking a bit more

127

browned than the other. We didn't say anything else until she'd walked away.

"Are there cedar thickets near the pipeline?" Emma asked.

Chuck nodded. "They're all over down here."

"Great," I said, picking up a slice of pepperoni pizza. Kalamata olives for breakfast just seemed a bridge to far. "You ever seen a whistling-wampus?"

"No."

Emma finished chewing a bite of pizza and asked, "What about a gally-wampus?"

"That I've seen," Chuck said. "Like I said, we have quite a few in the southern parts of Missouri."

"What are we dealing with?" Emma asked. "Are tranquilizers going to be enough?"

"Reckon so. It's not like you're trying to bring down one of those armored gowrows."

I blew out a breath. "Yeah, that didn't work so well."

"You all just need to camp out by the shore at night. You'll see a gally-wampus soon enough."

"We did that last night," I said, frowning at a particularly stringy bite of cheese. The crust crunched, and the pepperoni did nothing but complement the buttery dough. "That's damn good."

Emma grunted and picked up another piece.

"You're missing out on the olives," Chuck said.

I frowned at his deluxe pizza from hell. "Another time."

"Suit yourself. You had to have seen the gally-wampus last night. They swim up through those bends at all hours. Easy to mistake them for the wake of a boat the way they move."

I shook my head. "Didn't see one."

"We did see a hinge-tailed bingbuffer though!" Emma said, taking another sip of coffee. "That was somewhat terrifying."

"You saw a *what?*" Chuck asked. "I've been in this area for almost three years, and I've never seen a bingbuffer."

"They're huge," I said.

"Crushed Mason's ATV in one go," Emma said.

Chuck raised his eyebrows. "Seriously? Did you see it pick up any stones?"

I nodded. "And it killed a raccoon while we watched."

"Buffed the bing right out of it," Emma said. She smiled when Chuck flashed her a confused look.

"You saw a hinge-tailed bingbuffer hunting?" He spread his hands and laughed. "That is *amazing!* Did you record it? Are you going to use it on the show?"

"Yeah," Emma said. "It's not the clearest shot since I was really just hoping to not die, but that actually works out for the show."

"You have to let me see it."

"Later," I said. "It sounds like we need to get back to the river and watch for wampuses."

Chuck's excitement waned a little bit, but then he started to smile. I was beginning to think the guy should never play poker. Ever.

"Don't you want to wait until evening?" Chuck asked. "You'll be much more likely to find them if you do."

"Not a bad idea." I glanced at Emma. "We could head out to the pipeline in the meantime. Take a look around where those workers were killed."

"Now you're talking," Chuck said, sliding two laminated IDs across the table. "You're both officially state pipeline investigators."

"Is that even a real thing?" Emma asked, frowning at the ID. "I would have thought it would be pipeline inspectors."

Chuck cursed. "I knew that didn't sound right." He waved his hands. "Don't worry about it. Those boys won't give a damn, so long as you don't issue any citations."

"We'll try to resist," I said, clipping the ID to my shirt pocket.

We finished up brunch, mapped out the GPS coordinates Chuck provided, and headed off in pursuit of the gally-wampus.

4

Highway 213 led us north toward Galena, showering us with alternating views of heavily-forested Missouri hills and wide open fields. A few small motels peppered the highway in the literal middle of nowhere, and I wondered where they found their customer base.

"Seems like a lot of motels out here," I said.

"That one rents canoes," Emma said as we drove by another motel that I was fairly certain was out of business.

A short bridge carried us over Railey Creek. The creek flowed into the James River, and I caught a glimpse of the convergence as we passed by. Ivy crawled down the sheer rocks that flanked our right, while the river made intermittent appearances through the twisted trees on our left.

The highway ended at a sheer stone bluff, one that had been cut from the earth decades before. We took a left onto Highway 176 and passed quickly over the James again.

"It's beautiful," Emma said, watching the river bed with its sand-bars and flood plain pass by below us.

"That it is."

Galena vanished in a heartbeat. The GPS gave up when we reached a gravel road, telling us to make a U-turn in fifteen feet, and then immediately repeating itself. Thankfully, it wasn't hard to find what we were looking for from there. A few bouncy minutes rattling down into the backwoods, and the torn crime scene tape was plain to see.

Emma frowned at the GPS map on my phone. "I think we're close to where we saw the bingbuffer. Just on the other side of the river and upstream a bit."

"Not sure if that's a good thing or a terrible thing," I said, closing the truck's squeaky door and frowning at the scene in front of us. I grabbed some sulfur powder through the open window and started patting down my waistline and socks. I had zero desire to walk out of here looking like a tick farm.

"Looks like private property on the other side of the road," I said. "Don't be surprised if someone shows up with a shotgun to politely ask us what the hell we're doing on their land."

"I think that's happened all of once, Mason. Thank you for reminding me every time we're near private property though. I'd probably forget if it wasn't for—"

The unmistakable rack of a slide sounded behind us. "Three seconds to tell me what the fuck y'all doing here."

Emma squeaked at the shotgun leveled at my gut.

"Pipeline inspectors," I said after a deep breath, slowly pointing to the badge on my chest, and then silently cursing myself for not remembering it said investigator. "You'll want to lower that boom stick, unless you want the feds crawling all over your land."

The shotgun fell enough that it would probably just take my foot off at the ankle.

"I don't need no more feds out here. Last I seen of them they was looking at that latest kill."

Emma frowned and glanced at me. "You mean the pipeline worker that died."

"Oh she's a smart one."

Emma turned about five shades of furious red in three seconds.

"Mister," I said. "It's been a long day, and I'd really rather not—"

"You came onto *my* land with this dumb bitch, and I didn't ask for no pipeline to—"

The man looked confused when a hollow pop sounded, and the tranquilizer dart sunk into his neck. I suspected he was trying to reach up and grab the cylinder, but his motor skills were already suffering. He frowned and worked his mouth a bit. My brain scrambled for an explanation, but then Emma literally kicked him in the ass, and the man fell down into a heap.

I blinked. A couple times.

"He'll be out at least ten minutes," Emma said, loading another dart into her tranquilizer rifle. "Asshole."

I held my hand out, speechless.

"Oh, relax. It's no more than you accidentally shot yourself with in the arm last year."

"But he's an old man!" I said.

"Tough folks out here," she said, giving me a knowing look.

"Jesus. Prop him up. Make sure he doesn't choke on his tongue, yeah? And hide the dart for God's sake. Tell him it was the biggest damn mosquito you ever seen."

"You think I'm babysitting him, Mason?" Emma said, her eyes narrowing.

"*Hell* yes! You shot the man with a tranquilizer dart meant to take down a wampus!"

"Whatever," she muttered and rolled her eyes.

I waited for her to prop the old man up before I headed toward the broken crime scene line. What I'd thought was a dense forest broke away into a cedar thicket not thirty feet in. The sparse ground cover of the woods gave in to a tangle of flowers and grass on the flat patch of land.

A black cylinder sat at the opposite side of the clearing. Most of the pipelines were underground, but parts of them often surfaced, and some of them did so in unusual places. A steel fence, bent and twisted, formed a perimeter around a handful of old shutoff valves. I flinched when I saw what was waiting.

The mess of what had happened here hadn't been completely washed away in the rain showers. Humans didn't do this sort of thing to other humans. Not with enough violence and power to rend the earth beneath their victim. To send entrails so high up into the forest's canopy that the police hadn't bothered to bring them down was a special kind of awful.

I passed by the remaining gore soaking the ground only to find another patch on the southern edge of the thicket, nearest the river. Something large shifted in the shadows of my peripheral vision, sending my heartrate through the roof. It was about then I realized I was in the hunting ground of a whistling-wampus, by myself, with only a tranquilizer pistol at my side.

I'd seen all I needed to of the crime scene. No wolf had done this. No panther. A bear probably could have pulled it off, but why would it fling viscera into the trees? The tranquilizer felt woefully inadequate in my hand as I slid it free from its holster.

I kept my eyes on the tangled underbrush around my feet, but glanced at the edge of the thicket as often as I could. The shadows didn't move again, and it took a great deal of self-control not to shout for Emma.

My skin crawled as I crashed back into the woods, indecision still crawling through my brain. Every flash of sunlight and flicker of darkness became a beast set on murdering me. Only, if it was a whistling-wampus, wouldn't it whistle first?

I hadn't finished contemplating that conundrum when I broke free from the tree line, just in time to hear Emma say, "And you wouldn't have *believed* the size of that mosquito. Like a damn lawn dart, it was."

The mud-covered man grunted. "Lost my cousin to one of those back in the seventies. Came down right on his head, it did. I still have the set that done it."

Emma stared at the man in what I believed to be a mixture of awe and outright horror. "And you're sure you're okay?"

"Oh yeah, I've taken worse tumbles off my tractor." He pressed gently on the wound in his neck and frowned at the drying blood that came away on his fingers.

"You dropped your shotgun," Emma said, handing it back to him.

"Thank you, miss. And I do apologize for threatening y'all like that. We've had a lot of … a lot of unfriendly faces around, and some of them ain't human."

I tried not to look too interested while I appraised just how out-of-his-mind this guy was. "I'm Mason," I said. "That's Emma."

"Name's Clarence. Clarence Ellbrach. This here's my family's farm. Or it least it was until my pa sold half of it to the pipeline."

"Eminent domain?" Emma asked.

Clarence spat. "Y'all not as stupid as you look. Feds ain't welcome here, and that's why."

If his family had been here for generations, he might know a lot more than he'd let on, although I supposed the non-human comment was pretty out there already. I weighed my options and decided to see if I could keep the old man talking.

"How long's your family been here?"

Clarence paused for a second. I expected a vague answer, but instead he came back with, "My pa's side of the family been here since 1838. Settled in Hermann when Edward Hermann himself lived there. Moved here not much more than a year later, 1840 it was."

"You ever heard of a gally-wampus around these parts?" I asked.

The old man huffed out a laugh. "Common as bobcats and copperheads. You poke around those thickets, you won't miss their tracks. Quiet as a big cat goes, but they trample the brambles like nothing I seen."

"Ever see anything else?" Emma asked.

Clarence pursed his lips, the skin around his mouth wrinkling up like a sun-dried slab of jerky. "Reckon so. Some of it I hope I never see again."

"Like a bingbuffer?" Emma said, pressing the point.

Clarence eyed Emma for a moment, before responding a bit more forcefully than I'd expected. "You stay away from him, hear?" He turned a frown on Emma. "My family's known that bingbuffer for three generations. That's a gentle giant right there. Wouldn't hurt a fly."

The image of the exploding raccoon running through my mind said otherwise.

"You're asking if I know what killed those men." Clarence gestured toward the thicket with his shotgun. That'd be the whistling-wampus of Reeds Spring. And you'll be lucky if it don't kill you first."

I fought back a grimace. It was one thing to hypothesize about what might have killed those workers, but it was quite another to have someone confirm it *was*, in fact, one of nature's best ambush predators.

"Can you tell us anything about it?" I asked.

Clarence rested the butt of his shotgun on his boot and folded his hands over the barrels. My imagination immediately showed me a highlight reel of Clarence blowing his own arms off. Thankfully, the old man's voice brought me back into the moment.

"You don't go killing no gally-wampus now, hear?"

"How can we tell the difference?" Emma asked.

"Well, one's a big ass cat that moves like a mink. The other's a big ass cat that moves like a mink and whistles."

"Thanks?" Emma said, unable to stop her eyebrow's slow climb.

Clarence gave her a sideways grin that was two teeth short of a full set. "The only whistling-wampus I ever seen was as black as oil. The only thing you'll see coming are fangs and eyes. You'll find it in the shadows, less it finds you first." He thumped the shotgun on his foot twice and then nodded to each of us. "Y'all take care now. We have enough bodies in the holler already."

He turned and left. We watched him go without another word.

"Was that helpful?" Emma asked. "I'm honestly not sure."

"Maybe because you shot him with a tranquilizer?"

Emma scowled. "I pulled the dart out before it could deliver a full dose."

"Let's see about renting another ATV, which we'll leave parked on the trail this time, and setup down by the river again."

"Why?" Emma said. "Shouldn't we setup here?"

135

I looked back toward the thicket where I'd seen the remnants of the dead men. "A wampus won't hunt where it sleeps. I want to check the trails. We might find some tracks, and if we're lucky, we'll catch sight of a gally-wampus."

"Oh sure," Emma said. "And if we're really lucky, we won't get shredded by a giant whistling cat."

5

W e failed miserably in locating an ATV for rent, so I rode on the back of Emma's again once we parked the truck. It didn't seem like such a long ride while the sun was still up, but the thought of a whistling-wampus being anywhere nearby kept my nerves in a constantly frazzled state.

It took some serious doing to get a man's entrails into the canopy of a full-grown forest.

We parked the ATV by our tree stand, in the underbrush at the end of the trail.

Emma adjusted her belt and eyed the gun case when I picked it up. "Sure you want to carry around all three barrels?"

I glanced at the case. I had a .357 barrel with two magazines for the Magnum Research Desert Eagle, plus three magazines each for the .44 and .50 caliber barrels. "If I was going to leave anything, it would probably be the extra .44 long colt magazines, but I'd rather have them and not need them."

Emma shrugged. "It's your boat anchor. I don't think Clarence was lying about that whistling-wampus."

"Neither do I," I said, "but do we really know that's what killed those men?"

"Pretty damn sure," Emma said in a patronizing tone. "Yeah."

"Besides, you have that Taurus .454 holstered under your arm. I know your anti-tank pistol will keep me safe."

"Shut up, Mason."

I caught her smile before she turned away, but she didn't give me any more grief about preferring to keep the tranquilizer rifle at the ready. I left its smaller brother in the case. Whatever we ran into, I didn't want to be stuck with the smaller darts in the tranquilizer pistol.

The tree stand was still secure, but the ATV was gone. That gave me pause. "I'm not hallucinating, right?" I gestured at the empty patch behind the tree stand.

"What happened to the ATV?" Emma asked.

I shrugged. "Did Noah send a cleanup team? Seems a bit premature."

"They left the tree stand, so I don't think it was a cleanup."

Himari might know more, being she liked to spy on most of us and was essentially Noah's communication hub, so I sent her a quick text. My phone rang a second later.

"Himari?" Emma asked

I nodded.

"I sent them," Himari said before I could even offer a greeting. Her voice sounded tinny with the waterproof phone case I was using.

"Why?" I asked. "We're stuck down here for at least another night."

"That ATV was right by the river," Himari said, delivering her entire following spiel in one breath. "You want all the fishes to die, Mason? *Do you?* All that gas and oil just leaking into the groundwater? No no no."

"Thanks, kid."

"No problem. Now don't die. And tell Emma hi!" She ended the call.

"Himari says hi," I said. "She called the cleanup crew so the fluids from the ATV wouldn't pollute the groundwater."

Emma chuckled. "That kid."

I smiled and slid my phone into a pocket.

"Are we looking for gally-wampuses or whistling-wampuses?" Emma asked, looking at the tree line near the river's bend.

"Does it matter?" I asked, giving the supports of the tree stand a shake. The structure didn't budge, which reminded me just how bulky that hinge-tailed bingbuffer had been.

When Emma didn't answer, I turned to find her eyebrow judging me.

"What?" I said.

"Are you asking if it matters whether we're hunting an ambush predator known for killing men, or a kid-friendly—if somewhat destructive—giant cat?"

I blinked. Twice. "Fair point."

"If it's an ambush predator," Emma said, "we're going to need to bait it. Otherwise we'll be the bait."

"You're right, but if we aren't the bait, we'll have to wait for the pipeline workers to go back on the clock."

Emma cursed. "We can't do that, Mason."

"I know. Let's look around this side of the river some more. The old man seemed pretty sure the area is packed full of gally-wampuses. And if there's enough here to keep that bingbuffer fed ..." I trailed off with a shrug.

Emma nodded and adjusted her backpack.

I walked toward the edge of the riverbank where we'd seen the raccoon come out of the forest. Raccoons liked the sun more than most people thought, and I had a hunch that a giant raccoon may stay close to a clearing that received a lot of sunlight, especially if the edges of the tree line were warm.

"How far away do you think we are from the cedar thicket where those men were killed?" I asked, glancing over my shoulder and eyeing the far bank.

"Unless I'm reading the map on the GPS wrong, it's right up the creek there. Maybe a half mile?"

"Well," I said, "it'll be a lot longer than that when we have to drive around half the damn county to get there."

I turned my attention back to the shadowy forest on our side of the riverbank. Sure enough, a slightly overgrown, but very defined path wound its way between the towering trunks and branches of oaks and evergreens.

Emma stepped up beside me. "You think that's a path from a gally-wampus?"

"Could be. Could be from a family of them. Could be from boar, too."

"Wild boar?" Emma asked, her eyes flashing from side to side. "Here?"

"You sound more nervous about some pigs than you do about a whistling-wampus."

"How big are the boars?"

I crouched beneath a low tree limb and started down the foliage-obscured trail. "I know you don't like wild boars, but we really have bigger things to worry about."

"Says the man who's terrified of centipedes."

"Terrified is a strong word."

"Mortally fearful? Is that a condition? Seems like it should be if it's not."

I pushed an evergreen branch out of the way, the needles digging into my palm before they gave way to a slightly sticky mass of sap near the wood. Once Emma passed, I released the branch with a snap. It sprang back into its natural position.

We wove deeper into the woods, following a shallow switchback until the canopy grew thick enough to cover the entirety of the forest floor in perpetual shadow.

"Ugh, sap," I said, scrubbing another palmful on my jeans.

Emma ducked under a low oak branch. "At least it's not on the Bronco. Nothing more tedious than scrubbing sap off an antique paint job."

I ignored her not-so-subtle jab at my valiant steed. We entered a clearing in the middle of the woods. It wasn't a thicket, as the forest still loomed full and thick above us, but the clearing was shockingly, well, clear.

"What is this?" I asked.

"The ground is smoothed away in spots," Emma said, crouching down to study the striations in the damp dirt. She held her hand out to the widest lines and holes in the dirt. "Mason, these are tracks."

"What?" I said. "I don't see prints."

"Get your tranquilizer out."

I didn't wait. The rifle almost sprang into my hand as I pulled it off my shoulder.

"Look closer. You see the claw marks?"

"No," I said, my focus jumping between the odd pattern on the ground and the forest around us. I paced beside Emma, watching every shadow, every shifting branch. We'd almost circled the massive clearing when I looked down, and everything came into focus. "Shit."

"How big would it have to be?" Emma asked. "It's what I think it is, isn't it?"

"You think it's a heavy furry mammal with paws large enough to gut a deer in one shot?"

"Dragging its belly low to the ground, obscuring its own tracks," Emma said, finishing my train of thought.

"We need to go," I said, my heartbeat suddenly pounding in my ears. We'd walked right into something's lair. "We'll set up a camera and—"

"*Mason*," Emma hissed, her fingers clamping down on my arm like a vise. "Up."

I raised my eyes, catching the brief swish of tail on a branch some fifteen feet above us. Once I knew it was there, I couldn't unsee it, but its camouflage had been near-perfect.

"Don't run," I said, fighting my instincts as they kicked in. Would a gally-wampus behave like a bobcat? Or should we actually run screaming? Most of the folks I'd met that said they'd encountered a gally-wampus clearly hadn't.

It swished its tail again, raising a broad head that looked more like a lynx than a bobcat, but much larger than either species.

Something clicked beside me, and I almost shouted when I saw Emma had the camera trained on the gally-wampus.

"Are you insane?" I hissed.

"What?" Emma hissed back. "If we get eaten it'll be like one of those terrible horror movies where they find a camera with the whole story conveniently recorded. Only it'll be real, and we'll be dead."

That didn't make me feel much better, especially now that the gally-wampus's attention was all for the camera. I watched in awe as the massive creature lowered itself via the tree trunk, one wide paw in front of the other in utter silence.

Outside of the deeper shadows of its perch, I could make out the same spotted fur coloring as a bobcat, with the wide mutton chops on its face like a lynx. Bright yellow eyes roved the area, the gally-wampus pausing to eye the woods before focusing on me and Emma in turn. Its tufted ears swiveled from side to side, lowering slightly only to spring straight up again.

The gally-wampus took three quick steps toward us, sniffed the air, and cocked its head to the side.

"Mason?" Emma said, her voice rising as the massive wampus took a few slow strides closer to us.

"No sudden movements." I kept my eyes locked on its ears. If it was anything like the cats it resembled, its ears would tell me when and if I needed to fire a tranquilizer. If I was wrong ... I shook my head. Meeting new critters wasn't the time for doubt.

"Mason," Emma hissed, drawing out my name, and then the gally-wampus was on her.

6

I 'd seen wild animals respond with curiosity or outright hostility
when they encountered a human in their territory, but this was
something different.

Emma squealed as the gally-wampus rammed its head into her gut,
rubbing on her like she was a long-lost owner, and the wampus was
overjoyed to have her found again. It rubbed its head down to Emma's
thigh before running the length of its body down her side. Emma
didn't move, and I wasn't sure if she was even breathing at that point.

The gally-wampus finished twining around Emma, and then head-
butted me, rubbing its long body along my jeans and leaving so much
fur behind I was pretty sure Sonny the sasquatch would be able to
stitch a new pair of briefs out of it.

I held my hand out as the wampus circled me and smiled when the
broad head nuzzled my palm, and then proceeded to run its back
across my forearm.

"Mason," Emma said, her voice drawing the gally-wampus back to
her. "Why is it acting like a giant house cat?"

I grinned, letting the wampus's fur run between my fingers, soft as
any big cat I'd ever had the pleasure of meeting. "Someone's been
feeding her if I had to guess."

"Hi Kitty," Emma said as the gally-wampus padded back over to her. Emma grunted when the headbutt knocked her to the ground, sitting her flat on her ass. "Hey!" Emma squawked, but the wampus kept rubbing her head against Emma's chest, practically drowning Emma in a cloud of fur.

When the gally-wampus flopped onto Emma's lap and smacked her lips, I lost it. The clearing filled with my own unhinged, hysterical laughter, and the mottled tail casually swished back and forth on top of a somewhat flattened Emma.

"Mason," Emma hissed, trying to push what was likely two-hundred-and-fifty pounds of wampus off her legs. Instead, the gally-wampus turned to lick her face, apparently mistaking Emma's valiant efforts for a good scratching.

"Who's a good girl?" I said, walking slowly up to the gally-wampus's side. She kept one eye on me, which was great. Startling anything this big, like I could have with my little outburst of laughter, could end badly for everyone involved.

I slid a small can of tuna out of my backpack, thinking it would probably appeal to the giant cryptid feline more than the jerky, seeds, or dried fruit. As soon as I pulled the lid off, her giant golden eyes locked onto me. She popped up from the ground like she had the legs of a nigh-behind, and by the time I'd finished tapping the fish out into my hand, she locked onto my wrist. And by *locked onto my wrist*, I mean my *entire* hand was in her mouth.

"Mason!" Emma said, reaching for her gun.

I shook my head, wondering if that was the stupidest response I could possibly have as I looked down at the giant mouth of deadly teeth currently engulfing my entire hand and a good chunk of my forearm. I winced when the wampus's teeth cut into my palm a bit, but then all I could feel was the warm wriggling of a giant, sandpaper-like tongue.

She released my arm and smacked her lips, looking up at me expectantly.

"Look at her left leg," Emma said.

I stepped to the right a little to get a better angle and winced at the raw patch of skin. A rough scab had formed, entangled with her fur and what looked like a burgeoning infection.

"Call her."

Emma clicked a few times with her tongue, and when the gally-wampus shifted its attention to her, I swung the tranquilizer rifle up and fired. It popped like the plunger being ripped out of a large hypodermic needle.

The dart smacked into her right rear leg. She shook her tail a few times and scratched at the dart, but it held its ground. I pulled out another can of tuna and smacked the contents into my palm, holding it out to the gally-wampus.

This time she gently licked the strong-scented tuna off my hand and let me scratch her behind the ear. Emma did the same, and the gally-wampus slowly lowered herself to the ground, resting her head on top of her massive paws.

"Was that safe?" Emma asked. "Obviously, shooting her while we're standing next to her wasn't, but the dose I mean?"

"Should be." I ran my fingers through the tuft on the gally-wampus's ear. She flicked her ear the first couple times I made contact, but then slowly stopped responding as the tranquilizer took hold. "We need to look at that wound."

Emma nodded and carefully pulled the wampus's paw forward, stretching the wound out enough to give us a clear view. "Looks like it was an abscess," she said. "Possibly bite marks around it. And if those are bite marks, I'm guessing these are from something's claws."

I studied the long pale bald spots that led away from the wound. "You're right."

Emma pushed on the pad of the gally-wampus's foot. "Are you seeing those claws?"

"Like a damned dinosaur," I said, snapping a quick picture of the wound. I texted it to Himari. She'd get it to Doc. I wasn't sure if he'd want to risk taking my calls after the last time I'd dragged him into something. If the man knew how to work on a gowrow and put a cone of shame on an Ozark howler, I was pretty sure he could help us with this one, too.

10 sec, Himari texted back.

The screen on my phone flashed a moment before it vibrated. "Hello?" I said, turning on the speaker phone.

"Mason," Doc said, a surprising lack of irritation in his voice. "What is that a picture of?"

"A big cat?" I said, raising my voice slightly at the end.

Doc laughed quietly. "We're secure. Himari shipped me this phone by courier. If she says it's untraceable—"

"It is," I finished.

"Good. Save the number in case you need me in the future." Doc paused. "In case a cryptid you found needs me."

I smiled slightly at the rephrasing. "It's a gally-wampus."

"You in the Ozarks again?"

"Yeah."

"Figures. They've had a resurgence there. Not sure why, but the CCD is estimating the population to be almost sixty."

"That's practically a city by cryptid standards," Emma said. "So what can we do?"

"What do you have with you?"

Emma struggled with her backpack and pulled out a small white first aid case. "Not a lot. Maybe enough gauze to wrap around her leg a few times."

"Scissors?"

"Yes." Emma held up a pair a scissors that looked to be bent in the middle. I had a vivid flash of a nurse cutting my jeans off with scissors much like those after a very angry raccoon had gotten ahold of my calf. It wasn't a raccoon...

"Good," Doc said. "It looks like an abscess, but I honestly think it may be healing already. Is it hot to the touch?"

Emma pressed her palm gently to the wound, and then moved her hand to an undamaged part of the gally-wampus's leg. "Slightly, but I do mean only slightly."

"Excellent. Flush the wound a bit. Lay some gauze around the edges, just to soften up the scabs and crust in her fur. Wait five minutes, and then trim the edges out. It should keep her from tearing it open again. If she spends too much time in the water, it may open up, but that's the best thing you can do in the field right now."

"Thanks Doc," Emma said, already soaking the gauze and gently applying it.

"You two be careful. If the gally-wampus population is on the rise, I wouldn't be surprised if there are far more unpleasant things nearby."

I suspected Doc didn't know how right he was. I thanked him and ended the call before texting our thanks to Himari. She responded with smiling cat emoji number two hundred and forty-two.

Emma trimmed the worst of the matted fur away until the edges of the scab were smooth and flush with the bald patches of the wound. "That's as good as were going to get."

"What are we going to do with her now?" I asked. "This feels too exposed to just leave her."

"I don't think we're carrying her very far." Emma ran her fingers through the gally-wampus's ruff. "We'll wait for her to wake up."

"Good idea," I said, gently removing the dart before stashing it in a narrow sharps container. I pulled out a bag of jerky and gnawed on a few pieces while we waited. The sun started its slow dive into the tree line before I felt the eyes in the shadows.

7

Something rumbled, and the acoustics of the field made it impossible to tell where it was coming from. The hair standing up on the back of my neck told me I might prefer not to know.

"She's purring," Emma said, running her hand down the gallywampus again.

"Something's here," I said.

Emma unbuckled the snap on the holster for her pistol. She didn't draw it, instead going back to petting our very large patient. "Where?"

"Not sure. I can't ... holy shit."

Eyes, golden and huge, materialized in the darkness of the forest, focused with an intensity that put my nerves into overdrive. Lithe forms slunk through the shadows, their eyes vanishing and reappearing at such random patterns that I couldn't begin to guess how many bodies there were.

"Mason," Emma said in a hushed whisper. "Behind you."

"And you," I said, admiring the fact she had her camera up when I glanced her way again.

"She's waking up," Emma said, backing away from the gallywampus slightly.

"Mason Dixon, it's what's for dinner." Sometimes I said weird stuff when I was stressed, or about to die, which was generally stressful. I moved slowly, wondering if I could slide my backpack off and reload before—"

Emma screamed, and while I was pretty sure it was my name, it came out in a throat-tearing screech.

A quick glance showed me the wampus charging from behind, raising its paw to make quick work of my fragile underbelly. I barely got the backpack up before the first strike hit me hard enough to put me on the ground. Horrible visions of entrails in trees flashed through my mind. I gasped when the breath left my lungs, thankful for whatever soft vegetation my head had rebounded off of.

Emma raised the Taurus .454 into the air and fired. I didn't see her do it, but the bell ringing in my head told me all I needed to know. The vegetation beneath my skull moved, and then bucked, flinging me into Emma like a ragdoll.

We both went down in a tangled heap, thankfully free of bullet wounds. It was then that I realized I'd actually landed on the gally-wampus. The newcomers had hesitated at the gunshot, but they didn't run.

The wampus that had knocked me down moved to strike again, its eyes locked on Emma's prone form.

"No!" I shouted, scrambling up into an aggressive stance. It might give Emma a chance. She could fire another shot. Maybe scare them off, save herself. Best case scenario, I figured I'd die fast.

The wampus leapt.

Something roared beside me, and the gally-wampus we'd patched up barreled into my attacker, sending the larger, darker wampus barrel rolling toward the tree line. The golden eyes all around us froze, watching the encounter with what appeared to be cold detachment.

"I think I'll name you Claw," I said, speaking to the gally-wampus like a completely rational person.

She looked back at me, then raised her paw and smacked the other gally-wampus's head so hard it thunked against a tree trunk like a coconut. The second wampus crashed to the ground limp, but its chest still rose and fell.

"Claw didn't kill it," I said, glancing back at Emma, who for some insane reason had picked up the camera again.

Claw watched the downed gally-wampus for a brief time, and then all but strutted back over to rub her head against my thigh and bowl Emma over onto the ground again. The other wampuses filtered into the clearing, most patterned with the same spots as Claw, but a few verging on being striped like a tiger.

One lingered in the back, its fur almost a solid gray, vanishing into the shadows at the edge of the woods. Within a minute, we were surrounded by gally-wampuses sprawled out across the odd patterns in the dirt.

It hadn't been one wampus that had made the massive circular pattern in the mud and earth; it was a goddamned company of them.

"Mason," Emma said. "How do we get out of here without dying?"

"Claw already asserted her dominance. I'm pretty sure as long as she lets us go, the others won't bother us. Unless there are strays in the woods. Then, you know, claws, death, and kibble."

Emma blinked at me.

"Claw," I said.

The gally-wampus looked up, swiveling her tufted ears at me.

"We have to go. So you take care of yourself and try not to steal too many campers' cans of tuna."

She chuffed at me and rested her head on her paws again.

I didn't bother trying to slip into my backpack, instead opting to carry it in my left hand. Emma followed, weaving between lazy gally-wampus tails and doing our damnedest to be quiet.

I managed to snap branches in the underbrush on each of the first three steps I took into the woods. We were almost out of sight of the company of cryptids when the eeriest sound I'd ever heard echoed through the woods.

A whistle.

Like an old man singing an ancient tune he'd forgotten the words to, the melody carried, rising and falling. The gally-wampuses all perked up, staring at the opposite side of the clearing from where we'd left.

"Move," I said.

Emma gave me a sharp nod as I swung the backpack over my shoulder again and tightened the strap on the tranquilizer rifle. She put up the camera, leaving her hand free to reload the spent round of the .454.

We walked as quietly as we could, but with the light fading and us not wanting to use flashlights, we weren't very quiet.

Relief flooded me to my bones when we were back on the ATV. We had extra ammo, more firepower, and I felt a lot more secure because of it.

"That was the whistling-wampus out there," Emma said.

"Don't see what else it could've been."

"And it killed all of those men?"

I grimaced. "Seems likely."

"Are we hunting tonight?" Emma asked.

"Hell no. Back to the truck. Back to the motel. We need sleep, and we are *not* hunting a whistling-wampus in the dark."

"Good. We can send the footage to Himari. See if she sees anything we missed."

"If she wasn't watching the entire time you mean."

Emma barked out a humorless laugh. "No doubt."

Hey, kid," Emma said when Himari answered the phone. "Did you see any of the video tonight?"

Himari groaned. "No, my great grandma is here. We've been watching Chinese soap operas, Emma. Do you know how much I hate Chinese soap operas?" She paused. "Better than American soap operas at least. But still!"

"So sorry for your torture," Emma said. "At least you didn't get almost eaten by gally-wampuses tonight."

"What!" Himari barked out.

"Can you look the footage over when you get a chance?" I asked. "You can see our new friend, Claw."

"Is it cute?" Himari asked. "Or are you setting me up to look at exploded body parts again. That was not funny, Mason. Not funny."

"That was an accident," I said, leaning closer to the phone. "I told you that was an accident."

"I know!" Himari snapped. "I saw all the exploded parts!"

Emma covered a laugh when I mouthed the word *help* at her.

"Look for a dark colored wampus in the background," Emma said. "It wasn't acting quite like the others. Maybe Doc could help?"

"I will go watch the video," Himari said. "Great grandma is sleeping now. Bye."

The line clicked off, and Emma burst into laughter. "I love that girl."

8

I'd planned on getting up early the next morning, but the phone blaring at us at 3:30 a.m. was just not acceptable. I silenced the ringer and rolled over, yanking the edge of the blanket up around me like a collar.

The phone bleated at me again.

"Just answer it," Emma mumbled from the other bed.

I sighed and fumbled with my phone; the screen lit up like a lighthouse in the dark. "Noah? What the hell is Noah calling us at 3:30 in the damn morning for?" I put it on speaker.

"Mason," Father Noah said, sounding irritatingly awake. "Himari tells me there's an oil spill near the field where those men were killed."

My dead of night grogginess vanished in a heartbeat. I cursed and clenched my fist. This wasn't the first time there'd been a spill in one of the Missouri pipelines. We'd seen it in the Ozarks before, Rolla, and more places than I cared to remember. Now it was in Stone County.

"Are you sure it's the same place?" I said, hoping somehow the message had been mixed up, but Himari's voice popped onto the line, too.

"Exact same place," she said. "By the edge of the woods."

I cursed. "We were just there. I didn't see anything out of the ordinary by the river." Well, other than the giant steel fence that'd been twisted up like a pretzel.

Emma sat up on the edge of her bed, rubbing at her eyes. The phone's light turned her into a ghostly silhouette to my unfocused eyes.

"How bad?" Emma asked.

"Bad enough," Noah said.

"Why call us?" I asked. "What can we do about a burst pipeline?"

"You can help clean it up," Noah said. "I've already spoken to Larry, and he's getting a tanker truck ready. He might have hesitated, but once he saw the footage of the gally-wampuses, he didn't argue."

I frowned at the phone. "Larry knows how to clean up an oil spill? I don't think we can put the oil back into a tanker truck, Noah."

"The spill isn't far from McCord Bend," Father Noah said, like I hadn't spoken. "They either get it contained, or the James will be dead for years."

"That's bad," I said. "How big is the pipeline? Big enough to destroy the ecosystem and chase away that entire company of gally-wampuses?" It wasn't a question, really. I already knew the answer.

"Reckon so. Get ahold of Larry. He's sending help."

Himari snickered.

"What is it?" I asked. "What aren't you telling me?"

"Don't call the authorities," Father Noah said.

"What the hell is Larry sending our way? Himari?"

"I won't ruin the surprise," she said, as though she were merely refusing to give up the goods on a surprise birthday party.

I took a deep breath. "I'll call you when I know more."

"Use caution, Mason. Whatever killed those men is still in the area." Noah ended the call.

"That could take years to clean up," Emma said. "And it still wouldn't be the same."

"I know."

She flipped the light on and grimaced when the sun, which was actually a tiny light bulb, appeared in our room. "We've seen more gally-wampuses here than anyone's seen in any other city in the entire

154

state. Do you think they've been attacking the workers because they're polluting the river?"

I shrugged. "I wouldn't write anything off, but we just don't know enough. And if that's the case, what the hell spooked them out in that clearing?"

"Shit, I forgot to ask them where we're meeting Larry." I unlocked my phone to call Noah back when a text from Himari popped up.

Meet Larry here: Casey's General Store Ozark MO. 1 hour.

"Was she listening to us?" Emma asked. "Sometimes she creeps me out."

I smiled and let the GPS on my phone plan a route. "It's straight up 160 to 65. Let's get some coffee and hit the road."

"How long of a drive is it?"

"Thirty minutes."

"Good," Emma said, stripping off her pajamas as she shuffled into the bathroom. "I'm taking a shower."

I made a pot of coffee in the surprisingly nice kitchenette while Emma finished a quick shower. She tied her hair back in a damp ponytail, and we yawned our way to the car, under-caffeinated and sleep deprived. At least we had a half-full thermos of coffee with us.

Emma stretched as we bounced back onto the road. It wasn't long before we hit the highway, surrounded by nothing but the occasional flash of headlights and the clouds obscuring the stars above.

"I hate driving at night," Emma said. "Every road looks the same. I know there are hills and trees and rivers around us, but I can't see anything past our headlights."

"Don't worry," I said. "We'll be at the gas station soon enough, and then you'll be able to see everything. Probably a lot of bugs, too."

"Maybe a centipede?"

I caught her sly smile when I glanced over.

I didn't have much doubt about which truck was Larry's when we pulled into the parking lot, the rusted beast idling in a no parking zone. It looked more like a rat rod under construction than a tanker truck.

"I'd pictured something a little different than that," Emma said as I pulled up and parked beside the old truck.

Larry rolled his window down with a hand crank and smiled, his sun-worn face crinkling around his eyes. "Good to see you two. A little surprised to see two young'uns up for such a beautiful morning though."

"Is that a 1936?" Emma asked, leaning over me a bit as I chugged the rest of my lukewarm coffee. I needed a new thermos.

"She's a '35 actually," Larry said, patting the side of the truck.

"Can you even get fuel for her at a station like this?" Emma asked.

Larry tilted his head to the side in a kind of half-shrug. "I had to do some work. Some of the hoses got eaten up, and not by any of my boarders, mind you. Got a water separator installed before the carburetor. Been running like that some five years now." Larry frowned. "Ten maybe?"

"My dad has an old '66 Mustang," Emma said. "He runs it with a flex-fuel filter, and that helps quite a bit."

Larry nodded and tapped the side of the truck again. "I might have to try that, too."

I eyed the flared fenders flanking the narrow grill and the five spoke wheels. Larry grinned from a rounded cab that rose behind a flat hood. The rusted cylinder mounted on the back of the truck looked like it might fall apart at any moment, and I guess my concern showed.

"She'll hold together," Larry said. "Don't you worry about that."

Something thumped in the back of the truck, something inside that old rusted tank.

"What the hell did you bring?" I asked.

Larry frowned. "Didn't Himari tell y'all?"

Emma shook her head.

Larry hopped out of the truck and gestured for us to follow, tucking his thumbs into the straps of his overalls. We walked to the rear of the tanker truck, and something banged against the sides of the metal cylinder again.

"Take it easy," Larry said, thumping the sides of the tanker. He stepped on one of the wheel spokes and pulled himself up onto the flat bed of the truck like a man a quarter his age. He shuffled down close to the cab and motioned for Emma.

She made it look easy, while I flailed, almost fell on my ass, and probably made it look a lot harder than it should have been. Once we were all relatively stable on top of the truck, Larry glanced around. Apparently satisfied, he popped the hinged cover off the middle of the tank.

"What the hell!" I said as a pale tentacle lashed out, rising from the void. Emma stared wide-eyed at the black orb that floated to the top of the tank, set in the pale flesh of the creature's head.

"It don't mean no harm," Larry said, fishing a small bottle of oil out of his pocket. He unscrewed the top and let the tentacle snatch it away, the entire creature vanishing into the depths of the tanker.

"What the hell?" Emma said, echoing the same question that was still going through my head. "Was that a squid?"

It all clicked in my head from there, and my gaze snapped to Larry. "It's an oil pit squid!"

Larry smacked the cover closed and grinned at me. "That it is. Got a few in there. Buggers are hard to catch."

"What are they?" Emma asked.

"They're almost unknown," I said. "They found some hatchlings in Anderson, Indiana, in the nineties." I glanced back at the tanker truck. "These are a bit bigger."

"A bit," Larry said with a chuckle. "These're from that same shoal of squids. Cost me a lot in trade." He frowned slightly. "Reckon it was worth it though, considering they eat oil like my ma used to drink sassafras tea."

Emma shook her head. "Of course they will. Why wouldn't they?"

She shook her head again. "So, they're like the ocean bacteria that eats oil, but a squid?"

"No one's quite sure," Larry said with a nod. "Reckon they're more like those Proteobacteria than they are squids. Right you are about that."

I blinked. It was easy to forget how damn smart Larry was, especially when he was in full-on Missouri farmer mode. Lots of folks underestimate farmers, and I should know better. Larry took care of some of the rarest creatures in the world, and was damn good at it.

"Well, let's go," Larry said, hopping off the truck. "That oil spill's not getting no smaller."

9

I hate these damn earpieces," Larry muttered into his phone.

"Sorry," Emma said. "We couldn't hear you on the speaker phone."

"Alright," he said. "Now tell me where we're going."

"248 west out of Galena," Emma said. "There's a gravel road that'll take us down to the pipeline."

"So what do we do?" I asked.

"Evacuate the tank into the river," Larry said. "Best at the edge of the spill downstream. Is that pipeline Emma mentioned right where the break is?"

"We think so," I said. "Not exactly sure."

"We need to go further out," Larry said. "Get downstream of it."

I wracked my brain on that. An oil spill, not far from Reeds Spring, a town I'd spent more than one night in while my grandmother taught me to fish along the James River. And now a damn spill was threatening all of it. I tried to remember the landscape after that bend, the towns that followed, the places we'd dig for worms.

"Emma," I said, "see if Noland Hollow shows up on the GPS."

She typed it in and nodded. "It doesn't look like we have a road all the way in, but it's close."

"What's the GPS saying?" I asked from the driver's seat.

Emma leaned back in her seat and stretched her arms, one palm against the dashboard. "It'd be really nice if we could get a decent night's sleep on one of these trips, Mason."

"All part of the charm," I said with a small smile. I glanced over to see the dot on the phone.

"So?" Larry said. "Where we going?"

"Right," Emma said. "Take 248 to 173 south. Then ... well, I think we might be cutting through someone's yard."

"Well," Larry said. "Let's hope they're sleeping, or not home this morning. I'm taking this damned headset off. Don't be driving like some idiot now. I'm following *you*."

The line went dead, and I exchanged a grin with Emma.

"I really don't think he likes that headset," she said.

"Nope. Not one bit."

I thought about stopping and asking permission to cut through someone's yard, but oil spills weren't exactly patient disasters. Trespassing was a good way to get shot in the rural Midwest, but letting an entire ecosystem die because of that risk didn't rub me the right way.

"No lights on in the house," Emma said as we bounced onto the gravel drive that led in one side of the property, and appeared to lead to a boat dock, according to the GPS.

Larry was running in the dark, too, though we sure as hell weren't running silently with that old tanker truck, or my old Bronco for that matter. I squeezed the steering wheel, hoping the property owners wouldn't be trigger happy if we did wake them up and praying we'd gotten down fast enough to get the squids into the water.

The shadowy tree line broke to either side of the gravel road, and we pulled up close to the wooden remnants of what might have been a boat dock fifty years before. I closed the truck door slowly.

Emma slammed hers.

"Emma," I said. "You want to keep it down a little?"

"Are you serious, Mason? We just drove a truck that's one step away from belonging in a Mad Max movie through someone's yard. Slamming the door isn't going to matter." She raised the camera. "Now smile and say something nice."

I must have been scowling, or still standing there like an idiot from her lecture, because she lowered the camera.

"What?" I said.

She pointed behind me.

I turned to find Larry swinging the truck around near the woods, coming within inches of the trees on either side. The engine roared, pushing the tanker up to rest the rear end just above the river's edge.

Larry hopped out, checked his positioning, and nodded. "Sometimes my time spent driving trucks seems like time well spent."

"You think?" I said. I turned to Emma. "You okay?"

"You know I don't like trespassing, Mason. Let's just get out of here."

Larry shined a flashlight that could have blinded an airline pilot thirty thousand feet up. He frowned at the river and walked a few feet, swinging the beam up and down stream. "Oil's passed by already. Not far, but far enough."

"We need to get further downstream?" I asked.

Larry shook his head. "No. Stand back now. I'm letting the squids out, and you don't want to get tangled up in that mess." He glanced at us. "Put these gloves on. I don't want you jumping in with bare hands if something goes wrong. One of them oil pit squids latches onto your skin, you're having a bad day."

The glove reached my elbow, and part of me wondered how bad a thing the gap between my sleeve and the glove was. I flexed my fingers, frowning at the limited range of motion.

"Hope we don't need to shoot anything," Emma said.

"We can't leave the whistling-wampus here," I said.

"You mean to catch it?" Larry said.

"It could be the last one. We shouldn't kill it." I gritted my teeth, and my cheek twitched. "How do we hunt it?"

"Bait," Larry said. "It's the *supreme* ambush hunter."

"Right," Emma said, fishing a twisted section of driftwood out of the water, "and where do we find volunteers for that?"

I took a deep breath. "We don't have to."

Larry threw a release after we shifted the bulk of the debris out of the way, sending a gusher of water and pale creatures plunging into the river. Larry raised something in his hand, and a thin beam of green light lanced through the water.

"What is that?" I asked.

"Is that a laser pointer?" Emma asked.

"Sure as shit," Larry said with a grin. "Watch the water."

Emma and I both did. I didn't understand what I was seeing until Larry shifted the green laser in the river, and a surge of pale flesh flowed after it. When the largest squid reached the far edge of the surface oil, Larry cut the laser pointer and turned on his floodlight, I mean flashlight, again.

"They'll start there," he said. "Work their way back up to the source."

In the brighter light, I could see that some of them had a reddish hue, but it was wrong. It didn't look like a natural color on a squid. Of course, these things were swimming in a fresh water river, eating oil, and not dying, so I should probably reserve my judgements.

"Look at the big one," Emma said.

I didn't have to ask her which one she meant. A monster of a squid, which I suspected to be the squid that had snacked on Larry's oil bottle, surged through the middle of the river. Its body swelled as we watched, until countless tendrils exploded out from its core, worming and writhing through the oil-soaked surface, all still attached to the center of the beast.

"What the fuck!" Emma said.

My head dipped slightly in awe. The tendrils wrapped around each other, drawing in a tremendous amount of oil and guiding it back to the gaping maw that would have been a beak on an actual squid. Some of the more remote appendages pushed the surface oil to the smaller squids, their more conservative forms expanding into multiple tentacles, but nothing like the monster in the middle of the river.

"They don't eat people, right?" Emma said, looking hopefully at Larry.

"Long as they ain't covered in oil, I reckon they're safe."

We watched the squids for a time as they followed the oil a bit farther upstream, leaving a clean break between the pollution and the water flowing toward the lakes. I couldn't get used to seeing the largest of them occasionally exploding, for lack of a better word, and judging by her curses, Emma couldn't either.

"How do we get them back in the truck?" I asked. "I assume we're not setting them free?"

"Definitely not," Larry said. "Those buggers will bore through stone to get to an oil deposit."

"But they're safe for humans?" Emma asked skeptically.

Larry grinned. "Got a pump mounted on the tanker truck." He walked the fingers of his right hand along his other palm. "Don't want them running out of food. They'll chase oil. Just drop in some bait at the edge of the river and suck them right up."

I frowned at the mass of writing tentacles moving upstream. "How in the hell will those things fit in there?"

"They shrink," Larry said. "Defensive instincts cause them to ball up. Y'all need to stop worrying so much, but we do need to move upstream. Where's the spill coming from?"

"It's a creek near the top of the bend," Emma said.

"What's the GPS say?" I asked.

Emma punched in the coordinates and frowned. "Ten-minute drive, but it's showing almost a mile of hiking through the woods. That's not right though. We got the Bronco much closer."

"We did. It's probably not recognizing that gravel road. But the creek's on the opposite side of that thicket we were in. No way we're getting the tanker truck through there."

Emma cursed.

"Don't you worry," Larry said as he walked back to the tanker and opened the passenger door. He dragged what appeared to be a gray duffel bag out of the tanker truck's cab. "It'll be faster if we take the boat."

"Boat?" Emma said, raising a skeptical eyebrow.

"Yes," Larry said, "grab the trolling motor off the shotgun rack."

Emma wasn't the only one with a skeptical eyebrow at that point. I stuck my head into the rusty cab and blew out a laugh. Tucked into an oversized rung on the shotgun rack was, indeed, a trolling motor. I loosened the Velcro straps and pulled it down.

Larry had pulled what looked like an oversized air mattress out of the duffel bag along with a handheld cordless inflator.

"That's going to take forever," Emma groaned.

"Stop fretting," Larry said. "This is a custom job." He clipped the inflator to the air mattress, er, boat, and pulled the trigger. The inflator revved up like a sort of quiet jet engine, and I'd be lying if I said I didn't take a step back.

It wasn't instantaneous by any means, but it wasn't more than a few minutes before Emma was helping Larry lower the gray boat into the river by the old dock.

"That's a raft," I said.

"Just climb in already," Larry said. "Sooner we start, sooner you get out."

While I couldn't argue that logic, putting three people into a boat we just inflated with what amounted to a bicycle pump felt a little crazy.

Emma secured the holster under her arm and the one at her side with her tranquilizer pistol before she climbed in. We didn't have much in the way of portable extra ammo, but I kept a few rounds in what amounted to a camouflaged fanny pack.

"That's surprisingly solid," Emma said, pushing on the edge of the inflated boat.

Larry nodded as he fired up the trolling motor. "That it is."

I stepped onto the edge of the dock before lowering myself gently into the boat. "It's a raft." I crossed my legs and sat in the middle of the floor, grabbing onto one of the oars Larry had mounted to the side.

Larry revved the motor, and we slowly made progress against the current. "I can't see. Hit that flashlight, Emma."

She picked up the portable lighthouse from the floor of the boat and clicked it on. Ten bajillion lumens lit up the river ahead of us.

Larry frowned and watched the water before he said, "I see them. Keep that light on. I don't want to run over any of them squids with this motor."

He cut the power about ten feet downstream from the nearest squid. The water roiled and splashed with the explosions of tentacles while the creatures ate their fill. Inertia carried us past the first, but we started slowing soon after.

"Well?" Larry said. "Oars ain't there for decoration."

Emma glanced back at me. She popped off the oar on the left side of the boat, and I grabbed the right, wrapping my fingers around the grip and the throat before plunging the blade into the river.

"Try not to smack those squid," Larry said. "They're resilient as a gowrow, but can be a bit skittish."

Emma let her camera hang from a thick strap around her neck and started rowing on the opposite side of the boat, with a great deal more grace than I had.

"Damn, y'all need to stay in sync!" Larry poked me in the shoulder. "We're almost going in circles now."

Our rhythm wasn't nearly so bad as that, but we *had* drifted toward the opposite shore a bit. Larry started coaching us like a drill sergeant, and things got back on track. Emma and I had both worked up quite a sweat by the time we passed the remaining squids, and Larry lowered the trolling motor back into the river.

10

We dragged the boat up onto the narrow rocky shore of the creek. Larry trailed a thin rope to tie it off, and we plunged into the woods.

"Lights," Emma said, putting her phone away and gesturing at the deeper woods. The trees grew sparser, and some sort of artificial light glowed nearby.

"Could be the workers," I said. I stepped over a thick tree root and glanced at Larry. "Are you sure you don't want to wait for the squids at the creek?"

He shook his head. "We need to make sure that leak is locked down. There's enough oil in that creek to make me think it's still bleeding like a stuck pig."

"And what are we going to do about it?" Emma asked. "Mason and I sure as hell don't know anything about pipeline leaks."

"Reckon that's why I'm here," Larry said with a smile. He pushed forward, ducking a tree branch and leading the way into the nearby thicket. "You young folks don't have no sense when it comes to mechanical things."

"Tree stand," Emma said before she punctuated it with two fake coughs.

"Shut up," I said, holding back a small smile.

"Shit," Larry said, coming to a dead stop when we cleared the edge of the thicket.

It was easy to see the pipe that had been blown out, or torn out, just beyond the two valves behind the secured steel fence crowned with spirals of barbed wire. At least, that's what it used to be. Now the gate was torn from its hinges, and a tangled mess of barbed wire led away into the woods.

Emma leaned closer to the carnage. "That's even more torn up than it was earlier today." She ran her finger along a strip of mangled metal. "Something with claws did this. Big claws."

Larry shook his head, and we all started toward the enclosure. The shutoff valve looked old, aged to fine rusted patina. A slow trickle of oil ran from the destroyed pipe, but someone had managed to shut it off.

"Pass me the flashlight," I said, holding my hand out.

Emma did, and I flipped it on, cursing when the tracks showed plainly on the bare earth near the enclosure, vanishing into the grasses.

"Gally-wampus tracks," Emma said, crouching down to look at the mixture of oil and blood footprints.

"Someone opened the gate with a key," I said, pointing to the unlocked chain on the ground. "Then what? Tried to lock themselves inside this cage, only to have something rip the door off?"

"No wampus cat is that strong," Larry said.

"Noah said there are sasquatches in the area," Emma said. "Could they?"

That gave Larry pause. He grimaced and leaned closer to the mangled metal. "I don't know. That's *steel*. And it's been twisted around like it ain't no tougher than a coat hanger."

I traced the gally-wampus tracks back into the enclosure. "There's a pipe wrench in there." I paused and frowned. "A gigantic pipe wrench."

Larry didn't hesitate. "Good. Let's shut that off the rest of the way. Then the linemen can take their sweet time."

"Does that mean the repairmen have already been here?"

Larry looked down at the blood and oil. "Hope not."

Emma slipped past the mangled fence ahead of us and reached up to the wheel attached to the valve. "Can't we just use this?"

Larry nodded. "Yes, but it won't seal as well. Wheel's not wide enough." He scooped up the wrench and grunted. "That's thirty pounds if it's five." He whistled and slid it up under the valve, closing the wrench until it didn't move.

"You two, pull from that side. I'll push."

I grabbed the base of the wrench, while Emma took the middle. Larry placed his hands between either of ours, and there was still room to spare with the wrench being so insanely long.

"Go," he said.

Emma and I leaned back while Larry pushed. It didn't budge at first, but it finally gave with a high-pitched shriek. We didn't make it an eighth of a turn before it stopped cold. Larry shooed us and watched the flow diminish from the blown-out pipeline. His face wrinkled into a smile.

"Look at that. No more trickle." He unscrewed the wrench and leaned it against the line below the valve.

I looked back at the blood on the ground and pulled out my phone, flipping over to Himari's message thread. *Pipeline's shut off. Are the repairmen supposed to be here?*

She sent back: *First crew, yes.*

"Shit," I said. "Himari says the first crew should have been here."

Emma crouched down by the blood and oil and shook her head. "If they were human, they didn't survive this."

My phone buzzed with another text. *Crew hasn't checked in. Noah says leave.*

"Mason," Emma hissed.

I looked up in time to see a shadow circling us at the edge of the tree line, low to the ground and nearly dark as the night around us. Except for its golden eyes.

"That's the dark gally-wampus we saw with the others," Emma said. "Same gray socks."

The gray fur around its paws was plain to see when Emma aimed the flashlight at it. Still, the gally-wampus kept up its slow, stalking circle.

"No way that gally-wampus did this," Larry said. "Too small. Why isn't she running from that light?"

Emma's hand settled on her gun.

I touched her shoulder. "Don't shoot it."

"If it comes to eat us, I am damn well shooting it."

Everything, everyone, grew still. Only the wampus moved. The river rushed in the distance while the creek meandered behind us. The sudden acrid stench of rotting flesh choked out the subtle smell of oil and the nearby river.

It wasn't the first time I'd been hit by such a thick scent. I remembered that pungent fur and the hulking beast that followed it. My mind crashed back to that night, the night we lost Dylan, only to be pulled into the now when the silence gave way to something else.

The stillness broke to the sounds of a discordant whistle. It started almost like a catcall, a *whoo-hoo* you might imagine when a woman walks past a construction site with no harassment policies, and then it changed, growing shrill and grating and terrible. It didn't take much of an imagination to picture that whistle as a screaming child or a hunter in distress. Dissonant harmonics crunched together like an un-tuned banjo.

"Jesus in a holler," Larry said, his back suddenly rigid and his gaze roaming the perimeter of the thicket.

The gally-wampus's ears flattened, and it vanished into the woods outside the cage at a near sprint.

"Christ," Larry said. "That wampus is terrified. We're leaving. Now."

"What was that?" Emma said.

The hairs along my arms stood up, and I couldn't shake the feeling of being watched. "We go quick. Don't run. Emma, watch the river. Larry, eyes on the other side of the clearing. I'll take point. Liberal zone of fire, but for God's sake, don't shoot each other. Or me."

We kept a brisk pace, leaving the oil and blood behind in the short walk to the tree line that felt like fifteen minutes instead of two. We passed through the woods without incident, exiting onto the shore a little short on breath, but no worse for wear. My feet sank into a patch of mud on the bank as we pushed the boat back into the water.

Emma hopped into the bow once more while I flailed at the edge of the water, the cold river having deflated the sides a bit, making it harder to climb up. Finally, I made it, my jeans soaked through to the knees. I rubbed at them, as if that would somehow warm the chill from my shins.

"Squids are here," Larry said, pointing up the creek a bit.

"How the hell are we getting them back?" I asked.

He opened a small box in the corner of the inflatable boat to reveal a few pints of bottled oil. "Bait. It's always bait with river monsters. Remember that."

Something yelped and thrashed in the creek. My heart hammered in my chest when something large and furry batted away the pale flesh of an expanded oil pit squid, dozens of thin tentacles writhing and snapping away. The gray gally-wampus hurtled out of the creek onto the opposite shore, running a short arc around the cluster of squids before plunging back into the water.

"Don't shoot," Larry said when Emma and I both went for our guns.

The gally-wampus surged through the water, its body slithering in a rapid swaying motion as if it were a giant mink. Matted fur and golden eyes closed on us, and then passed in a flurry. The only sign the wampus had been there at all was a quiet wake in the water, and a retreating shadow downstream.

"It wasn't after us," I said, wondering what the heck it had been doing here in the first place. "And why was it alone?"

The whistle sounded again, closer this time, more human.

Larry cursed and fumbled one of the oil bottles open. He leaned forward and handed it to Emma. "As soon as we're in the middle of the crick, start pouring." He shifted the box closer to me with his foot as his hand revved the trolling motor.

The dissonant *whoo-hoo* became a *yoo-hoo,* and the flesh on my scalp crawled at the grating sound.

A low buzz became a high-pitched whine as Larry pushed the little motor as hard as it would go. Emma dumped the oil in, but we didn't wait to see if the squids were following. I doubt Larry liked the idea of leaving them behind.

"How fast can they swim?" I asked.

"Keep the trail narrow," Larry said. "They'll catch up."

Emma gestured for another bottle. I unscrewed the cap, tore off the foil seal, and passed it over. "They'll eat the plastic, right?"

"Yes," Larry said. "They'll eat most anything petroleum based."

She dropped the first bottle and seamlessly started pouring with the next.

We were back in the main current of the river before I looked back again, the whistling fading behind us. Only a shadow remained. I wasn't sure I'd seen it at all, until the dark form sank into the black forest around it.

11

We made it back to the tanker truck and wrestled the boat up onto the shore.

"If we hear that again," Larry said, "leave the boat. Get in your car and get out. Like a damned banshee that was."

Emma cursed and hefted the boat up when Larry pulled the trolling motor off.

"You two like risking your ass," Larry said with a laugh. "Not much doubt y'all, that there's a whistling-wampus." He hurried back to the cab of his truck and hung the trolling motor on the gun rack.

I helped Emma pull the boat the rest of the way up onto the grass, and we started opening the air valves to deflate it.

Larry pulled a hose off the back of the tanker truck that looked wide enough to stick my head in. He caught me staring and held the end of it up. "This'll suck those squids right up. We'll be out of here in a flash."

We let the boat deflate a bit more before Larry told us to stop. "Just roll it up a bit and stuff it in the front. I don't need it back in that damn bag right now."

Emma gathered it up in her arms and stuffed it into the cab. We both met Larry back down by the river. He pointed out to the water, and I could see the pale forms of the oil pit squids following the thin trail of oil we'd left.

Larry looked between the river and the tanker truck and frowned.

"What is it?" I asked.

"It'll be loud. The pump, I mean."

"I don't think we have a choice," Emma said. "Unless you want to leave the squids behind?"

Larry shook his head. "They can be hellacious on the environment. Built for living in oil, and they'll dig for it something fierce. You end up with sinkholes and collapsed roads, collapsed *homes*." He dropped the pump onto the ground. "Y'all start your truck."

I nodded. "We'll be ready to run."

Emma hesitated, and then held her hand out for the keys. I tossed them over, and she jogged to the Bronco. Larry's tanker roared to life a moment before Emma had the Bronco started. He threw the switch for the pump, and I realized at that point there was no way we'd hear something coming.

Larry poured some oil out around the broken dock, and it was like blood in the water for a starving shark. The pulsing mass of oil pit squids surged toward us, splashing water into the air as they clambered over one another.

Emma turned the Bronco around so we'd be pointed toward the narrow path into that unfortunate yard again. No one had come to threaten us, and I was beginning to think we'd lucked out on that front. At least we'd lucked out on one front.

"Keep an eye out," Larry said. "If anything's chasing us, it's likely to come from the north along the bank, or cross the river."

The three of us stood at the shore, waiting for the squids to get just close enough. Emma swept the opposite shore with the flashlight for about a minute until Larry plunged the end of the pump into the water.

Nothing happened.

"Oh shit," Larry said. "I didn't prime the damn pump." He left the nozzle in the water and hurried back to the tanker, grabbing a smaller hose. I watched in some confusion as water sprayed from the smaller hose into part of the larger pump Larry had just unscrewed. Apparently satisfied, he closed the pump a moment later, and the motor roared into a different kind of life.

The hose jerked in the river. Larry hefted it up and angled it into the small inlet created by the collapsed boat dock. It was teeming with a frenzy of oil pit squids. Squids vanished up the wide hose one by one with a sucking pop. Larry continued vacuuming up all the remaining oil he could see before shutting down the engine.

"Go," he said as he collapsed the hose into the back of the tanker. "We need to go."

"Where to?" I asked.

Larry glanced up. "I'm taking the squids back home. Y'all should get the hell out of here. Call DEMON. You don't know what a whistling-wampus can do."

"Larry," I said. "*I* am the guy DEMON calls. If we catch it, can you relocate it?"

"Are you insane?" Emma snapped.

Larry frowned and shook his head. "Maybe, but later. We shouldn't be in the open."

"Alright. Call when you're back."

Larry nodded and climbed into his truck. It was in gear and moving by the time Emma and I loaded up into the Bronco.

We followed the tanker truck back to the highway and had a mercifully uneventful trip back to the motel.

Emma and I sat in the parking lot of the motel, staring out the windshield at the modest building while the Bronco's engine ticked and whined as it cooled down.

"I want a drink," Emma said.

I blew out a breath and nodded. "Good plan."

We dragged our gear inside and locked the door. Another half hour passed, and Emma pulled out a bottle of Maker's Mark that had barely been cracked open.

"Neat?"

I nodded, and she poured more than we needed to drink into two glasses.

My phone buzzed a few sips in.

"Is that Larry already?" Emma asked.

I glanced down at the text and shook my head. "Himari. Asking us to call. That seems ... unusually polite."

The phone didn't have a chance to ring before she answered, "Mason, that gally-wampus is a half-breed."

"What wampus?" I asked.

"The dark one, on the video. Isn't that why Emma was recording it?"

"Uh," Emma said, "I wasn't really thinking that far ahead."

"You need to stay away," Himari said. "Doc says it's probably only half gally-wampus."

"Okay," Emma said. "What's the other half?"

I cursed under my breath and took another sip of bourbon as realization dawned. It felt good, burning just enough in a welcome Kentucky hug as it made its way to my stomach.

Himari and I spoke at the same time, "Whistling-wampus."

"Are you saying it killed those workers?" Emma asked.

"I doubt it," I said. "It was too shy around us. One of its parents must be in the pack of gally-wampuses. Maybe that's why it stayed outside the company?"

"And the other parent is the whistling-wampus," Himari said.

"Is that even possible?" Emma asked.

"I don't know," I said. "No one knows enough about their biology. I doubt even Doc knows for sure. We may be able to study those gally-wampuses, but even then, how many whistlers are left? Just this one?"

"Don't die," Himari said.

Emma laughed weakly and ran her fingers through her hair. "So, we catch it or we kill it."

"Right," I said, surprised at Emma's change in demeanor about the idea of capturing the whistling-wampus. "We can't leave it running around."

"Larry said to call DEMON," Emma said. "Maybe we should."

I grimaced. I didn't want to involve anyone at a federal level if we could avoid it. "Let's wait until we hear from Larry."

"Speak of the devil," Himari said. "I'll conference him in." The line clicked, buzzed, and came back. "Mason?"

"Yep."

"Larry?" she asked.

"Here."

"Okay," Himari said, "so how is Mason going to capture the murdery monster without getting murdered?"

"Y'all need to listen, and listen good. I only know one vet that ever even seen a whistling-wampus. Tranqs don't work, at least not as good as they should. Unless she was lying to me."

Larry trailed off, mumbling something to himself.

"Larry?" Himari said, drawing his name out.

"I'm here, I'm here. 10.0 cc, Mason. If y'all are trying to catch this thing, you need to knock it out cold."

"Won't that kill it?" Emma asked, glancing between me and the phone.

"Ten point oh cc," Larry said, emphasizing every syllable. "And if it ain't down in three minutes, hit it again. All wampuses are fast, and you're a half step shy of bonkers to try this."

"How do we transport it?" I asked.

Larry cursed, and I could picture him shaking his head. "Don't, unless you have a *very* sturdy cage in that Bronco. Call me. Wrap it in something soft, like a blanket like you did those gowrows. Tie it down if you have to."

"Thanks, Larry," I said.

"You two be careful. Lost enough friends these past years."

"We will," Emma said.

Larry hung up without saying anything else.

"Weird," Himari said, "it's like he likes you two."

"Goodbye, Himari," Emma said with a small laugh.

"I want pictures!"

"We'll get them," I said. "Just you wait."

12

W e were back at Reeds Spring Pizza Co. the next morning —early afternoon if I'm being honest—when I read the text out loud from Himari. "Maintenance crew will be at the pipeline by 2:00."

"You think the …" Emma trailed off and looked around us. The server was filling a mug behind the bar, and the nearest table was animatedly discussing the terrible end of their last Dungeons & Dragons game. Emma leaned close anyway. "Do you think the whistling-wampus will be hunting in daylight?"

I tilted my head to the side a bit and gave a half shrug. "It's possible. The last worker that died wasn't found until after nightfall, but his shift ended well before sunset. We should probably be settled by 3:00."

Emma sighed and ran her hand over her inspector ID. "Doesn't give us much time to set up." She let the badge flop against her chest and opted for the pizza on the table in front of her. She took another bite, and her expression soured. "I can't believe we're using them as bait."

"If it makes you feel any better, we'll be bait, too."

Emma snorted a laugh. "Much better, Mason. Thanks."

We finished what was quickly becoming my favorite pizza in the entire state of Missouri, except perhaps for a small pizzeria near Saint Louis called Talayna's. I wondered if Emma felt the same, or if I was just scrambling to hold on to our last few minutes of normalcy before we started hunting a maneater.

We squared up with the server and walked out to the Bronco a few minutes later.

"So glad we put that tree stand up on the wrong side of the river," Emma said.

I laughed quietly and hung my head. "You want to move it to the other side? It's super easy and a flash to assemble, says the salesman."

"I want to leave it there until it rusts away into nothing. Too bad it's not closer to the pipeline though."

"I know, but we'll have the woods for cover." We bounced through a particularly large rut in the gravel road, and I was somewhat surprised that the trailer remained attached.

"I still don't understand how this is going to work, Mason. It's an ambush predator. It whistles to lure people in. Why in the hell would it abandon that strategy?"

"Because it already has," I said. "It didn't lure those men into the woods around the thicket. It slaughtered them in the open. At least, I seriously doubt it killed them in the woods and dragged them back into the clearing."

Emma took a deep breath. "I know. It makes sense when you look at it like that, but why is it doing it? No one's seen a whistling-wampus in decades. Why now? What changed?"

I steered the Bronco back onto the edge of Clarence Ellbrach's farm. I didn't think the old man would mind. We'd already passed the shotgun test, even if it *had* required a tranquilizer dart.

We slid out of the Bronco and grabbed our gun cases from the back. This time I brought more than my tranquilizer rifle. The Magnum Research Desert Eagle along with its barrels was a reassuring weight in my left hand.

Emma led the way into the woods. No eerie calm greeted us today, only the raucous cursing of hard work and underpaid repairmen. We were halfway through the thicket and closing in on the half-destroyed pipeline before the workers noticed they weren't alone anymore.

The nearest, an odd mix of beer gut and biceps that looked like they could bend steel, shouted a warm greeting. "What the *fuck* you think you're doing out here? This is private land."

Emma held up her newly-minted badge. "Pipeline inspectors. Mister Ellbrach was concerned about all the noise on *his* property."

"Ma'am," the man said, his demeanor switching gears like a squirrel on hot asphalt in the dead of summer. "We thought y'all weren't supposed to be here." He paused. "Like you were civilians. You'd be surprised how many folks go wandering where they shouldn't. Get themselves hurt."

I almost had whiplash at that point from his suddenly nice personality. Apparently, inspectors either intimidated these guys, or they'd been instructed to scare off anyone who showed up.

A smaller man, probably in his early thirties with short hair and thick glasses stepped up beside the first. "I'm Dale; this is Jeffrey. Sorry for the harsh greeting."

"This is Emma, and I'm Mason," I said with a nod.

"Three men have died out here," Dale said. "We're a little on edge."

Three men? I wondered. *Did they not know about the crew from yesterday?*

"Don't worry about it," Emma said.

"Thanks. We have quite a bit more work to do on the line before it's ready for an inspector. Would you like us to call you when it's ready?"

Emma shook her head. "We'll wait out here. It's a nice day to hike through the woods."

Jeffrey frowned slightly. "Watch yourself for ticks. Bad this year."

"We're wearing sulfur powder," I said.

The bigger man nodded. "Glad to hear you ain't dumb." He spat on the ground and walked back into the twisted cage of steel. Dale followed.

"That could've gone worse," Emma said.

"No doubt." I glanced down at our gun cases. "They didn't even ask what we were carrying."

"I think it's pretty obvious they're guns," Emma said as we turned to walk to the edge of the thicket. "What now?"

"We wait."

We'd been in the shade of the thicket's edge for almost an hour when Dale wandered across the clearing to us. He glanced over his shoulder, and I knew conspiratorial body language when I saw it.

"You two with the CCD?" he whispered.

Emma gave him a small smile. "The what?"

Dale hesitated, most likely weighing his options. "Friends with Chuck?"

At that, I gave a short nod. "You too?"

"I'm a friend, yeah, but I'm barely in the CCD. I guess I kind of am? Like an honorary agent or something?" He shook his head. "Anyway, I'd like to be full time, but I don't know jack about, uh, rare animals, you know? I'm an okay shot, but I couldn't track a deer through a parking lot."

"It's good to know your limits," Emma said with a much broader smile.

Dale frowned.

"What do you know about what's happening?" I asked.

"I know it's a whistling-wampus," Dale said, his eyes widening a bit as he spoke. "They're one of the rarest of the wampus cats."

"One of the deadliest, too," I said.

Dale looked around the thicket as he nodded. "I know. You think it will come back?"

"It's been here twice," Emma said. "This is either its hunting ground, or the pipeline is close to its lair. Just let us know if you hear anything? Or see anything?"

"I will," Dale said, starting back toward the other two workers when Jeffrey shouted his name.

I waited until he was out of earshot. "Is Chuck just telling random people about the CCD?"

Emma looked away as she smiled. "I don't think so, Mason. I'm pretty sure that guy is a friend of Chuck's."

"How could you possibly know that?"

"Does he look like the pipeline workers? Their arms look like they could crush Dale's skull like a bad infomercial. Dale's small, and someone sent him out here to keep an eye on the workers. Who else but Chuck?"

It made sense, what Emma was saying. "But why send him out here without backup?"

"We're the backup, dumbass."

"Oh."

"I bet Dale is locked and loaded under those baggy overalls. Not to mention his orange vest is about two sizes too big."

I glanced at Emma. "This is why you do people and I do cryptids."

"Yes, it is."

We spent almost two more hours in the shadow of the forest before we noticed the change.

13

It started with the insects. The constant buzz of honeybees and the flurry of dragonflies cleared. I didn't think much of it until the hollow crunching and occasional thump of a squirrel freeing a nut vanished.

The birds were the last to give in to the silence, until the only sounds were the footsteps and clanging of the maintenance workers and the rustling of the leaves around us.

Everyone froze when the wail pierced the uncanny silence. A woman's scream; a baby's whine; a dissonant, terrible, growl.

"In the cage!" I heard Dale shout. "Stay in the cage!" He slammed the newly-minted steel door closed, locking the workers in, but I had serious doubts about the repaired gate's ability to stop a whistling-wampus.

I kicked open my gun case, slinging the holster for the Magnum Research Desert Eagle over my shoulder while gripping the tranquilizer rifle like it was a lifeline. Emma slipped her holster on, keeping the .454 in easy reach while she primed her tranquilizer rifle.

We walked side by side into the middle of the field. This was the plan. The maintenance workers had been bait, yes, but we were the first line of defense. They were inside a steel fence, and we were easy pickings.

The two maintenance workers started yelling at Dale, and I watched with some amusement when Dale flipped a badge out. Jeffrey's volume increased exponentially, and I cursed when the man slammed Dale into the fence.

Emma moved toward them to help, but we needn't have worried.

Dale twisted Jeffrey's arm up behind the larger man's back and leveraged Jeffrey's face into the steel barricade. When Jeffrey tried to kick out at Dale, he was rewarded with a quick trip into the mud. Dale had the man zip-tied faster than my eyes could follow. The other maintenance worker just held his hands up and backed away.

"I think he's good," Emma said.

"Uh, yeah," I said, beginning to think Dale's bumbling agent act had been just that.

The howl of the whistling-wampus changed again, into a stuttering, maniacal laughter. Emma shivered, and I was close behind. The grating sound continued for almost ten full seconds, then cut off abruptly.

"I swear it was moving," Emma said. "Close to the river, now ..." she traced the tree line with her finger, "over there."

I nodded. "I think you're right."

The distress call sounded again, the dissonant chords gone, replaced by the squeal of a wounded boar.

"What the fuck is that!" Jeffrey cried out.

A branch shook near the cage, and the wail echoed through the clearing again.

"Jesus, it's behind them," Emma said in a hurried whisper. "I don't have a shot."

"Can you even see it?"

Darkness moved against the tree line, and the maintenance worker who I hadn't met screamed, throwing himself against the side of the steel fence closest to us.

The shadow chittered and made a horrible sound, like the high-pitched laughing of a toddler until it shattered into the scream of an injured girl. The branches low to the ground shook, and a hulking form slammed into the steel fence, only to vanish back into the tree line in the span of a heartbeat.

"Away from the fence!" Dale shouted, dragging Jeffrey closer to the valves.

Emma and I did the opposite, closing on the metal barrier that kept them relatively safe, but not safe enough.

"Did you see it?" I asked as we got closer.

"Yeah," Dale said. "It's a big bastard. Looks like a gally-wampus, but Christ, the claws on that thing!"

"We need to get you out of there," I said. "If you get a break, take it. I don't care what shape Emma and I are in. You see an opportunity, run."

"You taking it down?" Dale asked.

"Tranqs," I said. "We're taking it alive."

Dale's expression twisted up, and I was fairly sure he thought we were nuts. Maybe he was right, but I wasn't putting something as rare as a whistling-wampus down unless we'd tried absolutely everything else.

"You should get a net cannon," Dale said. "Keeps them tangled up while the tranquilizer takes effect."

I blinked, now quite sure the bumbling agent act was only an act.

"He has a good point," Emma said, "although I don't think we're going to find a net cannon in the middle of a thicket."

The dissonant echo of *whoo-hoo* started up again.

"I don't think I'll ever be able to hear a catcall the same way again," Emma said, keeping her rifle trained on the woods. "And I already despised them."

The *whoo-hoo* broke into short whistles. Either the whistling-wampus was throwing its voice, or it was moving. While I didn't completely put the idea of throwing its voice out of the realm of possibility, it seemed much more likely that the wampus was moving.

"I'm going to untie you now," Dale said, looking down at Jeffrey. "Don't run yet. Don't attack me, or I'll tie you up again. We stay in this cage until the inspectors clear the area."

"Inspectors my ass," Jeffrey mumbled, but he didn't make a move after Dale untied him.

The shadows moved in the forest, and Emma didn't wait to see what was next. She fired, her tranquilizer rifle popping with the burst of air. The dart thunked into something hard, and I had little doubt it was a tree. The calls of the whistling-wampus cut off, and deeper in the woods, a form wove between the trunks, low to the ground.

Emma cursed and reloaded.

"It's here," I said, losing track of the racing shadow.

"We need to run!" Jeffrey shouted, pushing at his co-worker, shouting at Dale to open the gate.

Dale stared the larger man down, and Jeffrey backed off a half-step. "Not yet."

The earth beneath my boots may have been relatively flat, but clumps of grass and barely-concealed stones threatened to roll my ankles as I strafed the tree line with the tranquilizer gun. Emma reloaded, keeping her eyes on the forest. Five minutes passed. Emma and I stalked the thicket in the eerie silence before it fractured once more.

The haunting cry of the whistling-wampus shifted, the wail of distress roaming from the north over to the east, closer to our car. Emma glanced at the steel fence and then back to me. This was their chance.

"Get out of here!" I shouted at Dale. They scrambled, one tripping and crashing into the mud before finding his feet and fleeing past us. Dale went last, following them with what looked like 9 mm in his hand. I hoped he had something larger on him if they didn't make a clean escape.

If we were wrong, if this whistling-wampus wasn't hunting alone, another of those men would die. Maybe all of them would.

"Center of the thicket," I said, and Emma followed, both of us keeping our tranquilizer rifles aimed at the eastern edge of the tree line. Once we were there, Emma pulled at my arm, dragging us up against the steel fence around the pipeline.

"Smart," I said.

"I know," Emma said, and we let the conversation die.

The one thing that wasn't smart, I realized as I checked my pocket for extra darts, was that I'd left most of them in the gun case at the other side of the thicket. I only had two rounds on me, and as big as that shadow had been, I wasn't sure if that would be enough. Ten cc wasn't going to kill it. Hell, ten cc might not even knock it out.

A dissonant, stuttering cry started up again, and it was almost on top of us. A thick branch at the tree line bent down, and golden eyes set in a furry black face caught the fading sunlight. I cursed and raised the barrel of my rifle, barely aiming before I pulled the trigger.

Emma's rifle popped a second after mine, and the whistling-wampus's wail turned into a cat tail under a rocking chair cry of pain. I unhinged the butt of the tranquilizer rifle and reloaded as the tree's branches shook, firing a second shot the moment it was primed.

The branch the wampus had been on bounced, breaking a few twigs and leaves loose, but the whistling-wampus itself was nowhere to be seen.

"One shot left," I muttered.

"Did we hit it twice?" Emma asked. "Is that too much?"

I shook my head. "I don't know. But it's fast. And it's huge. And it can climb the goddamned trees, Emma." I blew out a breath and eyed the gun case across the thicket. "I'm going for the gun case. You stay here."

Emma didn't raise her eyes from the tree line. She kept her back planted on the fence, and I started walking back to the case. My gut screamed at me to bring the Desert Eagle up and defend myself like a sane person, but I didn't want to kill the whistling-wampus.

I should have listened to my gut.

14

It broke from the woods screaming, the ear-piercing cry like a thousand nails on a chalkboard, rattling my head until I couldn't think straight, much less aim straight. The black fur streaked into the thicket, golden eyes locked onto mine so it seemed its head didn't move even as its body sped toward me.

The tranquilizer rifle fired with a hollow pop. I thought there was a chance it might have connected with the whistling-wampus's hindquarters. It reared up, flexing its paw.

I threw myself backward. I didn't much care whether or not the tranquilizer had hit after the claws caught my forearm. Fiery pain erupted above my wrist. I didn't know how bad it was, but I knew it for damn sure wasn't good. I got in a lucky block when the wampus swiped at me again, but the tranquilizer rifle skittered away into the grass.

Emma's .454 thundered through the clearing, and the whistling wampus raced back into the tree line.

I scrambled over to my downed rifle and ran to the gun case.

"Mason!" Emma said. "Your arm!"

"I can still move," I shouted back. "It's fine. It'll be fine." My arm dripped a significant amount of blood, but nothing was spurting.

Usually, I only needed stitches when things were spurting. I wrapped what I hoped was a clean cloth from the gun case around my arm and twisted it into place, at least slowing the blood loss.

I scooped up another tranquilizer, mystified at how the wampus was still moving. When I went to reload, I finally saw the damage that had been done to the rifle. The CO_2 cartridge had been snapped off, along with the port to lock in a new one. I cursed and reached for the tranquilizer pistol at the far end of the case.

"Mason," Emma hissed.

I glanced over my shoulder and froze. The black shadow had reappeared, slower perhaps, but its eyes were still locked onto me. Ready to kill. Its cry echoed through the thicket again, the terrible wail of a child in distress.

The whistling-wampus stumbled, and I could have sworn it tilted to the side, a half-step, a stumble. The tranquilizer was working. This towering cat had finally been hit with enough to bring it down.

This was going to work. We'd be able to capture it and get it to Larry. We could tie it up in the blanket, and that would keep the rope from cutting into its legs.

Something cracked in the woods behind me. A gunshot? Had they missed? Who was shooting?

"Emma?" I said.

"It wasn't me." She circled behind the whistling-wampus, cutting off its retreat.

The wampus sprinted at me, flat out, like it had been fired out of a goddamned cannon, its explosive movement catching me off guard. I'd expected it to fall over. It hadn't.

A thunderous splintering of wood crashed behind me, and the whistling-wampus leapt, extending claws that would have made a velociraptor proud. I didn't understand what was happening. How, after all we'd done, all we'd survived, this airborne shadow of tooth and claw was going to spell my end.

Whistling of a different sort roared through the thicket. The stone hit hard enough to crush a car. What it did to that wampus, the streaks of gore and explosion of viscera, was not something that would soon leave my memory. I blinked the blood from my eyes, trying to understand what had happened, when the hinge-tailed bing-buffer trundled into the thicket.

It snuffled and puffed, casually uprooting a tree that could have survived a collision with a semi. I didn't move, my back stuck against the trunk behind me like glue. A brief survey with nothing but my eyes showed me Emma, frozen a few feet away. The carcass of the whistling-wampus lay crumpled at her feet.

The hinge-tailed bingbuffer didn't seem to mind at all. Its towering bulk passed me by with little more than a glance from its huge black eye. It scooped up its prey with its giant tail, rolling it up, and holding it in the air. Its nostrils expanded, sniffing at Emma a few times before it licked her from chest to forehead with a pink tongue that wouldn't have been out of place on a whale.

I bit my lip, my fear turning to a near psychotic need to laugh as the beast trundled back toward the river. Its body shimmered, and I gawked at the massive form as its skin rippled and blended almost seamlessly with the shadows of the forest. The only hint it was still moving was a flicker, like movement caught from the corner of my eye.

"Eww," Emma said, wiping at her face and drawing my attention away. "Just … eww. I guess we don't have to worry about that whistling-wampus killing another worker."

The bingbuffer had cleansed almost every splash of blood from the area around Emma with its massive tongue. It was hard to reconcile that those beasts could leave almost no trace behind. The toppled tree was the only real evidence, and most folks here would chalk that up to thunderstorms.

"I guess not," I said, the manic need to laugh thankfully subsiding.

"I need a shower, Mason. I may not have ever needed a shower more than I need a shower right now."

"Least we can do," I said, wincing as I flexed my arm. "Now that the workers are safe again."

A voice boomed from the shadows of the forest—basso, eloquent, composed—and my skin crawled with every syllable.

"It was those workers who killed his mate."

"What in the ever-loving hell was that?" Emma said, sidling up beside me. She briefly inspected my makeshift bandage before brandishing her .454.

"You would take the life of an innocent creature for defending its family? I had heard better of you, hunter."

The wind bearing down into the thicket shifted, the blood and musk replaced with a stench like a skunk thrown into a tire fire. My mind reeled as memories surfaced like a geyser. Dylan, the monsters in the woods, my friend's cold dead eyes ...

I fought the panic down. I'd had enough close calls since that night to learn how to control my emotions. It's not that I didn't panic, I just redirected the energy. Instead of freezing in place, I swept the barrel of the Desert Eagle across the tree line behind me.

"Do you not remember me, human? For I remember you." The shadow walked between the trees, vanishing and reappearing in the dim sunlight. It stepped forward, letting the crown of its wide head bathe in the dying light, its fur so black my eyes tried to tell me it was a hole in reality.

"Momo."

I couldn't shake the conversation I'd had with Sonny. Momo wasn't a sasquatch, and the sasquatches didn't quite know what exactly Momo's species was. But they knew it liked to hunt for sport, and it had taken more than one human trophy.

"You are famous among the sasquatches," the creature said. "They speak of you as though you are a savior of all the cryptids." It spat the word, as though the very name cryptid offended him in the worst of ways.

"You killed Dylan."

The shadow's chest expanded with a terrible, slow laugh. "I have killed many things. Should you fire that weapon, I will kill your female."

My index finger fell away from the trigger. I didn't think the .44 long colt magazine I had loaded for the smaller caliber barrel on the Desert Eagle would be enough to down something as large as Momo.

He'd likely have more than enough time to tear our arms off and beat us into a pulp with them. But Momo was talking. He wasn't killing us.

"What do you want?" I asked.

"A truce."

I hesitated. Whatever I'd thought he might say, that sure as hell wasn't it. Sonny had warned me that the Missouri Monster was notoriously violent, and what few creatures like Momo he'd encountered, their diplomacy amounted to *the survivor is always right.*

When I didn't respond, Momo said, "I have no desire to hunt humans who show respect." Momo tilted his head to the side, the dying sun catching his eyes so they burned with a deep red light.

"And what of the rest of the humans?" I asked.

The black line of Momo's lips twitched. I had no idea if it was a frown, a smile, or something else on his alien face. "I will defend myself."

A basso rumble filled the clearing, and this time I could tell it was laughter.

His red eyes swept to Emma. "Fire if you dare, child. You will not survive it. Larger men with larger guns have tried." Momo's gaze rose to the heavens before sliding back down to me. "What do we do now, hunter?"

Something must have pressed the *I must be invincible today* button in my brain, because what I said was, "Prove what you say."

Momo's eyes narrowed, and the movement was disturbingly inhuman on his pumpkin-shaped head.

We didn't move, waiting for the massive creature to respond.

"I have found this day most interesting," he said, breaking the silence. "Save the pride of whistling-wampuses. For without their guardian to teach them, they will not survive life in the Ozarks."

He looked toward the northwest, past the fenced area with the valves. "Follow the cries."

Momo said no more, turning and vanishing into the forest with only a few steps. The woods weren't thick enough here to conceal a towering sasquatch-like beast, but he was gone nonetheless.

Emma let out a string of curses, and I ran a shaky hand through my hair.

"We should get the hell out of here," I said. "That thing used analogies, Emma, what in the ever-loving fuck?"

She shook her head. "I don't know. I don't know, Mason." She glanced toward the fence, where Momo had been watching. "How bad is your arm?"

I raised the barrel of the Desert Eagle experimentally. "It burns, but the bleeding has stopped I think, or at least slowed." I eyed the gun case, wondering if we should really pack up and run, but my initial instinct to flee was gradually being overcome by my curiosity.

"I know that look," Emma said. "One quick sweep, and then we're getting you to a hospital."

I nodded, and we started toward the steel fence.

15

Nothing unusual leapt out at us, literally or figuratively, when we explored the area around the pipeline.

"There's nothing here," Emma said, stopping at the tree line on the other side of the fenced station.

"I know." I turned to face the trees, checking the compass on my phone. "Let's go a little further."

"Into the woods?"

I nodded, and waded into the darkness of a forest that would soon be as black as the night sky. "Wish we had Larry's flashlight cannon," I muttered as I ran my head into yet another tree branch.

Emma kept her flashlight aimed at the ground in front of us, which was probably the smarter thing to do, being that the forest floor hid a great deal of treacherous footing.

Leaves and twigs crunched and cracked beneath our boots. The underbrush grew thicker after a quarter mile or so, and I cursed when a bramble caught the bandage on my arm, pulling at the recently-formed scab.

"Let me help," Emma said, batting my good hand away. She broke a couple thorns away. "Almost got it." Emma had me untangled in moments, but the silence while she worked was enough to hear a quiet cry on the wind.

Emma shivered. "We're following that, aren't we?"

I nodded.

The compass told us we were still headed northwest, and I stayed on track, leading Emma and her flashlight through more underbrush until it gave way to another thicket. I froze and stared at the old structure, lit by moonlight and the last embers of the setting sun.

"You have got to be kidding me," I said. The small barn was more of a shack, and I suspected it had been built in the 1800s, the wood gone to gray and the entire structure casually leaning against a tall oak tree. Pieces of wood lay strewn around it, and I had little doubt a strong gust of wind could collapse the entire thing.

We walked closer, side by side, circling around the corner of the barn that wasn't leaning on the oak tree. The old door was half broken away, showing tiny flecks of color that may have been red paint in the past, but just as easily could have been mold.

The break in the door created a tall and narrow entrance to the black interior. A frenzy of movement exploded inside the barn when Emma shined her light, but I didn't see anything. The darkness still held too many secrets. I couldn't tell if the sounds had come from raccoons, or something we should be much more concerned about.

"Oh, Mason ..." Emma held her hand up to her mouth.

I followed her gaze to the edge of the thicket, where the pitch black furry hide of a whistling-wampus had been hung to dry, its edges woven through with a stained twine. I didn't need to see what was scattered about the log beneath it to know that men had slaughtered it and tanned its hide.

We walked a few steps toward the remains, and the thick stench of old tanning oil reached my nose. The hide had already been salted and oiled, so why string it up again?

A disturbing whine rose as we stepped closer to the old shack. At first only a whisper that wandered through the rustling leaves, but it grew into a dissonant wail. But not the wail of an experienced hunter ...

I exchanged a glance with Emma and said quietly, "I'm going in first. Keep the light in front of you."

She slid her gun from its holster, and while my first instinct was to protest, I didn't once I considered what this day had brought us. I made sure the Desert Eagle was secure in my own holster, and ducked into the darkness of the old shack.

Something shuffled beside me and sprinted toward the back of the small barn. It sprinted at me again, and sprinted back again. On the third sweep, Emma's flashlight caught the golden eyes and gray fur of the dark gally-wampus.

My good friend Claw wasn't here to chase the wampus away this time, but she didn't appear hostile. She charged at me again, rubbing her head on my leg before dashing back into the corner of the shack, ears almost straight up in the air.

Emma ducked in behind me. "Is that ..."

I nodded.

The gally-wampus charged at me again, hesitated, and then sank her teeth into my jeans with a surprising amount of care, tugging at my leg so that I'd either follow, or get dragged to where she wanted me.

"Okay," I said, "okay." I patted her back as softly as I could. She stiffened, but slowly relaxed and tugged on my jeans again.

That terrible, dissonant cry rose again from inside the shack.

The gally-wampus let go and dashed into the darkness.

"Come on," I said, pulling at Emma's sleeve in what struck me as a fairly amusing reflection of the gally-wampus tugging on my jeans.

Emma took a deep breath and followed, her flashlight showing ancient farm implements, some long since turned to rust, hung along the supports and old wood of the interior. The floor shifted from gravel to dirt to soft grasses. We rounded the corner of what looked like an old stable, and I froze.

"Oh my God," Emma said. "Oh my God."

The dark gally-wampus was on her side, a mixed litter of jet black wampuses and mixed black and gray babies clamored to feed. The gally-wampus, well, *meowed* at us, for lack of a better term, and I sat my ass on the ground.

Pressure built at the back of my eyes as I realized what Momo had said was true. The workers, or the hunters, or someone had killed the sire's mate, skinned her, and hung her up outside. These were more intelligent than any common prey. The dark gally-wampus may have become his new mate, started a new pride, but the sire had come back for revenge.

"Look at the older ones," Emma said, drawing me away from that horrible train of thought. Fur as black as the heavens at night gave way to small golden eyes that whined and pawed at their much smaller, much grayer siblings.

"Mason?" Emma asked, crouching down beside me. "Are you okay?"

"Fine," I said, my voice a little shaky. "I just ... I don't think Momo was lying. I think that's their mother strung up outside. At least the mother of the larger ones."

Emma cursed and looked back toward the entrance to the shack. "We can't do anything for her now, but we can still help her pride."

"Jesus." I pulled out my phone and texted Himari, making sure the volume was silenced. *Send Larry. Send him now. We have baby kittens.*

That's redundant, she responded.

Baby whistling-wampuses. Now, Himari.

Babies! Send pic!

"What now?" Emma asked.

"We stay with them. Make sure nothing comes for them in the night before Larry gets here, and then we go home."

"Aren't *they* what people usually fear coming in the night?"

I laughed quietly. "Yes, but maybe it's people *they* should have feared." I leaned back and rested my hand on an old log, watching the family of wampuses. The dark gally-wampus raised its head and purred, vibrating the air all around us before settling back to the ground.

Emma slid down the wall on the other side, holstering her .454. "Uh, Mason. Don't look, but you might want to move your hand ..."

16

I shifted the log and watched in awful fascination as a red head popped up over the edge, thick antennae probing the air, followed by a flurry of a half dozen legs, and then again by dozens more. I froze, staring at the awful specter of a giant red-headed centipede, its brown carapace darker than the rotting wood it rested on, and I suspected as black as the soul it didn't have.

"Mason?" Emma said.

"Centipede," I hissed, all thoughts of the nearby wampuses fled as I stared at the horrible little monster.

"I *tried* to tell you." She leaned over next to me and snorted. Emma held out a gloved hand and actually let the thing *walk up onto her arm.*

"You should kill it," I said.

Emma raised an eyebrow. "What is it with you and these things?"

"Have you ever been bit by one?" I asked, my voice rising slightly. "Even their legs can sting you, just by walking! Why are you letting it walk on you? What kind of hellbeast can sting you *by walking?*"

One of the whistling-wampuses snorted, and I liked to think it was in agreement. The nearest of the larger kittens stalked toward Emma, its body weaving in a clumsy rendition of its parents' graceful, stealthy strides.

ERIC R. ASHER

"It's so adorable," Emma said, and then the wampus pounced, snatching up the centipede with a horrible crunch and a tiny whine of victory. The wampus bobbed its head as it chewed, sure to suck up every last leg.

"It's ... less adorable," Emma said with a frown.

"Oh, I like him," I said, making quiet clucking noises.

The whistling-wampus turned its face to me, a smattering of legs still sticking out of its mouth.

"If you don't name him Legs," Emma said, "I'm going to be sorely disappointed."

"Sure, but how can you tell them apart?"

"Legs has gray in his eyebrows," Emma said.

"I don't think they have eyebrows," I said with a small frown. Legs wandered closer and sniffed at my hand. He raised his head just enough that I could see the pale streaks of fur that Emma had called eyebrows. "Oh."

The small wampus ran back to his brothers and sisters, nesting by his mother.

We waited in the dim light of the shack for almost two hours before we heard the rumble of a truck outside. The dark gally-wampus raised her head, ears springing forward, and then flattening again when a car door slammed.

"Mason? Emma?"

"It's Larry," I said. I turned to the flighty gally-wampus. "It's a friend."

Emma shined the flashlight at the entrance to the old shack. It didn't take long before I heard footsteps approaching, and Larry ducked through the torn-up entrance.

"Himari said y'all found a kitten."

I frowned. "Is that all she said?"

"Well, yeah, should she have ..." He trailed off, frozen in place when he saw the pride huddled in the corner. "So she's a half-breed after all." I had little doubt he was talking about the dark gally-wampus.

"What do we do?" I asked.

"That her mate outside?" Larry asked.

I shook my head. "Best we can guess, it was the former mate of the sire."

He cursed and turned away. "Well, damn. She might be alright on her own out here, but we already seen the gally-wampuses reject her on Emma's video." Larry pinched the bridge of his nose. "Guess we can see how they like gowrow. I don't know anyone who raises whistling-wampuses."

On cue, a soccer-ball shaped gowrow came hurtling through the hole in the shack's entrance.

"Brain!" Larry hissed. "No! I told you to wait in the truck."

Emma turned just in time to see the gowrow before Brain plowed into her, scratching at her chest like a *very* excited puppy. Brain bounded over to me, swung back to lick Emma, and then froze, staring at the pride of wampuses.

"Smart buggers," Larry said. "Brain figured out how to open doors in the cave. He figured out the car doors a week later." He sighed like an exhausted parent.

"What happened to Sid and Nancy?" Emma asked as she scratched the gowrow's head. She gave Larry a knowing smile.

"Stubborn critters," Larry said. "Won't answer to any names but Pinky and Brain. I gave up after a couple weeks, and Chuck gave me quite a ribbing over that. So you can just stop right now."

The whistling-wampuses noticed Brain one by one and stared at the much-larger cryptid with squeaking apprehension. The dark gally-wampus raised her head, sized up Brain, and was apparently not impressed. She flopped back down and flicked her tail.

Legs, however, strode right up to the gowrow and started sniffing. Brain raised her neck, twitching her head back and forth like she had *no* idea how to respond to a curious ball of fur. Legs climbed up onto the gowrow's spiky back, and Brain froze.

The gowrow craned her head backward and upside down, eyeing Legs as best she could. Apparently deciding this was all just fine, Brain wandered back out of the shack, a purring Legs fastened securely to her back.

199

Larry watched them go. "Y'all, that was not exactly what I had in mind. I have some big cat carriers in the truck. I think we could fit the whole pride in one, but I can't keep them forever. Too many cryptids in my orchard as it is."

The dark gray gally-wampus ushered her kittens and the whistling-wampuses past us, heading toward the hole in the door, the smaller wampuses stumbling after the gowrow and their trailblazing brother.

"I don't think that's going to be necessary," I said.

Larry frowned slightly before shuffling out the door just ahead of the wampuses. "We can try it without, the back's reinforced and all, I just don't want them getting scared and hurting each other."

Emma and I followed the last of the pride into the field. I'd half expected to see them scattering, running into the woods only to fall prey to the hinge-tailed bingbuffer or some other predator.

I couldn't have been more wrong.

The gally-wampus ushered the pride after Brain and Legs. Wherever those two went, the rest of the kittens stumbled after them.

"Well shit," Larry said. He popped open the rear door and waited. And waited. "*Brain.*" The gowrow perked up, sprinting at Larry with unbridled enthusiasm, until she seemed to remember she sucked at stopping.

The scaly soccer ball plowed into Larry's shins, sending Legs spiraling into the air only to land softly on Brain's head. The gowrow huffed and hopped up into the truck. And by hopped, I mean clawed hopelessly until Larry picked her up and helped her in.

"Help the rest in?" Larry asked, looking away. "I'm going to get their mother's pelt. It's not much, but I reckon it might bring them some comfort cleaned up."

"Are you sure?" Emma asked. "That's just ... grisly."

Larry offered a small smile. "Missy, we stuff our dead full of chemicals and cram them in a comfortable box. I'm sure they'll make do."

The mother gally-wampus hopped into the truck and followed Legs with his new best friend. Three jet black whistlers leapt into the back of the truck with little effort. A whine started when the smaller kittens couldn't leap quite high enough. They hopped and flailed into the air a bit, then splatted onto the grass with even less grace than Brain.

I moved slowly, not wanting to upset the dark gray gally-wampus, but she didn't seem to mind at all when I picked the first of the pride up and set her on the back of the truck. The kitten sniffed at the back of the enclosed truck and made a straight line for her mother.

Emma picked up the second, which proceeded to bite her hand repeatedly.

"Good job not dropping him and getting mauled by his mom," I said when she set him down in the back.

"Thanks," she said dryly. The next one licked the little bloody bites on Emma's palm and purred like a lawnmower.

"Where will you take them?" I asked.

"My orchard for now, I guess," he said, scratching his head. "I don't think they'll be a threat to the sasquatches. Maybe Sonny will have some ideas." Larry swung the door closed as slowly as he could before locking it.

"You have a whole pride in there," I said. "Maybe the last pride in the world."

"I know it, Mason. I'll take care of them, y'all don't worry about that."

"You know, there's a guy that owns the farm on the other side of the road you came in on. His family's been caring for a hinge-tailed bingbuffer for three generations."

"Really?" Larry asked, sounding impressed.

I nodded. "I bet he could take some of those wampuses under his wing."

"Well, alright," Larry said. "Reckon I could stand to talk to a local about the wampuses. They usually know more than any old book about these cryptids."

My phone buzzed in my pocket, the ringer still silent. I read Himari's text and frowned.

DEMON coming to clean site. Get out.

C ome on Mason," Emma said. "We met those DEMON
agents at Larry's place that weren't bad. I rather liked Agent
Amy. And Bubba was ... Bubba was interesting, too."

"I know," I said. "I liked both of them, but we're not talking about
those two. We're talking about cleaners. This place is going to get
reset. You won't know wampuses were here, you won't know the
maintenance workers died here, everything that's happened is going
to get buried. Not to mention that Stewart guy was a real ass. You
think he's technically Chuck's boss in the CCD?"

"Stewart." Emma made a disgusted noise. "I should have gotten
more footage."

"No," I said. "Even if you had, we couldn't use it. If Himari's right—
and Himari is always right, the little brat—we need to get the hell out
of here."

Emma picked up her gun case, slid a few extra shells into her
pockets, and said, "You're making them sound like the mob."

"It's apt. They don't want their business known by the world at
large. And why would they? They deal with things the public can't
handle. Emma, *we* deal with things the public can't handle."

She slowed a bit, obviously chewing something over in her mind.

"I can see that. We edit the shows so someone who already knows things could probably tell what we're doing is real. But everyone else would think it's a hoax."

"Exactly." I snapped my gun case closed with the mangled tranquilizer rifle. "Now let's get out of here before we end up with the worst case of 'I told you so' in our storied working relationship."

I started walking toward the river when Emma cleared her throat.

"What?" I asked, glancing back.

"The car's that way."

I blinked slowly. "Holy shit, I was going for the boat."

Emma smiled, and we hurried out of the thicket, making the short trip back to the Bronco with only a few stumbles under the cover of night. I could have sworn I heard the quiet hum of a black DEMON helicopter in the distance.

We drove up the gravel road, leaving Larry to be regaled by Clarence's stories of the bingbuffer at the Ellbrach farm. I was relieved that the old man had agreed to take on at least some of the wampuses. I didn't know how many more creatures Larry could really handle at his orchard.

I didn't turn the lights on until we were back on 248, headed for Reeds Spring. Emma was asleep by the time we made it back to the motel. I woke her to help her into the room, but I didn't make it much longer than that.

We slept for hours until the phone rang the next morning. I stared at the blurry phone screen, trying to focus my eyes. It was one of those times I could have sworn I'd silenced the ringer, but apparently, I'd only thought about it. I answered the call when my brain finally registered who the contact named "The High and Mighty Hypocrite" was.

"Noah," I mumbled, half in greeting and half in irritation that he'd called so early. "What time is it?" I may have been able to make out the contact name, but reading the tiny number that actually told me the time? Not so much.

"It's 11:45 a.m., Mason."

I blinked. "It's what?"

"It's *noon*," he said, clearly annoyed at that point. "You were supposed to check in two hours ago."

I tried to remember any hint of an actual schedule of checking in with Noah, and failed. "Sorry?"

"Mason, you shouldn't have stayed in that motel. I just got grilled by DEMON. They want to know where you are, what business you have with Larry, and whether you are *once again* transporting cryptids illegally."

At this point, I was wide awake. Emma had rolled over on her bed and was squinting up at me. I flipped the phone to speaker.

"Why was DEMON even here?" I asked.

"Oh," Noah said, "you'll love this. Someone overheard the CCD's plant in the maintenance crew talking to Chuck. They called the *police*."

I groaned and set the phone on the nightstand between the beds.

"Yes, Mason, do you know how long it takes for DEMON to find out about a police report with the words whistling-wampus in it? *Do you?* I've been making excuses for you half the damn night, Mason. This is not my job."

Emma frowned and whispered, "That's kind of exactly his job, isn't it?"

"Emma," Noah said, "Mason's phone has an extremely good mic."

She bit her lips, and I grinned at her.

Noah took a deep breath. "It's fine. Everything's fine now. But you *are not* transporting cryptids, right?"

Emma leaned into the phone as she spoke, sleep still heavy in her voice. "I can honestly say we're not transporting cryptids."

"Good," Noah said. "Good."

A text message popped up on my screen from Himari. *Dem Ears is a terrible album. I don't know why you recommended it.*

I frowned and tilted the screen toward Emma before letting it rest on the nightstand again.

"DEMON?" she mouthed at me.

I nodded.

"Thanks for letting me know you didn't transport anything," Noah said.

I hesitated, wondering how much I should push my luck. "I'm licensed by the CCD, Noah. Why would it matter if I was relocating a cryptid?"

"That's a good point, Mason. That's a damn good point. It might have something to do with a new statute in DEMON's bylaws."

Static burst onto the line, and words were exchanged that I couldn't understand. It cleared long enough for me to catch the last of it.

"… out there risking their lives! They *deserve* to know what you …"

I scooped the phone up and texted Himari. *What was that? Could you hear them?*

Yah. New bylaw. Any cryptid posing significant danger to local peeps can be put down.

"They can't do that. You can cut the bullshit," I shouted into the phone, partially unhinged by what Himari had texted. "What you're doing is like declaring a hunting season on endangered animals!"

Himari texted again. *Uh oh. DEMON agent looks freaked you heard that. Here look.*

A small box appeared on my phone, showing me Noah's office, and Agent Stewart of the CCD, looking like an ass in his suit as per usual.

"Stewart," I hissed into the phone.

"I told you no video calls!" Stewart said, clearly flustered. It was probably good he assumed Noah had accidentally enabled video, and he didn't know Himari had jacked us all in to Noah's home security system.

"I didn't," Noah said, completely killing our excuse in five seconds flat.

"They're in Noah's home," Emma said, frowning at the picture. Her face fractured into a smile that always spelled trouble. She leaned into the microphone. "Did you invite him into your home?"

"Not exactly," Noah said.

"Did he have a warrant to search your property? The CCD doesn't operate outside of local police jurisdiction."

Noah perked up.

Stewart's fairly calm demeanor cracked. "I don't need a warrant when someone is suspected of hiding the illegal transport of cryptids!"

"Oh, you're probably right," Emma said. "That's good since this surveillance video will be on the news tonight. Copy it now."

Stewart looked frantically around the room, digging through Noah's bookcase and eyeing the picture frames on the wall.

Done, Himari texted a minute later.

"We already have a copy," Emma said. "Now get out of our friend's house."

Stewart froze, glancing between the phone and Noah. His expression flashed into a snarl, and then he was completely composed again, adjusting the buttons on his suit. "I'll have to discuss this with my superiors at DEMON. I'd hoped you could be civilized, but we clearly need to pursue other channels."

Himari texted again. *Look look look. Talked to Chuck.* A photo of a document appeared on my phone, a short section highlighted, and the CCD logo clearly visible in the corner.

I forwarded the image to Noah's phone.

"You can ask him to leave now," I said.

"It's just GPS coordinates in the location," Noah said, frowning.

"Read lower."

"Stone County? *All* of Stone County is marked as a cryptid preservation?" His concern changed into a smile. Section 9CCD 13-3.442 Purpose: This rule establishes a permit for CCD agent transport of endangered cryptids. To exercise the privileges of a Class X wildlife caretaker. Authority: Any licensed agent may transport cryptids between any border, sanctioned or not, to preserve the life or species of said cryptid." He started to read the amendments cited, but stopped, and set his phone down.

Noah turned to Stewart and said simply, "Get out."

Stewart tugged on the bottom of his suit jacket, turned sharply, and strode out of Noah's office. The front door slammed a moment later, and the faint sounds of an engine starting reached Noah's speaker phone.

"Thank you," Noah said. He glanced up at the wall and looked into the surveillance camera hidden in his clock. "And Himari, while I appreciate what you did, we're going to have to have a talk. But not tonight. Tonight, just … thank you."

The video feed dropped off my phone.

"Mason?" Noah said.

"Still here," I said.

"What actually happened?"

So I told him about the raccoon and the hinge-tailed bingbuffer, the oil pit squids, Larry's rescue of the mixed pride of wampuses, and our new friend Clarence.

"Well done. The workers will be safe then."

"Should be," I said before I muted the phone. "Should I tell him about Momo?"

Emma grimaced and shrugged. "I don't know. You could just tell him what the workers did to that family of whistling-wampuses. He doesn't have to know where you heard it."

Momo was an uncertainty, a source of information that proved to be true, but to say I didn't trust Momo would be a vast understatement.

I unmuted the phone. "Noah, the construction workers who died, at least two of them shot and killed a whistling-wampus."

"What?"

"Not the worst of it." I told him about the scene, about the skinned mate and the pride that had adopted the half breed.

"Lord help them," Noah said. "They're safe now."

"They are," Emma said, "and they seem to like the gowrows, too. At least the one gowrow that we know they've met so far."

"Good job, both of you. Now, get out of that motel before I end up having to pay for another night. Your checkout time is past."

I thought about asking if he'd already taken care of paying for our flattened ATV but thought better of it. We ended the call, packed up our things, and made one last stop by the pizzeria.

C huck was at the same table we'd seen him at just the day before, happily munching on his olive-drenched pizza.

Emma made a disgusted noise and took a seat at the opposite side of the table from Chuck.

"Hey guys," Chuck said. He grinned at Emma. "The cheese bread is olive free. Dig in."

Emma narrowed her eyes, the suspicion practically dripping off her. She grabbed some cheese bread and tore it in half, making a show out of checking for olives. "So, Chuck, why are we here?"

Chuck furrowed his brow. "You asked *me* here." He glanced at me. "Didn't you?"

Emma laughed and took a bite of bread. "I'm just giving you hell. Since your friend Dale got us tied up with Agent Stewart of DEMON, who then illegally invaded *our* boss's home."

Chuck's eyes got wider with every word until he choked on his pizza. He wiped his mouth hurriedly and said, "What are you talking about? I gave Himari the CCD code. That got you out of it, didn't it?"

We gave him the story, and he flopped back into his chair, staring at his pizza. "I can't believe Dale let civilians overhear that."

Emma ordered a pepperoni pizza while we waited for Chuck to

become responsive again, and I ordered an Italian grinder. Pizza is great, but too many days in a row and it's just no.

The server walked away, and Chuck leaned forward, running a hand over his beard. "That's why Stewart got involved and Himari needed the code? That's ... oh man, I'm sorry. I'll talk to Dale about that. I mean, I will *talk* to Dale about that. As far as civilians are concerned, we don't exist. It's why your show is such a great cover."

"Watched by millions," Emma said between bites of cheese bread.

I smacked my lips and gave her my best side-eye.

"I appreciate the help," I said, leaning forward. "It got Stewart out of Noah's house in a flash. I just don't want to see it come back on you when it shouldn't have been an issue in the first place."

"Oh, man, don't worry about it. This isn't the first time Dale did something stupid. I'll take care of it."

I nodded.

We ate in relative silence once our food arrived. I was surprised at just how good the grinder was—crispy bread, melted cheese, and some fantastically greasy meat. Chuck regaled us with his best chaw-green stories.

Apparently, the little guy we'd met the month before had a whole litter of tobacco-stealing pups, and they'd laid siege to a discount tobacco store.

"You wouldn't have believed the shopkeeper's face," Chuck said with a laugh. "He has this pallet of high-end chew, and it is just *riddled* with baby chawgreens. I've never seen one of those things ill tempered, you know how docile that one you met is, but you get between a chawgreen and its babies, whoo boy."

"Bad?" Emma asked.

Chuck nodded. "Stitches for days. Although I reckon he shouldn't have gone after one of those babies with a broom. Big mistake."

"Where'd you take them?" I asked.

"Just back to their little burrow in Columbia. Thought about taking them to a tobacco farm. You think that would work?"

"I doubt it," I said. "You'd be better off taking them to a tobacco factory. They'll eat the cast offs and the bad batches. They probably won't eat tobacco unless it's good and dried out at this point."

Chuck nodded. "I was thinking the same thing. I'll think on it. They should be safe in the meantime though, right?"

"Just keep some cans close to the burrow," Emma said. "Food will keep just about anything from wandering too much."

Chuck frowned a bit, nodding slowly as he finished his last piece of pizza. "Damn good idea. Thanks. But can I ask you a question?"

"Sure," I said when Emma didn't respond.

"Why do it, man? Some of those cryptids are deadly. I mean, save what we can, and the ones that don't mean no harm, but some of them are just cold-blooded killers."

Chuck had helped our cause, working for the CCD as he did, and I liked to think he didn't mean that to sound as bad as it sounded, so I didn't lecture him outright.

"Look, it doesn't matter how dangerous these cryptids are. Humans are still the apex predator on this planet, and I'll do my damnedest to keep those endangered animals from going extinct. Some of these cryptids have been around for thousands of years, or more. We don't really know how they impact the environment around them. You really want to find out by letting them all die?"

"No, no, that's not what I meant at all."

"You should say what you mean," Emma said. "It helps keep people from getting confused." She pushed her pizza pan closer to Chuck. "Take a slice, it's good." I fought a small smile down, seeing her ploy for what it was. Always pair criticism with a compliment, and if you don't have a compliment, use food. That had been her mom's philosophy when we were kids.

"We'll do better, man," Chuck said. "We will."

"I think you will, too," Emma said. "And the whole state will be better for it."

This time I did smile. She'd found her compliment, a vote of confidence in the CCD agent, and Chuck sat up just a little straighter for it.

I finished the grinder before squaring up the check. Emma insisted on paying for Chuck's meal, too, and I wasn't going to argue. Really,

Noah would be paying, and Noah owed Chuck. We said our goodbyes and headed back outside.

"Should we record another outro?" Emma asked, rubbing her thumb on the camera strap hanging from her shoulder.

"We got one in the woods, right?"

She nodded. "With the bingbuffer, in fact."

"Let's just stick with that. We can edit it later if we need to. I don't think we want people to know where we were. That hinge-tailed bingbuffer could be unintentionally hazardous."

"You think?" she said with a lopsided smile.

"Momo tested us," I said. "But what did we gain by saving those whistling-wampuses and their half-breed siblings?"

"What do you mean?" Emma asked, heat rising in her voice. "We *saved* them. They won't die out. They have a chance to start a whole new pride, and Clarence will be there to help."

"I know. I mean, what about Momo? Did he mean he'll leave humanity alone? Or just give us a break for a while? I don't understand what Momo wants."

"Maybe we should have told Noah?"

I frowned, wondering if we should have done just that. But we didn't know enough to worry. I crossed my arms and took a deep breath. "Momo's killed people. He freely admitted to it. And none of it changes the fact Momo killed Dylan."

She frowned at that, and we stood in silence for a time, watching the occasional car drive by in the sleepy little town. Things hadn't exactly gone as planned, though nothing ever follows a plan all the way to the end.

"Well," Emma said, breaking the quiet around us, "whatever happens, that was different."

I smiled, and we climbed back into the Bronco, heading toward Larry's place to see a load of howlers, some very round reptiles, and a much-needed shower.

THE END

III

MASON DIXON & THE GHOST DINOSAUR

1

Y ou knew the trolls would find you eventually," Emma said, smacking the tripod on one of the trap cameras with her fist.

"It's just uncalled for," I said. "Of course everything looks fake. It's not an excuse to be so vile."

"Well maybe you should take it as a compliment," Emma said.

I grumbled and kicked at the gravel on the side of the road. It probably wouldn't have annoyed me so much, seeing a dozen nasty comments on our latest video, but that was more comments than we'd had in a while, and it could be seriously irritating when all you heard from was trolls.

My earpiece crackled to life. "I can find those trolls for you in five minutes."

I laughed and shook my head. "No, Himari. Just let it go."

"Just let it go?" Himari said. "I don't think so, Mason. We have blood, sweat, and CGI in those videos."

I exchanged a glance with Emma.

"Sounds like Himari's going to take care of it," she said. The last leg of the tripod broke free, and Emma slid it back into place. This was our third, or maybe even our fourth, trip out to the old abandoned road. It was one of those places that was so remote, you were never really sure if you'd be able to find it the next time. But this place was home to one of the most consistent sightings of an elusive creature called the side-hill hoofer.

"Maybe that thing doesn't live here anymore," Emma said. "We've been to the top of the hill and back down. And this isn't much of a hill. How many hours of footage do we have now?"

I rubbed at the back of my neck and frowned. "With today's? I don't know. Must be close to two hundred. Let's just shoot a quick intro clip."

"Another one?" Emma asked, turning away from the trap camera she'd mounted.

"Always another one. At least until we're dead."

Emma smirked and walked back to the Bronco to grab her camera. A minute later, she had it on her shoulder, had the mic ready to go, and gave me the thumbs up.

"We're back with another mission," I said. "Some of you were asking about the side-hill hoofer, so I thought we'd go find one. Now, this is an odd critter in the tales, and we know those stories are never wrong. Or at least not *entirely* wrong."

I crouched down so Emma could catch the odd tracks we'd seen in the mud by the road. "Now, I've never seen a hoofer myself, so I can't say if these tracks are from one, but they certainly aren't from anything I'm familiar with." I pointed to the imprint in the mud, an oblong thing with what almost looked like a single hoof or claw.

Emma kneeled to get the shot level with me again.

"We probably won't know until we find it. But this is flat ground, and the stories say the hoofer lives its life on the hills. That's the only way they can stay balanced since their left legs are always shorter than their right, or vice versa. I've heard told it's one crazy fight when a hoofer going left runs into a hoofer going right. They're terrible climbers, so it ends up being more like nature's version of king of the hill. It's going to be a fun hunt, my friends, so stay with us until we find that side-hill hoofer."

Emma flipped a switch and lowered the camera. "Might have been the best take yet."

I took a deep breath and blew it out while Emma started packing the camera up.

"Okay I got them," Himari said, her metallic voice echoing in my ear.

"Got who?" I asked.

"The trolls!"

I blinked. "And what did you get exactly?"

"Email addresses, IP's, and in a moment … there we go! Home addresses."

"Well, that's terrifying."

"What are you going to do with that?" Emma asked.

"What are *we* going to do with that you mean," Himari said. "We're going to get on a plane and go Jay and Silent Bob on their ass."

I laughed. "Isn't that a little before your time? Was that in the nineties?"

"No way," Emma said. "It had to be after that. Still before Himari's time."

"You mean because my body isn't falling apart like you two old bastards?"

"Watch it, kid," Emma said.

Himari unleashed a giggle that could only be described as evil. "No, no, you're right. It's one of my brother's favorite movies. I don't usually watch classic cinema."

"Classic cinema?" I said, a little exasperation in my voice. "We're not that old, Himari."

I glanced at Emma as I slid the second to last camera into its carrying case.

"What the hell?" Himari said. The rapid staccato bursts of Himari's keyboard echoed over the headset. "O-M-G! Almost all of the trolls are Noah!"

"Noah?" I said. "I'm pretty sure he has better things to do than leave disparaging comments on his hunters' videos." I'd known Noah for a few years. He was our connection to the church, or at least the part of the church that paid us to eliminate the more dangerous monsters of Missouri. They weren't thrilled that Emma and I usually rescued the critters instead of killing them, but trolling us online didn't seem like Noah's style.

"I guess someone could have spoofed his IP," Himari said. "Or just taken over his account. But this looks clean. It's his address, his IP, and it's routed through the VPN that I set up for him."

"Mason," Emma hissed.

"It's no big deal," I said as I snapped shut the latches on the camera case. I turned back to Emma and frowned. "What is it?"

Emma stared past me, over me. She took two slow steps backwards, reaching for the tranquilizer pistol holstered at her waist.

"What's behind me?" I asked.

Emma shook her head slowly and didn't respond.

"Emma?" I whispered.

Emma raised her other hand. I realized she had a small cell phone camera pointed in my direction.

I turned slowly and found... nothing. Nothing until it moved. In an instant, I understood why our cameras hadn't found anything. I understood why the trap cameras hadn't been triggered and why nothing had been caught on film. "It's freaking invisible."

Anytime it stopped moving, the starlight shot through it with no distortion. But when it did move, the slight rolling aberration was almost too subtle to see. A blast of hot breath tousled my hair. The subtle distortion loomed far above my head.

"What is that?" Himari asked. Her voice squawked through the earpiece.

"Not. Now." I hissed out the side of my mouth.

Not five feet from me, the gravel shifted. The realization of how large this thing was sent a shiver down my spine.

The illusion hiding the creature shimmered and slowly fell. Inch by inch, rubbery scales of flesh replaced what had appeared to be an empty space. And instead of some bizarre-looking creature with the inefficient anatomy of a side-hill hoofer, we were staring eye to eye with what amounted to a Tyrannosaurus Rex.

The trap camera flashed, and the rex swung its massive head back to study the tiny bit of technology with the blinding light. The trap camera fired again and again as the dinosaur flinched away.

"Truck. Now." I wasn't sure if Jurassic Park had been right about standing still so a dinosaur couldn't see you, but I figured this was as good a time as any to put it to the test. More specifically, the motion test.

Emma and I ran like hell. We covered a good 50 feet before Emma spoke, trying to catch her breath. "That's fifteen feet of dinosaur, Mason. That is a goddamned dinosaur!"

"Just run!"

We were within two dozen feet of the truck before the creature grew bored of the flashing camera and decided to just step on it. While the loss of the expensive lenses didn't make me happy, I figured Noah would cover them. What really didn't make me happy was the rex was now fully focused on us. And yet I still wondered if maybe the SD card survived.

I cursed when the rex took two steps toward us and broke into a sprint.

2

W e were three quarters of the way to the truck when the thing behind us unleashed a sound somewhere between the roar of a lion and the stuttering squawk of a giant chicken. If I hadn't been worried about our imminent demise, I probably would've laughed at it.

Emma was already inside the cab by the time I threw open the driver side door. She leaned across the cab toward the ignition. The old Bronco roared to life, and Pinky the gowrow sleeping on the bench between us perked his head up just a little.

The rex let out another stuttering squawk, and I dropped the Bronco into drive. Pinky raised his head, looked out the back window at the dinosaur closing in on us, and promptly went back to sleep.

Old Broncos don't have a lot in the way of speed off the line, and I cringed at the sound of the back window shattering. Twisted metal shrieked as claws, or possibly teeth, found a hold in the rear door. I swerved as sharply as I dared and breathed a sigh of relief when the giant stumbled off to the side of the road behind us.

I mashed the accelerator and contemplated using the button for the nitrous. It added some serious kick when you needed speed. One problem with using it, though, was you couldn't really turn. And this was a winding, overgrown deathtrap as it was. A boost of nitrous was more likely to send us into a tree than it was to help us escape the rampaging dinosaur.

I almost missed the shimmer in the headlights in front of us. "Hold on!"

I swerved hard to the left, taking the Bronco off the road, and away from the teeth that materialized from nowhere.

"How many of these things are there!" Emma shouted as she braced herself against the dashboard.

"Why can't the ones that want to kill us ever be stupid?" I said, shaking my head. "Blocking the middle of the road both ways..." We bounced off into the ravine on the shoulder and onto an ancient gravel road.

"Where the hell are we going?" Emma asked.

"West!"

"Those things are going to be faster off-road than we are," Emma said, glancing out the destroyed back window. "And they can turn invisible, Mason."

"Are you dead?" Himari squawked in my ear.

"No, Himari," I said. "Any ideas on how to avoid invisible dinosaurs?"

"You said you're going back west?" she asked, keyboard clicking in the background.

"I don't know where we can go to get away from these things."

"You picked a good road. From what I see on the satellite, you're only two mouse cursors away from a ghost town."

"How far is a mouse cursor?" Emma asked.

Himari didn't answer.

"Himari?" Emma asked.

"I don't know. It doesn't look far, though. It's not scaling."

The trees and underbrush in the rearview mirror suddenly parted before being flattened to the ground. We slipped beneath a low hanging oak branch, and it squealed as it scraped the top of the Bronco. Whichever dinosaur was crashing through the woods behind us smacked into the branch, and the branch held. I watched as a flurry of something sharp cut the tree to ribbons, and the thick log fell to the earth.

"Himari," I said. "Find us a building we can hole up in. Preferably something we can drive the Bronco straight into. An old garage, an old department store with a loading dock, I don't care. These things are just too close for us to get out and run away."

"Highway," Emma said.

"Where you're at?" Himari said. "Not likely. Closest thing to a highway there is an old gravel road."

"And we're already on that. So what's your plan?" Emma asked.

"Unless you have a better idea," I said. We hit a monstrous rut in the old road. The Bronco jerked hard enough to bounce my head into the ceiling. "I think the potholes here may be almost as bad as 255 back in Illinois."

Emma snorted a nervous laugh. "They have a lot less dinosaurs there."

"I think I have two places for you," Himari said. "One of them *is* an old body shop, and the other used to be a hardware store. It might have a loading dock."

"The body shop should at least have a bay," Emma said. "If we're lucky, they might even have a basement for the pits."

I ground my teeth and nodded, trying to decide between the two options while I swerved around another massive rut. "Directions to the body shop."

"It's a little bit further," Himari said. "You're going to come out of the woods on what used to be Main Street. Turn left at the second street and it's right at the end of that block. You won't even have to turn. You should see it straight ahead."

The squawking roar of the creature rose around us, and branches shook in the distant woods we'd passed, barely lit by our surviving taillights. We smashed through the edge of the tree line, leaving the decayed gravel road behind in exchange for what I imagined was a well-kept brick road in the past. Now, it felt like we were driving over speedbumps. Emma held her hands out flush against the dashboard, and Pinky finally woke from the jarring rhythm of the road.

The gowrow perked up, tilting his angled head from one side to the other.

We took a hard left at the second street, and a quick glance over my shoulder showed me the tree line separating behind us and at least one of the dinosaurs charging forward.

I'd been to some old ghost towns before, but this was different. This looked like a town that boomed in the 40s or 50s before everyone moved on. Rusted chassis and the remnants of a ruined bike rack sat at an odd angle in the road. A few old cars had been left to decay in front of what had to be the body shop.

"Watch it," Emma said, pointing to a downed street light that blended in dangerously well with the dirt-covered road. I swerved around the shattered glass top and drifted back to the center of the street. Our tires squealed as they crushed something, and we bounced from brick onto crushed concrete and back onto brick. Pinky looked behind us and let out a small hiccup of a bark. Emma turned around and cursed.

"It's right on us. We're not going to have time to open the damn garage doors."

"We won't have to," I said. "We'll go through them."

"You think that thing's strong enough to tear through the walls?" Emma asked.

"I sure as hell hope not."

Pinky let out a longer, higher pitch bark. I glanced up at the rearview mirror and cursed. Outside of the woods, the thing was fast. Now I could see both dinosaurs charging down the road behind us, their camouflage fully engaged, but their positions betrayed by the explosions of brick and clouds of dirt at their feet. They didn't need to dodge the debris in the streets—they simply stepped on it and flattened it to the ground.

"Hold on," I said. "I really hope that door isn't reinforced."

I braced myself on the steering wheel, and Emma crossed her arms, placing her trust in the safety belt. Pinky hopped down off the seat and forced his way up underneath Emma's legs.

A quick glance at the mirror showed the beasts closing on us, their steps kicking up old dirt and debris as they crushed another lamppost. "Grab guns, food, leave the rest."

"I'm not leaving my damn camera," Emma said.

I wasn't going to argue. Besides, it was right about then we hit the door.

3

The door resisted for a split second. I almost had a heart attack before the metal gave way. The old aluminum door slammed down to the ground, revealing more than one interior bay and what I suspected were the stairs to the basement Emma had been hoping for. I slammed the Bronco into park, leaving the back end nearly flush with the doorway so the things chasing us would have to pull the entire car out to get around. Or I supposed they might be able to step on it thoroughly enough to flatten it into a metal pancake, or crash through the second bay door.

My mind flashed back to when the hinge-tailed bingbuffer had stepped on our ATV and turned it into a literal metal pancake. I didn't want to see what these creatures could do. We flew out of the Bronco. Emma snatched two cases out of the back seat before dashing into the interior of the body shop. I looked up in time to see the first of the dinosaurs reach the intersection across from us. I cursed, grabbed the cooler and a case of my own, and followed Emma in.

"Pinky, no!" I shouted.

The gowrow circled around behind Emma to face down one of the rampaging creatures.

"Pinky!"

The second shout got the gowrow's attention, and the knot in my chest unwound a hair when Pinky dashed back across the concrete floor. Getting tangled up beneath our feet was a much better option than getting mauled by ghost dinosaurs.

"Why did we agree to watch the gowrow this week?" I shouted.

"Because Larry's juggling the wampuses and can't keep them from fighting with Pinky."

"I know," I grumbled. "This is just really bad timing."

Emma threw open the door I thought would lead to the staircase. Instead, I stared blankly at a disheveled back office. Emma cursed, shook her head, and led the way to a door further into the body shop. She swung this one open, and dust-covered stairs vanished into the shadows below us.

"Sure the basement is the best idea?" I asked, and a moment later, the squeal of rending metal and the thunk of claws on brick filled the space around us.

Neither of us said anything else. Emma led the way down the stairs, lighting the way with the flashlight on her phone.

"Look at the size of that wolf spider," Emma said, flashing her light at the furry arachnid with a leg span like a saucer. I raised an eyebrow when its eyes reflected the light.

Pinky trundled forward and snatched up the spider, happily crunching on the unfortunate creature.

"Well then," Emma said. "I guess we won't have to worry about spiders while we're down here."

The dinosaurs roared above us. Something slammed into the ground, shattering and crashing into the basement through one of the bays.

I hoped Emma was right.

I frowned at my phone, staring at the text Himari had sent over from an old collection of folktales.

"I don't see what else it could be," I said.

"Jimplicutes," Himari said. "It's the only thing that makes sense."

"I don't know if I'd say it makes sense," Emma muttered.

"What do you know about them?" Himari asked.

"The old stories say a jimplicute could bite the neck of a man and drink his blood," I said. "But, if those things were truly as large as they seemed, I don't think they'd have trouble snapping a head off in one quick chomp."

"You're telling me these are invisible bloodsucking dinosaurs?" Emma said, sliding her phone into her pocket. Something shuffled around above us and we both froze.

"Sounds like they are," I said. "If we're right, they should leave at daybreak."

"They don't like the sun," Himari said.

Emma sighed and crossed her arms.

I'm not sure how long we spent anxiously watching the dim rectangles of light at the far end of the basement, but we eventually started to nod off. I cursed and shook my head. "We can't both fall asleep."

"We have a watchdog," Emma said. She patted Pinky on the head. The gowrow gave its chortling semblance of a purr.

"Right. The scaly soccer ball. How could I forget?"

I pulled one of the gun cases closer to me and lifted the lid. I was happy to see I'd grabbed the case with the fifty-caliber magazines, but I honestly wasn't sure if they'd be big enough to do anything at all to those jimplicutes out front. Maybe we got a lucky shot and hit one in the eye, but for all I knew, that might just piss it off.

I closed the case and locked it again, sliding one of the magazines into my pocket just to be safe. I'd been caught without ammunition before and it wasn't something I cared to repeat.

"I'm guessing if the tranquilizers didn't work on the gowrow," Emma said, "we probably won't be tranquilizing one of those beasts?"

"To say the least. Those scales looked tough."

"So, how sure are we that they're nocturnal?" Emma asked.

"Pretty sure," I said. "That's one of the few facts that all the legends have in common. They only come out at night, and the only recorded attacks on people have been at night."

"Let's just hope they're right," Emma said. "You want to record a segment? Pass the time a little?"

I eyed the snoring gowrow beside Emma and shrugged. "Let's do it."

We were almost set up when one of the dinosaurs stuck its snout down inside a bay at the other end of the basement. It didn't get quite low enough that it could see inside, but it was close enough that I could see the nostrils flare and just make out the scaly flesh shifting from side to side as the monster bared its teeth.

"I got it," Emma said, nodding at her camera. "I think it's a pretty good shot. I'm going to keep the light dim. It should still be enough to see your silhouette, but hopefully not enough to attract too much attention from the dinosaurs."

I nodded.

Emma pointed the camera at me, raising it just a hair so it was looking down at me when the light turned on. "Go."

"Welcome back," I said, easily slipping back into my onscreen personality. "We may have lost one of our cameras, or maybe more than one, and we didn't find the side-hill hoofer, but we found a jimplicute!" I lowered my voice, muttering, "And unfortunately, we found two."

Apparently the light was enough, or the sound of my voice, as one of the dinosaurs released another cackling bark.

"You hear that? That's them. They have us pinned down in an old body shop. We're safe here in the basement..." I slowly looked from one side to the other, then turned back to the camera. "Or so we hope."

"This is the first time I've ever seen one of these monsters. Big. I mean, really big. If I had to say what it looks like, and you may have been able to see this from the video, it's like a Tyrannosaurus Rex. Except, if you know the stories of the jimplicutes, they're said to be more like a vampire. Biting the necks of travelers, only coming out at night, but I'll tell you what – if that thing bit your neck, you wouldn't be telling a story about it."

One of the jimplicute's claws fished down through the far bay. I was confident now that it wouldn't be able to fit into basement. It could barely get its head down, much less its thick legs.

"Keep your distance," I said, keeping my eyes on the claws in the distance. "They may be real, but they're also some of the most dangerous creatures we've found so far. I think it's coming back." I quickly turned my head to the left and then snapped back to the camera. "Remember, just because it's only a story doesn't mean it won't eat you. Be safe out there."

"Never gets old," Emma said, snapping the camera's flash bar closed. "You think about being a game show host? I feel like you have the skills."

"Thanks?"

Pinky was wide awake again. The gowrow looked up at me, then extended a long pink tongue to lick her own eyeball.

"That's gross."

The gowrow chuffed.

Emma sighed and patted the gowrow's head. "All we need to do is release the nice video of this little girl and we could retire."

"Retire?" I laughed. "Who was the last person to make money from actual footage of a cryptid? Loch Ness? Bigfoot? A yeti? None of the above?"

"Yeah, yeah. Still though, I think with Himari's help, we could swing that into something profitable. Maybe get a nicer camera mount. Or a tripod whose leg doesn't get stuck?"

"Or a Bronco that still has a back half?" I said.

Emma laughed quietly, and the jimplicutes chattered above us.

E mma took the first watch, but I'd be lying if I said I got anything more than a few restful minutes of sleep. It felt like I'd barely closed my eyes before she tapped me on the knee.

"I'm done," she said. "Need a nap."

I nodded and rubbed the exhaustion from my eyes. "Anything new?"

Emma shook her head. "Haven't heard a noise in quite a while. Other than Pinky snoring." She curled up next to the gowrow, yawned, and was out before I could think of anything else to ask her. My grandfather had told me stories of trench warfare, where the soldiers were so exhausted they had to sleep, but the war wouldn't let up around them. I wondered if it was something like this, only with more explosions, and death. I shuddered at the thought.

About the time I was wishing I would've grabbed the cup of cold coffee instead of the gun case from the Bronco, the light at the far end of the basement changed. At first, I thought was my imagination, but the shadows moved, and slowly the dim light brightened.

I double checked the Desert Eagle holstered under my left arm and the extra magazine in my pocket before heading toward the stairs. I figured I'd let Emma sleep for a couple more minutes before dragging her up into the light. I still didn't know if we could use the car or if all that was left was a mangled hunk of steel.

Now that the strongest light source wasn't the stars or Emma's phone, I could see well enough in the dark corridors of the basement to make my way back upstairs. I paused at the steel door at the top, only a narrow window letting me see a thin slice of the space beyond and waited.

I moved as slowly as I could tolerate, my only company the sharp scent of rust and the constant need to fight off a sneeze. The hinges on the door remained quiet, and I silently thanked them as I stepped out into the body shop. Now that I wasn't rushing through the shop with the single goal of not dying, I could see the old storefront had been abandoned without being emptied out.

The parts room off to the side was stocked with the rows upon rows of old engine parts. I wondered how many of them were still good being in the musty old building. And I wondered what the salvage rules were for old abandoned ghost towns. My folks had made a great deal of money flipping antique cars and parts at local flea markets and swap meets.

I turned back to the task at hand, checking every corner, every wall, for any tiny line of distortion in my vision. Whatever the jimplicutes used to camouflage themselves, I now understood why they were referred to as ghosts. I'd barely been able to see the one standing right in front of us, and if it hadn't moved, I doubted I ever would've seen it. Even then, I needed Emma to point it out, except for the brief time it had dropped the camouflage. Why had it done that?

I kept to the walls, pondering the dinosaurs' behavior, and figuring the walls gave me two advantages. One, nothing was going to be able to sneak up behind me. Two, if the thing was hiding against the wall, I'd run into it. At least Emma and Pinky could get away after my dying screams woke them up. I tried to turn my brain away from that grisly line of thought. I also began to question the intelligence of coming upstairs alone.

But, my worst fears didn't bear any fruit. I circled the entire shop without running in to any old dinosaurs. Except maybe my Bronco. The truck was a lot worse for wear. I was happy to see all four tires were still inflated, but the back had essentially been turned in to a pickup truck. The roof was peeled back like a sardine can and at least one of the jimplicutes had dug through the cargo. I hoped my latest tranquilizer rifle was still okay, as it would probably cost more to replace it than the Bronco. The second bay door was torn down, and I suspected that had been responsible for a great deal of the racket we'd heard.

I turned my attention back to the Bronco. The key waited in the ignition. I turned it slightly, relieved to see the dashboard lights come on. I turned it back to off and started picking up some of our cases that had been scattered across the ground.

One of the gun cases had been crushed flat. I was going to need a cutting torch to get into that thing, then a gunsmith to fix whatever had been inside. I wasn't 100% sure which case it was, being so bent out of shape.

Our plastic cases had fared better. A few had bite and claw marks, but only a couple had been broken open. Apparently, when the dinosaurs hadn't found snacks inside, they were quick to disregard the rest.

The left rear wheel well was the biggest problem. Part of the fender had been folded down until it was touching the tire. I pulled on a pair of old leather gloves that I plucked from the back of the Bronco and yanked the mangled metal far enough away from the tire that I thought it was unlikely it would cut the rubber. A few shallow gouges showed in the side wall, but nothing had punctured it.

I snatched a bag of Cheetos out of the front seat and headed back toward the basement. I'd only made it about halfway when the basement door flew open and a very worried looking Emma popped her head out. "Mason," she snapped. "I thought you were dead. What the hell are you doing?"

"They're gone," I said, crunching down on a handful of Cheetos. "Breakfast?" I shook the bag at her.

At first, she frowned, then she nodded. Pinky shot out around her legs and hurried over to the Bronco.

"Is our ride dead?" Emma asked.

"It still has power. It doesn't look like they attacked the engine, although I didn't try to turn it over."

Emma eyed the old truck. "Yeah, we're just driving a convertible back."

"Pretty much."

"No sign of the jimplicutes though?" Emma asked as we walked toward the Bronco.

I shook my head. "No, but there's no doubt they were here. Makes me wonder how no one found evidence of them before. I mean, look at the claw marks in the side of the truck. What do people think if they see something like that?"

"Maybe they think a forklift ran into it?" Emma said. "Ran into it about fifty times?"

I shrugged. "Who knows. Could be."

I hopped up in the driver's seat and turned the key. The Bronco sputtered and did nothing. I cursed, turned the key again, and the engine roared to life.

"Thank God."

I pulled my phone out, and Emma hopped into the passenger seat with Pinky.

"I have about fifty missed texts from Himari. I think she thinks we're dead."

"Well tell her we're not," Emma said. "Then let's get home. Or at least to a more up to date body shop."

"Right."

I texted Himari, *Still alive. Thanks for the help.*

I already bought a funeral dress, came back a moment later.

I held my phone up to Emma and she let out a short laugh.

I put the Bronco in gear. It protested for a moment, but the squealing gave way to momentum, and we bounced our way out of the old ghost town.

4

———

W e made it back to a body shop and dropped the Bronco off, and I'd be lying if I said I wasn't amused by the shocked expressions on the estimators' faces. By the time they were done tallying up the damage, I was under no illusions that it would be cheaper to just buy a new truck. But, even though the Bronco was totaled from an insurance perspective, that didn't mean I wanted to spend the time to hunt down an entire new truck. It took a little bribery, but the shop eventually agreed to replace the body, because the frame was still intact. I'd have to pay for most of it out of pocket, since what I'd be getting from insurance would basically be the blue book value. At this point, I suspected that was probably about a hundred dollars. And the thought of explaining it to my insurance company... I pinched the bridge of my nose.

"You think Noah and the church will pay for some of this?" Emma asked. "We were on the job."

I shrugged. "They'll probably give us some kind hazard pay, but for the most part I suspect I'm on my own. I'll ask Himari to check on it later. For now, we need to get to Larry's and pick up your movie date."

Emma nodded and said, "As long as whatever we're doing doesn't involve going back and messing with the jimplicutes, I'm good."

"I don't know that there's really anything we can do about them," I said. "I'm pretty sure the art of transporting dinosaurs has been lost to the ages."

Pinky forced his head up between the seats and rested it on the console. Emma patted the gowrow's snout and leaned back.

"Don't scratch the seat," I said. "This is a rental. We have to give it back."

I glanced down in time to see the gowrow rolling his eyes at me. I'm sure it was just the angle I was sitting at, and the way he was eyeing the bag of beef jerky on the floor, but it still made me laugh.

"Jimplicutes don't strike me as the kind of creature that would get along with the gowrows," Emma said.

"To say the least."

"I feel like the body shop we dropped the Bronco off at may have seen some weird shit over the years," Emma said. "I mean, they were shocked at first, sure, but they agreed to fix it."

"How far out from Larry's are we now?" I asked.

Emma glanced at her phone and said, "Not far now. Only about a half hour or so. We should be hitting the highway soon."

"And then I guess we'll find out how bad of an idea this is," I said.

The GPS was dead on. Another half hour put us in Brumley, where we once more traversed the old rusted swinging bridges. It never got less unnerving, suspended on the wobbly old cables, flanked by rust and the creak of a stressed structure.

I turned right onto the drive into the woods, and it took us by the bend in the Missouri River before dumping us out at the front gates of Larry's Orchard Extravaganza.

"You hungry?" I asked, looking in the rearview mirror at the gowrow excitedly hopping around on the back seat. I really hoped he was being careful with his claws.

I turned off the ignition and we climbed out of our khaki beast. Emma barely had the back door open before Pinky flung it wide, and the scaly soccer ball waddled off into the Orchard in a hurry. I suspected many apples were about to meet their doom.

"Mason?" Larry's voice said.

I looked around, trying to find the old man, and it took me a minute because he was camouflaged up in his tree stand.

"You hunting?" I asked.

"Come on," Larry said. "This is where I sleep and these are my pajamas."

Emma chuckled and grabbed some of the larger equipment cases out of the back. "You mind if we leave some of this here?"

"Not at all."

"You sure it's okay to bring Pinky back already?" I asked. "I don't want him giving you and the wampuses trouble."

Larry shook his head. "If it wasn't fine, Mason, I wouldn't have said it was fine."

A shadow lumbered through the woods behind Larry's tree stand. I smiled as Old Willie caught up to Pinky and nudged the little gowrow. Pinky yapped at the beast, as if Old Willie couldn't squash him in one careless step.

Old Willie wasn't alone. A smaller and only slightly less imposing silhouette grew more defined as the figure walked closer. Sonny raised a furry arm and said, "Greetings."

"Y'all be careful now," Larry said. "It might be Halloween, but don't be stupid about it."

"I believe I've done this enough times to avoid making a scene," Sonny said, still in the shadows of the trees.

Emma barked out a laugh as Sonny fully cleared the edge of the woods. Once he was in the light, and his costume was revealed in full, I wasn't sure if I was more impressed or more concerned that maybe this wasn't a great idea.

"Chewbacca," I said.

Sonny plucked at the bandolier crossing his chest and gave me a wide smile. "Let's get the next misfit," Emma said.

"And there were two jimplicutes?" Sonny asked after we finished telling him the tale of our escape.

"At least two that we saw," Emma said. "And that was more than enough for me."

"When I encounter anything that is trying to eat me," Sonny said, "it is generally more than enough. Even if it's only one."

"What the hell is going to try to eat you out here?" I asked.

"Bears, bingbuffers, whistling-wampus, the occasional nigh behind."

"You've actually seen a nigh behind?" Emma asked, turning to look back at Sonny.

"Certainly more than I've seen of jimplicutes."

"Legend says a nigh behind can eat a man in one bite," I said.

"Perhaps a slight exaggeration," Sonny said. "I suspect, with the larger ones, it would still take two bites."

"Well that's not terrifying," Emma said.

I guided my khaki Suburban, aka family tank, into a small neighborhood outside Columbia, Missouri. The houses here were large, but the yards were well kept with the shrubs trimmed into exacting geometric patterns. It made my head hurt just thinking about the effort it would take to maintain something like that.

"I'll text her," Emma said.

We only had to wait about two minutes after Emma sent the text before the front door swung open and a very peppy Himari streaked toward us.

She popped the back door open opposite Sonny and hopped in.

"What are you wearing?" I asked.

"Mason," Himari said. "I'm dressed as Mononoke."

"It's fantastic," Emma said. "Did you make it all yourself? The detail is amazing."

"Mom stitched the throw for me. It's actually fur. I was just going to use fake fur, because sometimes people get a little weird about fur, but this was an old rug we made from roadkill, so I didn't feel too bad about it."

I took a deep breath. "Okay, let's do this. Let's take the hacker and the sasquatch to the movies."

W e parked outside the old theatre, one that I hadn't been to in years. I wondered if it would have the old flat seating instead of the stadium seating that had become the standard in modern theatres. We hadn't made it three feet inside the front door before a group stopped Sonny to take a picture with them, and while we were waiting for that to finish, another couple stopped Himari.

"I love your Ashitaka," Himari said, complementing the young boy with the recurve bow standing beside her.

"Thanks!" the boy said.

"We're in theatre six," Himari said, turning back to me and Emma. Sonny had been stopped by yet another group to take photos. I heard one of the kids whisper that his face didn't look quite right for Chewbacca, but the rest of him was perfect. Sonny thanked him, and we moved on.

The scent of popcorn followed us through the hall. The old theatre still had some Hollywood flare. Decorative pieces hung on the walls, and crown molding that looked fit for one of the Fox Theatres ran just below the ceiling.

It was there, along the ornate trim, that I saw something move. I wasn't sure if it was a rat or squirrel, but it seemed to be moving at speed, and backwards. I frowned and shook my head, and when I looked again, it was gone.

I kept my eyes on the ceiling as we moved into the theatre and made our way to our seats. I didn't see anything else moving along the rafters, and I eventually wrote it off as an overactive imagination and perhaps a little lingering trauma from being chased by ghost dinosaurs. The theatre itself *had* been updated, and I followed Sonny and Himari down to the first row of the middle section.

"You have to be close," Himari said. "It's the only way you can truly appreciate the detail. Oh, and especially if it's a 3D showing? Then you have to be in the front row."

"I haven't seen anything in 3D," Sonny said.

"Oh, we'll have to fix that," Himari said. She turned to me and Emma. "What are you two doing after this? I'm sure they're showing something in 3D."

I exchanged a glance with Emma. She shrugged.

"We'll see how it goes, kid," I said.

"Oh, they're in," Himari whispered conspiratorially.

"I can still hear you," I said.

"That's okay," she said. "I know you're in."

The lights dimmed and the movie began.

I hadn't seen much anime over the years, other than what Emma had shown me. And she usually showed me movies with giant monsters and far-fetched creatures, and I guess that proved she knew my tastes.

This movie was subtler. It still had monsters and legends and things that ought not exist, but there was more to it. There was more depth, more character, and I suddenly had an urge to see everything else the screenwriter had done.

It was about the time the strange demon worms started wriggling out of the boar on screen that a couple released some startled shouts behind us. While I thought some people might find the imagery a little disturbing, I didn't think it called for quite so much drama. After the sounds died down, and another few voices joined the chorus, I suspected there was something more going on.

The noise died away and the movie continued. Every so often, another movie patron would make another surprised squeak and I couldn't understand why. It was intermittent all the way until the end of the film, and as the credits rolled, something climbed up the back of the screen. A pale silhouette that I'd almost missed in the credits.

"What was that?" Himari asked. "Something just brushed my

ankle." She bent down and snatched something up with uncanny speed. Himari gasped.

"What is that?" Sonny asked.

"It's adorable!" Himari said. I stared at the thing in her hands. At first, it looked like a squirrel, but it had a large ball in its tail that it was bouncing up and down. It gave its tail one mighty snap, and the ball hit the seat in front of it and launched the squirrel into the air, pulling out of my Himari's grasp.

"That's a zigmal," I said. "What's a zigmal doing in a movie theatre?"

Someone in the back of the movie theatre screamed, and this time, I stood up and turned to look. As the lights came back on, it became clear the zigmal Himari had caught wasn't the only one in the room. A small horde of them were dancing across the tops of the seatbacks, occasionally bouncing off peoples' heads, flying in erratic patterns when they hit their tails on something to launch themselves into the air.

"Their tails are quite tasty," Sonny said. "Chewy, but in a good way. I highly recommend trying one."

"That's horrible," Himari said, utter horror etched across her face. "That's like eating the family gerbil. Why would you do that?"

Someone shouted, "Rats!" I figured this wasn't the appropriate time to correct them. Although I didn't suspect the presence of squirrels or rats to do much for the attendance at the movie theatre.

I watched the chaos unfold as the audience surged toward the exit all at once. I hoped no one would get injured in the crush, and I tried very hard not to laugh as half a dozen of the zigmals slammed their tails against the ground and sailed backwards through the air.

"We need to get them out of here," Emma said. "This place will go out of business if word gets around they have a rat infestation."

"Just a few pictures," I said, almost dropping my phone in the excitement of catching a zigmal in the wild. Well, sort of in the wild.

"Might I suggest trapping them inside this room for now," Sonny said.

"They've already been behind the screen," Himari said. "I imagine they're already in the ductwork and maybe the walls."

"But why?" Emma asked. "Zigmals are just supposed to be attracted to lumber yards."

"That makes sense," Himari said. "Used to be a lumberyard about three quarters of a mile from here. It just closed down a month or two ago. They've probably been looking for a new place to live."

"Regardless," I said, "let's get the doors closed up there so we can try to get a better idea how many are in here." My mind slipped back to the shadow that had been surging across the crown molding out front. "Actually, I think they may already be outside. I think I saw one on our way in. Let's go take a look."

The folks who were apparently most terrified of rodents had exited the theatre, screaming as they went. A few stragglers had only left a moment before us, apparently fascinated by the strange zigmal tails as some of them hopped up to look at the humans before skittering off into the shadows.

We stayed over to the left, taking the ramp up a narrow incline to the theatre doors closest to us. A tall man with thinning hair stopped me as we exited. "You're him, aren't you?"

"Sorry?" I said.

"The monster hunter. You're Mason Dixon."

"Oh Lord," Emma muttered.

"I don't mean to disturb you, I was only hoping you might be able to help get rid of all the squirrels. Some folks are calling them rats and that will be terrible for my business."

"You're the owner?" Emma asked.

The man nodded. "Greg Randall, Randall Theatres."

Himari pushed her way up between me and Sonny. "Of course, we'll help! Any theatre that would show such fantastic movies deserves the best. Or, in this case, whoever happens to be available."

"Hey," I said. "I feel like maybe you've been talking Emma too much."

"Or just enough," Sonny said.

Some of the zigmals chittered above us. I glanced up to see one bouncing its tail off the seat up against the wall and then rocketing off in the shadows. "How in the hell are we going to catch those?"

"Catch them?" Randall asked. "Just kill them. Kill them all."

"They're bit rare for that," I said.

"I don't care what you do," the theatre owner said. "Just get them out of here. Please. You can come see movies for free whenever you like. Just get rid of them!"

"Free movies," Himari whispered, her eyes widening as the theatre owner walked away.

One of the zigmals bounced off the wall and then bounced off my head before landing on Sonny's shoulder. It rooted around the sasquatch's fur before bounding down the hallway.

"Only at the cost of your dignity," Emma said.

I narrowed my eyes.

5

—————

We need bait," I said.

"Zigmals like nuts, right?" Emma asked.

I nodded. "So Sonny just needs to take his loincloth off."

"I don't think I like this plan," Sonny said.

I flashed him a grin.

"Gross," Himari said. "There's a little organic pantry two doors down."

I nodded. "Okay, get peanuts, peanut butter, and any walnuts they have. We need a lot."

"What are you going to do?" Himari asked.

"Hopefully I'll figure that out by the time you get back."

Emma made a disgusted sound, but I knew she was on my side. She pulled a small wad of twenties out and handed it to Himari. "Just get whatever this will buy. Hopefully it will be enough."

"Okay!" Himari said, and she jogged down the hall, vanishing toward the entrance to the theatre.

"This has been an interesting Halloween," Sonny said. "I hope the other sasquatches are having a less... memorable time."

I blew out a breath. "Me too."

"So, what *is* the plan?" Emma asked.

"I have no idea. I wasn't lying when I told Himari I just hoped we'd have it figured out by the time she got back." I frowned at the potentially stupid thought that popped into my head. "I've got an idea. We're going to need some nets."

"I am not one to question your expertise," Sonny said. "But, I believe you may need more than that to catch small horde of zigmals."

"Not like a butterfly net," I said. "Like a big fishing net, or any kind of mesh cloth should do. As long as it can't tear too easily."

Sonny glanced back into the theatre, eyeing the large screen. "Let me talk to the owner. I may have an idea."

I nodded.

"Pull the suburban around," Sonny said. "Back it up to the front door. Actually, don't do that. Back it up to the door that leads into the hallway. I think it's the emergency exit in the alley beside us."

"If that's really just an alley," Emma said, "there's no way I can back the suburban up."

"See what you can do," I said. "If it doesn't fit, it doesn't fit. Find something else." I tossed her the keys as Sonny vanished inside.

Emma nodded and headed toward the parking lot while I got to work on the door that led to the side alley.

I was relieved to see the door would open wide enough and came to a rest almost flush with the wall. It would make this madcap idea a little bit smoother. Sonny carried back an old movie screen, as apparently the owner had recently replaced it to go with his new digital projector. With a little cutting, we created a square hole with flaps leading through the doorway and into the back of the SUV.

"You think this will work?" Sonny asked.

"It was your idea," Emma said.

"I didn't change it by much," I said.

Emma nodded. "So if it doesn't work we get to blame you. So that kind of means even if it doesn't work, it kind of worked, because I really enjoy blaming things on you."

Himari giggled and handed me a huge jar of organic peanut butter. I set it in the back of the suburban.

"I hope that cargo netting will hold." Even if we got most of the zigmals in the back of the suburban, I was a little afraid they'd chew right through the netting, and then we'd have quite a mess of a road trip on the highway.

Himari unscrewed the second giant jar of peanut butter and handed it to Sonny. The sasquatch looked down at it and said, "I really don't like this part of the plan, Mason."

"Just make a couple quick runs through each of the theatres. If any of the zigmals haven't taken our bait, I doubt they'll be able to resist."

Sonny frowned, sighed, and smeared some of the peanut butter on either of his shoulders. The sasquatch made a disgusted noise. "This is awful. I am sure we could have used Himari. The peanut butter would have come off much easier."

"Oh, I don't think you'll have a problem with that," I said under my breath.

"What?" Sonny said.

"I said good luck. Or something."

The sasquatch stuffed the jar back into Himari's hands and set off down the hall.

"Okay," Emma said, "let me make sure I have this right." She pointed down the hall, then back to the suburban. We're setting up the nuts just in this hall, the peanut butter on Sonny, and the peanut butter in the suburban."

I nodded. "Right, the zigmals love peanut butter."

"So they follow either Sonny or the giant pile of walnuts, and then you're hoping they'll go down the screen into the back of suburban to feast on the giant jar of peanut butter."

"That's about it," I said.

"This is the best Halloween ever," Himari said, grinning wide enough that I worried about her current state of mind. I supposed that wasn't much different than any other day.

"You must've had a weird childhood," Emma said.

I clapped my hands together. "Let's do this."

Half a dozen zigmals came bouncing out of the nearest theatre door when Himari started cracking open the bags of walnuts and spreading them across the ground. I followed her lead, and a few furry snouts sniffed the air at the next door. Further down the hall, I saw the scenario repeated, except instead of coming toward us, they ran toward the other end of the building and slammed their tails into the ground, bouncing off the walls, ceiling, and the floor in crazy, erratic patterns.

For a moment, I didn't understand why, until I heard the sasquatch bellow. And I was pretty sure no one would mistake the sound for something coming out of a set of human lungs. Sonny exploded from the last theatre door, a crushed jar of peanut butter in his left-hand and at least a dozen zigmals perched on his shoulder digging into his fur.

"Mason!" Sonny bellowed.

"That seems to be working well," Emma said.

The sasquatch charged toward us. He flailed his arms, nearly clipping the theatre owner as he jogged into the hallway to see what the commotion was. Or at least what the *new* commotion was.

"I bet that's what it would look like if wamp rats ever attacked Chewbacca," Himari said. She gave a sage nod.

Emma burst into laughter as Sonny bounced off one of the walls trying to fling the zigmals off, only to have them leap right back at him.

Finally, Sonny reached us, and a few of the zigmals gave up clinging to the mad sasquatch in order to dive into the small clusters of walnuts strewn across the ground. Sonny's grunts were joined by the sounds of dozens of cracking nuts and chittering zigmals.

Sonny dove into the back of the suburban, several zigmals chasing him like he held the last jar of peanut butter in the apocalypse. He grabbed a towel and started pulling the peanut butter out of his fur, or at least what little bit was left that the zigmals hadn't already picked out. He threw the towel in the corner, and it looked like half the fur jumped off his body as the zigmals bounced toward the towel.

Sonny hopped out and stared at the growing bouncing ball of zigmals, and then glowered at me.

"I'm thinking," I said.

The back of the suburban had turned into a churning mass of zigmals. There was only one more in the hallway that hadn't taken the bait. It seemed a little skittish, bouncing slightly on its tail before skittering up to Sonny's foot and then dashing away. I popped open the last bag of walnuts and poured some into my hand, holding it out toward the zigmal. I expected to have to wait quite some time as the last little rodent sniffed the air. Instead, it slammed its tail into the ground and sailed in a graceful backwards arc, catching the back of my hand with its claws. It wasn't much larger than a squirrel, and a bit smaller than some of the other fluffy-tailed rodents I'd seen, closer to the size of a flying squirrel. It had the same soft webbing that stretched between its legs, which explained how they were able to glide a bit after they launched themselves with their bouncy tails.

The zigmal looked up at me with big black eyes, and then started crunching on the walnuts in my hand. I walked over to the suburban, threw the rest of the nuts into the back with the zigmals, and set the critter on my hand down in the corner as it stared hesitantly at the mass of fur inside the suburban.

"I think that's all of them," Emma said.

"If it's not," I said, "they'll just have to let us know later. Chase them out themselves. I don't think we're fitting anything else inside that suburban."

"Unless you want it in your lap," Emma said.

"They're so cute," Himari said.

"That is a matter of opinion," Sonny said. "An opinion I do not share at the moment."

I pulled the screen down that we had used as a ramp and closed the back doors of the suburban.

"Their home closed," I said. "We need to find them a new one."

"The new lumber yard's not too far," Himari said. "It's just a mile or so off Stadium."

Stadium was one of the main roads in Columbia, and it wasn't far from the old theatre. "All right, hop in, let's go deliver some rodents."

"Thank you!" The manager said as he peered around the corner. "I don't know what I would've done without you."

"Let us know if you have any more trouble," I said. "You can email us through the website or message us through YouTube. We'll be around."

"If you ever want to see a movie, you can come here for free. I thank you. I'm afraid my patrons may be afraid to come back. If word gets out about a rat infestation …"

"Rats," I said. "Right."

Emma rummaged through her camera bag and pulled out a small stack of business card-sized promo cards. "Here. Hand some of these out to your customers. That lists all the sites you can find about Mason's monster hunting. Don't tell them you had rats. Tell them you had cryptids."

I pursed my lips and nodded. "Not a bad idea! You can get some old monster movies and do a marathon. Really sell it. Talked to the journalists at the university. Maybe you can get a student to take you on as a thesis project."

The manger took the cards and raised what I suspected to be a skeptical eyebrow. "I might have to try that." He hesitated, his eyes on Sonny. "That's not a costume is it?"

"It's actually a painstakingly well-made costume," Sonny said, pulling at the bandolier on his shoulder. "I may have irritated my sisters, requiring the level of detail that I did. The silver just wasn't right on the first one, but by the time they wove the fourth, it was perfect.

The manager gave Sonny an uncertain nod. We slipped through the exit and climbed into the suburban full of zigmals.

6

The explosion of motion and chittering bouncing balls of fur in the back of the suburban cut off the instant we made a sharp turn and pulled back onto the road.

"What are they doing back there?" I asked.

Himari craned her neck around to look through the netting in the back. "That's weird. They're all sitting in orderly rows, waving their tales around."

"A defense mechanism perhaps," Sonny said. "Though they do not seem to be baring their teeth or making any kind of aggressive movements."

"Or they might be trying to distract us from the one that's chewing through the net," Himari said.

"What?" I said. "The cargo net?"

"What other net would it be?" Emma asked.

"How far to the lumber yard? Minutes, I mean."

Emma's phone lit up, and I suspected she was searching the lumber yard. "We're only five minutes out."

I nodded slowly. We made it to Stadium and the net held. We were halfway down the side street, with the lumber yard in sight, when the first zigmal broke through. I was worried the critters were going to bounce up and obscure my view of the road or a torrent of them would do the same, but I needn't have worried.

Sonny bellowed a curse, and the horde pounced on him. As one thread of the net gave way, more zigmals followed, until they were pouring over Himari to get to the remaining peanut butter in Sonny's fur. Himari giggled and tried to pet each one as they flew by, while Sonny tried his best not to just smash them all.

"I want to crush them!"

"Almost there," I said through a choked laugh.

Sonny roared and made to smash a small cluster of zigmals, but Himari grabbed his arm. "You think peanut butter is hard to get out?" she shouted over the din of rodents.

The normally-benevolent sasquatch grumbled and lowered his arm.

We pulled into the lumberyard a minute later. They were closed, and I could still see the security cameras up on the four corners of the building. I suspected there would be more back in the yards. I turned off to the left and curved around one of the stockpiles, angling for a more remote area of the property.

"They have a sawmill," Emma said.

"That's good," I said. "Zigmals are supposed to like those."

"What if this territory has already been claimed by another clan of these bouncing irritations?" Sonny asked, his face barely visible through the mass of zigmals.

"I'm sure they can sort that out for themselves," I said. "Besides, how many of these things can that really be around Columbia?"

"Plenty," Sonny grumbled.

As soon as I stopped the car, all the zigmals started bouncing around again. They streaked past Sonny, ricocheted off the windshield, and landed on Emma with a thud, before bouncing off my head.

"Okay," I said, "I think that's about enough."

Himari threw open the back door and shouted, "Come on, we have to warn Ashitaka!" In the same breath, she ripped open a bag of walnuts, and all the zigmals immediately focused on her. They leapt and bounced and surged out of the back of the suburban. Some of them were still trapped behind the net, and I hurried to the back to open the rear gate.

Himari, still wearing her Mononoke cosplay, dashed into the shadows of the lumberyard, a small army of zigmals bouncing around behind her.

I laughed and shook my head as Sonny crawled out of the back. "I have bald spots," the sasquatch said. "Those monsters chewed bald spots into my fur."

"I'm sure you'll get hazard pay for that," Emma said. She lowered her phone once Himari and the zigmals had fully disappeared from view.

"Oh, great," I muttered. I pointed toward the edge of the lumberyard. "Is that a coyote?"

"You think they'll be a problem for the zigmals?" Emma asked.

"I'm a little more concerned they'll be a problem for the Himaris," I muttered as I opted to grab the Desert Eagle out of the back of the truck as well.

"I'll get her," Sonny said. "Contact Larry to ask about the zigmals. I don't think the CCD will appreciate it if you manage to annihilate an entire horde of these rare creatures." The sarcasm dripping from Sonny's voice made me grin.

I called Larry and waited for him to pick up.

"What is it, Mason?" Larry asked after the third ring.

"Do coyotes eat zigmals?"

"You found zigmals?" Larry asked. "I haven't seen a zigmal in forty years."

"We found ... a lot of zigmals. We're dropping them off at a local lumberyard, but we noticed there's a coyote here to."

"Don't worry about the zigmals," Larry said. "If they feel threatened by that coyote, or that coyote's stupid enough to eat one of them, that coyote is going to have a hell of a headache."

"What do you mean?"

"Zigmals can use their tails for weapons, too. Reckon they could knock that coyote out cold."

A vision of Sonny being pummeled by the zigmals flashed through my mind, while the zigmals dug the peanut butter out of his fur. That may have been unpleasant for him. "Thanks, Larry. Everything else good?"

"Everything except that one wampus you named Legs. I swear, he can't sleep unless he's on top of a gowrow. Found him nestled between the spikes on Old Willie's back earlier today. But yeah, Mason, everything is good."

Sonny howled in the distance, and I quickly said goodbye to Larry before stashing my phone.

"Sonny!" I shouted. I tried to focus on where Sonny's howl had come from, rushing forward and rounding a stack of lumber before I froze in my tracks, staring at the *thing* in the distance. It looked like a butcher had tied a bunch of flanks and pork loin together to make some kind of twisted scarecrow of flesh, only the thing was moving.

"Mason, what the hell is that?" Emma asked, skidding to a stop beside me.

If she hadn't spoken, I wouldn't have known it was her. I couldn't tear my gaze away from the monstrosity closing once again on Sonny. I fumbled at the holster under my arm and cursed when the button stuck. I wrenched it open with a snap and raised the Desert Eagle.

"You cannot harm the raw head with your toys," a voice boomed from above me.

I flinched at the sound. I had the safety off, and the Desert Eagle leveled at the monstrosity attacking Sonny before I spared a glance for the shadow perched on the lumber pile beside me. Deep red eyes glowed in the ambient light cast by the security lamps posted around the lumber yard.

"Momo?" I said stupidly. He ignored my surprised question. He also ignored the gun I was now pointing at him. Generally, when Momo surprised people, someone ended up dead. When the monster didn't move, I lowered the gun. "What the hell are you doing here?"

"Following that," he said with a nod toward Sonny and the raw head, "though it's the witches who make them you need the most caution with."

The raw head released a barking squeal, like some twisted cross of a giant boar and a black bear. It swung the raw meat of its makeshift fist and connected with Sonny's shoulder. The raw head may not have been as tall or broad as Sonny, but the sasquatch went down in a heap. Sonny scrambled away as best he could, favoring his shoulder, and I worried for the damage he'd incurred.

I gritted my teeth, took a deep breath, and pulled the trigger as I exhaled. The Desert Eagle barked in my hand and a chunk of flesh exploded from the raw head's shoulder. Momo had been right. The raw head didn't so much as flinch, didn't so much as hesitate at the mass of flesh that had exploded from its body. Instead, it stalked toward Sonny.

I took three more quick shots, two of which hit the raw head, and one that shattered a two by four in the stack behind the raw head.

"Okay," Emma said, "if we can't shoot the damn thing, then what can we do?"

"You need to feed it to its predators."

"What the hell feeds on a raw head?" Emma snapped.

I flinched at the savage tone in her voice, half expecting Momo to tear our heads off.

Instead, the monster simply looked down at Emma, as if contemplating his words. "I believe you already know. For you stink of them." Momo almost spat the words.

"We smell like zigmals," I muttered. "And it doesn't look like they're eating the raw head. Maybe if he was made of acorns. But he's not."

"The jimplicutes," Emma said, her voice trailing off.

"Indeed," Momo said, nodding his head toward Emma. "Though I do not think your sasquatch can survive escorting the raw head to the nearest pack of jimplicutes."

"Oh hell no," I said. "You have to be kidding. You expect Sonny to lead this thing all the way back down to that town on foot? That's an hour drive from here."

"As I said, I do not think your sasquatch could survive it."

A white cape flared in the corner of my vision. Himari dashed through the opening between two piles of untreated lumber. She wrapped her arms around Sonny's and tugged at the sasquatch.

"Run, you fool," Himari said. "Get back to the truck."

"Help us," I said, looking up at Momo.

The monster cocked its head to the side, eyes narrowed. "I would find it much more enjoyable to watch the raw head have its way with you, so that I may rid this place of more than one parasite this night."

Yellow teeth gleamed in the moonlight beneath Momo's red eyes, but the expression faltered. What appeared to be a frown etched its way across the monster face. "I would exchange a favor for one task. Treat with the sasquatches on my behalf, and I will give you a favor with the raw head. They have long held a grudge due to my... hunting practices."

"That's going to be kind of hard if our only sasquatch dies," Emma spat. "Maybe you should save him? We don't really know anyone else that's in with the sasquatch packs."

Momo said nothing. He simply sprang from the wood pile and charged at the raw head. "Return to the jimplicutes in three hours," Momo bellowed as he closed on the creature. "I will give you proof of the raw head's destruction, and you will negotiate for my people."

It was that moment that Sonny noticed Momo. He instantly picked up Himari and placed himself between the diminutive girl and the notorious monster.

"You have nothing to fear from me this night, sasquatch," Momo said. The raw head reared up and swung a fist made of hooves at Momo. The monster batted the cloven fist away and connected with a quick uppercut that sent a concussion through the lumber yard. The raw head stumbled backwards before collecting itself and charging at Momo. "Leave this place," Momo said, looking at Sonny. "Go with your friends and I shall follow."

"What the fuck is happening," Himari said when Sonny scooped her up and ran, or at least limped hurriedly, back toward us.

"How bad?" Emma asked, hopelessly trying to prop up the sasquatch.

He shook his head. "A sprain, at worst. I am sure. Why does that devil fight for us?"

"Well," I said, "we may have made a deal with him."

We jogged back toward the rental, keeping a slow pace so that Sonny could keep up. The sounds of the raw head and Momo clashing in the lumber yard rose up all around us, bouncing through the strange acoustics.

A panicked zigmal zipped back and forth on Sonny's shoulder. It dug into his fur, and I suspected it was looking for more peanut butter. A moment later it thumped its tail on Sonny's shoulder and rocketed off into the darkness.

"What do you intend?" Sonny asked.

"Momo wants us to meet him where we found the jimplicutes."

Sonny blinked at me as we closed on the truck. We were silent for a brief time, listening to the grunts of Momo and the unnatural cry of the raw head.

"Momo seems to think he can get that thing down there."

"Take heed," Sonny said as he pulled the back passenger door open. "He would not help you if there is not something of greater value in it for him."

Himari jumped inside behind him while Emma and I climbed in the front.

"He wants you to put in a good word for him and his people," I said.

"With the sasquatches?" Sonny asked, clearly astonished.

I nodded and started the car.

"My words will carry little weight against the history between Momo and the packs," Sonny said as we backed out of the lumberyard. The dim lights around the yard went out, and an eerie silence fell all around us.

Something chittered in the back seat. I glanced in the rearview to see Himari digging through her cloak. "It's one of the zigmals she said. "I think he might be hurt."

"Hold on to him for now," I said. "We'll see if Larry knows anything about them."

"Where to?" Emma asked.

"We're taking Himari home," I said.

"No way!" Himari said. "This is the most fun I've had in a year."

"This is not fun, young one," Sonny said. "This is dangerous, and you do not want the attention of the one called Momo."

"Like I said," Himari said with a smirk. "Fun."

7

We were only ten minutes from Himari's place, and I'd feel better once she was back inside her own home. If she thought Momo was fun, I'd hate to see what she thought of the jimplicutes.

"We aren't armed with anything that can take down those dinosaurs," Emma said.

"We're not going to take them down," I said. "For all we know those may be the last two left in the entire state."

"I think it is more likely those are the last two left in the entire country," Sonny said. "But, they are dangerous, and I do not think they would differentiate between someone who would come onto their land to kill them and an innocent child who had wandered too far."

I frowned, thinking back on our encounter with the ghost dinosaurs. "I think you may both be wrong. We basically barged into their nest with floodlights blazing. What else should we expect to happen?"

"Well," Emma said, "we mostly thought that we wouldn't actually find ghost dinosaurs because they were just supposed to be a story."

"I don't mean to state the obvious," Sonny said, "but you have a sasquatch in your back seat."

257

"He does have a point," Himari said.

I glanced up at the rearview mirror and glared at Himari. "That's not helping, kid."

"You're dumping me back off at my parents' house. I don't think I need to be helpful at this point."

I laughed, and my angry façade fractured. "Fair enough. But there's no way in hell we're taking you to see the jimplicutes, Himari. I'm not explaining to your mom how you got eaten by a ghost dinosaur."

"Hopefully I'll get to explain to her how *you* got eaten by a jimplicute," Himari said, flashing a huge grin.

I glared back at her again as we pulled into Himari's driveway a few minutes later, the suspension squeaking in the rental as we passed over the gutter. Himari hopped out and cradled the zigmal in her balled-up cloak.

"What should I feed him?"

"I would start with wood and peanut butter," Sonny said. "They did seem rather fond of that."

"At least you don't have too many bald spots," Himari said. And with that, she slammed the door and jogged over to the front of her house. She waved goodbye before vanishing inside.

"How angry was the little one with you?" Sonny asked.

"I don't think she's really that angry," Emma said. "I think she just wants to see the ghost dinosaurs. And who wouldn't?"

"I wouldn't," I muttered.

It was only a few more minutes before we were back on the highway, our GPS set for the coordinates that would return us to the long-forgotten town.

"What gets me," Emma said after an hour had passed, "is that Momo said to meet him there in three hours. But it's going to take us two hours to *drive* there. He's seriously going to drag that thing all that way? Almost as fast as we can drive there? I don't get it."

"Momo has a deep respect for the natural world," Sonny said, "but he himself is not natural. It has long been suspected that Momo is a creation of the witches, or some darker spirit, born onto our plain for a purpose no one truly understands."

"You're talking about magic, aren't you?" I asked. "I've heard stories, but I just don't know, Sonny. I've seen some weird stuff, but magic?"

"Mason," Emma said slowly, "we just saw a dismembered barbecue fighting a sasquatch. There's no way that raw head was natural. There's nothing in this world that can be cut apart only to stitch itself back together! And not just pull itself back together but include parts of other beings, too." Emma shivered.

"I don't know," I said. "Look at some of the parasites out there. There's stuff that can literally take over the nervous system of other creatures. It could be something like that. Like the fungus that takes over an ant? Or something creepier, like a tarantula wasp?"

"I believe you stretch yourself," Sonny said. "There have long been witches in these lands. And most of them are good people. My pack has been friends with several witches for many decades, centuries even. But what you think of as a witch may not be what drives the raw head. I have never known a witch to use such dark magic, unless she had been wronged in a terrible way."

"That doesn't particularly make me feel better, Sonny," I said.

"I wasn't trying to make you feel better, Mason," Sonny said. "I was only trying to make you understand what may be lying in wait."

"Lying in wait?" Emma asked. "Are you saying a witch is behind the jimplicutes, too?"

"No," Sonny said. "Ask yourself, why was Momo at the lumber yard? And the raw head happened to be there too? What if it was the witch that sent the raw head after Momo and the creature simply mistook me for one who looked so similar to me?"

I cursed under my breath. "Not much we can do about that now. How bad is your arm?"

Sonny rolled his shoulder and tilted his head from one side to the other. "It's functional. I may be sore for a few days, but I will be fine."

"If a witch sent the raw head after Momo," Emma said, "you think that's why he was so confident about being able to get it to follow him? You think he already knew somehow?"

"It is a possibility," Sonny said. "Raw heads are extremely intelligent in many regards, some far more so than others, not unlike humans or sasquatches." Sonny rubbed his chin. "They're formed from magic, but they are also susceptible to it. It's quite possible that a creature such as that, sent after Momo, could be confused by my presence. It is hard to tell without knowing what compulsion drives it."

I exchanged a glance with Emma. The crease on her forehead reflected the growing uncertainty in my gut.

T he delay we expected in Momo's arrival gave us more than enough time to swing by Grits and Grenades, one of the strangest yet most awesome diners slash gun stores I'd ever been to. And I'd been to quite a few. The grits were good, served with cheese as they should be, and the guns were... well, whatever you needed.

"Mason," the clerk behind the register said as we walked inside. "You here to buy or rent?"

"I guess that depends," I said. "You have anything that can take down large game? I mean, extremely large game?"

"Larger than your friend there in the sasquatch costume?" James asked. He raised a salt-and-pepper eyebrow. "Best damn costume I've seen in quite some years."

I glanced back and almost cringed when I saw Sonny walking into the store. I guess it was still Halloween, but it was bold. Especially with all the guns around.

"You definitely won the office competition this year," I said.

"What office?" James asked.

I gave him an awkward smile.

"We need something that can tranquilize an alligator," Emma said, breaking the loaded silence.

"An alligator? In Missouri?"

"That's right," I said, my brain racing to make up a story that made sense with Emma's request. "There's a little alligator farm up north. One of those exotic zoos you see all over the state. You know the type?"

James nodded and gave an annoyed, "Mmmhmm. Some of those

zoos should be shut down. The animals don't deserve to be locked up like that."

"Well, they had a huge saltwater gator that got away," Emma said. "It's not good. But, they don't want to put it down."

"You still have those fancy safari tranquilizer rifles, don't you?" James asked.

I thought back to the time I tried to shoot a gowrow with one of those and it hadn't really done shit. "I shot something similar with that. It... didn't do the job."

"You just need better darts," James said.

"We still have one of the rifles in the truck," Emma said, her focus switching from James to me and back. She stepped up beside me with Sonny.

"That is a fantastic costume," James said.

Sonny grinned at the man, and James looked a little unnerved when the sasquatch revealed his all-too-real set of rather sharp teeth. I suppose that made sense. Sonny had some rather large fangs that looked extremely good for prosthetics, considering they weren't actually prosthetics.

"Darts?" Emma said.

James nodded quickly. "Right, right. You should be on one of those, like, makeup reality shows or something." He started toward the back, gave one more look over his shoulder at Sonny, and then vanished through a squeaky wood door.

Emma looked up at Sonny. "I think you passed the test."

"It's why this is my favorite time of year."

"I bet he could totally pull it off at a comic con too," I said. "He'd fit right in with some of the cosplayers. Just another Chewbacca on the floor."

James came back a moment later and handed us two darts. They didn't look much different than the darts we already had, which I guess made sense since he said they'd work in the tranquilizer rifles we already had. I frowned slightly, and I guess James noticed.

"Oh, don't worry," James said. "These are *a lot* different. The needle is made of titanium. So, when this hits and the injector goes off, that needle's not going to bend. They're a lot more expensive, but you can reuse them as long as the mechanism doesn't break. Once that happens, it's almost as cheap to just buy new ones."

I nodded. "How much?"

"Fifty each."

"Not bad," I said as I handed him the credit card we used to expense everything back to Noah. I did wonder what the father might think of a hundred dollars for two tranquilizer darts, and the more I thought about it, I wondered if we needed more. If we needed to put down two of those jimplicutes, we only had two shots. This maybe wasn't the best idea.

"You have any more?" I asked.

"Maybe one," James said. "We don't really have a high demand for them. Especially when you can get the regular darts so cheap."

"We'll take it," Emma said, clearly echoing my own thoughts.

James grabbed the other dart and rang us up.

"Would you mind if I took a picture with you?" James asked, looking up at Sonny. "I have to show my nieces your costume."

"Not at all," Sonny said.

James stepped out from behind the counter, and Sonny gave him a kind of awkward half hug that enveloped the smaller man. Emma snickered as she lined up the shot and snapped the photo.

James ran a hand down Sonny's upper arm and marveled at the fur. "Is that real? Be careful if you go into the cities. There's people around here that really don't like fur. Seen more than one protester tossing paint at some old lady in a fur coat."

"That is not as frustrating as peanut butter," Sonny said.

James gave him a confused look, while Emma and I choked back a laugh.

"I bet they wouldn't be so quick to trash those coats if they realized how much they were worth."

"I don't think it's the money that worries them," Emma said. "But fur has been used in a lot of cultures for a lot of years."

"Oh, you don't have to tell me," James said. "I doubt those millennial vegan types give much thought to what living back in the day would've been like. People made coats out of other people back then."

Sonny just blinked at James.

"Thanks again," I said, bouncing the bag in my hand. "We'll see you around."

We made our way out the door before James started up on a tirade about Communists and Democrats and space aliens.

———

"You do take me to the most interesting places," Sonny said, leaning up between the seats.

"And you haven't even seen the ghost dinosaurs yet," Emma said.

"They aren't ghosts," I said, shaking my head.

"That's what they call them in the folktales," Emma said, "and I tend to believe the folktales."

"Good Lord," I said. "Just because it's Halloween doesn't mean those were ghosts. It doesn't mean there's some hedge witch, or green witch, or whatever color witch, reanimating hog corpses to create a raw head."

"I believe this stage is called denial," Emma said.

"I tend to agree," Sonny said.

I frowned at him in the rearview mirror as I merged onto a smaller and less maintained highway.

"All the things we've seen," Emma said, "and you're still so weird about magic."

I blew out a breath, unable to hide my exasperation. "Look, I know there's some weird shit out there. There's some shit we've seen that we can't explain, but you can't honestly tell me you think it's magic. *Magic!* Come on."

"Mason Dixon, skeptic," Sonny said. "Never thought I'd see the day."

"Look at the time," Emma said. "It's getting late. How close are we?"

I glanced down at the clock. It was damn late. "We don't know what time those things wake up," I said, trying to remember exactly when the sun would set.

"I am excited," Sonny said. "A Halloween party with ghost dinosaurs, and witches, and monster hunters."

"And Momo," I muttered.

"I am less excited about him," Sonny said.

"I'm a little worried about how excited you are about ghost dinosaurs," Emma said. "They're not exactly... entertaining."

"Far more entertaining than bobbing for apples with a group of sasquatches," Sonny said. "That is not exactly a challenge when your teeth are as sharp as ours."

"Or your mouth's as big as yours," Emma said, unable to stop at a snicker from escaping her mouth.

"You've spent too much time with Mason. I thought you above such terrible jokes."

We drove the rest of the way in relative silence, aside from occasional puns thrown out by Emma, as if she needed to prove to the sasquatch just how poor our humor was. I was pretty sure we were far past that point, though.

The suspension of the rental truck rattled as we turned off the highway. The path up the hill didn't seem as rough now that we weren't racing away from dinosaurs. It was like any other worn-down road. A few bumps, a couple sasquatch grunts when Sonny's head bounced off the roof, but other than that, it was a wonderfully uneventful ride.

8

The abandoned town felt different now. We drove slowly across the broken-up streets. Our headlights flashed across damage and destruction in the storefronts, the abandoned cars, and the fractured curbs, that I now realized had come from the jimplicutes. Their claws and footprints were too large for an everyday observer to comprehend what they were actually looking at, but the rends in the rusted metal and gashes in the sidewalk couldn't have come from much of anything else.

"This place is creepy," Sonny said. "It's perfect."

"I'm officially worried," I said. "How many horror movies have you watched lately, Sonny?"

"Quite a few," Sonny said. "But, those weren't nearly as exciting as one of the short films that my pack worked on."

"What?" Emma said. "What do you mean your pack worked on a short film?"

I saw Sonny's eyes flash back and forth in the rearview mirror, taking in the darkness all around us. "We are not so different from you. We have our own art, and some of us are more technologically minded than others."

"You mean you literally make movies," Emma said.

"Oh yes," Sonny said. "Some of the elders think it's ridiculous. Tell us it's a senseless hobby. I guess it all started when some of the pack wanted to make one of those shaky videos of a sasquatch sighting."

Emma snorted a laugh. "You mean to tell me that your *actual* sasquatch pack made a found footage movie of sasquatches."

Sonny pondered that for a moment, and then said, "Yes!"

"Aren't you a little worried people might find that and think it's real?" I asked.

"Absolutely not," Sonny said. "Our movie was filmed in HD. It's crystal clear. Nothing like those terrible films so many of your cryptozoologists have. It took a great deal of effort to blur things out to a proper level."

"What's it called?" I asked.

"Rage of the Bigfoot."

"That's just amazing," Emma said. She glanced at me. "Where are you going?" She leaned forward, as though it would let her see past the edge of our headlights.

"Back to the garage," I said. "We can hole up there, and we know the jimplicutes can't get to us."

"They can still get to the car," Emma said.

"I paid for full coverage."

"You can't be serious," Sonny said.

I flashed him an evil grin and slowed the truck as we continued down Main Street, the wheels bouncing through potholes, causing Emma to grunt as she latched the case sitting in her lap.

"I think you may have missed one of the potholes back there," Emma said. "If you want to circle back around just to make sure you hit every one, I think we have time."

"Funny," I said.

I didn't say anything more on the matter, but I did slow down and pay particularly close attention to some of the deeper divots in the road. A few minutes more, and we pulled into the old body shop. I could still see the dents in the wall and the crumbled bricks near the entrance where the dinosaurs had slammed in the wall. Instead of parking in the entrance, this time, I pulled all the way into the garage and pulled to the right until the truck was nearly even with the stairs that led to the pits.

"We aren't going to be able to see much once we turn the lights off," Sonny said. "Did you bring lanterns?"

"Lanterns?" I said.

I could almost hear Emma roll her eyes. "You know he means a flashlight. Don't be a jackhole."

"What's a jackhole?" Sonny asked.

"I'll tell you about it when you're older," I said.

I walked around to the back of the truck and pulled the hatch open. I slid out the case with the tranquilizer rifle and grabbed the backpack that held the Desert Eagle and extra magazines. I eyed the case with the extra barrels, but I didn't think I wanted to shoot anything at the jimplicutes other than a fifty caliber, so I left the rest of the truck.

"What the hell are we doing out here, Mason?" Emma asked.

"Trying not to get ourselves killed," I said.

"A worthy pursuit," Sonny said, taking a heavy Maglite from Emma when she handed it to him.

I hit a button on the side of my phone and checked the time. "We only have about twenty minutes before Momo is supposed to be here. Let's setup a bolthole downstairs and then we can figure out a good observation point upstairs."

Emma lifted her chin, and I followed her gaze.

An ancient iron catwalk stretched around much of the second floor. And at the far end, it stopped just below one of the old broken out windows. It was still black where rust hadn't chewed too far into it.

"That definitely looks like it will hold our weight and not collapse and kill us all," I said.

"Sonny," Emma said. "Do you mind waiting on the ground?"

"Of course not," Sonny said. "As a sensible sasquatch, I wouldn't be caught dead standing on that rusty old deathtrap anyway."

"I'm glad one of us has some sense," I said.

"You have put on a few pounds this past year," Emma said. "Maybe you should stay down here, too."

"Hey," I said.

"I wasn't going to say anything ..." Sonny said as he trailed off. "But you do look a little soft, Mason."

"You two are just a riot." I muttered.

Emma handed over her case filled with the new tranquilizer darts along with the bottles of the actual drug. "Take this to the basement with Mason. I'll check out the catwalk. If it looks too rickety, we'll just find some other place to post up."

Emma clicked her own Maglite on and headed toward the far corner of the shop.

"All right," I said. "Let's head downstairs. The sooner we get set up, the sooner we can scrape Emma's remains off the floor."

"Your morbidity would be frowned on among my people," Sonny said. "It is an old saying of our kind that if you joke about such disaster, you invite it."

"Well, I guess it's a good thing it's just a saying," I said, pulling the old steel door open to the staircase. I let Sonny head down before me, as he had the light, and I didn't want to have to walk through my own shadow when I couldn't see what was in front of us. The sasquatch took the stairs two at a time and I had to hurry to keep up with him.

"You see where the bays are at the end of the hall there?" I said as we reached the bottom of the stairs.

Sonny nodded.

"We'll set up behind them. The jimplicutes can't reach us through those bays, and we're close enough to the door that we can reach our stash in a hurry."

"A sound strategy."

Something clanged and clattered up above us, and Sonny and I both froze. The silence was broken a moment later by an impressive string of curses echoing down through the bay holes from Emma.

I hurried down to the closest bay until I could see up and out to the catwalk. Emma was hunched over, working at something closer to the wall.

"You okay?" I shouted.

"Yeah..." Emma muttered. "I think I might just need a tetanus shot."

"We just had those," I said. "So you should be good."

Emma let out a humorless laugh. "I forgot about that. Hurt like a bitch."

"That it did," I said with a smile. "The more important question is, did that racket alert one of the ghost dinosaurs and sentence us to an early grave?"

"Ha, ha, ha," Emma said.

"It hardly seems appropriate to jest about such things," Sonny said. "It would be quite easy for one of those jimplicutes to kill one of you, from what you've described."

"One of us?" Emma asked, rattling around on the catwalk. "You think it couldn't run you down?"

"Oh, I am certain it could," Sonny said. "But, I am also certain I can run faster than you."

I laughed and cracked open the gun case that held the tranquilizer rifle. I lifted out two of the titanium-needled darts and filled them before flipping the chamber open in the stock and dropping one into the rifle. After an unfortunate mishap with an underpowered, overused CO_2 cartridge, we had started unloading after every hunt. I snapped a fresh CO_2 cartridge onto the rifle and checked the pressure gauge.

"You are still carrying the Desert Eagle," Sonny said.

I patted the holstered pistol under my jacket. "Hell yes. These things ripped apart our car. I'd hate to see what would happen if they got a hold of one of us. But I'm not taking a shot unless I absolutely have to. Plus, it might slow down the raw head."

"That is doubtful."

I took the two remaining darts and slid them into an elastic loop on the outside of the holster for my pistol. I'd normally keep them tucked snugly into the holders on the side of the rifle's stock, but after our experience with the wampus, and the tranquilizer rifle getting mangled, I always wanted to be sure I had one on me. Aside from that, we only had three.

"You look troubled," Sonny said, sliding an old steel crate sideways in the hallway. I didn't know what he thought that would stop, but he looked happy with his handiwork.

"Three shots. Emma and I are both good, but there are two of those jimplicutes. Even if we make a good shot, it may not be enough to put them down. It may just piss them off."

"Always a risk," Sonny said.

Boots rang out on the old steel stairs before I heard the door open behind us and the footsteps grew louder.

"All set?" Emma asked.

I nodded.

"What's the crate for?" Emma asked.

"You never know when you may need to slow something down," Sonny said. "I always prefer to be prepared."

"Always a Boy Scout," Emma said.

"I am neither of those things," Sonny said. "Though if you're referring to the strange organization of youth that is based around a system of badges, I suppose there may be some truth to your words."

I exchanged a grin with Emma, and we headed upstairs to wait. We didn't have to wait long, before the horrible cries of the raw head crawled through the abandoned town.

Emma returned to her perch on the catwalk above us when we made our way back upstairs. Sonny stood on the opposite side of the garage door from me. He insisted on taking the far side, as he could outrun either of us.

"See anything?" I asked. I drummed my fingers on the barrel of the tranquilizer rifle.

"Nothing yet," Emma said. "Seems like those cries are getting louder though." She hesitated, and her voice turned into a harsh whisper. "Wait. Something's out there."

I tilted my head a fraction of an inch, so I could see more of the street outside the old body shop. At first, I saw nothing but the starlit town, cut through by the low angle of the moonlight. A high-pitched squeal joined the unnatural cry of the raw head. As I watched, one of the rusted-out junkyard cars on the street sank toward the ground, screeching on rusted old springs. The rear trunk showed signs of crushing, until whatever had been there stepped away. A small ripple, a tiny wave at the corner of my vision, was all I could make out.

Emma said what we all knew. "Jimplicutes."

We studied the street in silence. After a time, once I understood what I was looking for, I could spot the dinosaurs even when they were standing still. There were at least two on the street, but a few strange disturbances in my vision made me think there might be a third.

Sonny leaned further out into the open garage door. One of the invisible forms that had been pacing back and forth across the street froze. I slowly eased my way back into the shadows, making myself as small as possible, before frantically waving Sonny to back the hell up.

The sasquatch hesitated. But he seemed to figure out what I was trying to tell him. He, too, slowly sank back into the shadow beside the doorway. It was only a narrow strip of stone, perhaps three feet wide, but it was enough to hide the sasquatch entirely.

The disturbance in the air rose and fell, as if the dinosaur was standing tall before lowering its head to sniff at the old broken-up street. If these things were as isolated as I believed they were, I was sure our scents stood out like a beacon.

The wavy form of the jimplicute grew larger, and Emma hissed, "It's coming."

From my position, I was pretty sure I could slip unnoticed back toward the stairwell, but Sonny would have to cross the open ground. With nothing between him and the dinosaur, I had little doubt that the creature would see him. And if it saw him, well, we'd seen how jimplicutes felt about intruders in their area.

I raised the tranquilizer rifle and aimed for the heart of the dinosaur's faded form.

The cries of the raw head broke the strained silence, and the wavy visage of the dinosaur froze. It moved violently, and the gouges in the pavement turned quickly, and I realized it was now facing the other direction. I let my finger rest near the trigger, but I did not move.

Something huge and unnatural let out a roar that fell somewhere between a lion and the squawk of a very large bird.

Another creature echoed it, and the jimplicute closest to us surged down the street. Dust and bits of stone exploded from the thing's footfalls. A pitch black shadow sprinted out of an alley down the street, and I glimpsed Momo as the raw head chased after him.

Momo moved with the deadly grace of an apex predator. I hadn't really expected the musclebound tower of fur to be quite so agile. Aside from his speed, he would dodge and slide away from something I couldn't see.

The horrible sight of the raw head stomping down the street after him, before suddenly flying backwards when an invisible force hit it, told me all I needed to know. Momo had evaded one of the ghost dinosaurs and momentum did the rest.

The horrible squawk of the jimplicute joined the snuffling rage of the raw head, and I stared at the scene unfolding before us. The raw head raised a cloven fist and brought it down with tremendous force. Another roaring squawk sounded from down the street, and the invisible form of the dinosaur started to take shape.

Blood trailed from the thing's skin, rivulets staining its translucent form. The more the jimplicute fell and charged and fell again, the more dirt got stuck in the blood, and the easier it was to see where it stood as it faced the raw head. The rex may have towered over the raw head, but every time the jimplicute ducked its head to attack, it put itself into striking range of the raw head.

The bloody form of the dinosaur backpedaled, slipping away from another blow from the raw head. I marveled at the exchange. The move hadn't been to avoid the damage the raw head may have inflicted; the jimplicute was baiting the creature into taking one more step. The other dinosaur snapped its jaws closed and the raw head squealed as teeth tore into it. The raw head landed a quick blow on the side of the jimplicute's head, and the ghost dinosaur snapped its jaws to the side. It flung the raw head in a huge arc, until the creature crashed to the earth not twenty feet outside of the body shop.

I cursed.

The raw head regained its feet and turned bloody eyes toward us. I grew fairly certain staying out of it wasn't going to be an option. A shadowy mountain of fur some ten feet high moved between us, stalking toward the raw head.

"Stay inside," Momo said. He slammed his fist into the raw head's face, and what had been torn open by the jimplicutes ruptured under the blow. Whatever force held the thing together kept it animated, but it was not immune to damage.

Momo retreated to the shadows as quickly as he had appeared, making way for the dinosaur that was barreling down the street. Claws dug into the old asphalt, sending sprays of debris into the air, until at last the monster's bloody teeth reached out toward the raw head. But the raw head was learning. The body of meat didn't move quickly, but it moved with purpose. The raw head tilted itself to one side, dodging the gaping teeth of the dinosaur, and landed a crushing blow on the side of its jaw. Something broke, a horrible crack filling the air around us. The jimplicute's scream of pain was an absolute horror that crawled and reeled through.

Apparently satisfied with its work, the raw head turned back toward the old body shop. I bit my tongue so I didn't curse under my breath. It had seen us all right, and the mangled jigsaw puzzle of flesh stalked toward us.

We already knew nothing we had on us was taking down the raw head. We'd already seen it shrug off bullets, and now we'd seen it retain most of its function after practically being bitten in half by a goddamned dinosaur. Hiding in the shop may have been a great idea to avoid the jimplicutes, but the raw head could easily fit into the bays.

The raw head was only about ten feet out now, and I could just barely see one of the translucent dinosaurs hovering over its injured brethren. They appeared to have lost all interest in the raw head, and Momo was nowhere to be seen.

Sonny grunted as he stepped into the moonlit doorway. Something sailed over the raw head and shattered against one of the jimpli-cutes. It took me a moment to realize Sonny was chucking old bricks and stone that the dinosaurs had torn off the wall the last time we were here. The debris shattered against the creatures, and before the raw head could reach us, the jimplicute charged.

9

It only took me a moment to realize that a creature that size moving at that speed was going to have a crap ton of inertia.

"Fall back," I snapped, stepping backwards through the shadows

Sonny sprinted toward me, clearing the doorway a moment before the ghost dinosaur crashed through it, carrying the raw head in its mouth. The raw head pummeled the rex over and over, releasing a string of unearthly howls. But the dinosaur had its jaws sunken into the flesh of the walking barbecue.

The ghost dinosaur tightened its jaws and shook the raw head. The motion was violent enough that it would have killed any mortal creature. While the raw head may have been made up of pieces of a mortal creature, whatever it was now was something else.

Bone cracked and meat tore. The jimplicute slammed the raw head onto the ground and stepped on it with a clawed foot. A wide wound opened in the thing's chest. The dinosaur bowed its head and latched on the top of the raw head, pulling and stretching while the thing beneath its grasp howled and fought but ultimately broke.

The horrible crunch of torn gristle echoed around us. The rex hurled a piece of the raw head into the air. It crashed down on the catwalk beside Emma. The metal supports squealed at the sudden addition of the weight of the raw head.

Emma cursed as a bolt anchoring her section of the catwalk to the wall shuddered and sheared off. She backpedaled as the floor gave out from under her. Still, the raw head moved. It dragged itself toward Emma on that rickety old stretch of metal, cloven fists grappling with the twisted metal as the raw head pulled itself upwards.

The sharp bark of Emma's gunfire filled the old body shop a moment later.

Momo returned, battling a jimplicute just outside the bay doors. But, while he distracted one, it did nothing to occupy the other already inside the shop. The second rex stalked toward the catwalk, focusing on the mangled remnants of the raw head clawing to get to Emma.

"Get out of there!" I shouted.

Emma fired once more into the broken raw head before she shifted her aim. One more gunshot echoed through the store, and the bolts she'd aimed for shattered. A second section of the old metal catwalk creaked, then gave way in earnest. It crashed into the dinosaur's snout as Emma raced back down the stairs.

The rex caught the struggling raw head and a section of steel flooring in its jaws. Unable to penetrate the honeycombed catwalk, the ghost dinosaur proceeded to simply smash the raw head into a gory paste, forcing bits of the walking barbecue through the grate like a sausage press.

We continued backing away until we were all at the door that would lead us back down to the pit. It was only then that I noticed the disturbance in the corner of the shop.

"There's another one in here," I said.

Sonny's nostrils flared. He shook his head. "I only smell the two."

"There's something there."

Emma stared at the corner of the old body shop. At first, I thought I might have been mistaken, as nothing moved.

But then my vision stirred.

Emma cursed. "That's too small to be a jimplicute."

Momo's voice boomed from outside the bay doors. "It's the witch!"

"Downstairs," I snapped. "Now!"

I'd raised my voice too much, and the jimplicute in the garage turned to face us.

"Now!" I said, flinging the door open. Emma shot down the stairs first, followed closely by Sonny. The jimplicute sprinted across the body shop. I practically dove in after Sonny, feeling the impact as the jimplicute tore away part of the wall above me. Old cinderblock rained down, and I felt it cut into my shoulder. Rubble threatened to my roll my ankles as the jimplicute roared above us and littered the staircase with debris.

The quiet crack of a low caliber pistol echoed through the corridor around us.

"Get down!" Emma shouted as she pulled on my arm, bringing me into a crashing heap behind the steel box Sonny had so carefully placed in the hallway. This was one of those days I was happy the sasquatch had more foresight than I did.

"You get one warning shot," the gravelly voice of an old woman boomed. "The raw head. Why'd my raw head come for you?"

"*Her* raw head?" Emma whispered.

"Witch," Sonny said.

"Witch?" I said, catching a glimpse of an angry wrinkled face standing in the starlit shaft of light at the other end of the pit. "It's just a woman with a gun."

"A woman who's a very good shot," the old woman said.

I cursed under my breath.

The jimplicute roared above us. The witch frowned and looked up through the bay. "What has them so riled up?"

"Dinner?" Emma muttered.

The old woman turned her attention back to us. "They already ate my raw head. What the hell has them so riled up?"

"Probably Momo," I said.

The old woman laughed under her breath, but the gun didn't waver. "I thought there was a skunk around here. I didn't realize that old monster was about."

"The raw head was yours?" I asked.

"I summoned him," the old woman said. "The raw head was a monster. He was made to take care of those who done wrong to my family. Murdered our livestock. Tried to chase us off our land. "

"You know that wasn't us though, right?" Emma asked.

"I suspected," the old woman said, lowering her gun. "Stand up where I can see you."

I stood up slowly. "Stay down. If she shoots me, shoot her back."

The old woman smiled and she looked amused. The expression threw me off.

"You don't have much sense, threatening us magic folk. I could make things bad for you and yours... if I wanted."

"I don't believe in magic tricks."

"They ain't tricks, boy."

"Mason," Sonny said, "she is a witch. I can smell it."

"Stand up, sasquatch."

Sonny joined me before Emma let out a muffled curse and joined us both.

"You're definitely from Missouri," the woman said, "wearing those ridiculous sasquatch pants."

"They are not pants," Sonny said, looking down at his midsection.

The old woman laughed. "I met the squatches down South. They do enjoy their... ventilation."

My eyebrows crawled higher on my forehead.

"I followed y'all from the lumberyard. I know you didn't kill my raw head. I know you didn't kill my hogs. I was somewhat surprised to see you rescuing all those zigmals."

"If you knew that," Sonny said, "why did you have the raw head attack us?"

"You can't believe everything you read in the legends, son. I can guide a raw head somewhat, but raw heads will attack what they deem fit."

"That doesn't sound safe," I said.

The old woman barked out a laugh. "Of course it's not safe. Those raw heads are the closest thing to a demon of vengeance I can summon. It was supposed take out my neighbor, and then come back to be laid to rest." The woman frowned. "It didn't quite listen."

"You sent it to kill your neighbor?" Emma said, disbelief plain in her voice.

"I'm in the middle of nowhere, honey. My neighbor lives about three miles down a crappy gravel road. Doesn't even look much like the road to be honest."

"He can't be that bad," Emma said.

The old woman harrumphed. "Not that bad? How would you feel if someone came to your house and slaughtered your pets? Just wrapped their grimy paws around something you love and snatched it right out of this world."

Emma recoiled at the woman's words, and she wasn't the only one.

"You had a boar as a pet?" I asked.

"Two of them," the woman said. "Two of the smartest damn critters I ever knew. Until I found them strung up on the Smith farm. Not even in their barn, mind you. Just hung up and gutted on the side of the road, dangling from one of their big walnut trees."

One of the jimplicutes barked above us and the old woman took a casual step to the side, narrowly avoiding a bloody claw as it swiped down through the bay. She spoke like anyone else, but she sure as hell didn't move like anyone I knew. I narrowed my eyes.

The old woman laughed. "I resurrect my hogs and you don't bat an eye, but I show you these old hips can still dance and then you're curious." She laughed again, and it blended in with the cry of a jimplicute, sending a shiver down my spine.

"You planning on using that tranquilizer gun?" The old woman asked. "You plan on Momo walking out of here alive, you better do something."

Sonny laid a paw on my shoulder and squeezed, breaking me out of my trance like state.

"Listen to the witch. Do not break your word to Momo." He paused. "I will not let you break your word to Momo."

I shook my head. "You can still vouch for Momo if he's a little dismembered."

Regardless, I checked the pressure on the tranquilizer gun, and turned it up. The needle sat near the red, and I hoped it would be enough to penetrate the jimplicutes' thick hide.

"I do not believe you understand what Momo's people are like," Sonny said. "They will mark you a traitor to your word. You promised to speak to the sasquatches on his behalf, promised *I* would speak for him. If that word is broken, they *will* hunt you down."

I cursed and exchanged a glance with Emma.

She nodded. "Go."

With that, I sprinted for the debris-strewn stairs, hoping I wouldn't find a bloody fur rug carved out of Momo's hide when I got there.

W hile I knew Sonny and Emma had their eyes on the old woman, I couldn't help but wish one of them was with me. It had been a long time since I'd walked into a stupidly dangerous situation by myself. I had no illusions that if one of those jimplicutes got angry enough, it could tear its way into those bays. The catwalk had crumbled with a small impact, and if this place wasn't built up to a decent code, its support structure might not be much better off.

I eased the door open, lifting up on the knob to try to take some of the weight off of the hinges. I hoped to prevent them from squeaking too loud, and I breathed a sigh of relief when it opened wide enough for me to slip out with barely a creak.

The roar of Momo and the cry of the jimplicute was a thunder upstairs. I stayed low, keeping to the shadows as best I could as I moved to the front of the truck. I'd parked at just enough of an angle, that I could rest my hand on the hood, and the barrel of the tranquilizer rifle could clear the windshield. It didn't give me a huge angle to fire through, but I didn't need it to be. The jimplicute was massive, moving with a terrible speed, and now that its claws were dirty, I could see the strikes as they flashed out at Momo. It gave me a stark understanding of how quickly these things could dismember us.

I flipped the safety off on the tranquilizer rifle. I took two deep breaths, waiting for the towering form to turn toward Momo and give me the widest possible target. The tranquilizer dart popped, and a burst of air sent the titanium dart streaking out of the shop to smack into the jimplicute's flank. The skin rippled where the flesh had been hit, changing colors briefly before settling back into its translucent state.

I frowned, realizing that its skin wasn't really translucent at all, more like the camouflage on an octopus. It was the only thing that made sense. These things weren't bending light—they were masterful camouflage artists. Momo narrowly dodged a lunge from the jimplicute, but the move cost him his position. The dinosaur thrashed its head to the side and caught the mountain of black fur in the shoulder. The sasquatch-like creature flailed and slammed into the wall. No new blood or slashes appeared in Momo's fur, which told me the teeth of the jimplicute had missed.

I didn't know how long Momo would be able to keep up, how long he'd be able to keep ahead of the dinosaur, and I only hoped it was long enough for the tranquilizer to take effect. Even as I thought it, I started loading the next dart. I adjusted the pressure, opened the stock, and slid the next dart inside before locking it all down.

If that other jimplicute was still outside, there was no way in hell I was sneaking around the one in the garage to get a shot at it. But if it snuck up on Momo, it might eviscerate him before he ever saw it. Instead I headed for the surviving section of the catwalk. I crept up it slowly, thankful for the fact it was still almost entirely in shadow. I was perhaps even more thankful that the remains of the raw head had fallen to the ground. I made it to the nearest broken window, which gave me a clear view of the street below. What I saw made my skin crawl.

10

I was pretty sure I understood why the jimplicutes haunted this place. At the corner of the side street, where the shadows met the starlight, the small skull of a juvenile jimplicute rested on the old street. If they grew at a rate like most reptiles, the long dead jimplicute was a fraction of the age of the one Momo was fighting. And while I hadn't gotten a good look at the other living jimplicute, I suspected it was much the same.

Even as I raised the tranquilizer rifle, I wondered how long that runt had been out there, left to rot away in the street of a long-forgotten town. I'd heard of stranger things being left out in plain sight, but looking at the old, dirt-covered bones, I didn't understand how no one could've seen it before. Or maybe they had, and just hadn't lived to tell about it.

I swept the barrel of the tranquilizer rifle across my field of view. Nothing moved outside the shop, nothing appeared to be waiting to ambush Momo, or us, when we'd walk out of the old body shop. But the jimplicutes were hard to spot, so I kept my eyes unfocused, trying to catch even the slightest glimmer of movement or the tiniest distortion of the light. The frantic pace of the fight between Momo and the dinosaur below me lessened.

What had been ferocious, deliberate strikes became lazy flails and sloppy blows that ended in the bloodied form of the rex stumbling forward several rapid steps. Its massive head cracked against the wall, and the catwalk shook beneath my feet. The loud ringing of metal caused a commotion outside. From the corner of my eye, I saw a shadow move. The other jimplicute had been near the bones of its young brethren.

The wonder of whether these creatures would simply murder whatever happened to get close to them fled in a heartbeat. I watched the wavy light in my vision pace back and forth, guarding the old bones as if they were crying out for help. I ground my teeth and stifled a curse. I'd seen that behavior before in a dozen different animals I'd studied. Even the gowrows showed that protective instinct to their young. These things weren't mindless killers, they were a close-knit family, as protective of each other as any human or animal pack.

I let out a slow breath and followed the pacing jimplicute in the sights. If I was wrong about the distance, the tranquilizer dart wouldn't have a chance of penetrating its hide. My elevation threw me off, and I couldn't be sure, but I hoped I was right. The pop of the tranquilizer rifle sent the dart hissing into the blackness. I didn't hear the impact, but I saw the ripple of flesh in the jimplicute's camouflage when the dart impacted it.

I turned my attention back to the interior of the building when the jimplicute below me groaned. It blew out one more angry breath at Momo, then slumped into unconsciousness.

The jimplicute out in the street paced for a few minutes until the tranquilizer took hold, and it, too, settled to the ground. I looked over my shoulder, between the rails of the catwalk, and was surprised to see Momo gently inspecting the dinosaur he'd been fighting so ferociously.

Momo glanced up at me, as though he felt my eyes on his back. "I am afraid the raw head fractured this one's jaw," he said. "It could not open its mouth completely, and it will not survive without the ability to eat its prey."

"Son of a bitch," I snapped. I hurried down the stairs to the catwalk and shouted, "All clear!"

I made my way over to Momo as the jimplicute's camouflage started to fade. It stopped me dead in my tracks.

What I had only seen in glimpses and outlines slowly became a living, breathing dinosaur. Where I expected the thick hide of a reptile, like a crocodile, I instead found rubbery flesh more like an octopus, mimicked camouflage and all. But as its muscles relaxed and consciousness left it entirely, a streak of brilliant feathers fell loose across its back, a single stripe from its massive head to its log-like tail, a burst of color on an otherwise plain-colored creature.

"Holy shit," Emma said as she stepped up beside me. "It looks like a Tyrannosaurus Rex, but squishy."

I gave her a small smile. "Momo said the jaw looks like its broken. From the raw head." I gave the witch a sharp look as she sidled up beside Emma.

"It was not me who brought my pet to fight these things."

"Regardless," Momo said, "this creature will suffer and die because of your magics. You should be marked and destroyed."

The old woman gave a knowing laugh. "You'd like that, wouldn't you?"

"Let us end this creature's suffering," Momo said.

I was surprised by his words, the words of the creature known as the Missouri monster. But I suppose every story I'd heard about him had been one of swift brutality. The creatures that had died at his hand had not suffered long, even my friend, though I'd never forgive him for killing Dylan. People and animals alike had met very quick ends.

"We're not putting it down," I said as I pulled out my phone.

"There is nothing else that can be done."

"We'll see," I said. The line picked up on the third ring, and Larry's very grumpy, very tired voice echoed across the line.

"Somebody better be dead, Mason," Larry said between yawns.

"Even better," I said. "Is Doc still staying with you?"

"Yes," Larry said, drawing the word out, making the suspicion in his voice plain to hear.

Doc was the best damn cryptid vet I knew. Anyone Larry trusted with the gowrows was someone I'd trust too.

"You know that old abandoned town about fifteen minutes from you?" I asked.

Larry's voice lowered. "What have you done, Mason?"

"Well, we have two jimplicutes unconscious up here. One of them has been beaten up a bit by a raw head. Looks like its jaw may have been broken."

"What in the hell, Mason," Larry said. "What do you want us to do, perform surgery in the middle of some old ghost town?"

"No, actually, we have it in an old body shop. So it's not out in the middle of the old town at all."

Larry let out an exasperated sigh. "You know that town's in dispute, right? The sasquatches laid claim to it, but they've had trouble with Momo and his people. Things have got nasty around there." My eyes landed on Momo. He didn't react to Larry's words, but he didn't dispute them either. Somehow that didn't surprise me, as I began to see the monster's actual motivations.

"Just get here soon as you can," I said. "We only have one more dose of the tranquilizers, but it's all a guessing game with these things. They're huge, and I don't know how long they'll stay under."

"We'll bring some of our own, Mason. Just don't move."

"We'll be waiting."

———

I looked up from the now-snoring jimplicute, somewhat surprised to still see Momo inside the shop. Apparently Momo didn't miss me studying him.

"If you have a question, ask it now."

"Why are you still here?"

"If I were to leave now, I would likely be killed before I was able to return to my home."

"Killed by what?" Emma asked. "The jimplicutes are out like a light."

"These creatures are not the true threat in this town."

"You're cunning," Sonny said, a growl in his words. "But, you take more of a risk than I expected."

Momo inclined his head toward Sonny. "But I trust you will keep your word."

"It was not my word," Sonny said. "However, I will not allow you to sully the name of Mason. Or any of my friends here."

The old woman standing on the other side of Sonny frowned up at the sasquatch. "What exactly did you promise this overgrown, tick-ridden, murdering fleabag?"

Well, that told me where the old witch stood in relation to Momo. I blinked at my own thoughts. For the first time, I'd thought of her as a witch.

"Mason made a promise," Sonny said.

"A promise of what? Answer me, sasquatch."

Sonny looked down on the old witch. "On my honor, I will speak to the sasquatch packs, so that Momo may have free reign through our territory without being challenged."

"No sasquatch can make that promise," the witch said. She barked out a harsh laugh. "You might earn yourself free passage around Sonny's people, but that will hardly do you any good around the more violent packs."

"They are the only pack that concerns me at the moment," Momo said.

A shadow crossed in front of the bay doors before it spoke. "As well we should be."

"Who is that?" I whispered out of the side of my mouth to Emma.

"Sonny's boss?" she replied, somewhat louder than I would have preferred.

The sasquatch striding toward us hesitated. "I would hardly refer to myself as a boss."

"A boss with really good hearing?" Emma whispered back.

"This is not how I would have preferred to meet your acquaintances," the newcomer said, glancing at Sonny.

Sonny bowed his head. "And it is not how I wished you to have met them either. Mason did not realize what he was promising."

My mind was racing now, trying to understand just how far out of line my agreement with Momo had been. I couldn't let anyone hurt Sonny.

"If this is like a fight to the death or honor type thing," I said, gesturing wildly, "we can just shoot Momo and be done with it. That's fine."

Momo bared his teeth in the semblance of a terrible smile. "You can try."

The casual confidence in the monster's voice was unnerving to say the least. And the fact that anything could be unnerving after seeing that walking barbecue fighting a ghost dinosaur, well, it had been a strange night.

The newcomer took a deep breath and cast his gaze down toward the witch standing beside Sonny. "You must use more caution, Augusta. You use bold magic, in a time where magic has been long forgotten."

For some reason, it was there, standing with a sasquatch talking about magic, that I finally started to believe it.

"I am sorry, Frederick," she said, nodding her head. "If this one had not interfered," she gestured at Momo, "the Smiths would have been dead, and the raw head would have been laid to rest."

"That's not exactly an argument," Frederick said.

"This old woman just wants her peace."

"We shall discuss it later. I overheard the phone call and I know Larry is on his way. We do not need more witnesses than this. Speak your plea, demon."

Momo narrowed his eyes. "Choose your words carefully, Frederick." He hesitated before he continued. "Or I may misunderstand you."

"He did help us this night," Sonny said. "He saved me from the raw head."

Frederick nodded.

"I seek only passage," Momo said. "And the rights to homestead in the old town."

"Homestead?" Frederick asked. "Here? With the jimplicutes? You do realize they are protected? You will not be able to drive them away from this place."

Momo nodded. "And I will not harm them, unless they seek to harm me first."

"You've been fighting them all night," I snapped. "What do you mean, you won't harm them?"

"I have not," Momo said, "and I will not."

His reddish orange glowing eyes locked onto mine, and I'll freely admit that I looked away first.

"Homesteading would give me the rights to the ground and what lies beneath it," Momo said.

"We are aware of the old mines," Frederick said, frowning slightly at Momo. "There is nothing of value there for us. The gold is long since gone, and what few other minerals remain are not worth the risk of our seeking."

"Grant me passage between here and Louisiana, Missouri. I will ask no more of you after that. I will not attack you or yours, and I will war only to defend myself."

"What say you?" Frederick asked, turning to Sonny.

Sonny frowned, and his furry brow drew together. He was clearly contemplating Momo's words as much as I was, trying to find the trap. I couldn't believe that Momo only wanted this place as a home. I'd spent too many years hating this creature, knowing that he was the reason for my friend's death. But, now? Now, I almost believed him.

"I have seen no ill will from Momo in this regard," Sonny said, and it was probably about the nicest thing Sonny would ever say about Momo.

Frederick nodded. "So be it. We grant you passage and the right to homestead here. But, you must not harm the jimplicutes. They are scarce and there are few left."

Frederick held his fist up in the air as if he was signaling a stop. My jaw slackened when the shadows came to life and a small horde of sasquatches filtered back into the light, only to vanish into the shadows of the forest.

"I know what drove the jimplicutes mad," Momo said. "One of their calves was killed here. It is still out in the open."

"I was not aware of that," Frederick said.

Sonny frowned at Frederick. "How could you not be? We've had sasquatches all over this place. Somebody had to have noticed."

"It is quite possible that if they noticed," Frederick said, "they did not understand the repercussions."

"Is there anything we can do?" I asked.

"I'm quite sure Momo has already planned on it," Frederick said. "Wise of you not to mention that before our bargain."

"No offense was intended," Momo said. "It was time for me to move."

Frederick studied him for a time and then nodded. A truck rumbled in the distance, and I had little doubt that Larry and the vet were almost here.

"I will leave you now," Frederick said. "We have much to discuss when you return home, Sonny." He turned to me and Emma. "You are welcome in our home, though I hope when next you return, it will be with more favorable guests."

"I will free the young one for burial," Momo said.

Frederick nodded. "If you do it quickly, I am sure the two that are sleeping would be thankful."

Frederick left without another word, his fur blending in with the brick walls before it vanished into the darkness.

"Speak of this to no one," Momo said. "I will take care of the calf and remove the remnants of the building that collapsed on it, so the jimplicutes can bury their own. Perhaps then they will finally move on."

Sonny nodded slowly. "It is a good plan. Even if they don't leave, they will not be so violent in their mourning."

Momo nodded and turned to me. "Keep your doctors away from me. I am not here to be studied like some pet gowrow."

I blinked at Momo, as the now-silent creature strode out through

ERIC R. ASHER

the mangled garage doors and walked toward the skeleton of the young jimplicute.

"I feel like I should apologize," I said.

"You need not," Sonny said. "There's no way you could have known about our culture."

"What do you expect from some fool monster hunter," Augusta said, straightening the tattered old shawl around her shoulders.

"Mason is a friend," Sonny said. "A friend who could have been killed by your raw head."

Augusta harrumphed. "No one would've been in danger from that raw head if Momo hadn't led it away from the Smith farm. Maybe that's the real question you should be asking yourself. Why would that thing do that?"

Sonny frowned.

"You don't think he just wanted this place as a home?" Emma asked. "And it's sitting on top of a mine?"

"It's more of an old cave system than an actual mine," Sonny said. "But, I understand what you mean."

"You think he engineered our encounter with the raw head to manipulate us?" I asked. "That leads me to a question that I really don't like—how in the hell did he know we'd be at that lumberyard?"

Light cut through the darkness when one of Larry's old trucks turned onto the street. The headlights bounced and swerved as Larry slammed through potholes and barely dodged the debris strewn all around.

———————

The truck doors squeaked as Larry stepped out and his boots splashed into a nearly dried-up puddle of water. He straightened his overalls and opened the back door. A very round, scaly reptile rocketed out of the back seat. She looked bigger than the last time I'd seen her, and I supposed that shouldn't be so surprising considering how large some of the old gowrows were.

"Brain!" Emma said. The gowrow veered around me and barreled into Emma, excitedly huffing and rubbing her neck on Emma like she was a cat. I suspected the gowrow may have been spending more than a little time with the wampuses we'd rescued.

"Mason," Larry said, staring at the massive form of the jimplicute. "What in the seven hells have you gotten into?"

Doc wasted no time, passing Larry and walking up to the jimplicute's head. He frowned at the cut where the raw head had struck the jimplicute's jaw. "Are you sure it's broken?"

"It stopped opening its jaw as wide," I said.

"That doesn't sound like such a bad thing," Emma said. "It looks big enough to eat someone whole."

Doc gave her a small smile. "Not quite that large, but yes, it's an imposing sight." He ran his hand along the jimplicute's jawline and frowned. His fingertips focused around the wound and traced their way back up to where the jaw met the rest of the skull. "The line seems intact. I don't think its jaw is broken, but something is distended here," he said, indicating a bulge in the corner of the reptilian face. "I believe its jaw is dislocated."

"That's good," Larry said. "You should be able to set it then, right?"

"Assuming it's hinged like any other reptile, sure. But we don't know if it is. Trying to force the bone back into place might injure the jimplicute further or disable it to the point that it will starve to death."

"It's a predator," Larry said. "If we don't fix that jaw, it's going to starve to death anyway."

"I need an x-ray," Doc said, prodding at the jaw.

"How long has it been under now?" Larry asked.

"Maybe half an hour," I said.

"Dosage?" Doc asked. Emma ran down a list of which tranquilizers she loaded the darts with, and I showed him the remaining unused dart.

"A rough estimate," Doc said, "I doubt we have more than another fifteen to twenty minutes of safety. I don't want to injure this animal further."

"The skull," Emma said, her voice rising. "Get a picture of the skull.".

"Hell yes," I said, fumbling my phone out of my pocket. "You all stay here. There are... unfriendly things around."

I heard Larry say, "What in the hell is that boy talking about," as I dashed out into the street.

I jogged the two blocks to where I knew the young jimplicute's body was. I heard Momo rustling through the debris, the sound of stone dropping on concrete and the clanging of heavy metal on the pavement filling the air.

"I told you not to follow me," Momo said.

"You actually said not to tell our friends about you. And I didn't. I just need a picture of the jimplicute's skull. We have a vet here that might be able to help."

Momo let out a sound that was somewhere between a sigh and a growl. "It is still buried enough that I do not believe you can see the hinge of the jaw."

I blinked at the monster. Momo's awareness and perception of what we were doing, without us actually telling him what we were doing, showed an intelligence behind those glowing eyes that was unnerving.

"I will raise the steel from the side, take your photo quickly, and leave this place."

I didn't say anything more. I just waited for Momo to show me just how terrifyingly strong he was. He lifted a crumbled I-beam the way I would've lifted a hundred-pound bag of cement. I leaned down, getting closer to Momo. The pungent stench of the ancient creature enveloped me. I snapped three quick photos and backed away.

"Thank you."

Momo looked at me for a time, and then turned back to his work of unearthing the jimplicute's body.

I hurried back to the shop and handed my phone to Doc.

"Where in the– how did you– oh, whatever." He shook his head. Doc zoomed in and scrolled and shifted, studying the line of the jaw and what little desiccated flesh was left around it. After a few minutes, he nodded to himself.

"I'm glad we had these photos. Look at the hinge in the jaw—the socket is grooved at an odd angle. We could've caused far more damage trying to pop it in like an alligator's jaw. I believe the raw head hit the right angle, to simply pop these two bones apart."

"I hope we don't need that kind of force to put it back," Augusta said. "Those raw heads are terribly strong."

Doc crouched over the massive jawbone and wiggled it a bit. "It's not too bad. I think two or three of us can do this. Mason..." Doc looked up and rethought his words. "Sonny, you get the front of the jaw and push when I tell you. The rest of you stand by me, and when I tell you, push down here." He patted the rear part of the distended flesh.

We all lined up where Doc had indicated. The jimplicute breathed evenly, but I had no idea how to judge if its heart rate was rising. Doc didn't seem concerned, and that lent me some small semblance of reassurance.

Doc checked the alignment of where Sonny was standing, and the rest of us made ready to push. He nodded to himself and said, "On three." Sonny leaned into the jaw slightly, preparing himself. Doc counted down, and then it was time.

Sonny growled, and the massive jaw shifted beneath the force he applied to it. The strange flesh felt like rubbery scales beneath my fingers, but the thought left my mind when Doc shouted, "Down!"

Emma and I both grunted as we leaned into the back of the jaw. At first, I was afraid nothing was happening, but then something crunched, and a muted pop sent a vibration from the jawbone into my arms. I could actually see the change in the jawline, and the smile on Doc's face was no small thing.

"Lucky boy," Doc said, patting the jimplicute on the cheek. "That would've been a slow death."

"I have something to say," Larry said, standing up on the other side of the jimplicute's head. "I'm not taking any of these buggers back to my farm. And that's final."

I grinned at the old man and he gave me a sour look in return.

"I'd never dream of it," I said.

Pinky chuffed beside me before following Brain over to Doc, and I stared at the gowrow in betrayal.

What do you intend to do?" Augusta asked. "There isn't enough space to get your truck out of here. Not past this sleeping beast."

I glanced between the jimplicute and the bay doors, and knew she was right. "I guess we're camping out in the pits so we can see what happens."

"Where did you find the skull?" Larry asked.

"I can't tell you," I said. "I promised I wouldn't."

"It is a matter of honor," Sonny said. "Perhaps one day we may speak of it, but not today." He added weight to his closing words, as if urging Larry to drop it without having to speak Momo's name.

The old man took the hint, but Doc still looked curious. "Well, if you change your mind, I'd love to see it."

Sonny ran a hand across the jimplicute's snout. "Let them bury their child. They at least deserve that."

"Deserve is a pretty strong word," Larry said. He started packing up the small medical bag he tended to carry with him that was loaded with various tranquilizers and half a dozen different needles. "Who knows how many people those things have killed over the years."

"And who knows how many of those things the people killed," Sonny said.

Larry paused and looked up at Sonny. "I meant no disrespect."

Sonny looked like he was going to say more, but instead, he let the conversation drop. "You should go before they awaken. Even if they do not harm you, your truck is in their way. I must discuss some things with my pack, but I will return."

Larry scrunched up his nose. "All right. You all try to stay out of trouble for the rest of the night," he said with a nod to me and Emma. "And don't get on the wrong side of the witch." He tipped a hat that he wasn't wearing to Augusta.

"Aren't you the savvy one?" she said with a wicked grin.

"I'm just not a skeptic like my friend here."

"Mason," Doc said, "call me if you need. The jimplicute might have some bruising, but it should recover well enough. I can honestly say that's the first time I've ever seen one."

"Most people that have ever seen one," Augusta said, "never knew they saw one."

"Fair enough."

With that, Larry and Doc took their leave.

"Are we seriously going to wait here for this thing to wake up?" Augusta asked.

"Absolutely," I said.

"You want to set up the cameras?" Emma asked.

"Do I want to set up the cameras?" I said, enunciating each word. "Hell. Yes."

It wasn't hard to slip back into my more outgoing personality. I didn't know what it was about nearly being eaten and coming face-to-face with the monster that had hurt so many. But sometimes it made things easier. Like I needed an escape, so the mask slid into place with less effort.

Emma counted down on her fingers. Three. Two. One. She pointed at me.

I crouched in the corner, acting ignorant of what was around me, as if I didn't even see the camera that was right over my shoulder. I spun quickly in place, pulling a finger up to my lips, calling for silence. I whispered into the camera. "You won't believe it. You won't believe what we found in the wreckage of a forgotten town."

I gestured for the camera to follow me, and I hurried up the staircase, turning into the dimly lit bay where the jimplicute still slumbered. I figured we had a good five minutes before the thing woke up. Its heartrate was getting faster and we needed to be quick. Augusta was apparently the smart one, waiting in the safety of the pits.

Emma's footsteps padded along behind me, and I could tell by the way the light swung back and forth over my shoulder that she was panning the room, most likely for the eeriest angle she could find.

"Now this isn't something you see every day," I said. I raised my voice, emphasizing my somewhat fake good humor. "In fact, even if you did see one of these, you probably wouldn't know it. They have the best camouflage I've ever encountered, so good that they're practically invisible. But if something is *practically* invisible, I can still find it."

I stepped to the side, making a wide gesture toward what looked like a gelatinous lump in the dim starlight. I walked down the length of the jimplicute, carefully staying away from the more defined features of the creature, so the film would look really *really* fake.

"You can see it breathing, just look at it. How high its chest is getting? How large must its lungs be? To get that kind of height out of every breath? Look at the claws," I said, showing one of the bloodied appendages. Emma gave a thumbs up, so I knew she'd have the film just out of focus enough no one would suspect that we were, in fact, in the same room as a jimplicute. Or at least not many people would.

"The claws on its feet are even larger, but I can't reach them. They're in the back corner behind the sleeping behemoth. But I can tell you this, I saw one of these things step on a car and cut it right in half. Like nothing you've ever seen."

The jimplicute snorted a breath. And I didn't have to fake the near-panic that rose up in my chest. "That's our cue to get the hell out of here," I said. "So remember, while you're exploring, just because something can eat you in one bite doesn't mean it will. Stay safe out there!"

Emma shut the camera off, and the darkness was nearly blinding. She flipped the flashlight on a moment later and I hurried around the jimplicute to join her.

"Let's go," she whispered. "It's definitely moving now."

We hurried away from the massive form, and before the light left the jimplicute in total darkness, I saw the claw at the end of its arm flex.

A s apprehensive as Augusta had seemed about us stupidly going up to film around the unconscious jimplicute, she appeared more than happy to settle in beside us and watch the video feed of our night vision camera.

"You have footage of this thing," Augusta said. "And yet people won't believe it's real?"

"We have footage of a lot of things," Emma said. "We really try not to scare the hell out of the general public. A lot of the stuff on Mason's show is either fake or intentionally blurry."

"How can you afford all this?" Augusta asked.

"That's a little personal," Emma said.

"I know you're not making that kind of money off of some internet nonsense."

Augusta wasn't wrong, we certainly weren't making millions off of the show, though we *had* accrued a decent following. Some people seemed to be in it for the laughs, and some of them seemed to be in it because they yearned for some greater truth. And based on a few of the comments on a couple of the episodes, I was pretty sure Bubba's friend Skeeter was also a viewer. That made me wonder how many other monster hunters out there might be watching our show, with either the knowledge that what we were doing was actually real, or just wanting to laugh at some of our very bad decisions.

"It's getting up," Emma said, pointing to the rear of the massive creature. Some of the details could be hard to make out on the strange contrast of the night vision camera, but Emma was always quick to identify something on the screen. A few pixels shifted around for another few seconds before I could finally make out what she was talking about. The jimplicute had rolled completely onto its stomach before pulling its massive hind legs up underneath its belly. A moment later, it was standing.

"Wow," Augusta whispered under her breath.

I just stared, watching in complete fascination as the green light rippled on the screen, and then the jimplicute partially vanished.

Emma brought a menu up on the tablet to switch to an infrared FLIR view. I was surprised the jimplicute didn't stand out better than it did. I didn't know if that had something to do with being a cold-blooded creature, but I didn't think the jimplicute's strange camouflage would be able to mask it from a FLIR.

It listed to the side, one massive clawed foot snapping out to catch its unwieldy form. The head swiveled and the jimplicute turned slowly in place, as if it was studying every facet of the body shop, be it for prey, or danger.

The strange barking roar of the jimplicute echoed through the pits around us. I smiled at the gaping jaws of the creature above us. The jimplicute outside the body shop barked in response. I released the breath I hadn't realized I was holding when the jimplicute above our heads made its way back outside.

"Amazing," I said. "I wasn't sure if Doc would be able to fix something that large."

"How long has he been working on Old Willie?" Emma asked, bringing up the massive gowrow at Larry's farm.

I nodded. "Fair point. Willie might not be as tall as these things, but he certainly has the mass."

I caught movement out of the corner of my eye as Augusta dropped a small pouch into a pocket on her sweater.

I must've frowned at her, because she rubbed her hands together and her gaze flashed between me and Emma.

"I wasn't sure if you hurt that thing," she said. "I don't like people hurting animals."

"Yeah? And if we would have?" I glanced down at the pocket where she'd dropped the pouch.

"You would've had a bad day," Augusta said.

"Well that's not terrifying," Emma said.

I still didn't really know how much I believed Augusta was a witch. But I'd seen the raw head, and I'd seen the remains of the thing, and it sure as hell wasn't anything natural. Like slabs of pork stitched together. I shivered, met Augusta's gaze for a moment, and then let it drop.

"The question now," I said, "how long do we wait before we head upstairs?"

"I'm prepared to stay here for a good solid week," Augusta said.

"Sounds good to me," Emma said.

"I'm going to head up to the catwalk," I said. "I could see the bones of the calf from the window when I was up there before."

"Grab the FLIR on your way," Emma said. "That showed the jimplicute better than anything else. Unless it's not camouflaging itself, in which case any old camera will do."

I nodded. I didn't really think any old camera would do in the pitch black of the late night, which was quickly becoming early morning.

"You think Momo already finished?" Emma asked. "He hasn't had that much time."

"Considering his strength, I wouldn't be surprised by much of anything."

Emma nodded. "Be careful."

I was halfway up the stairs when I heard the strange howling wail.

12

I snatched the FLIR camera off the back of the truck where Emma had mounted it. As much as I'd planned to stay quiet on the catwalk, I took the stairs two at a time, not really pondering the intelligence of putting all that extra force on the rickety old structure. I breathed a sigh of relief when I reached the top and it hadn't collapsed under my weight.

I hurried to the broken-out pane of glass and aimed at the FLIR toward the old bones. I cursed under my breath and watched wide-eyed as some of the skeleton floated away. The moonlight wasn't enough to see things clearly outside of the FLIR, but I could see the movement in the distance with my naked eye, and see that the floating bones were falling near the edge of the forest. Momo was nowhere to be seen, but I felt a strange spark of appreciation for what the monster had done.

The jimplicutes passed each other in the road, dropping their camouflage for a moment and rubbing their heads together, before one returned to the forest and the other returned for more bones. I wasn't sure how long I watched them, maybe fifteen minutes, maybe twenty. Emma quietly and carefully crept up beside me at some point and stared at the FLIR screen in silence.

We watched until there was nothing left to watch. All the bones had been pulled away from the collapsed building, freed by Momo. The jimplicutes had covered the hole they'd dug for the bones. And before they left, they pushed an old tree over, leaving it to fall onto the grave.

When the movement had stopped, and silence reigned over the old abandoned town once more, Emma spoke. "They buried it. Like humans would bury it."

I shut the camera off and turned to her. "I've never seen anything like it. Never."

"The time has passed," a voice said from below us.

I squinted at the shadows over the edge of the catwalk. Augusta stood there, looking out the old garage doors. "I believe this place will be safe for now. This is a good place for the dead to rest."

I frowned, looking at the cement floor, expecting to find the remnants of the old raw head. But there weren't any. "Did the jimplicutes carry that raw head off?" I asked.

"I sure didn't see it," Emma said.

The witch just gave us a broad smile. "I appreciate what you did here," she said. "Perhaps I'll ask my grandson to help me look up some of your videos. I never could figure out where the tape went in one of those damn computers."

"Now you're just screwing with us," Emma said.

"It's what I do best, missy. You kids take care of yourselves out there. There are bad things afoot. I don't trust that Momo."

"You really a witch?" I asked. "Can you show us a trick?"

She let out a soft laugh. "I suspect, even if I did, you'd think it was all show."

"I wouldn't say that," I started to say, but I trailed off, speechless.

Something like a shaft of moonlight brightened around the old woman, reflecting on every bit of dust and debris in the air. But when it was gone, so was the witch.

"Well that's scary as hell," Emma said.

I just stared at the empty space where Augusta had been.

S o, is Sonny coming back or what?" I asked as we packed up the last of the cameras. Emma kept a small handheld job with her in the front seat, so she could get a little close-up footage when we drove by the wreckage of the old building.

"I'll text him again. I'm sure he's fine."

"Did I say I was worried? I don't think I said I was worried. I'm more worried about Himari and that zigmal..." I muttered.

I slowly backed the truck up and managed to slip out between the pits and the falling catwalk without too much of an issue. It was a short drive over to the building Momo had picked apart so the jimplicutes could bury their calf. Emma hopped out and started filming the ruins as the sun slowly started to rise in the distance.

"You want to splice some of this in?" Emma asked.

I leaned back in my seat and frowned. I didn't really feel much like slipping back into my more annoying personality. "We can just dub over it later. Let's get the footage and get out of here."

Emma's phone buzzed on the console next to me. I picked it up and looked at the text message. Sonny had finally responded. *I'll be staying with pack tonight. Do not wait for me.*

"Sonny's good," I said. "Maybe getting some lectures from his elders, but he's good."

"And whose fault is that?" Emma asked. When I didn't respond, she raised her eyebrows.

"Yeah, yeah. I know, I know."

"You want to film the grave?"

I looked out the window, where the jimplicutes had buried their calf, and the earth now rested so peacefully with a fallen log to mark the spot. It was clear enough that a viewer might be able to find it. I didn't want that to happen. I wasn't usually that sentimental about dead things, but I felt like the jimplicutes had been through enough. Their calf deserved peace.

"No," I said. "Let it rest."

Emma gave me a small smile as we pulled away and left the old town behind.

M ason," Emma said. "It's late, or early, and the jimplicute completely pancaked that camera."

"Leave no tech behind," I said as I guided the rental down the overgrown road.

We were back on the narrow stretch of unmaintained highway a while later. The remains of the camera weren't hard to find, being that the shattered lens and housing had exploded across half the road. The tripod looked nearly identical to the pancaked handlebars of the ATV we'd lost to the bingbuffer.

I scooped the remains up and frowned at them. I couldn't tell where the slot for the memory card was, much less whether it was intact.

"Found it?" Emma asked as she climbed out of the rental and stretched.

"Yeah, but it's smashed."

She let out a small laugh and joined me at the side of the road. "A dinosaur stepped on it, Mason. Of course it's smashed."

I tilted my head to the side.

"Give it to Himari," Emma said. "She might be able to pull something out of that wreck."

I nodded and turned back toward the rental before freezing in my tracks.

Emma didn't say anything for a moment, just followed my gaze back to the hill that led into the woods. Her voice was a whisper. "That's the biggest damn fox I've ever seen."

The fox cocked its head to the side and took a few steps through the underbrush, its eyes staying on us. The sunlight caught the back of its head before a wide flat tail rippled out behind it. It looked like a beaver's tail.

"It's a hoofer," I said, dumbstruck that the creature we'd been looking for before the jimplicutes chased us had come for a visit.

"I don't have a camera," Emma said, eyeing the rental before turning her attention back to the side-hill hoofer.

"Doesn't matter," I said. "Just watch."

And we did. The hoofer nosed at the underbrush, glanced at us one last time, and trotted off toward the waiting shadows. It passed through a clearing, and I couldn't stop the smile when I saw its two stubby left legs balancing higher on the hill and its longer right legs keeping it upright on the incline.

"Can it really just run in circles?" Emma asked.

"It's a wide hill," I said. "It could take that hoofer a day to walk all the way around it."

We watched it until the tail vanished and the sun crept just a little higher.

I'm about five minutes from passing out," Emma said as we finally made it back onto a modern highway. "We driving all the way back home?"

"We can stop at a hotel in Columbia," I said. "Or we could just stop at Waffle House."

"Waffle House," Emma and I said together.

I exchanged a grin with her, and then promptly yawned.

It only took another ten minutes or so to make it to the Waffle House right off Highway 70. Columbia was very much a college town, and I suspected most of the patrons in the restaurant had been up for as long as we had. Emma ordered her usual scattered, smothered, and chunked, and I ordered my normal boring plate of hashbrowns, eggs, and a waffle.

"Let's call Himari," Emma said.

I nodded and slid a Bluetooth headset over my ear before flipping it on. Emma did the same, and we were both synced up to her tablet a moment later. She set it on the edge of the table, so at that angle, we were the only ones who could see the screen. The phone rang three times before I remembered just how early it was.

Himari picked up a moment later. To say she looked tired, would be a bit of an understatement. "Mason? Emma? What happened?"

"We just wanted to call and check up on you," I said. "And we left a... rather flat camera in your mailbox. How are you?"

"Who cares about me?" Himari said. "What happened with the jimplicutes? And the raw head? I'll check the camera later. And I can't believe neither one of you are dead!"

Himari looked more awake with every sentence, and I was somewhat jealous that someone could wake up that fast without coffee.

"We'll tell you," Emma said. "But how is the zigmal? Is everything okay?"

"Oh yes, he's fine. Larry came by with Doc. We're going to try giving him the same diet as a sugar glider and see how he recovers."

I frowned at the screen. "You mean you still have the zigmal?"

Himari grinned and nodded quickly. She turned her camera so I could see the surprisingly large cage in the background. "Yes. Lots of room to run around in that cage. He'll be fine. He can't fall from a great height and hurt his leg again."

Emma snickered. "I think Himari just adopted a cryptid. I'm quite sure we won't have a problem explaining that to Noah. I'm sure it'll be just fine."

I groaned.

Emma pulled her laptop out and connected the camera. "I'm uploading videos to you now. You'll see one part where the night vision camera and the FLIR are synchronized. I think there might be some really good stuff in there."

"I can't wait!" Himari said.

"That's just because you weren't there," I said. "That raw head was terrifying. And when it was fighting the jimplicutes?" I shook my head.

"It actually fought them?" Himari said, unable to keep the excitement from her voice. "Like, you got to see two kaiju going head-to-head? In person!"

"You know what generally happens when people see kaiju going head-to-head?" Emma said. "They get dead. They get very dead."

"It's the best," Himari said.

I blinked at the screen. "Well, then, I'm glad we have video for you."

"I think we probably have enough for another episode once Mason does some voiceovers. You mind getting some editing done while you're up watching your zigmal?"

"His name is Stripe," Himari said.

"Like the gremlin?" I asked.

"Exactly!" Himari said. "I love those things."

"Let's just hope that's not an omen," I muttered. I saw our server heading out from behind the counter with two plates piled high. "Our food is coming, Himari, we have to go."

"Okay, I'll talk to you guys later."

"Himari," Emma said. "If you find Sonny or any of his people in there, edit them out."

"Will do!" The screen went black a moment later, and Emma shut down the tablet.

"Here you two go," the server said, sliding a platter to each of us. Emma had awkwardly stacked all her gear off to the edge of the table. The server eyed it for a moment, but I suspect she had seen much stranger things at five in the morning than some fancy cameras.

"Aren't you glad I set those cameras up now?" Emma asked.

I stared at the images flashing by on the tablet screen. Emma had caught part of the fight between the jimplicute and the raw head and the picture was clear. It could completely change our understanding of the jimplicutes and how they moved and how their camouflage worked. I'd have to get the video to Larry and Doc. I suspected they would find it most fascinating.

I nodded. "It's great. I think we're gonna have a hell of an episode after this."

"Yes indeed," Emma said, stuffing a bite of sloppy hashbrowns into her face. "So, when do you want to call Noah?"

"Tomorrow."

"Tomorrow like this morning? Or tomorrow like definitely not today?"

I gave Emma a knowing smile.

THE END

IV

MASON DIXON & THE
GOWROW'S LAST STAND

1

E   mma poured her third cup of coffee. She ripped open a
    packet of powdered creamer, screwed the lid back on her
    mug, and gave the concoction a violent shake before
checking the focus and batteries on her camera gear.

"Feeling better?" I asked.

Emma narrowed her eyes. "Mason, we got out here while I could
still see stars in the sky. That's not even early, that's still last night."

"The beds at that B&B were pretty good though."

"I don't care how good the bed is, I'm still not falling asleep at
seven at night."

"Especially if you start binge watching a new series."

She blew out a breath and sipped at her coffee. "One day you'll
realize the rest of the world needs sleep. You're a damn mutant."

I leaned forward to get a better view out of our blind. "I get it. But
Himari found two sightings of the jackalope on that board."

My headset crackled to life, and the clacking of a mechanical
keyboard sounded in the background. "Make that three sightings,
Mason."

I turned to look at Emma, but she was already scowling at me,
having heard the same message from Himari.

"I can't believe we're out here hunting a jackalope. How do you know some college kids didn't just glue some antlers onto a rabbit?"

Movement drew my gaze across the field. Something low to the ground zipped through the shadows.

"There aren't many creatures as wasteful as a jackalope. Except people, maybe. Jackalopes kill for sport, and I don't exactly know why."

"Mason, if this is some ridiculous practical joke you dragged me out here for, I'm just going to kill you this time."

Himari chuckled over the headset. "Sounds like she figured you out."

"Himari," I said, making an effort to keep my voice even. "You aren't helping."

"Oh, you say that now. But as soon as you need help with any kind of tech, who are you going to call, Mason? It better not be me, because I'm going to go work for the CCD."

I pinched the bridge of my nose.

Emma sipped at her coffee, looking smug. "I've seen enough weird shit with you that I wouldn't be surprised if there's actually a jacka-lope out here. But telling me it's a murder machine? Something the size of a rabbit that kills for fun? You're yanking my chain."

I shook my head. "You saw that cow out in the field. It would take a man hours to skin something like that. And I don't care how much you don't like your neighbor, no one's going to skin a cow and leave the meat to rot."

"Maybe it's a vegetarian who doesn't like their neighbor."

"What? That makes literally no sense, Emma."

"You've never met a vegetarian hunter? And I don't mean someone that hunts vegetarians and tries to get them to eat meat. Those people are assholes."

I didn't respond for a moment, watching a family of possums make their way up a neighboring tree. "I've known a few competition shooters. But I can't say I've met a vegetarian hunter."

"I'm sure they're out there," I muttered, rubbing at my eyes. "And probably a lot more of them than jackalopes. But this isn't some steakhouse critter, Emma. The Missouri jackalope is different than a great many you'll find in other states."

"You sound ridiculous."

I scowled at Emma. "Just drink your coffee."

We sat in mutual irritation for a time, Himari occasionally breaking in with some other nugget of research she found on the jackalopes. A pair of deer and now two cows had been mutilated in the past few days.

The tabloids had already gotten a hold of it. One had twisted the story into a tale about chupacabras coming up into Missouri, and another spun a classic tale of alien saucers harvesting cows for intergalactic fuel. Lord help me. If only they knew what creatures actually lurked in the woods of rural Missouri.

Camped out on the edge of a farmer's field in what appeared to be the middle of nowhere came with some advantages. Being halfway between Jamestown and Lupus meant we weren't far from Jefferson City. Sometimes it was nice to actually stay at a hotel chain where you knew what you were getting, but it was hard to beat a good B&B.

That didn't change the fact we were up and out before dawn. This was our second day watching the field, and if I was being honest with myself I was concerned we weren't going to find anything.

It hadn't been long before I wished we hadn't found anything. The second cow's head had been gnawed off, and while the conservation agents may not have recognized the teeth marks, I did. There was a Missouri jackalope in the region, and we needed to trap it, or far more animals were going to fall to the predator.

"Are you fucking kidding me?" Emma muttered, slowly setting down her coffee mug and raising a primed tranquilizer rifle to her shoulder.

"What?" I leaned closer to her, trying to get an angle and what she was looking at.

Emma flipped the safety off on the tranquilizer rifle.

But all I could see was a bobcat walking the edge of the woods before it leapt to pounce on top of some unseen prey. "I don't think we have to worry about …"

Emma gagged when the bobcat all but exploded. Something squeaked like a guinea pig and shiny red antlers coated in gore caught the early sunlight. It hopped back and forth, cutting pieces off the bobcat with every movement, until all that remained was blood and fur.

Calming her gag reflex, Emma didn't wait. She gave the trigger a steady pull. A puff of compressed CO_2 sent a titanium dart streaking across the field. I was a good shot, but Emma rarely missed. Today was no different.

The dart found its target, but instead of the jackalope preening at its wound, it charged directly at our tent.

"Oh shit!" Emma snapped, scampering away from the blind as the red and white ball of murder hurtled toward us.

I was afraid if I shot the jackalope again it would be too much tranquilizer, and we might kill it. But at the same time, I was worried if it got three hops closer to us, we weren't going to survive the encounter.

But even as I leveled my tranquilizer gun at the jackalope, it went limp in mid-leap, crashing onto the grass field face first and sliding the last 10 feet into our blind, its knife-like antlers cutting through the fabric at my feet.

"It went down fast. That may have been too much tranquilizer." I couldn't hide the small tremor in my voice from the adrenaline.

"That's a fucked up circle of life." Emma toed the antlers with her boot.

My headset crackled to life and Himari started to sing.

"Don't you dare," I said.

She sighed, apparently put upon by my request not to mock us further.

I pulled the edge of the blind toward me, freeing the jackalope and giving me my first good look at the creature. Sprawled out as it was I could've easily mistaken it for jackrabbit, some two feet in length from nose to tail.

But the weight was wrong as I slid the critter closer. The texture of the fur wasn't as soft, and its head was far too heavy, weighed down by thick bones and antlers and a bite strength to rival an alligator.

"Pass me the pool noodle." I picked up a rag and wiped down the antlers only to look up and find Emma with the camera out, pointed at me and the jackalope.

"And tell me again what you need the pool noodle for."

I narrowed my eyes at Emma before slipping into my other personality. It was the one people were used to seeing on our videos, and not the more serious side of the conservationist who'd thought they were about to be impaled by a jackalope.

So I went through my thoughts out loud, lifting the jackalope's head up so viewers could see where the antlers met the skull, and see that there wasn't anything like a headband holding the horns in place.

Bad taxidermy graced almost every steakhouse in the state, with only a few missing the staple of a fake jackalope. It meant we didn't have to make this video look as fake, because people would already assume it was fake.

"And these horns are sharp. Boy oh boy are they sharp." I took the pool noodle as Emma slid it over to me and then sliced off an eight-inch section against one of the horns. "Now, given a little time and enough effort a jackalope could work their way through a pool noodle easily enough. This is just a safe way to transport them without hurting them."

I slid a chunk of pool noodle over each of the curved knife-like horns. On top of each I added a copious layer of duct tape. I looked back up to the camera when I was done. "Now, if you see one of these suckers in the wild, you keep your distance. If you leave them alone, they'll leave you alone. But if you're out with an animal, you get them back inside as fast as you can. A jackalope is a predator like few other animals."

I went through my usual signoff and waited for Emma to lower the camera.

"I guess this is where you say I told you so."

I shook my head. "Neither one of us got stabbed. I'm quite happy with how this morning went." It took a moment to get the jackalope wrapped up in a blanket, and then Emma helped me maneuver it into a wire carrier.

"Are his horns going to fit through that cage?" Emma frowned and stuck her finger through the top of the wire carrier.

"Maybe. But it will take him a while to work through the pool noodle and the duct tape. I doubt he could more than nick your finger."

Emma took a deep breath and flopped back onto her field chair. "Well, we caught it. Now what do you want to do with it? I doubt Larry is going to want a jackalope running around the orchard."

"Definitely not."

Himari's voice came alive in my ear. "But he's *adorable*. I can keep him as a pet. Just bring him to my house!"

"Himari, no."

"Mason," she said, dragging my name out. "Have I not done a good job taking care of the zigmal? I think I have."

Emma chuckled under her breath as she started to pack up the contents of our blind. "That zigmal would be a two-bite snack for a jackalope. At least from what I'm seeing here."

"We can just send him to Momo," I muttered.

Emma barked out a laugh. "I'm sure Momo would like you even more after that."

Two quick beeps in my headset let me know I had another call coming in. "Hold on, Himari." I glanced down at my phone. "It looks like Larry's calling. I'll get back to you in a minute."

I didn't wait for her response as I clicked over to Larry. "This is Mason."

"Mason! I've got a problem at the orchard. I heard from Chuck. Chuck from the CCD? He says DEMON's moving against the orchard."

I frowned at Larry's words. "What do you mean? Moving what?"

"Moving on it. Like attacking it! And I don't have much time to get ready. I can't just leave all the cryptids here, Mason. You've got to help me get them out of here."

Larry's words were coming out so fast I was having a hard time understanding him. The old man was panicked, and panic was not something I associated with Larry Townsend. Anyone who could take care of gowrows and wampuses without a care in the world was not someone who was prone to panic.

"What the hell?" Emma whispered.

I shrugged. "Did Chuck say anything else, Larry?"

"Not really. He thinks maybe DEMON wants to weaponize the cryptids. Does that make any sense to you?"

I thought about the size of Old Willie, and how much damage one of those giant gowrows could do on a battlefield. Thought about the prowess of the wampus, and the destructive power of things that even Larry didn't keep in his orchard, like the hinge-tailed bingbuffer.

"It makes a little bit of sense. A terrible kind of sense. Shit."

"Just come and help me. Please."

I nodded to myself. "Let me talk to Chuck. I need to find out if he knows anything else. Maybe we have time, or maybe he made a mistake."

"I wish he had Mason, but I don't think so. Between the Church and DEMON, you knew someone was going to come for these animals. It was only a matter of time."

"I'll get back to you as soon as I talk to Chuck."

I hung up and met Emma's gaze. Whatever was happening, it wasn't good. And whatever was coming, we were about to be standing in the middle of the storm.

2

———————

After a frustrating five-minute conversation with Chuck, I finally gave in. We headed north on Highway 179 and hopped on Highway 70 headed east toward Columbia.

"Don't get mad at Chuck."

"Himari, I'm not mad at Chuck. I just wish he would've told us what we needed to know so we could save some time and get down to the orchard."

"But Chuck's right. DEMON could be listening to everything you say when you're talking to him. The CCD is part of them, and you know they have some of the best intel out there. Chuck was right."

I switched lanes and passed a slow-moving car. It looked like it had a king-size mattress strapped to the top, and I was fairly certain the car's shape would never quite be the same again.

"Emma, is he scowling?"

Emma eyed me for a moment before she said yes.

Himari blew out an exasperated breath. "Sometimes you're worse than the kids I babysit. Grow up, Mason."

I looked at Emma with my jaw a little slack. "She's in her terrible late teens now, isn't she? Our little girl."

"Oh, don't you even start with that shit. My parents are ninjas with guilt trips. Listening to you is like amateur hour. Now, are you going to bring me that jackalope? That's the more important question here."

"Himari! No! I wasn't exaggerating when I said the thing could cut your hand off. Now imagine the guilt trip your parents would give me about *that.*"

Emma burst into laughter while Himari whined a little bit more before finally acknowledging the fact she wasn't going to have a pet jackalope.

"Fine. I wouldn't want them to eat my zigmals anyway."

I frowned and signaled as we passed the tanker truck. "Was that plural?"

"Gotta go!"

And with that the line went dead, and the quiet electronic buzz of my headset faded to nothing.

I glanced over at Emma who was biting her lips trying not to laugh. "How many does she have?"

"Honestly, Mason, I thought it was just two. But maybe they fell in love and decided to have a nuclear family. They breed as fast as squirrels? Hopefully not as fast as rabbits. Do jackalopes breed as fast as rabbits?"

I grumbled under my breath and choked the life out of the steering wheel beneath my fingers. We could worry about that later, for now we needed to get to Chuck's, and find out just what he knew about DEMON and Larry's orchard.

———

There were few hours in the day when downtown Columbia was dead, but the crack of dawn qualified. Most of the stores wouldn't be open for a few more hours, and the traffic had more in common with a zombie apocalypse than rush hour.

We made our way down between brick buildings and flashing signals before finally turning onto 9th Street. It wasn't far to the club, and it was quite an easy thing to find a space to leave the car. On concert night you might have to walk a couple blocks, but I suspected most concertgoers would just be getting into their hangovers at that time of the morning.

"What are you doing?" I asked.

Emma looked up from the back of the car as she lifted the cage for the jackalope. "Well, I'm not leaving him in the car. How long are we going to be in there? How hot is the car going to get?"

I raised a finger about to argue with Emma, but if I was being honest, I had no idea. I grabbed a sack off the back seat that held an array of snacks that might appeal to the jackalope and led the way to the club.

The heavily tinted doors were locked except for the one on the far left. We went through into the darkness of the entryway. It wasn't until we rounded the corner by the bar that I could see the lights down by the stage.

The jackalope thumped its rear leg in rapid succession like a rabbit signaling danger.

"It's okay, buddy," Emma said tapping the top of the cage.

I suspected the jackalope didn't find the tapping on the top of its cage to be very reassuring. His foot kept bumping as we walked up the stairs that led to the stage and followed the lights around to the back.

"Mason?" A voice said, echoing around us. "I'm downstairs."

Emma and I made our way to the green room, and the hidden door that Chuck had propped open. The place was a little better decorated since the last time we'd been there. Photos of the Missouri wilderness sat side-by-side with old illustrations of folklore monsters. Some of them I had little doubt people had seen the creatures they were illustrating. But others looked like little more than a child's drawing, the stuff of nightmares, and the face of Momo.

Emma sat the cage down on Chuck's desk and nodded to him. Whatever the CCD agent had been about to say, he trailed off as he stared at the jackalope.

"Those aren't real." He pointed at the cage, and then recoiled when the jackalope's jaws spread wide and lunged at him. They snapped closed before the jackalope backed its butt up into the corner of the cage as close to Emma as it could get.

Emma gave him a tight smile. "Yeah... It's pretty real. So what is it you couldn't tell us over the phone? And if you couldn't tell us over the phone are you really going to tell us sitting here in your office?"

"I already swept for bugs. If there's anything here, I think it's in my phone. And it's probably not a bug, but malware."

There was a time I would've thought Chuck was just being paranoid. But I'd seen and heard enough of what DEMON was capable of, not to mention the Church, that spying wouldn't have surprised me.

"That's it?" Himari asked, my headset popping back into life. "I could've dumped you all into an encrypted chat room to get around that."

"I'll let you know what we find out. But for now I'm turning you off."

"Mason —"

But before Himari said anything more I turned the headset off and slid it into my front pocket. I powered my phone completely off as Emma did the same.

Chuck nodded. "I stashed mine in the safe. Turned off, the batteries out, which is a huge pain in the ass to do by the way, and it's not going to be able to hear shit through that steel."

I watched in half horror and half fascination as Emma reached through the bars of the jackalope's cage and scratched the ruff of its neck. It twisted a bit, rubbing the pool noodles against her fingers, before settling in for a good scratch.

I slowly raised an eyebrow before turning back to Chuck. "Now tell us what you know. We have to get down to Larry's orchard."

Chuck slid some papers around on his desk and pulled out a handwritten note that looked like so much chicken scratch. "Noah tipped off some new middle-management prick over at DEMON. Said prick is looking to make a name for himself in research."

I knew where Chuck was going with that before he even finished talking.

"And what would be more memorable than research done on cryptids?" Chuck shook his head. "It's disgusting, Mason. How rare are those animals? And it's not like they're going to be bringing them into captivity to breed them. They'll do what they can to weaponize them."

"Weaponize them!" Emma scoffed. "What do they think they're going to do with them? The more dangerous cryptids are practically weapons already. We had to put pool noodles on this jackalope for fuck's sake."

Chuck shrugged. "Would it be that hard to train them? I doubt it would be much more difficult than taming bears or big cats. You could bait a gowrow with a sack of apples."

I rubbed at the stubble on my face. "Fair point. But if DEMON thinks there's a new venom or paralyzing agent to get their hands on, or a poison to be made from cryptid blood, maybe that's all the incentive they need."

I rummaged through the sack I'd brought down with us and pulled out a length of carrot. Emma took it and held it out to the jackalope. He snatched it out of her hands and snapped it in half with two quick bites. Emma let out a quiet laugh as the carrot started to disappear into the jackalope's mouth, only to be spat out across the cage.

"You're thinking too small." Chuck leaned forward and balled his fists. "All they have to do is drop a gowrow or a wampus in the middle of a populated city. Simple as that, they can throw it under quarantine. Martial law on demand."

"They wouldn't do that."

"Mason, they already have. Everything Larry told you is true. DEMON has rezoned the orchard. They're redrawing the sasquatch lands without negotiating, using the presence of cryptids as an excuse to quarantine the area. They're going to set up a base of operations there. A front line against the Momos moving into the abandoned city."

I blinked at Chuck. "Momos? Plural?"

Chuck cursed under his breath. "You haven't been talking to Sonny, have you?"

I exchanged a glance with Emma. She grimaced and said, "Maybe he was more pissed than he let on about your pledge to Momo."

"It doesn't matter right now. You need to get in touch with the sasquatches. DEMON is going to come for them when they get done with Momo. They'll burn Larry's orchard to the ground, and God only knows what they'll do with those cryptids."

"Got any good news?" I muttered.

"The only reason DEMON knows about your pledge to Momo is Noah. And now that information made its way up to someone I don't know, someone named Director Shaw. You promised Momo that abandoned town, and DEMON has taken issue with it. Momo and his people have been on their watchlist for decades. Now they're planning to bulldoze the abandoned town, and use your pledge as an excuse to do it. DEMON sold you out."

"Fuck." There hadn't been much doubt in my mind that Larry was right to be worried, but what Chuck was telling us was far worse than the old man had led me to believe.

Emma put her hand on my knee. "Let's get moving. We need to be at the orchard. There's no way Larry can evacuate all the cryptids by himself before DEMON gets there. Even with our help I don't know if we can do that Mason."

I nodded slowly. Emma was right. We probably didn't have that kind of time. But that begged another question. "Chuck. How much time do we have to evacuate the orchard?"

Chuck frowned. "I can't be positive, Mason. It's not like they gave me an exact time on the raid, I'd say you have two days at most. But that might be a stretch. I think they're going after Momo first."

If what Chuck was saying was true, DEMON was going to be at the orchard at nightfall tomorrow. We didn't have the trucks or the equipment to move the larger gowrows.

"We need Sonny." I spun the keys to the Bronco around my index finger before snapping my fist closed around them. "And I hate to say it, but I think we need to talk to Momo. If we don't warn him about what's coming, it's as good as pulling the trigger ourselves. I gave him my word. Let's move."

3

———————

"I'm sorry I didn't think about this earlier, Mason." The clacking of Himari's keyboard sounded like a hailstorm in the background. "I can't guarantee what people are doing on the other end, but I can certainly get your calls and data encrypted." She ran down a list of apps and instructions, but finally gave me three simple steps to open an encrypted app for calls.

Emma followed her instructions, and in no time the line to Sonny was ringing.

Someone took a deep breath on the other end of the line. "I do not have a house to sell. I have not applied for any new credit accounts. If this is the FBI, just come and arrest me. Please do not call —"

"Sonny, it's Mason and Emma."

The sasquatch paused. "My apologies. I am not sure how my number made it out into the world of telemarketers, but the flood of calls has been trying." Sonny said "telemarketers" the way a preacher said "the devil." And I could relate.

I exchanged a glance with Emma. "I'm sorry I haven't been in touch with you. We talked to Chuck from the CCD."

"I have spoken with Chuck fairly regularly. We have been keeping

324

an eye on the town Momo has made his home after you granted it to him. The place you fought the jimplicutes."

I let out a low laugh. "Yeah, I remember. Look, Sonny, I know I put you in a bad place with that pledge to Momo. And I'm sorry about that. But Chuck said there's a lot more going on in Momo's little town than we knew about."

"There is." Sonny took a deep breath. "I am not angry with you, Mason. You did what you thought best, without understanding the ramifications of what you had agreed to. But now I fear my people will pay the price for your impulsiveness."

I squeezed the steering wheel and ground my teeth together. "I want to help where I can. Chuck says there's more than one Momo in that town now?"

"Yes. A small family of them has taken up residence there. I expected them to be a much larger problem than they have been. They have hosted the sasquatches in the town multiple times without conflict now. Momo did want access to the old mines, but it would seem more than that he wanted a place away from humans."

"To raise a family?" Emma asked.

"In so many words, yes."

Emma blew out a breath. "Did Chuck tell you what's happening? With DEMON and the orchard?"

"A bit. He suspects that the rezoning will result in a conflict."

"You could say that," I muttered. "DEMON is moving on the orchard in the next forty-eight hours. We need your help, Sonny. We need to get as many of those cryptids out as we can, and we don't have the manpower, or 'squatch power, to do it."

Sonny was silent for a time. "So the devil shows its horns. I will help you, Mason, and we will spare what creatures we can. I can be at the orchard in a few hours."

"How fast can you be at Momo's little town?" I asked.

Sonny's fur crackled in the phone and I suspected he wasn't sure how to respond to that. "You mean to meet with Momo? The one who killed your friend?"

"Yes. Yes, I do. Because the other thing that Chuck told me is once

DEMON has the orchard as a staging ground, they're coming for Momo. And I doubt very seriously anyone else inside that town is going to survive it. DEMON is nothing if not thorough."

"That makes no sense, Mason. DEMON has never been so overtly hostile toward the cryptids here. They have allowed the sasquatches to live in relative peace in many parts of this country. Why here? Why now?"

"Chuck can tell you more," Emma said. "But it sounds like they have some new middle management dickhead calling the shots. We think he wants to prove himself, and apparently this Director Shaw wants the cryptids for research. Or at least that's the excuse they're using."

Sonny sighed. "Mason, would it not be easier to simply throw yourself off a bridge?"

I barked out a laugh. "Sometimes it feels that way, Sonny. Sometimes it feels that way. Now how fast can you meet us at Momo's place? Emma and I will be there in less than an hour."

"I'll be there before you are. Meet me by the old garage. Be careful, Mason. Momo may seem more peaceful in these times, but I remember what he has been, and what he has done. Journey safe."

Sonny ended the call and I sank back into the driver's seat as we continued down the highway.

"It doesn't sound like he's too pissed at me."

Emma nodded. "Maybe he's had enough time to cool down. Or maybe his elders are just happy to get some time to study the Momos up close."

"Momos. Plural. Fuck."

T he anticipation of what was coming made time drag out. It felt like we'd been driving for a day as the roads slowly got worse, turning to worn asphalt, cracked concrete, and finally overgrown gravel.

I suspected if we looked hard enough, we might find remnants of the camera we'd lost to the jimplicute. There wasn't anything quite like coming face to face with something that was very much like a dinosaur.

We hit a pothole, and while my seatbelt kept me from hitting the steering wheel, I still managed to crack my head on the roof. The jackalope wasn't excited about the rough road either. It chittered and almost growled as we started up the hill through the woods. Emma leaned back and scratched him through the cage.

"It's okay, little buddy. Were just gonna go see a big scary monster."

"I really wish you wouldn't stick your fingers in that cage."

"Mason, I've seen you do far stupider things than scratch a jackalope. Besides, his horns are still shielded by those pool noodles."

"Yeah, but his teeth aren't." I remembered watching him take down that carrot, had a terrible vision of Emma's finger meeting the same fate. I shuddered and steered the truck into the old abandoned town.

It was strange to be back, and while I could see Momo had done a little bit to shift debris out of the road and clean out decades of dirt gathered on the sidewalks, the ruins of cars and brick and lampposts slashed to bits by the jimplicutes littered the side streets.

The old bricks still showed mold and discoloration from a lack of care over the years. It made me wonder where Momo was living in that town. Or if he'd made his home down in the caves that had been abandoned so long ago.

It wasn't long before we could see the garage at the end of the street, the tall bays covered once again by metal doors that had been torn down by the jimplicutes when we were last here. They were dented, and sloppy patches showed against the aluminum, but some care had been shown in restoring the old garage.

Emma leaned forward. "I would've expected Momo to just tear this place down and replant a forest or something."

I nodded. "It does make me wonder what he's up to. Is he really just turning the town into a home for his family?"

It was a strange thought, and one that ran at odds with my assumptions about the Missouri monster. Ever since Momo killed Dylan, I'd assumed the worst about the creature. It was hard not to when something killed someone important to you. But the more encounters we had with Momo, the more I wondered what had really happened on that stormy night.

I parked the Bronco at the intersection just in front of the garage. Emma hopped out, looking up at the old brick work in the façades of some of the buildings that had started to fall. It was turning out to be a cool day, so I left the windows down for the jackalope.

"Mason," a voice boomed.

It took me a moment to find the speaker, but over at the side of the garage stood Sonny, tall and furry as usual. I raised a hand in greeting before adjusting the holster that sat under my arm.

"I would not bring a gun to this meeting," Sonny said in a hushed voice as he walked over to us.

I glanced down at the holster. "Habit. It's just a tranquilizer." I undid the buckle and slid the holster off, leaving it on the front seat of the truck.

Sonny sniffed the air and then leaned into the truck. "Is that a jackalope?"

"Maybe."

Sonny slowly turned to look at me. "Sometimes I fear you are quite mad, Mason. What have you put on its horns?"

"Oh, it gets better," I said. "Emma's been petting it."

Sonny recoiled as if I'd slapped him. He turned slowly to Emma. "Are you insane? Jackalopes are violent and unpredictable."

Emma cocked an eyebrow. "The little furball worries you that much? You need to get out more."

Sonny held up his hands and turned away. "I know better than to argue with either of you. Now let's find Momo, so we can get the hell out of this place."

A breeze and a shadow rolled through the small town, but by the time I looked up to see what had flown by, it was already gone.

4

Sonny led the way into the old garage. I was a bit surprised when we passed the bays set into the ground and he turned toward the stairs that led to the basement. This was the place we'd huddled with the witch while the jimplicutes fought the rawhead.

The boxes had been moved from the hallway that led to the bays, and there may have been fewer cobwebs now, but there was new debris that waited in the shadows. An archway had been carved into the concrete wall, and dim light waited in the darkness beyond.

"What is that?" I asked.

"The way into the mines," Sonny said.

We shuffled through a short corridor that opened into an antechamber. It wasn't a large place, and it looked like the ceiling barely cleared Sonny's head. The room was bare except for a large plate set into the wall, and a strange thing to find in a cave sitting beside it.

"Is that a drum mallet?" Emma asked, picking up the pale rod with a large hammer at the end.

"It is. Think of it as a doorbell."

Sonny took the mallet from Emma and smacked it against the

large plate. It boomed like a gong, and the sound reverberated into a distance that I could not see. It was an odd thing, knowing that there was more space around us than what our eyes could show us.

"Now we wait."

It wasn't long before heavy footfalls approached. I was still unnerved by the fact I couldn't see where they were coming from, much like I couldn't tell how the gong had reverberated through the space around us. But a moment later the wall cracked open and swung away from us like a wide door.

Behind it, covered in fur as black as night, and eyes almost an iridescent red, stood Momo, the Missouri monster.

He eyed Sonny for a moment before looking in turn at Emma and me. "You were not invited to this place." Momo frowned. His shoulders relaxed a hair, and it was an unnervingly human movement.

The words came out of my mouth in a hurry. "There's a problem with DEMON. And we think it might affect you."

Momo didn't say anything for a time. Instead he was silent, as if carefully choosing every word before he spoke it. "You are aware of what lives in this town with me?"

I nodded. "Your family."

"Then understand, should this be a deception, the repercussions upon your body will be severe."

It was one of the strangest threats I'd ever heard, but the intent was clear enough. "My pledge didn't include that I would never set foot here again. I only ask that you speak to us, and then you can do what you want."

Momo inclined his head. "A reasonable request. Come, there is no reason for these caves to be a secret from you."

I exchanged a glance with Emma as Momo turned away and Sonny followed him through the doorway. She shrugged, and I knew exactly how she felt. We'd come to talk to Momo, and walking deeper into the cave, where we had little chance to escape, seemed like not the brightest idea.

But whatever my concerns had been, they vanished when we

turned the corner of the narrow corridor and I looked out upon something I never would have called a cave.

Stone that looked more like a spinal column traced a graceful arch across the ceiling where ribs branched out to an unimaginable width. We stood at the top of a staircase and I couldn't see how far down it went, as it turned every twenty steps and sank back into the wall before coming back into the light once more.

Wires had been draped across the chasm, stretching between light bulbs that didn't reach the depths of the shadows below. But it wasn't merely the size of the place that I had trouble wrapping my head around, but the dwellings carved into the walls.

They weren't sized for humans, as each doorway was more than enough for Momo's width and height. Whatever had built the place had either been far larger than humans, or built out of scale to what they needed. But I suspected it was the former.

"This is what I wanted the old city for." Momo gestured to the dwellings around the walls in the courtyard far below I could just make out as we traversed more stairs.

"What is this place?" Emma asked. "And how on earth is this supporting the town above us?"

Momo didn't turn back to look at us, instead gesturing to the spine-like arch and rib cage over our heads. "Your people once called this a slide rock bolter. A massive beast that once hunted in the mountains. But when they died, they often became the mountains themselves, buried beneath rock and earth over the centuries."

"I've heard of them," I said. "But to be honest, until I was standing inside of one, it seemed like one of the more ridiculous tales I'd heard."

Momo looked up at the skeleton above them. "If there is one thing I have learned of humans in my years, there is truth in many of your lies."

It wasn't until we reached the bottom that I realized we weren't alone. Furry black shadows, not much smaller than Momo himself, flitted through the doorways set into the cave walls.

Momo glanced back and answered the question I hadn't asked.

"My family is here. This was the home of our people for centuries before the humans came. After they drove us out, stories of where this place was hidden were lost to our ancestors. Once we found it again, it only seemed right to come home."

"You could have told that to the elders," Sonny said. "They would have been understanding without your deception."

"I prefer to take the path guaranteed as opposed to the path of possibility."

"You speak the words of our elders. They will not seek conflict with you. They have never sought that."

"You are wrong there, sasquatch. And one day you will see it. But for now, and for this time, if you offer an alliance I need to know why." Momo gestured to a heavy wooden table, polished to a dark sheen.

We each took a seat at one of the oversized chairs. It was an odd sensation, to have my feet dangling above the ground like a small child in a chair that was too large. Emma swung her feet back and forth, while Sonny sat comfortably.

Momo turned to Emma. "Tell me why they have come. I have less reason to distrust you."

Emma blinked at that. But to her credit, she didn't hesitate long. "Someone at the Church tipped off DEMON about Mason's pledge to you. About giving you this old town. It didn't take long for them to rezone the orchard where Larry protects the cryptids. You know who Larry is?"

Momo inclined his head. "He is one of the few humans I have tolerance for. One who seems to understand the balance all should maintain with nature."

"Well, DEMON is going to seize the orchard. We don't know exactly why. But we know they want to set up a base there, a base of operations where they can more easily attack you."

Momo leaned back, his gaze trailing from Emma to me. "I should kill you all. You would bring this down on my family."

I pursed my lips. "That would be one option. But hear me out, we did come here to warn you."

Sonny tapped his fingers on the table. "And to ask for your help."

I glanced between Emma and Sonny.

The sasquatch gestured to the cave around us. "You have space here, and in the town above us. Could we use it to shelter some of the cryptids from Larry's orchard?"

"Even if I agreed, most cryptids avoid us. We are known to them as predators, and few would look to us for shelter." Before Sonny could respond, Momo continued. "Your plan is flawed. You would only remove the cryptids from Larry's orchard to place them here, where DEMON is coming. You only delay the inevitable."

"Not if you fight with us," I said.

"Mason," Emma hissed. "What are you talking about? Fight?"

"If we can't get the cryptids out in time, DEMON is going to come for them. I'm not going to abandon all of those creatures in Larry's orchard. I'm not going to abandon Larry."

Emma started to argue more, but Momo cut her off.

"I will consider your words. I will not put my family at more risk than they are already in. But allowing DEMON into our home is unacceptable. I am willing to fight to keep them at bay."

"I still don't understand why they want this place," Sonny said.

Momo gestured toward the ceiling. "The bones above you. They've long since changed, their makeup now more metal and stone. The source of the precious minerals that were mined so long ago. I have a little doubt of what DEMON wants here."

Another Momo walked into the antechamber. This one was shorter, and when they spoke I was surprised at the submissive tone. "Apologies for the interruption. We have intruders above."

Momo turned to look at us. "Did you lead them here?"

"Who?" I asked.

Momo turned his attention back to the newcomer. "Tell us who they are."

"Of course. They dress in black. Tactical gear, and they do not appear to be armed with tranquilizers. They arrived on two black helicopters."

Momo stood up. "Go. Gather the others. You know what to do."

The smaller Momo bowed and hurried into the shadows.

"Did you lead them here?"

I shook my head. "Absolutely not. They're as big a threat to us as they are to you."

Momo's fur lifted into an unnatural grin. It had far more in common with the snarl of a predator than the expression on a human. "They are not a threat to us. Join us in the fight if you would. Or wait here while we remove them."

"We don't have our guns!" Emma said.

Momo slowly turned his head to me. "Why in the world do you not have guns?"

"Well," I started. "We thought it would be a little rude coming to your home uninvited and armed."

"Humans," Momo growled. "Your logic fails you at every turn in every situation." He waved us off. "Join the fight if you wish. You've given us your information and should you die we have no more need of you."

With that Momo stalked off into the darkened corridor after his kin.

Emma watched him go. "That was kind of nice and kind of insulting."

"DEMON's already here," Sonny said. "That means Chuck was wrong. They are not going to the orchard to use it as a staging ground. They're going there to take it by force."

"I'm afraid you're right." I curled my hand into a fist. "We're going to need to move faster than we thought."

Emma cursed under her breath when the first sounds of gunfire echoed through the cave far above us.

5

"Come on," I said. "If we just let Momo kill all those DEMON agents, this isn't going to go well." I hopped up from the table and hurried down the dim corridor the two Momos had taken.

"Mason," Sonny said. "If those agents have come here to kill Momo, he has every right to defend his home. Surely even the bylaws of DEMON make way for the rules of engagement."

Emma scoffed at that. "There are good people in DEMON, don't get me wrong. But if they've cooked up something with Noah and the Church, I don't trust them any more than I trust Momo. We're on dangerous ground, and I think you know it."

I didn't miss the slow incline of the path we were on. It wasn't long before my phone vibrated in my pocket. The screen showed me Himari's face looking panicked. I slid my headset on and answered.

"What is it? We have a bit of a problem at Momo's."

"I know!" Himari yelled. "I've been monitoring DEMON's comms. They're right on top of you."

The rapid staccato of gunfire sounded again, and Himari's voice broke up. Her voice returned as we ascended another staircase.

"They aren't using names. I'm not sure who's giving the order. But someone said to kill the humans. And I'm pretty sure the humans are you, Mason."

My steps slowed. "They wouldn't do that. They can't do that."

"Someone is fucking doing it. You need to get out of there."

"The child is correct."

I almost shrieked when the voice sounded right beside me. Another Momo was there, not much taller than me, with none of the musty scent I was so familiar with.

Once I gathered my wits I asked, "What do you mean?"

"We are more informed than you know." This Momo's voice was lighter, more fluid, almost feminine. "Momo has been in contact with DEMON for a great many years. There is a schism forming inside that organization. And I fear it may have reached its breaking point. And that bodes ill for all."

"Can we help?" I asked. "Do you have any weapons a human can wield?"

The Momo smiled down at me. The expression looked natural on her face, and in that moment I questioned everything I knew about Momo and his people. "Do not worry Mason Dixon. The jimplicutes will cleanse this place."

"The what now?"

A large hairy hand grabbed my shoulder and Sonny pulled me backwards. Above us, at the end of another slanted hall, bursts of gunfire intensified. And then the screams came. It was not the confident basso shouts of trained soldiers, but the cries and shrieks of terrified humans.

"Oh my God," Himari's voice sounded in my headset. "Oh my God oh my God oh my God. Something's killing them all."

It was then that I realized Himari didn't just hack the audio, but she had the video of DEMON's troops too. "Himari, don't watch. Himari, turn it off."

But the random shouting and cries and bursts of gunfire were joined by a terrible roar. The stone shook beneath our feet, and I had little doubt what was happening above us. I'd seen what the jimplicutes could do. What I didn't understand was why they were here, underground, with the Momos.

Two sharp whistles sounded as the gunfire died away. The smaller Momo was gone, and I didn't see where she went. Instead I hurried down the corridor to see if what I feared had come to pass.

At the top of that ramp, in the flickering light of the torch, stood Momo. The Momo I knew, the Momo I'd hunted for so long. Beside him was a ghostly silhouette that bristled and shifted as Momo patted its snout.

The jimplicute shook itself off but failed to dislodge the blood around its teeth. As I watched, the ghost dinosaur started up another ramp into the light of day that waited above.

But in the dimmer light of the chamber we stood in, I could see the corpses. Bulletproof vests that had been bitten through like they were so much tissue paper. Blank stares and the scent of iron, blood, and ruptured intestines choked the air around us.

Momo pulled the helmet from one of DEMON's soldiers and stared into the small camera mounted on the side of it. "You have one chance. Do not send your people here again." And with that, Momo crushed the helmet and the camera in his palm.

I stood there in silence as he made his way to each of the corpses and destroyed their cameras.

Momo shouted down another corridor. "Gather the bodies and burn them. The smell is bothering me."

I didn't wait to see who or what came to gather those bodies. I led the way up the ramp the jimplicute had taken. I needed fresh air, I needed to get away, and I needed to scrub that vision from my mind.

Sonny and Emma and I stood in the sunlight at the edge of the ramp. There was no sign of the jimplicute up top save for a few claw marks in the base of the trees. We were at the edge of the town there. None of us spoke as we started back toward the truck.

We almost made it there when Momo called out to us.

"You'll have my help with the cryptids. Whoever ordered this attack on my home has made an enemy this day."

One of the black choppers appeared overhead as it streaked into the distance. An explosion sounded out in the woods and a terrible smile twisted Momo's face. "Though I admit they have paid a price."

"You let the jimplicutes into your house," I said, at a loss for any words of more substance.

"They are not violent creatures unless subjected to terrible circumstances."

"I cannot say the same for you," Sonny said. "You invite violence and war wherever you go. Even into your own home."

Momo turned away. "One day you will understand, sasquatch. And on that day I hope you can embrace the violence you were once so capable of. Bring the cryptids from the orchard here." It was the last thing he said before he vanished back into the caves below.

I didn't say anything else until we reached the truck. Emma let Sonny take the front seat where he had at least a reasonable amount of legroom. I exchanged a glance with the sasquatch.

"What the hell just happened?"

"We have the ally we need, but do not want. That is what has happened, Mason. Now go, we must reach the orchard."

I put the truck in gear and started out of the town.

Emma put words to what I feared. "Momo just killed agents of DEMON. They're going to rain hell on this place. And they're going to start with the orchard. We have to get those cryptids out of there, and then we need to get far far away."

But Momo's town was supposed to be a safe haven for the cryptids. Now I worried DEMON might come for them anyway. But what other choice did we have? Some of the cryptids were too dangerous to be around humans, especially humans that didn't understand how to interact with them. And that could get them killed as surely as taunting a lion with a steak.

The only advantage we had was that Himari had intercepted their comms. They were going to kill Larry. And they were going to kill us if they could. Of that I had no doubt.

I pushed the accelerator to the floor, and we bounced back out onto the highway.

6

Sonny twisted around in his seat and watched Emma feed a long strip of beef jerky to the jackalope. "That is a dangerous animal."

Emma rolled her eyes. "That's what Mason keeps telling me. But do you see the pool noodles? He's not going to cut me." She reached her fingers farther into the cage and scratched the jackalope closer to his tail.

I caught Sonny's eyes as he turned back around and the sasquatch shook his head. "Look, I've taken my fair share of risks with cryptids, but I'd never mess with the jackalope."

"Wise of you," Sonny said.

"Ugh, boys."

"Now that I can agree with," Himari said, her voice booming over the Bluetooth speakers in the truck.

"Not helpful, kid," I said with a smile. I didn't want to turn the conversation back to what we had just witnessed, but we were short on time. "Himari, tell me again what you heard over the comms."

"I can do better than tell you. Let me pull up the recording."

Emma leaned forward. "You've been recording DEMON's feed? That's not going to go over well when they figure it out."

Himari puffed out a breath in exasperation. "I'm too good for that. Okay now, here it is. Best I can tell is the guy who talks first is the jackass Chuck was warning us about."

The recording sounded a little tinny, but it was easy enough to make out the words.

"No, you go in with tranquilizers. We need the cryptids for research."

"Be a lot easier if you just let us shoot everything," a gruff voice responded. "What about the caretaker? He's not going to be happy about us taking his animals."

"They aren't animals. They are cryptids. They are dangerous, and their caretaker should be treated as such."

"Sir?"

"The caretaker attacked first. You were only defending yourself. Kill any humans you find."

The hesitation in the second man's voice gave me some hope for the human race. But the man's response soured my stomach.

"Understood, sir." He might have bitten the words off, but there was resignation in that voice too.

Larry was in danger. They were all in danger. And now with what Momo had done? I shook my head. "That's enough, Himari."

"We need to move fast," Emma said. "We might have to leave the cryptids behind, Mason. We might need to get Larry out and run."

"Emma, if you don't want to be a part of this, I'll understand. I worked half my life to understand those creatures and protect them. I won't abandon them to what's coming."

"I'm with you," Sonny said.

Emma looked down at the jackalope and scratched at the side of the critter's face. "I'm with you too. Obviously. Let's just not die."

I rubbed at my shoulder as we made our way toward Brumley. To say I was feeling stressed was a gross understatement. Emma made some calls to a handful of people we could trust, and Sonny reached out to the sasquatches.

"It's a shame you don't have that farmer's number you shot with a tranquilizer dart," I said.

"That's helpful, Mason." Emma scowled at me in the rearview mirror.

"I try. The big cat rescue sounded promising. But I'm pretty sure they'll notice the wampuses aren't mountain lions when they get there though."

Emma shook her head. "The wampuses are probably the easiest thing to pass off at Larry's orchard. I still have no idea what we're going to do about the old gowrows. They're too big to fit in anything we have access to. Maybe we could rent one of those mobile home haulers. Stuff them inside of one."

I laughed at the idea, trying to picture Old Willie stuffed into half a mobile home while his head hung out one end and his tail out the other. "That might be a problem."

"I know," Emma muttered.

Sonny cleared his throat. "On the bright side, the sasquatches have agreed to monitor the perimeter of Momo's town."

"Do you think they'll go inside? If it comes to that?"

Sonny didn't answer for a time. "I am unsure. The idea of Momo being a potential ally is an intriguing one, but I do not trust him. And neither will my elders."

"I get that. Boy, do I get that."

"Mason?" Himari asked, her voice filling the truck around us. "I think we might have a problem."

"You have to be more specific. I think we have a lot of problems."

"I lost the comm channel. I think they found me."

My heart hammered in my chest. "What do you mean? Are they there? They've come for you?"

Himari laughed. "Not in real life. I mean they found the exploit and patched it. Whoever they have, they're good. But they're not going to find me in real life, Mason. I doubt they could track me through more than a couple VPNs, and I'm behind far more than that."

My eyes glazed over as Himari went through the details of her security layout. I was relatively savvy when it came to technical things, but Himari was throwing out acronyms that I had no idea what they meant. Sometimes it was easiest just to let her talk, especially when things were stressful. There was something calming about listening to someone speak at length on things they were passionate about.

I felt like our plan was only half formed when the Brumley swinging bridges came into view.

"Oh look," Emma said. "They still haven't fallen down."

"Maybe we'll get lucky and today will be the day. Then we won't have to worry about the orchard."

Sonny blinked at me. "I have never fully grasped the morbid humor humans often employ."

I smiled at the sasquatch as I slowed and eased the truck onto the bridge. The rusted cables and old wood groaned, but held, making a slow rhythmic thump as we continued across.

"It's like getting peanut butter in your fur and having zigmals clean it out for you."

Emma snorted from the back seat as the jackalope thumped in his cage

Sonny narrowed his eyes. "That was neither humorous nor pleasant. You are only reinforcing my observation."

I may have joked about it, but the old bridges did look like they could fall over at any moment. Some of the cables had small wires that had frayed, sprouting out like a rusted flower. I didn't have much doubt it was only a matter of time until they wouldn't hold much weight, much less the weight of the truck with the sasquatch in it.

Our tires thumped down on the opposite side of the bridge and I turned off onto a gravel path that looked like little more than an overgrown shoulder. Branches scraped the side of the truck as we made our way into the shadowy woods.

We were quiet except for the occasional warnings of the jackalope.

The shocks tried to keep up with the dips and ruts in the road, but it didn't do much to keep Sonny's head from bouncing against the ceiling every few seconds. The sasquatch eventually scowled and pushed his hand against the ceiling to keep from smacking his head repeatedly.

The gravel road swung out by a sandbar before dipping back into the tree line. It wasn't long before the forest thinned and we came out into a clearing where a worn painted sign hung above a white fence. Larry's Orchard Extravaganza.

I parked the truck just below the swinging sign and we all piled out. Normally it was quiet at the orchard. The cryptids who sheltered there avoided the entrance. But today I could hear the chaos at a distance.

I exchanged a glance with Sonny and Emma before grabbing my tranquilizer equipment and hurrying into the orchard. Emma threw a backpack on and grabbed the jackalope's cage.

"Grab those tubs out of the back would you, Sonny?" Emma asked.

The sasquatch picked up a large stack of plastic tubs and followed us through the woods. Larry's place wasn't laid out as precisely as the big commercial orchards. And that was very much by design. There were a few spots where you got a good view down a long row of trees. But for the most part everything was obscured, and it was a good way to keep the cryptids hidden.

I heard things snuffling through the underbrush, but nothing made itself known at first. We traversed the narrow path through the woods until we came to a long sloping hill. And only when we stepped out of the last line of apple trees did I finally see what had been following us through the field of fallen apples.

A scaly head popped up, its body plump and round at the end of its long neck. It had a large red apple in its mouth that it horked down in one quick gulp.

"Brain!" Emma said.

The gowrow charged at her, nearly knocking the cage out of her grasp as she rubbed at Emma's thigh enthusiastically.

"It's good to see you, girl. I can't scratch you now. Got a jackalope to carry."

Brain chuffed at Emma, looked up at Sonny, and then trotted over to me. I scratched at the softer scales on the underside of the gowrow's neck.

"Grown a bit, haven't you, girl? Not as fast as I would've thought. Especially considering how big Old Willie is. Maybe we were wrong about how old that gowrow is."

I pondered that for one merciful minute, distracted from the reason we were actually there. We reached the top of the hill, and the chaos of what waited below grew in volume.

"Holy shit," Sonny said.

I grinned at the sasquatch. "That's quite a sight." Near the bottom of the hill, the side of the mountain was opened like some massive garage door. Normally it was how Old Willie got in and out of the underground compound. But it looked like today Larry was trying to load every cryptid in his reach through that same door.

7

Two Ozark howlers prowled the area, their black fur and curved horns blending in with the shadows of the trees around them. Oddly they didn't attack the small yapping gowrow bounding around between them. I was surprised to see Pinky being so bold, as if he was familiar with the howlers.

"Fang," Sonny said, and there was a kind of confusion in his voice. The sasquatch squinted and frowned, taking in everything and everyone that waited below us. "Frederick."

Frederick was the name of one of the elders in Sonny's pack. A sasquatch we'd met when we first faced Momo and the jimplicutes in the old abandoned town. My gaze flicked across the field below until it landed on the sasquatch. His fur wasn't as dark as Sonny's, and in the daylight I could see a pale gray pattern near the sasquatch's ears.

I looked up at Sonny. "Frederick. As in *that* Frederick?"

"I do not know more than one Frederick." He started down the hill, circling to the right to avoid the opening below us. "I suppose that explains why Fang is here. He tends to stay near the sasquatch pack."

The hill vibrated beneath our feet and I wasn't surprised when Old Willie's long broad head appeared from the side of the mountain. It would be an easy thing to mistake the gowrow for a dragon. Perhaps a somewhat fat dragon, but a dragon nonetheless.

Brain lost interest in following us when she saw Old Willie. She darted down the hill, headed straight for the ancient gowrow.

Beyond Old Willie, hissing at Larry from a series of cages, was a family of a rather annoyed wampuses. The cats had grown even larger since the last time we saw them, but one remained outside of the cage, walking lazily beside Larry, the patterns in his fur telling me it was the wampus we'd named Legs.

Something chittered above us, and near the top of the canopy I could see a cluster of zigmals, easily mistaken for squirrels, rocketing through the branches as they bounced their tails and streaked through the air.

Emma's pace slowed and she cursed under her breath. "This is a mess. This is chaos. What in the hell is even happening?"

"I've been saying the same thing all damn day," a scratchy voice said, a shadow suddenly appearing beside them.

I took a step back to see around Emma, and I didn't hide my surprise at who I found standing there. "Augusta?"

One side of her mouth quirked up, a smile that could have easily been mistaken for a snarl. "At least you remembered my name."

I smiled nervously at the witch. "You didn't bring another rawhead did you?"

"But I see you're still a fool."

Emma snorted a laugh and followed Augusta as she led us the rest of the way down the hill.

"I'm surprised to see you're still with that boy."

"Oh, I'm not with him. This is just my job."

"Job? Oh yes, Frederick told me something about your videos on those Internets. Can't imagine people would actually pay to watch fake videos about cryptids. If you tried fake videos about magic? Now that sounds quite a bit more interesting."

I exchanged a glance with Emma. "That actually doesn't sound like a terrible idea. Maybe we should start a second channel, Emma."

"Oh yes," she muttered. "That's exactly what we need. Another channel to mislead people about more things. Woo."

"We don't entirely mislead people about everything." I slapped at my neck when something bit it. This close to the river, mosquitoes were an annoyance most of the day. "We give them good information. And maybe most importantly, we tell them to stay the hell away from cryptids."

Augusta harrumphed. "You ask me, humans are far more dangerous than cryptids. Might make more sense to switch your warnings around."

I shook my head. "It's not like cryptids are watching my show. That doesn't even make sense."

"I watch your show," Sonny said.

I raised my finger to protest, but words failed me. "Dammit."

Emma chuckled at that, only falling silent when we reached the bottom of the hill and Old Willie leaned over to sniff at our group. The gowrow didn't have the most pleasant odor, but I'd have to say an unwashed Momo still took the cake for bad smells.

Emma scratched Old Willie's jaw and the towering gowrow leaned into it a little too hard. The jackalope remained surprisingly calm as the gowrow knocked them over, and Emma fought to keep his cage upright.

It was the first time Augusta took note of the cage. "Do y'all have a jackalope in that thing? And what the hell is on its horns?"

"Pool noodle," Emma said with a grunt as she found her feet again. She patted Willie on the nose and the gowrow turned his attention back to Brain. Brain chuffed at us as if expressing her annoyance at distracting Old Willie.

"What in the seven hells is a pool noodle?"

"Long Styrofoam thing? You can kind of float on it in the water."

Augusta eyed the jackalope with some suspicion. Almost as much suspicion as the look she gave Emma.

It was about then that Larry finally noticed our arrival. He looked disheveled, his overalls stained with God only knew what. But he raised a hand in greeting regardless after handing off the carrying cases to Frederick.

I remembered quite distinctly how heavy those wampuses were. And was more than a little surprised at how easily Larry lifted and moved the cages. I returned Larry's greeting and wound his way past the gowrows and in between the Ozark howlers.

"Mason. Thanks for coming. You talked to Chuck I hear."

I nodded. "Did he call you?"

"From some number I didn't recognize. I assume it was one of those disposable phones."

Himari's voice came to life in my ear. "Oh, like a burner phone. It's like a spy movie, Mason, a *spy* movie."

I slowly massaged my forehead because the predicament we were in felt like anything but a spy movie. I turned my attention back to Larry. "What's the plan?"

"Frederick here brought a cattle car up. I have to admit I was surprised to see it. I was even more surprised he got it up the back road. You think the front road's in disrepair ..." Larry blew out a breath with a laugh.

"It certainly wasn't easy," Frederick said after he slid the wampus crates into a box truck. "I had to drag the trailer through more than one part. Thankfully Fang seems to be part ox."

I raised an eyebrow. "You're telling me you yoked an Ozark howler? And used him to help pull a trailer? And didn't get it on film?"

Sonny put a hand on my shoulder and slid in front of me. "I apologize, Frederick. Sometimes I fear Mason does not live in our reality."

Emma snickered at that.

"Regardless," I said. "How can we help?"

Larry put his hands on his hips and looked around the clearing. "We've got most of the wampuses loaded up, a couple kingdoodles, a handful of the zigmals I could actually catch, and two more howlers we had to tranquilize. The main problems now are what to do with Old Willie and Dolly. No trailer is going to hold both those gowrows. If DEMON knows what's here, the compound I mean, they'll get into the underground easily enough."

Even as Larry spoke, a kind of blue mist crept in along the ground like a fog being cast off from the river. It felt muggy in the clearing, humidity making the air heavy from the recent rains. Some of the ground had dried out, but with the traffic from the cryptids, other areas had turned into muddy sinkholes.

From one moment to the next, all of the cryptids fell silent. The only sound was a wind that whispered through the branches of the trees around us like some long-forgotten god exhaling.

Larry paused in that silence, cocking his head to the side, and it looked like he was straining to hear just as much as I was. The rustling of a small cluster of zigmals above us finally interrupted the quiet.

"That wasn't natural," Larry said. "What the devil is that mist? DEMON gassing us?"

"No." Augusta bent down and ran her fingers along the earth. "There is more magic than my own in this place."

Frederick reached out and laid a hand on Larry's shoulder. "My friend, I believe it may have been one of the most natural things in the world." He looked up toward the top of the hill. "That is no mist. Look again. It is a blessing. A blue summer haze breathed out by the snawfus itself."

I'd heard stories of the snawfus. I'd heard tales told of a great many things visiting with some of the rural communities in Missouri. But the snawfus was one that came up quite often. Sometimes it was a white deer and nothing more. But other tales told of a huge white beast with antlers formed of a peach tree, and sometimes an apple tree, but a benevolent creature to all who encountered it.

Perhaps the story I heard most often was that of an albino deer who traveled through the treetops, exhaling the blue summer haze across the Ozarks. Sometimes the snawfus would bestow a blessing, but a few said that every blessing came with a curse. It was one of the more magical creatures I'd heard described, but until I'd met Augusta I hadn't really believed in magic.

A shiver ran down my spine as the witch studied the tree line.

Larry clapped his hands together, breaking the moment. "If what Chuck says is right, we got one day to get all these critters out of here. Let's get to work."

And so we did.

8

O nce we had the box truck loaded up, well past dinnertime, Frederick and Sonny helped us drive it, and sometimes drag it, down the back road. The gravel eventually gave way to asphalt when we reached a small county road.

I had no idea exactly where we were, but Frederick was confident we were in the right spot based on Larry's directions. We stayed there for a time, listening to the wampuses whine in the back while fireflies lit up the late evening air.

We'd been there about thirty minutes when I started to get antsy. "Are you sure this is the right place? We haven't seen a single car go by."

Frederick gave me a look that made Emma belt out a stuttering laugh. "I'm fairly certain that is the point, Mason."

I pursed my lips and leaned against the box truck.

Sonny stepped closer to the road and then gestured for Frederick to hide. "Car. I think it might be them."

"Well then, I hope it's more than a car," I heard Frederick mutter as they retreated into the tree line. And he had a fair point.

About the time the sasquatches vanished into the vegetation, I could pick out the headlights Sonny had seen at a much greater distance. They turned off a road I couldn't make out and headed in our direction.

A knot of worry I hadn't realized was there untied itself when I saw the long cargo van pull up next to our box truck. An older woman hopped out of the driver's seat and nodded to us as she walked around and opened the side door. It slid open with a hiss, revealing a wide space and deep metal shelves to host an array of cages.

"What you caught?" She asked.

"Some panthers, I think," Emma said.

The woman from the big cat rescue raised an eyebrow. "That's what Larry told me, too. But Larry is fond of his crazy stories. Let's take a look."

I lifted the rear door on our box truck and the nearest wampus hissed at us. "Oh, stop that. She's a friend."

The woman cocked her head to the side. "One of the only friends these critters have left. I think we're the only big cat shelter around with a no kill policy."

"Did Larry tell you he'll be back for them later? After he gets his new property settled?"

"Something like that." She reached in and dragged the nearest metal cage to the edge of the truck. "Well, shit. You might just have a panther there. I thought they died out a long time ago."

Emma patted the top of the cage. "Be careful with them. They can be a bit ... bitey."

The woman grinned at her. "What's your name, girl?"

"Emma."

"You seem comfortable around these cats. You ever need yourself a job out this way, we're just a few miles outside Columbia. I'd be happy to have you. Larry's got my number. Just call up and ask for Annie."

She lifted the crate and waddled over to the van, sliding the first wampus in without much of a fuss. After she came back for the second one, Emma and I each grabbed one of the last crates. Annie loaded two more by the time we put ours down.

Once they were in and strapped down, Annie said her goodbyes and headed down the road. I waited until the taillights were gone before I turned towards the woods.

"Sonny, Frederick, she's gone."

The edge of the tree line shifted to the side as the sasquatches reappeared.

Emma brushed her hands off. "Well, that's all of the wampuses except Legs. And from what Larry was saying, Legs isn't going to leave his side."

More headlights appeared, except this time they were coming from the nearly invisible road we'd taken from Larry's. After a couple more minutes Larry's truck appeared beside us and the old man stepped out.

"Most of the smaller cryptids are loaded up. We can transfer them to the box truck, and you can take them down to Momo's place. If that ain't a weird thing to say."

Frederick nodded and started pulling crates off the back of Larry's truck and setting them gently into the box truck. I saw the kingdoodles and a tighter wire cage full of zigmals, but there was no sign of the younger gowrows or Legs.

Emma asked the same question I was thinking. "What about Pinky and Brain?"

Larry shook his head. "I can't get those two far away from Old Willie. They've taken to him like a couple of kids. We'll get them out of here tomorrow when Frederick comes back."

Frederick nodded as he pulled the back of the box truck closed. Metal cracked against metal and he locked the cryptids into the transport. "I'll be back as soon as I can. I'd like to make sure Momo isn't going to feed these cryptids to the jimplicutes."

Larry waived the thought off. "The jimplicutes aren't going to kill anything that's not a threat, or a snack. They left well enough alone, until Mason stuck his nose into their business."

"Hey," I started. "I didn't exactly just go sticking my nose into a jimplicute's business. We were looking for a side hill hoofer."

"You were looking for a side hill hoofer," Emma muttered. "I was just trying not to get stepped on by an invisible dinosaur."

I stared at Emma slack-jawed for a moment before I snapped my mouth closed. "Anyhow. Why don't we get back to the orchard and grab some dinner. Not to mention some sleep."

Larry nodded. He held out his hand and shook Frederick's before the older sasquatch climbed into the truck and headed down the road. "He's driving at night. I'm sure no one will notice a sasquatch on the highway."

"I wouldn't exactly call this a highway," Emma said.

Larry blew out a breath. "Fair enough. That's fair enough. Hop in the truck and I'll get you back to the orchard."

Emma and I climbed into the back while Sonny took the front seat. It wasn't a smooth ride back to the orchard, but I felt a little better knowing we'd gotten so many of the cryptids to safety.

"Pinky, get back here!" I shouted as the gowrow sprinted out the door once more. My shoulders sagged and I gasped for breath. It had taken me fifteen minutes to run the damn gowrow down, only to have him slip out the door once more with Legs.

Emma laughed at me and walked down the wide corridor carrying the cage for the jackalope with two gun cases balanced on top.

Larry sighed. "Leave him be. He'll be back soon enough. The gowrows tire out quite a bit faster than the wampuses."

It was easy to forget how large Larry's underground compound was. Old Willie fit in the corridor effortlessly. Beyond the massive gowrow, I could just make out the silhouette of Dolly. She wasn't quite as large as Old Willie, but still plenty large to give some humans a fright.

I followed Emma over to a table set close to the kitchen. Larry was just laying out some freshly microwaved chili and oyster crackers when we sat down. Sonny came out of the kitchen with two beers in each hand, followed by Augusta. The steins looked small compared to the sasquatch, and when he set it down in front of me I wasn't sure if I should drink the whole thing.

"It will help you sleep," the sasquatch said.

"And don't you worry," Larry said. "That's my own brew. That's none of that sasquatch brew that'll put you on the floor for a month."

Augusta almost purred. "Now, you want a good strong ale, nothing beats that sasquatch brew."

I raised an eyebrow. "Sonny, have you been holding out on us?"

The sasquatch grinned. "Another time, when there is a little less pressure on us."

Emma raised her stein and smiled. "You know we're going to hold you to that, right?"

9

Sleep didn't come easy. More than once I bolted awake, and not just from the cold metal of the cot digging into my back. It's hard to put into words just how loud a sasquatch can snore. Sonny was folded awkwardly into a corner of the underground compound, two blankets balled up next to him as he tried to outdo the snores of the giant gowrows in the next hall.

It made me wonder how the sasquatches managed to stay hidden. If they all snored like that, they'd be about as stealthy as an elephant in the woods. I chuckled to myself at that thought and rolled over.

Emma didn't seem to have any such issues falling asleep. She'd been out like a light every time I'd woken up. It wasn't the first time I was jealous of her ability to tune out the world around her when she was sleeping.

I drifted in and out of sleep for a few hours before I heard someone rattling around in the kitchen. I tossed off my covers and shuffled to the dim light in the doorway.

Larry stood inside, flipping bacon before cracking eggs that hissed in the bacon grease while a giant carafe of coffee brewed. He glanced back and offered me a smile when the door creaked open. "Grab a seat. You want two pancakes?"

Before I could answer, a scaly ball not much higher than Larry's knees started hopping up and down.

Larry patted Brain on the head. "I know you do, girl. Just give me a minute."

It wasn't long before there was far more food piled up on the table than I could ever eat. Larry's pancakes were glorious, light and fluffy and dripping with butter. And not that anyone could really screw up bacon, but Larry's was excellent.

I felt the table shake beneath my elbows and paused.

"Don't worry. That's just Old Willie waking up."

Emma and Sonny joined us a short time later. And while at first I thought Larry had made far too much food, Sonny proved just how much he could take down at breakfast. The sasquatch ended up with a little bit of syrup in his fur, which he frowned at before trying to scrape it out.

Larry tossed a few strips of bacon to Brain before she trotted off into the compound. It wasn't long before Fang appeared at the door, pleading eyes looking up at Sonny. But the horns of the Ozark howler couldn't fit through the kitchen door.

Sonny lobbed him a pancake and Fang followed Brain into the shadows.

"Where's Pinky?" I asked, the coffee finally starting to work its magic.

"He's around. Probably back with Old Willie still. Pinky has taken a liking to Willie's regular diet. But Brain? She is still all about the human food."

A high-pitched rapid staccato filled the room and echoed through the compound. Larry frowned and turned to the small bank of black and white monitors on the far end of the kitchen counter.

"What is it?" Sonny asked.

"Perimeter alarm." Larry leaned closer to the monitors. "Shit."

The change in Larry's tone sent a lance of ice down my spine. I hopped up, the old wooden chair screeching across the concrete floor. The monitors were dated, but it was easy enough to see what was on them.

At a glance I could make out four different groups of soldiers. They were spread across two of the monitor screens, but I couldn't tell where either was located.

"Where is that?" Emma asked, voicing the question I hadn't.

"Down by the river." Larry tapped on the upper left monitor. "And this other group, they're near the front of the orchard, not quite to the sign."

"Coming from two different directions," Sonny said.

I shook my head. "They'll come from more than that. We're not seeing everyone that's here." I banged my fist on the counter. "We were supposed to have another day."

"We need to leave," Sonny said. "We have rescued a great many of the cryptids, but I'm afraid there's nothing we can do for the others."

Larry looked back at the sasquatch. "Sonny, I'm not leaving them here. That's like asking me to abandon my family. I won't do it."

"Fuck," I snapped. "Larry, after what Momo did to those DEMON troops, they're not going to come in here like pacifists. They're going to shoot first and not really worry about what happens later."

Emma nodded. "Mason's right, we need to leave."

"I don't believe you." Larry put his hand on my shoulder. "These animals mean almost as much to you as they do to me. Are you going to leave Pinky and Brain here to die? To be used up in what-ever experiments these monsters want to do to them? I don't think so."

"They aren't monsters," Sonny said. "They're people. Soldiers given orders by someone who is our true enemy."

My phone buzzed in my pocket. I looked down at the screen and there was just one long text. It was my name over and over again from Himari. I called her and put it on speaker.

"You're surrounded, Mason. Larry's perimeter alarm is going off."

"I am aware, Himari."

"Then you need to go. Those mercenaries aren't going to want to do nice things to you."

I exchanged a glance with Emma and frowned. "Mercenaries?"

"Yes," Himari said, drawing the word out like I was an idiot. "Can't you see the black skulls on their vests? Those assholes are from Viper."

I almost snarled at the word. Viper was made up of the worst kind of people. Hunters who had grown bored with killing rare game for trophies and moved on to the rarest of creatures. They started hiring out as mercenaries for a thrill in their spare time. The few that I'd met over the years were remorseless sons of bitches with a love for killing people as much as cryptids.

DEMON had hired cryptid hunters. If we left now, everything at that orchard was going to die. DEMON might've thought they could control Viper, used them to secure whatever cryptids Larry still had at the orchard, but they didn't understand. Or at least I truly hoped they didn't understand what they'd done.

"Were those agents at Momo's Viper?" Emma asked.

I shrugged. "Fucking hell I hope so. Emma, I'm staying with Larry. Run. It would be the smarter thing to do."

"Fuck you, Mason. Aren't you glad we brought the guns in now?"

Considering Emma's response I thought it best to keep my mouth shut and be thankful I wasn't the only one staying behind to help Larry. I looked back to the monitors. The mercenaries from Viper were showing up on three different views now, but some were obscured by rolling white wisps.

"What's with the fog?" I asked.

Larry shook his head. "I don't know. It's not the right temperature for that kind of fog. Strange times, Mason. Strange times."

Emma grabbed my arm and dragged me out of the kitchen and over to the corner where we had our gun cases. I pulled out my tranquilizer rifle and a couple extra cartridges. We had a box full of tranqs that should take down a human in a few minutes. It was risky, and it could still kill them, but at least they were mercenaries. The darts should do well enough against a human.

I replaced the cartridge on Emma's tranquilizer pistol and passed it back to her before doing the same with my rifle.

She took it from me and loaded it. "Take your Desert Eagle."

"Emma, no. I'm not killing people intentionally. No matter how shitty they are."

Her pistol snapped closed and she holstered it before sliding a concealed revolver over her belt. "Take it. Just in case."

I grimaced before pulling out the Desert Eagle. It was a reassuring weight, but it soured my stomach to think about using it on a person.

"Only in an emergency."

Larry walked by us in dark camouflage overalls as he slid two rounds into a double-barreled shotgun. They popped like a can of chips before the breach snapped closed. He had a pump action strapped across his back, and I didn't think I'd ever seen the man look so determined.

"It would be best to surprise them." Sonny crouched down next to the wampus, Legs. Legs rubbed his head on the sasquatch before retreating into the wide hall where Old Willie stayed.

"Oh, they'll be surprised." And before any of us could reply to Larry, he pressed the button on the wall, and the massive door that secured us in the compound slid open.

The pair of mercenaries standing outside the door didn't look nearly as shocked as I'd hoped. They trained their rifles on Larry, but before anything else could happen, Old Willie charged out of the compound.

I didn't think the gowrow was actually trying to kill anyone. He seemed like a rather gentle beast, but the mountain of scales and broad head gave the mercenaries pause.

I heard the pop of air beside me when Emma fired. I saw the mercenary flinch when he reached up to grab something stuck in his neck. And while it didn't put him down immediately, he fled for the cover of the trees.

Left alone in the presence of the gowrow, the second mercenary turned to run. I raised my rifle and fired another dart. It caught the mercenary in the back of his unprotected arm.

Old Willie charged forward, his broad head swinging back and forth on a long neck as he studied the mercenaries. It felt as though an hour had gone by, but it was likely only a minute before I heard the first body hit the ground.

Larry looked over at me. "How much tranquilizer did you give him? Might as well just shoot him in the head."

"He'll live. Probably."

Augusta, still bleary-eyed from just waking up, walked up beside me and tapped her cane on the floor. "Subtler ways to knock a man out, you know?"

"I will restrain them," Sonny said as he sprinted toward the woods where the mercenaries had appeared.

I looked at Emma. "What the hell are we doing?"

"This was your idea. I am quite sure this was your idea."

Larry hissed. "Keep quiet. They're going to come this way. We need to be gone when they do."

I slid my headset on and texted Himari. If she could see Larry's feed, she might be able to keep us out of the worst of the trouble.

Instead of answering, Himari called. "I'm watching. The two you took down are the only ones I see on that side of the hill."

"Where are the rest?" I whispered.

"Two more by your car. And another pair by something that looks like an oil barrel?"

"Larry. Where do you have something that looks like an oil barrel?"

"Doesn't *look* like an oil barrel. It is an oil barrel. Keep the oil pit squids out there sometimes. Far side of the orchard, near the back road."

"Okay. We have two other teams Himari can see." I told them what she'd seen, and Larry nodded, clearly having a better idea of distance then Emma and I.

"The barrels are almost a ten-minute walk. We're safe enough from whoever is there. Take the two by your truck."

Pinky and Brain streaked by, following in Old Willie's footsteps while Dolly stayed behind in the compound.

We passed Sonny and found that he had tied the two mercenaries to a tree, stripped them of their gear, and fashioned a gag out of a grapevine. It would have to do for now.

"Stay together," Sonny said. "You do not move quietly through these woods. But I do. I will circle around behind the others to distract them."

And with that the sasquatch was off, headed toward the road that curved by the river. The rest of us went straight up the hill that would take us into the heart of the orchard and to the path back to the truck.

10

Halfway up the hill Larry changed his mind. "We should circle around, come at them from the side."

He took the lead as he knew the area better than any of us. We made it down to the river without an issue, and perhaps better than our angle of approach was the fact our footsteps were quieter on the gravel than the dead leaves.

I squeezed the stock of my tranquilizer rifle when something howled in the distance. It took a moment to realize it wasn't wolves, but that Fang was prowling the orchard somewhere. I hoped the Ozark howler had enough sense to avoid the mercenaries, and perhaps he would if he stuck close to Sonny.

Something pale and silent like a bird flitted through the trees above us. It moved too fast to be a person, so I put the distraction out of my mind. I studied the forest shadows around us as if staring hard enough would reveal any threat.

"I see another pair by the oil barrel," Himari said.

I didn't answer her. We were close enough now that I worried any sound might tip off the mercenaries by our truck. Caution was never a bad idea, but as we started up the hill toward the truck, I realized I may have been overly cautious.

Old Willie's heavy footsteps shook the trees as he passed between them. And the two armored figures at our truck had trained their full attention on the approaching cryptid. I could just make out what they were saying to one another.

"No response from red team. Something's approaching. Something big."

The second mercenary raised a rifle I didn't recognize. One thing I knew for sure, it wasn't a tranquilizer gun. A drum-like clip extended from the bottom and it was wide enough to hold an extremely powerful round.

My hand inched towards the Desert Eagle holstered under my arm. I curled my hand into a fist and made for the tranquilizer rifle instead. I wasn't ready to do what I'd seen Momo do.

The cages and miscellaneous cases that had been in the back of the truck were strewn about the ground. Their contents had been thrown out, haphazardly piled about the gravel parking lot.

It was about then I realized I'd lost track of Augusta. The witch was nowhere to be seen, and I wondered if she'd followed Sonny. But that didn't make sense. She'd been with us. Maybe she'd been the smartest of us and decided to leave. I couldn't fault her for that.

Himari's voice whispered in my ear, like she was worried about the mercenaries hearing her. "Another truck near the back entrance. There's more of them, Mason."

A deep basso howl sounded in the woods past the mercenaries. For a moment, they were distracted on two fronts, and I had little doubt that sound had come from Sonny.

I tapped Emma on the arm and raised my rifle. It was a long shot for her with a handgun, but we weren't going to get a better opportunity to put these mercenaries down. She dialed up her tranquilizer gun. It was as high as we could go without losing accuracy.

I nodded to her and pointed to the right.

Emma shifted her aim and waited.

The thunder of the gowrow crashing through the orchard slowed as the beast's head cleared the edge of the trees, and the howl quieted in the woods beyond. The mercenaries hesitated when the long jaws opened and the gowrow roared. It was the most aggressive I'd ever seen Old Willie. Like he knew these people shouldn't be here, like he understood they were a threat.

"Now," I whispered.

Both of the tranquilizer guns puffed within a split second of each other. I caught the mercenary in the neck, but I wasn't sure if Emma hit her target. She reloaded, primed the shot, and fired again.

The second mercenary swatted at his face only to yelp when his fingers caught the dart and ripped it out.

"Woods, now," Larry hissed.

We dipped into the edge of the tree line and waited. I knew it wouldn't be long before the tranquilizer took effect, but I never guessed it would be too late. By the time the first mercenary stumbled, the second pulled the trigger on his rifle.

The rapid staccato of the fully automatic rifle soured the air around us. Old Willie roared as the gunfire took him in the underbelly. I had no idea how bad the old gowrow was hurt, but he spun, his tail leveling apple trees before it clipped one of the mercenaries and the gowrow charged back into the orchard.

From the edge of the woods I could just make out the mercenary slumped over at the front of the truck. He tried to stand up and then collapsed, his leg at a terrible angle. The second made his way over to the first when a scream sounded from the edge of the woods.

I watched in confusion as a form armored in black sailed through the air, arms flailing before he crashed into the mercenaries' van. Yet another member of Viper sprinted out from the edge of the woods as the shadow of a sasquatch chased him. He fired wildly behind him, and Sonny broke off his pursuit, instead angling back into the orchard.

"Move and you're dead."

The rack of a pump action shotgun punctuated the threat. I thought about grabbing the Desert Eagle holstered under my arm. But I couldn't see where the barrel of the shotgun was aimed. If it was already on me, I'd be dead before I could draw my gun.

"Hands behind your back. Walk over to the truck. This would've been easier if you would have surrendered."

"You didn't so much as give us a chance to surrender," Larry said.

"Don't bullshit me, you piece of shit. We've already been briefed about you. Three strikes, old man."

Three strikes? What the hell was he talking about? I exchanged a glance with Larry as we slowly stood up and made our way toward the truck. He shook his head, as if answering the question I hadn't asked.

If someone had told Viper Larry was a threat, and had been warned multiple times, they were putting far more effort into the seizure of the orchard than I would've thought. I was worried that whoever the newcomer at DEMON was may be far more formidable than I'd hoped.

"Mason…" Himari said, panic plain in her voice. "Mason, there are two behind you. The one that did a Superman into the clearing is unconscious, or dead, and so are the two you tranqed."

A third was checking the others on the ground. A rough hand shoved me into the truck before spinning me around. The man wore a ballistic mask, and I couldn't make anything out in the early morning light.

He kicked Larry's legs out from under him and the caretaker hit the ground with a thump and a grunt.

"Hey!" Emma snapped.

The butt of the gun snapped forward so fast I barely had time to flinch. It caught Emma in the side of the head, and she crumpled on top of Larry. She cursed as she slowly sat up, blood running from her temple.

I sat down next to her waiting for them to tie us up, or at least restrain us. But all the man did was take the guns we had holstered on our person and toss them away.

"You should've left the guns," the third conscious mercenary said, a deep female voice. "You're going to need the blood spatter to make it look like a righteous kill."

"Fuck them." The first mercenary raised the shotgun and pointed it at my head. "How many more of those fucking things are here? I'm ready to napalm the whole fucking place."

"Go fuck yourself," Larry spat.

"Let's see if you're ready to talk after I splatter your friends all over you." The mercenary's finger moved from outside the trigger guard to settle onto the trigger itself.

I turned away from the gun. I had no desire to see the end coming. I'd always thought I'd get trampled by a cryptid when I got old and slow. Not get gunned down by a goddamned mercenary.

Emma squeezed me tight, leaned her bloody forehead against mine, and that's when I heard the squeak.

"What's this crazy bitch doing?" The female mercenary asked.

I cracked my eyes open and followed her gaze. Standing in the entrance to Larry's Orchard Extravaganza was Augusta. She leaned over a heavy wire cage, removing the reinforced latches.

"Get the hell out of here, lady. Take your rabbit somewhere else."

I stiffened when I realized fully what she was doing. Augusta opened the cage of the jackalope, and she removed the pool noodles from its horns.

"What the fuck?" The mercenary spat. "What the fuck is that?"

Augusta whispered something to the cryptid, and I watched in horror as the jackalope's jaws unhinged and it released a wail of a chittering cry.

The speed of the jackalope was almost impossible to follow. One moment it had been in the cage and Augusta's hands. And in the next, its antlers had pierced the breastplate of the mercenary's armor, and instead of words the man vomited blood.

"Holy fuck!" Emma shouted before tackling me as the shotgun went off. She pulled on my arm until Larry and I finally climbed to our feet and we sprinted toward the woods, scooping up our discarded guns. Another of the mercenaries tried to shoot the jacka-lope, but only managed to riddle their dying ally with more holes.

A glance back showed me the vicious spiral of the jackalope as it sank its fangs into another mercenary's neck and used the momentum to scythe through his spine with those deadly horns. As the man's head toppled to the ground, I began to understand that the pool noodles hadn't done jack shit to restrain the jackalope.

We ran.

11

B ack inside the orchard it wasn't hard to see which way Old Willie had gone. Even when the apple trees weren't broken over, it was easy enough to see the stains on the leaves. Dark crimson formed a trail that had me worried for the old gowrow.

"We need to get off this path." Larry slowed and studied the orchard around us. "This way."

We broke back toward the river. The woods had started to come alive again since the gunfire died down. It wasn't long before I saw zigmals zipping through the branches above us. What I hadn't expected was the two round gowrows herding them along the ground.

Pinky and Brain were both there, chasing the bouncing creatures like well-trained sheepdogs.

"What are they doing?" Emma asked as she wiped at the drying blood on her forehead.

"Trying to help," Larry said. "I've seen them do this more than once. Anytime there's a threat to the orchard, they gather up the smaller cryptids. They'll take them back to the compound, or further down the river."

For a brief second, I caught some relief from the panic of running from mercenaries. I wondered why the gowrows felt protective toward other cryptids. Wondered how they'd learned to herd creatures that were so much faster and more agile than them.

"Jackalope's still loose."

My gaze snapped to the left where I found Augusta moving like someone a fraction of her age. "You're looking spritely."

"It's a kind of magic. I can't keep this up forever. But if I need to run, I can do so well enough. More than I can say for those mercenaries back there."

Larry nodded. "Don't let down your guard yet. We're headed back to the oil reserves. Another squad of those bastards is back there."

I tapped on my headset. "Himari, can you still see them? We're headed toward the oil barrel now."

Her voice sounded shaky, but she answered soon enough. "I can see three of them. The fourth one's out of frame, but they have to be there somewhere. Be careful, Mason. That was too close. And ... I don't think I want a jackalope as a pet."

I smiled despite our situation and stayed close to Larry. "Another four mercenaries close to the oil barrel."

Larry tightened his grip on his shotgun. "Tranquilizers might not be enough, Mason. We might have to kill them."

"Settle down," Augusta said. "Sonny is still out in the woods with Fang. Neither one of you is made for killing people. Leave that to the adults."

I blinked at the old witch. I supposed it wasn't a huge stretch. She *had* summoned the rawhead to murder her neighbor. And I had no idea how old Augusta really was. If she'd lived long enough, she may have seen Missouri when it was still a frontier. I'd heard more than one rumor that witches had unnaturally long lives.

"We should've taken the truck and left," Emma said. "Mason, we are outgunned. In every sense of the word."

"We have Himari. Larry knows the orchard better than anybody. It gives us a slight edge."

Rapid gunfire sounded in the distance. The echo made it hard to pinpoint, as fast as it had come, it died away.

"I'd rather have a bigger gun," Emma muttered.

We were close enough to the river to hear it washing against the shore. It wasn't a loud sound, but I feared it would be enough to hide anyone closing on us from behind. Of course, by that same token, it would hide our own progress from whatever waited ahead.

"We take the mercenaries out of commission," Larry said. "Get the cryptids on the trailer, and drag it out of here."

It was a simple enough plan, but I was afraid it was too simple. The mercenaries had already gotten the better of us, and if Augusta hadn't released a homicidal jackalope, we might not be walking away.

I looked at the old witch. "Thanks for that, back there."

"Next time use your gun. If someone's about to kill you, you kill them. Even someone opposed to killing can make their peace with that."

"And you?"

She bared her teeth. "I'm not so opposed to killing when killing's needed."

"Suppose not," Larry said, glancing back at Augusta. "I'm a bit worried what that jackalope is going to get up to."

Augusta shook her head. "He'll be back to normal soon enough."

"What did you do to that thing?"

Augusta held her finger up to her lips in the shushing motion, but I didn't miss the sly smile she gave Larry.

Larry shook his head and continued on. I was quite certain we'd walked far enough to pass the entrance to the compound. Himari confirmed as much when I asked her, and that meant it wouldn't be long before we reached the oil barrels.

Something moved in the woods uphill from us, off to our left. Larry heard it first and froze, holding his hand out to stop us. We all watched the tree line, guns at the ready, until the lumbering furry shadow raised a hand in greeting, a horned shadow at his side.

I blew out a breath. "Sonny. Hell, man."

"You're too loud in the woods. And humans wonder why they do not find sasquatches. It is because you are easy to avoid."

"We can talk about our lack of stealth some other time. There are more pressing matters."

Sonny inclined his head and gestured for Larry to continue. We followed him like a loyal pack, slowing when he signaled and hurrying when his pace increased. It wasn't long before we smelled the fire. Wasn't long before the glow shone through the woods.

I cursed when we reached the small pond of oil, burning as it was.

"No," Larry hissed, hurrying out into the field.

"Larry, wait." I called to him as loud as I dared, knowing that even though we didn't see the mercenaries in our direct line of sight, they had to be nearby. He grabbed a fire extinguisher from the nearby shed, a red monster of a thing, dousing the fire as fast as he could.

He dropped the extinguisher as soon as the flames were out and scooped up the lid to the oil barrel to fish through the little pool. I could see the sigh of relief as he turned to us. "Squids are okay."

The sharp crack of gunfire echoed around the field. I didn't see the shooter. I only saw the savage grin of the man walking out from behind the shed. Saw the explosion of red mist from Larry's back as two rounds took him in the chest and he collapsed.

I dove for Emma as more gunfire sounded, feeling something like a bee sting in my right arm before pain and fire blossomed when we hit the ground. We both scrambled into the woods, taking shelter behind two massive trees.

Gunfire splintered the trunk around us. Whatever they were shooting was large caliber, and at the rate they were going they could cut through the damn tree with enough patience. And that was only if they decided not to take a few steps to the side and end us.

"Well, now I wish I would've brought a damn rawhead," Augusta muttered as she raced into the woods behind us.

Sonny's claws dug into the bark of a wide tree and he scurried up into the canopy faster than I would've thought possible. He may have been fast, and strong as hell, but he was no match for the hail of bullets coming our way.

I closed my eyes and took a deep breath as I drew the Desert Eagle. This wasn't what I was made for. Encounters with cryptids could be dangerous, but they didn't shoot at you, didn't shoot at your friends. How was I even supposed to fire back? Soon as I stuck my head out to get line of sight I'd be dead.

We stayed there, frozen as splinters of wood exploded around us and Emma curled up into a tighter ball to hide herself behind the tree as best she could. Between one step and the next, Augusta vanished. It was as though she had stepped into a shadow itself, and then it was just me and Emma.

The earth shook.

I didn't understand the roar I was hearing. I'd never heard anything like it. Branches and logs snapped and cracked as trees fell, and at the edge of the clearing, beneath his earthquake-like steps, appeared Old Willie.

The gowrow must have followed us back through the orchard all the way to the other side of the reserve. But he hadn't gotten there unscathed. My chest ached when I saw the round wounds in Old Willie's belly. Trails of blood leaked down the gowrow.

The distant shots we'd heard earlier ... I guess I knew what they were for now. But something was different about the gowrow. His eyes glowed, ragged breaths expanding and contracting like a hot air balloon inflating in seconds, and blood frothed at the corners of his mouth.

A shadow above us caught my eye. At first I thought it was Sonny moving through the canopy. But the fur was too pale, the head too broad. When I finally got a clear view of it I had no words.

Above us moved something that could not be. Standing on a branch that could not have supported its weight, stood a pale white deer crowned by massive antlers. It lowered its head, and as it breathed, a fine blue mist spread throughout the woods around us.

But as that mist reached Willie, the light in his eyes grew wilder, fiery, and when the gowrow unhinged its jaws, a maelstrom of flame roared over the two mercenaries on the far side of the field. There were no screams, there were no exclamations of shock or surprise. There was only fire and death in that place.

The other pair of mercenaries screamed at the far edge of the

372

clearing when they saw what happened. But it was the last mistake they ever made. Old Willie pivoted towards them and another burst of flame cut them down in an instant.

The fires retreated, and the gowrow stumbled forward, crashing to the earth as his last breaths escaped him. And there, beside Larry, the old beast fell still.

"Stay back!" Augusta shouted as she broke through the tree line on the other side of the clearing. I didn't understand how she'd gotten there.

I hadn't even realized I was crawling toward Larry. Hadn't realized Emma was right beside me, tears staining her cheeks. Two more mercenaries crossed into the field with guns raised as the snawfus descended through the branches, flowering vines twisting through its antlers as though they were snakes.

Time slowed around me and I tried to understand what I was seeing as the snawfus walked between Old Willie and Larry, the mists condensing around the gowrow until they trailed over to Larry. And as I watched, Old Willie decayed until he was no more than a skeleton wrapped in scales. But pale lightning crackled through the mist around Larry and the old man bolted upright gasping for breath, grasping at the wounds that should have killed him. *Had* killed him.

The mercenaries pulled their triggers as they took aim at the snawfus. But I didn't miss the rust devouring their rifles as the metal crumbled in their hands. Didn't miss the mushrooms springing up behind the snawfus as it walked quietly past the mercenaries. And I vomited as the mercenaries decayed while they were still alive, screaming as their flesh turned green and black and ruptured as it dried out. Their armor frayed as the earth churned, swallowing them beneath a ring of pale mushrooms.

The snawfus brushed a tree, and it withered to the ground, decay and rot overwhelming it as fast as new saplings rose to take its place. By the time the earth settled around us once more, littered with the corpses of men and cryptids alike, the snawfus was gone.

12

"Larry," I said, pleading with the man. "Larry, please take it easy."

He didn't respond at first. Instead he just loaded up another crate onto the trailer before heading back for yet another.

I cursed under my breath and grabbed a couple tubs of supplies and followed him to the trailer. This time Legs came with us. The wampus stayed close to Larry, and after the caretaker had set down the last crate, he scratched the wampus under his chin.

Emma stood toward the back rearranging the cages and tubs so she could secure them with the few ratchet straps we had.

"The boy is only worried about you," Augusta said, tapping her cane on the side of the trailer.

Larry stretched his back and closed his eyes before blowing out a breath. He gestured to the bloody holes in his shirt and the unmarred skin beneath it. "I got shot today. I should've been dead. I think I was dead."

Augusta shook her head. "Dying, yes. But not so dead, I don't think. A snawfus don't help the dead."

I didn't miss the shiver that ran down Larry's spine. "Look, we

374

don't know if Viper has more people here. Let's just get the truck loaded and get the hell out of here."

Pinky and Brain circled around Larry, sending up a high-pitched whine that seemed to cut the old man to the bone. I didn't miss his trembling lip as he crouched down and scratched the two young gowrows.

It didn't take long for me to realize the gowrows were mourning Old Willie just as much as Larry was.

He finally looked up at the witch, his eyes red. "And goddamnit, Augusta, I'd known Old Willie longer than most of my family. It leaves a hole like I can't describe."

Augusta gave him a sad smile. "I know. You just take care of the rest of your animals now. Things get better in time. Or at least less sharp."

I nodded to Larry. "Sonny is bringing Dolly up. Once we load her into the trailer we should be good to go."

"At least something's gone right today. I'll get the trailer down to the road before we load the gowrow in. I think it'll take her weight, but that won't much matter if it's sunk in the mud as soon as she steps in."

"Is there anything else you need out of the compound?" I asked.

Larry shook his head. "I've got a little box of personal stuff already loaded. That's good enough for now."

He didn't say anything more as he headed to the cab. I watched him pull forward and reverse to break the mud's hold on the tires. It wasn't looking too good until everything lurched and Emma squawked along with Pinky and Brain as she fell over next to the crates.

I smiled and turned back to the compound, heading inside to see how Sonny was doing. It was a long hallway that led from this side of the compound back to the huge door in the hillside.

Flickering fluorescent lights added to the slightly creepy corridor. It reminded me of an abandoned school I'd once explored with Dylan. Of course, that place hadn't had working lights, and the flickering had come from the dying batteries of our flashlights. It was a good memory, and bittersweet though it may have been, it was nice to hold onto.

I crossed out of the hall close to the kitchen. Sonny had the surviving members of Viper tied up there. They looked normal enough, but I didn't much like murderers for hire. We'd call the authorities once we were on the road.

Himari was already running photos we'd taken of Viper's people. We had video from Larry's surveillance system. Once we sent this to the Church and Chuck at the CCD, we'd know who our allies were soon enough. This wasn't the kind of evidence an organization could just write off.

I stopped at the front of the massive hall where Dolly and Old Willie had tended to shelter. "How's it going?"

I couldn't see Sonny, but I heard the sasquatch grunt. "After a great deal of bribery, I think she's finally moving."

Slowly the sasquatch came into the light, trailed by a looming shadow. Dolly wasn't exactly in a hurry to follow, but the sack of apples thrown over Sonny's back seemed to be providing some motivation.

I smiled at the pair and led them outside. We'd have to take the long way around, but that would give Larry enough time to reposition the trailer.

Dolly didn't shake the ground like Old Willie had. She bumped a tree on occasion, and sent the branches shivering, but other than that the gowrow was unnervingly silent. The idea that such a large beast could be so quiet was an unsettling thought. Dolly may have been a gentle giant, but other predators in the world weren't.

Sonny remained silent for a time until we passed the curve of the river and started over the hill that would take us to the outer road. "I only know of one sasquatch who claims to have met a snawfus. Mason, I still do not understand what I saw."

I tilted my head to the side. "I hear you. I think if we hadn't met Augusta in Momo's town, my brain might've broken seeing what we saw today."

"That is a creature of old magic. I do not believe it is good, or evil, it simply is."

"It saved Larry. It certainly can't be all bad."

"But it could have saved Old Willie. Could have spared the mercenaries, or killed us all. Frederick has told me stories of the snawfus. It has long been regarded as a force of nature more than a conscious entity. But it made choices today, Mason. And I do not know why."

"I doubt we'll ever know. The only human I've ever met who claimed to have seen the snawfus probably should have been in an institution."

My headset crackled. "That makes two of you."

I blew out a laugh. "Thanks, Himari."

"I have everything packaged up. You tell me when I should send it."

We made it over the hill and passed the clearing with the remains of Old Willie and the mercenaries. It felt like something I shouldn't have seen, like some dark secret in the world that wasn't meant for mankind.

I shook my head as we passed out of the field and turned my attention back to the conversation with Himari. "As soon as we have Dolly on the trailer, fire it off. And Himari?"

"Yeah?"

"Be sure Bubba gets a copy too."

"Consider it done. I'll copy Skeeter too."

It wasn't long before we passed the loading area for the trailer, deep ruts in the mud showing where Larry had more than one instance of trouble moving the truck. But we made it to the gravel, Dolly's heavy footfalls sinking into the rock and mud. And finally around another turn, the open trailer waited.

"About time," Emma said. "I was about to start worrying."

"The mercenaries are all tied up in the kitchen. Himari's got the package ready to go. We have Dolly. Things are about as good as they could be, considering."

"Considering we aren't dead?" Emma scoffed. "Yeah, you could say that."

Augusta grinned up at Emma before making her way around to

the truck's cab. Sonny led the gowrow to the back of the trailer. I was worried the ramp wouldn't hold her weight, or she'd be too wide for the truck, but Dolly trundled up the incline without an issue. The shocks protested, but they were made to withstand a full cattle car. Dolly ducked and fit inside well enough.

"She hardly has any space," Sonny said.

"Not too long a drive," Larry called back from the cab.

Sonny nodded. "I'll stay in the back. Just to be sure she doesn't panic." He called out to a horned shadow at the edge of the trees. Fang trotted off away from the orchard. "He'll be home soon enough. They do like to wander."

Emma pointed toward the front of the trailer. "If you need it, tranquilizers are in the top gray crate."

We locked Sonny in the back and then followed Augusta to the cab. Emma and I climbed into the back seat while the old witch took the front.

Larry eyed her. "Coming to Momo's with us?"

"Mmhmm. I'd rather like to see a family of Momos. Just be the icing on this fucked up day."

Larry grinned at Augusta and the truck jumped as he put it in gear.

I tapped my headset. "Himari. Send the package."

13

I listened to Himari hum about thirteen different spy movie theme songs as she started distributing the recordings, videos, and our assessment of what had happened. Once they were in Chuck's hands, I knew he'd get them to people who wouldn't try to sweep this under the rug. I half expected Father Noah to deny what had happened, as my trust in that man had eroded quite a bit of late.

It wasn't a terribly long drive to Momo's town, but it took some extra time as Larry stayed at the minimum speed limit. The highways weren't large, and were somewhat curvy in rural Missouri, and getting into trouble with the trailer out here would be a disaster.

Augusta had been quiet most of the trip. But there was one thing I wanted her opinion on. I leaned forward and tapped her on the arm. She glanced back and raised an eyebrow.

"What do you know about the snawfus?"

Augusta pursed her lips and gave me a small smile before turning her attention back to the road. "You've come a long way for not believing in magic when I first met you. Come a long way in a short time."

"Yeah, well, it's hard to deny some things when it's right in front of your face."

"The snawfus. It's an animal. A cryptid as you like to call them. But something you need to understand is that some of those cryptids are older than our collective memory. The witch who trained me had many stories."

I exchanged a glance with Emma. "But it's obviously not like any other cryptid we've encountered."

"Oh, of that I have no doubt. There are tales in many cultures of nature given form, and I believe that's what the snawfus is. A god in its own right, with the powers of life and death over its domain. But how it decides to use those powers?" Augusta shrugged.

"What it did. What we saw it do."

Larry rubbed at the back of his neck. "Didn't need to see it. Felt it. And I don't have the words for it."

I glanced down and looked back up at Augusta. "Magic. That's my word for it."

"You oversimplify. The creature like the snawfus is beyond us. It is not our place to know it, only see it as it wills. And count our lucky stars it didn't turn us into mulch."

"Now that's the voice of reason," Emma said. "We're alive. Let's just be happy for that."

And I *was* happy for that. But curiosity and cats and all that. Just being happy to be alive hadn't led me to chase Momo for years. Hadn't sent me after some of the most dangerous cryptids I could find. A want for knowledge and understanding did that. And that was a part of me I didn't think would ever change.

Larry stared up at the overgrown road that ran through the woods. Several parts of the road, more like trail, had branches encroaching on it. Not to mention deep ruts that could trap the trailer. "It's going to take a miracle to get through that."

Something banged around outside the truck and metal crashed down to the ground. Sonny appeared at the side of the cab. "Let me unload Dolly. That will free up half your weight."

Larry nodded and waited for the giant gowrow to back her way off the trailer. Once done, Sonny made his way back to the broken-up road in the woods. He picked up broken branches and piled them into the deeper ruts while we waited.

I frowned at Emma. "I feel like that sasquatch just outsmarted all of us."

"You should be used to that at this point," she said with a grin.

Dolly wandered around the edge of the road, sniffing at the vegetation before sampling some, spitting bits of it back out. Hopefully she'd find something she liked in the old town. The last thing we needed was for the gowrow to go wandering.

Sonny made his way back down the path. "I think that's about as good as you're gonna get."

Larry nodded. "Then it'll have to do. We ain't getting any younger."

"You can see where the jimplicutes snapped off some of the larger branches when we were running for our lives." I gestured to the tree line.

"And your point is?" Emma asked.

"I just wanted to point out how we were helping."

Larry glanced back at us. "You aren't helping."

Augusta snickered from the front seat, but she didn't say anything.

"Hold on." Larry put the truck in gear and Sonny stepped to the side. The engine roared, the idle rumble of the diesel lost to the sudden burst of power. The logs held in the first rut, but if I hadn't had my seatbelt on I would've been cracking my head on the roof. It was probably good Sonny wasn't sitting unrestrained in the trailer.

"Holy shit!" Emma squawked as she tried to hold onto the edge of the seat.

Larry didn't slow down as a tire spun through mud and caught on more logs and gravel before surging up onto the asphalt above. "Come on. Come on!"

My biggest concern was that the trailer would break off, and we'd end up having to carry all of those crates across the town by hand. Our inertia slowed, the trailer catching on trees and debris behind us before it finally bounced up onto the asphalt and we made our way onto the cobblestones beyond.

Larry eased up on his white knuckle grasp of the steering wheel. He looked into the mirror and I followed his gaze. Waddling up behind us was Dolly, flanked by Sonny. The gowrow seemed more curious than anything, sniffing at the ground and wandering over to the abandoned buildings.

Sonny hopped onto the running board and grabbed the edge of the window when Larry rolled it down. "Head straight down the road. We can park outside the old garage and see where Momo wants you from there."

Larry took it slow, the truck and trailer bouncing and squeaking down the road past the wrecked cars the jimplicutes had left behind. I took a deep breath as we turned the corner and the trailer came to a stop in front of the two-story bays of the repair shop.

"That was an adventure," Augusta said. "Now, let's find Momo, figure out what he's going to do with you all, and then get some food."

"Smartest thing I've heard all day," Emma said, following Augusta out the passenger door.

I slid up into the front seat and followed them out, stretching and looking around the town. If I didn't know about the underground lair here, I would've thought the place was still entirely abandoned.

Larry patted the hood of the truck. "So, you're telling me Momo is living in the caves under this place now?"

I nodded. "It gives your compound under the orchard a run for its money. A bit less reinforcement, but I think you'll be impressed."

Dolly wandered by, sniffing at the buildings, the old debris, and some of the broken windows. The gowrow didn't seem impressed, and continued on until she reached the other side of the woods.

"Will she be okay out here?" Emma asked.

"Dolly?" Larry looked toward the gowrow. "Oh sure, she was always the calm one. I don't think I've ever seen her butting heads with another cryptid."

Himari whispered in my ear. "What about the jimplicutes? Do gowrows and jimplicutes get along, Mason?"

Emma flashed me a grin, having heard the same commentary from Himari.

I shook my head. "I have no clue, Himari. I guess we'll find out soon enough."

"Find out what?" Larry asked.

"Himari was just asking if jimplicutes and gowrows get along."

Larry pursed his lips. "That's two kinds of cryptids like to avoid other cryptids. I don't think they'll have an issue."

"Well," Augusta said. "I suppose if they do, we can whip them up like gator bites."

I pointed at Augusta, started to say something, and then thought better of it. Sometimes I couldn't tell if the old witch was joking or not. But I suspected there was a bit of truth behind her jest.

"Let's find Momo." I led the way inside the garage, trailing back to the stairwell that took us down to the entrance to the caves. Augusta muttered something about not liking the dingy old garage, but no one said anything outside of that. We hadn't exactly shared a great experience the last time we all set foot in the garage together.

We crossed over from the smooth concrete beneath the bays to the rock of the cavern supported by the skeleton of an ancient cryptid. Larry whistled as we passed underneath it and started down the staircase.

"Hello?" I shouted as we continued down.

Words echoed back to me. "Join me at the table."

14

I t wasn't long before we reached the cave level where we'd met
with Momo the first time. He was already seated at the table. A
much smaller shadow, one that I wondered might be a child of
Momo's, peered out at us before vanishing through a small crawl
space.

"Surely you did not all need to come here?" Momo said, his voice
dripping with what I would've called disgust in a human. "Take a seat."

"I'll bother you as little as I can," Larry said as we sat down around
the table. "I appreciate you letting me bring the cryptids here."

"There are few humans I tolerate. But you are known to me, caretaker. Perhaps if more cared about the creatures they didn't understand, I may find humanity less trying."

Larry hesitated, perhaps wondering what the right thing to say
was, but I agreed with the tack that he took. "I only need to know
where you would like me to store the cages and feed. There's a good
amount in the truck, so we'll need a bit of space."

"The garage above will be fine. There's a secondary cave entrance
to the south the gowrows can use. The jimplicutes avoid the garage.
Likely due to our…unfortunate introduction."

Larry nodded. "Thank you. I do appreciate it." He hesitated and

MASON DIXON, MONSTER HUNTER

glanced at me before returning his attention to Momo. "If you ever need a vet for any of the cryptids here, I know a guy."

Momo tilted his head. "The man who reset the jimplicute's jaw?"

"The same."

"I will bear that in mind. You, and only you, are welcome to stay in one of the buildings above. It will likely need renovation, but the sewers and pipes are still intact. My family prefers modern conveniences like running water. Unnecessary in my opinion. A cold river is just as good."

Emma shivered. "Hell no it's not."

A deep voice spoke from the shadows. "You see? Even the humans have more sense than you."

Momo sank into his chair a fraction of an inch, and I suspected very much that was an argument he'd had with his family many times.

Sonny grinned at Emma. "I'll side with Momo in that argument. A cool spring over a face full of chemicals."

Augusta harrumphed. "I prefer to bathe in the blood of my enemies."

I blinked at the old witch. The delivery was so deadpan, it even gave Momo pause.

"Chuck's calling," Himari said, her voice metallic and loud and somewhat unexpected in that cave.

"Patch him in." I put the phone on speaker and set it closer to the center of the table before leaning over it. "Hey Chuck, it's Mason. I've got everyone here. Including Momo."

"Momo?" Chuck said. "Oh wow, that's incredible. Can he hear me? I've always been a big fan. My dad used to read me old folktales. Did you ever go looking for him? I mean, he stays better hidden than the sasquatches. It's incredible!"

Momo slowly raised his red gaze to me as Chuck rambled. "Is he always like this?"

I shrugged.

"Sorry." Chuck sounded a bit more focused after the interruption. "I get really excited about meeting new people. Not that I would call you people. But, um, never mind. I have an idea that you all need to hear."

Momo laid his hands out on the table and leaned back into his chair. "I am not in need of ideas. Should more of these mercenaries arrive, they will not leave alive. It is a plan that should work well enough."

There was a cold calculation in Momo's voice. It was an odd thing to hear so clearly coming from something that wasn't human.

"I get that," Chuck said. "Survival of the fittest. I bet that's something you can relate to. But here, think about this. The orchard was rezoned due to issues with the sasquatches. But you're outside of their agreement. You're not a sasquatch. Which means their zoning doesn't affect you."

"I fail to see how that is useful."

I nodded. "I'm with Momo on that. What's your point, Chuck?"

"What's the next largest population of cryptids in the area? It's wampuses. Ozark howlers are a close third, but I say we stick as large as we can. I say we try to get the orchard rezoned as a wampus sanctuary. It will have nothing to do with the sasquatches, and DEMON won't be able to leverage any agreements with them into ousting Larry. Because who better to look over a wampus sanctuary than Larry?"

Larry crossed his arms. "They'll see what we're trying to do if you do that. They might be assholes, but they ain't fools."

"In a manner of speaking," Chuck said. "But I'm talking about using their own red tape against them here. They won't be able to say no to this, without invalidating a dozen other arrangements that benefit them directly. Trust me. It won't be instant, you're going to have to stay away from the orchard for a time. But I think we can get you home, Larry."

The old caretaker bowed his head. "I can be patient. But I don't know how long Momo will want us around."

The old cryptid narrowed his eyes. "Stay out of our caves, outside of your gowrows. Take no more than what we offer, and I will have no quarrel with you. My offer to you to live in the city above will stand."

Chuck gasped. "You get to live there? In that town with the jimpli-cutes? And Momo? Goddamn, Larry, you have all the luck."

Larry leaned forward over the phone, propping himself up on his elbows. "Chuck, I got shot today. By a mercenary. I should've been dead, but for some snawfus laying his magic on me."

"All the luck."

Larry rolled his eyes in disgust and flopped back into his chair. "Never mind, Chuck. Never you mind."

"Chuck?" Himari's voice broke into the call. "Can you hear me?"

"I can."

"Sorry to join the call like that uninvited. Mason doesn't like to secure his phone. Anyway, can you file that action now? Get it into the system?"

"I can, but it's going to take months to get through the bureaucracy."

Himari laughed, and I could almost see her smile in my head. "That's what I'm here for. You get it into the system, and I'll move it *through* the system. Father Noah might have sold Larry out, but I have something better in mind."

"Noah?" I asked. "What are you going to do, Himari?"

"Well, I'm quite sure the reason DEMON was able to rezone the orchard with the Church's blessing was to free it up for this benevo-lent gesture of turning it into a wampus sanctuary. Now I just have to make their databases match that fact."

Chuck whistled over the phone. "Oh, you could get him into some shit over that."

"Chuck, Himari, get on it," I said. "It's a good idea. And you could get Larry back home. And maybe DEMON out of the damn orchard for now."

"But it was not DEMON who set foot in the orchard," Momo said. "Mercenaries can be denied. It is easy enough to obscure the truth."

"Not from me," Himari said, and I didn't miss the edge of mischief in her voice.

15

T he occasional flash of red eyes in the shadows was hard to miss as we worked to unload the truck. However good Momo was at keeping his family hidden, it was clear to me now that the children of his kind were just as curious as humans.

Sonny and Augusta dragged a mesh net over each of the bays. They didn't have any good anchor points, but the sasquatch sank steel hooks into the concrete with the help of a sledgehammer.

Larry looked over their handiwork as he set another crate in the corner. "Reckon that should hold. Course I might trip over those eye loops just as much as fall down the hole, but I suppose that's better."

"You think?" Emma asked. "Unless you have a snawfus around here to heal your broken neck. I'm guessing it's a lot better."

Larry looked at Emma wide-eyed.

"Sorry about that," I said. "She's a bit short on coffee right now."

Emma grumbled something else I couldn't quite make out, but I definitely caught the gist of it.

"Hell girl, you should've said something." Augusta closed her eyes and reached behind her head. I didn't understand exactly what was happening, but it almost looked like her hand had vanished behind a curtain. The air around her shimmered and resolved into a silver thermos. "I always have one in my cache."

Emma gestured uselessly at Augusta. "Are you serious? You just pull the thermos of coffee out of thin air?"

"No. I brewed it yesterday. It might be a little cool now, but I've always found caffeine more important than anything else."

"You're the best. You're so much better than Mason. I can't even explain to you how much better than Mason you are. You ever need a camera woman to make a show about magic, I'm your girl."

Sonny chuckled and moved to the last bay where he started hammering in another anchor.

Augusta patted Emma's shoulder. "If you're ever out in my neck of the woods again, feel free to drop by my cabin. Do you know your family line? Maybe we'll find a witch somewhere in your history."

"I don't know about a witch, but I have plenty of bitches in my family."

Larry hung his head and gave one short laugh. "I haven't had enough to drink to deal with this day. Sonny, when this is over, I'm going to need some of that sasquatch brew."

"You are not far from our village here. I am sure Frederick would welcome you. You are well known to the sasquatches, especially for what you've done for the cryptids. And perhaps now, when they hear you were blessed by the snawfus, it will be even more so."

I grabbed a cage with a large kingdoodle. The massive lizard could have been mistaken for a salamander if it wasn't for the sheer size. The doodle had a bandage around her tail. Something had managed to bite it before it escaped and lucked into Larry's protection.

It took another two hours rearranging the cages before Larry was happy with the garage. As exhausted as I was, I was happy to see him settling in.

"I guess with this straightened out, I need to go find a new place to stay in town."

Augusta nodded. "Momo said the old apartment building had running water. Might be a good place to start. But I'm not here to be your decorator. I'm going to get myself home."

Larry reached out his hand and shook Augusta's. "I appreciate your help. And you're sure that jackalope will be okay?"

"Reckon he will. Sometimes you just need to know the right words to unlock the darker parts of a creature. Not to mention a man."

"I'd be lying if I said you didn't disturb me a bit, miss. My daddy may have been an asshole, but my mom raised me right to judge people by their actions. Not just what they are."

Augusta smiled. "Actions are what make us who we are. When the mask slips, and you see what's hiding underneath, believe it."

With that, Augusta made her way out to the edge of the road. Between one step and the next, she vanished into shadow.

Larry grabbed a cot and a sleeping bag out of the back of the trailer. "You three don't need to stick around for this. I can find my own way into the apartments."

"Should you have need of me, call," Sonny said. "I'll be in Frederick's village for a time. He needs to know what has occurred here, and I'd prefer it come from me than a surprise from Momo."

Emma gave the sasquatch a hug before he left and then started over to Larry. "So, umm, we kind of left our truck at the orchard. Can we borrow yours?"

Larry's lips twitched. "Sure thing. I'll get the trailer disconnected. Then we can just grab that tub and you can help me up to my apartment. Payment for borrowing the truck."

I groaned, then followed Larry as Sonny left.

It didn't take long to get Larry settled. The place may have been dusty as hell, but it was in surprisingly good condition considering some of the buildings that had fallen down around town.

The pipes rattled for a bit when I tried the faucet in the pedestal sink, but after some sputtering, clear water flowed down the drain. Each of the four arms of the faucet was a tarnished silver with a plastic-like insert I was fairly certain was Bakelite.

I had little doubt Emma, with her love of antiques, was going to find quite a lot she liked about the apartment before we left. As if on cue, she barged into the bathroom carrying a strange pink box.

"Have you seen this place? I don't know what happened here, but it's like they left everything behind." She turned the box over in her hand to reveal the crank on the side.

"What is that?"

"I think it's an ice crusher."

I shook my hands off and dried them on my pants. "That massive thing is just to crush ice? People must've been really into their ice here."

"Didn't your parents have one of these? Or your grandparents? My parents had an electric one. Noisy as hell."

I followed her back into the kitchen where Larry had his head in the refrigerator. "I'm guessing that doesn't work?"

"It's making some noise, but it doesn't seem to be cooling anything. I can use it as an oversized cooler, but that's about it. If Himari's crazy plan works, maybe that will be good enough."

Larry liked to call anything that involved technology "crazy." Of course, looking around the old apartment that likely included many things once considered cutting edge, it wasn't so hard to think of breaching networks and firewalls and security systems crazy.

Larry closed the door to the fridge and turned around. "You two are welcome to stay here. We can't say if it's safe to go back to the orchard for your truck."

I nodded. "Himari hasn't seen any new activity on the monitors since the mercenaries freed themselves a couple hours ago. If nothing has tripped the motion sensors since then, not even cryptids, I think we'll be all right."

"Fair enough. But you keep your guns on you. We know those people are ready to murder. And I doubt a snawfus is going to save more than one of us in a day."

I grinned at Larry. It was insane to think that sentence had actually happened earlier that day. I'd feel better about returning to the orchard the sooner we got there. If Viper or DEMON was going to send more people in, the longer we waited, the more likely they were to show up.

Larry tossed me his keys and I snatched them out of the air. "You be careful with that truck. It might be old, but it has some power."

"Thanks, Larry. We'll be back as soon as we can."

Larry nodded, and we headed back down to the street where the truck waited, now detached from the trailer.

"Is this the stupidest thing we've ever done?" Emma asked.

"I doubt this is the stupidest thing we've done *today*," I muttered. "Let's go get the truck, and then I'd really like a shower."

16

Emma fidgeted with the radio. "One of us should have just taken the damn truck while we were there."

Himari's voice came to life in our headsets. "Emma? Are you feeling okay? That sounds like one of Mason's dumb ideas."

I barked out a laugh and grinned at Emma.

Emma narrowed her eyes. "I don't know what you're laughing at. I'm pretty sure that insult was far harsher on you."

I opened my mouth to say something, thought about it, and then suspected Emma may have been right.

"Think about it," Himari said. "You don't know if there were more mercenaries there. Hell, you still don't know if there are more mercenaries there. I mean, we don't see them on the camera, but maybe they're smart enough to avoid the cameras. Just because the ones you tied up finally escaped, doesn't mean they didn't come back."

"Himari, Himari!" I raised my voice as she continued to ignore me and rambled on. "You aren't talking us out of this. We have too many supplies strewn about that orchard to just leave them."

"Not to mention the camera," Emma said.

"We could probably replace the camera for less than some of those guns. Not to mention ammunition is ridiculously expensive right now."

Emma nodded. "But enough about us. How is your hack coming along?"

Himari groaned. "Don't call it a hack. It's not a hack. I'm just taking advantage of an exploit. Even DEMON's security can't keep their idiot users from clicking every link that comes through their email. Once Chuck told me who to send it to, it was just a matter of waiting."

"So how is your exploit going?" Emma asked.

"It's not a ... never mind. I'm adjusting priority now."

I exchanged a smile with Emma. "That's great, Himari. We're almost back to the orchard."

It wasn't long before the swinging bridges came into view. It was usually stressful crossing the old things, but I was far more preoccupied with what had happened earlier at the moment. We'd been attacked before, threatened at gunpoint, and I'd even seen my friends injured in the past. Today, though, today we'd lost Old Willie and almost Larry and I had no idea what kind of fallout there was going to be from Momo's actions against those mercenaries.

We bounced off the road and into the woods to take the path down by the river and back up the hill to the orchard's entrance. The mercenaries' transport was gone. I was half expecting all the supplies they'd thrown out of our truck to be gone too, but they were still there, haphazardly strewn across the ground.

I left Larry's truck running while Emma and I hopped out. "Let's just get everything we can back in the truck and get the hell out of here."

Emma nodded and gathered up the boxes and supplies that hadn't been ruined in the mud. There wasn't a point in taking some of the bandages and darts that were now covered in filth.

I opened the false floor in the rear of the truck, surprised to see all of our ammunition still intact.

Emma stacked up a crate next to me and peered inside. "They

didn't find it? Hell, that's some luck." She held out a mangled piece of metal. "Unfortunately, we're going to need a new camera."

I frowned at the wreckage. "What in the hell happened to that?"

"I'm pretty sure Old Willie stepped on it."

A small laugh escaped my lips as I closed the compartment in the back of the truck. "Let's get the rest in here and hit the road. You want to drive this or Larry's truck?"

"Oh, I'm driving Larry's truck. It's a rare chance to get to drive an old beast like that."

"Mason," Himari hissed. "I'm picking something up on the motion sensors. Seeing an alarm at Larry's. Get out of there."

I nodded to Emma and tossed her the keys. I silently crossed my fingers as I climbed into the truck and turned it over. The old Bronco roared to life as Emma turned Larry's truck around and led the way out of the orchard.

"Anything on the cameras?" I asked Himari.

"Nothing..." She trailed off. "Wait, oh, I think it might've just been a group of zigmals."

I'd feel better if that's all it was. But I wasn't sure if Larry's gear was actually sensitive enough to pick up something as small as a squirrel. A knot of tension untied itself in my gut as we bounced back onto the asphalt highway and headed back toward Momo's town.

We were only about thirty minutes away from getting Larry's truck back to him when Himari's voice came back over the speakers in the Bronco. "Chuck's calling. Let me patch him in."

"Let's hope it's good news," Emma muttered. It was odd to hear her voice coming over the speakers with Himari's as I followed her on the highway.

The line clicked twice as the calls joined.

"Chuck, I've got Mason and Emma on the line too."

"You aren't going to believe this," Chuck said. "I think this might actually work. I was on a conference call today and heard one of my supervisors getting their ass chewed out for leaving a priority one project in limbo."

"Seriously?" I asked. "Already?"

"Already for us," Chuck said. "But whoever audited their system, all they saw was a project that's been sitting there for six months that should've been completed six weeks ago."

Himari laughed. "That's what happens when you add the right paper trail in."

"Paper trail?" I asked.

"It's all digital now," Himari said. "And this part of the process is obviously not a priority. They don't even have an audit trail enabled. Once I figured out how they were mapping the tables in their database, it was easy enough to link the GUIDs together. All I had to do was copy and paste a few signatures, and we were all set."

"Uh, yeah," Chuck said. "That's exactly what I was thinking."

"That's great and all," Emma said. "But what does that mean?"

"That I can tell you. The new middle-management guy over at DEMON is in deep shit. Now I'm not saying whoever installed him won't be able to bail him out, but there are a lot of people very pissed off at him."

"And the orchard?"

"The rezoning has already been approved. It's a wampus sanctuary and Larry is eligible to apply for a cryptid veterinarian license through the CCD. Once he has that, he can keep whatever cryptid he wants in that orchard."

I blew out a breath and sank into the driver's seat. I could see Emma through the rear window of the large truck in front of me pump her fist. I knew exactly how she felt, as I'd been worried about what in the hell was going to happen with Larry after this.

"It's not all great," Chuck said. "There's still some bickering about what they're going to do with Momo. They keep talking about how he killed more people, and for some reason the word mercenary hasn't come up yet. I'm keeping my mouth shut for now, but Himari is helping me gather evidence."

Emma scoffed. "Evidence? What more do you need than the armor and weapons left behind? Or the surveillance video from Larry's orchard?"

But I remembered the armor, and how it had decayed under the touch of the snawfus, and how their weapons had crumbled to rust. It would be a hard argument to make, but perhaps there was still hope with the security video.

"Himari? Do you have Larry's feed backed up? It sounds like we may need those videos."

I could hear the keyboard clacking on the other end of the line. The mechanical beast Himari liked to type on wasn't the quietest thing. "I kept the recording from when you were there. I'll download what I can from the rest. I'm not sure if Larry actually has the storage online or not."

"As long as Viper didn't get their hands on it we should be okay," Emma said.

"We had them tied up in the kitchen right next to the monitors," I said. "I hope that didn't backfire."

Emma turned off the highway as we headed back to the abandoned town. "I didn't see anything that looked like a DVR or a cable box in there."

"A what?" Himari asked.

"Before your time. Before your darn fangled streaming services."

"Okay, grandpa," Himari said, and I didn't miss the laugh from Emma and Chuck.

"Guys," Chuck said. "I hate to run, but my break is about over. I'll contact you and Larry as soon as everything is finalized. The rezoning approvals have to go through a couple levels of bureaucracy, so even though it's basically done, I think avoiding the area for now is best."

"I'll let Larry know," I said. "Thanks for your help on this, Chuck. Truly."

We said our goodbyes and disconnected as the outskirts of the forest around the abandoned town came into view.

We both parked by the garage. Emma was careful to line the truck back up with the trailer so it would be easy for Larry to reattach it when he needed to. Pinky and Brain came sulking out of the garage to greet us with tempered enthusiasm.

Brain munched on a peach, and I wondered where she'd gotten it. Maybe one of those crates had more than Larry's supplies in them. But before I could ponder that for long, Dolly appeared at the end of the street, dragging along a branch filled with peaches.

The gowrows lost interest in snout pats and scratches as soon as the other gowrow appeared. They hurtled down the street after their elder.

Emma smiled as she watched them go. "I guess they found some food."

"Good. Maybe they'll get to go home to the orchard soon, but I won't be surprised if it takes a couple weeks for everything to go through. And I don't think Larry is going to want to push it until Chuck tells us the rezoning has been approved at all levels."

"I know," Emma said. "It would probably be good for us to keep our noses out of things for a little bit too."

I nodded in agreement as we made our way down a block and over to the old apartment complex. Larry's front door was two buildings down from where the young jimplicute skeleton had been buried.

Emma took the lead as we started up the stairs. She knocked on his front door a few times before I heard footsteps behind it. I was a little surprised when Larry opened the door to reveal a rather large wampus curled up on an old red couch. He glanced back at the big cat when he saw me staring.

"I went back down to the garage for a bit and Legs wouldn't stop following me. Thought he was going to claw through the door if I didn't open it." He gestured down to deep gouges in the wood.

"That's so adorable," Himari whispered over my headset. "Take a picture, Mason. Never mind, I'll take a screenshot."

I rubbed at my temples and followed Larry inside.

"We have some good news," Emma said.

Larry took a seat on the couch next to Legs and scratched the wampus behind the ears. "Oh?"

"It looks like Chuck and Himari pulled it off. But don't get too excited. It's going to take a little bit of time to be finalized, so you'll probably be stuck here for at least a couple weeks."

"Maybe longer, really," I said. "I don't think Chuck knows how long it's going to take to go through."

"So they canceled the zoning?"

"Not exactly." Emma shook her head. "Basically it's being rezoned into a wampus sanctuary."

"So it's not in sasquatch territory still?"

I shrugged. "It doesn't look like it. But the CCD is going to issue you a veterinary license for cryptids. Once you have that, you can bring whatever cryptid you want back into the orchard."

Larry pondered that for a moment before a wide smile tugged at the edges of his lips. He patted the wampus on the back and the big cat's purr shook the floorboards.

"Guess I'm never getting rid of Legs now." Larry let out a sigh, and I knew exactly how he felt.

E mma and I left shortly after, deciding to head to a fairly nearby hotel for a hot shower and some food. We always traveled with extra clothes, never knowing exactly how long we'd be gone, or how much muck we'd get into. And today had been full of muck.

I let Emma shower first once we were checked in. I had a phone call to make, and I didn't particularly want her to hear it. Sometimes it was easier to gamble when your friends weren't watching.

I sat at the foot of the bed while the phone rang. It wasn't long before Father Noah picked up. All he said was, "Hello?"

"Noah. It's Mason. I wanted to keep you informed on what happened today."

"Is this about the rezoning everyone is talking about with Larry's orchard?"

I kept my temper in check. "Which rezoning would you be referring to? Would it be the one where you sold Larry out to a group of mercenaries?"

Noah spluttered. I'd known the man long enough now that his tells were obvious. I already knew his denials before he said them, because his blatant lies were something to behold.

"You almost got us killed today."

"What are you talking about, Mason? I've shared information with our allies, as dictated with the agreements that we have in place with these organizations."

"I say this with the utmost respect. Cut the shit. Either you knew what was going on and you sold us out, sold Larry out, and put some of the rarest animals on this planet in harm's way, or you're just a fucking idiot."

"Mason –"

"No, Noah, I've had about enough. I think it's time we change the rules. I think it's time we do what I should've done in the first place. I'm starting my own agency as a consultant. You need me, you hire me. And you pay for it."

Noah didn't respond for a time. It was a gamble, and one I

should've discussed with Emma, but I wanted her to have deniability. This was the only way I could look out for the cryptids, while still getting intel from the Church and keeping that network alive.

"Traditionally we do not do this type of thing."

"We're a long fucking way from tradition. I don't know what's going on at DEMON, and I don't know why you keep feeding them information, but something is wrong inside that organization. And I'm afraid of what's going to happen when it all breaks open."

Noah took a deep breath. "They sent mercenaries to the orchard?"

"Yeah, that's who shot Larry." I bit my tongue before I said more. Noah didn't need to know about the snawfus. No one did.

"What!" Noah mumbled something under his breath I could've sworn was a curse. It would've been out of character for the man, but I suppose finding out that your inability to keep your mouth shut had gotten an ally shot could do that.

"He survived. He's in hiding for now. But I am done, Noah."

Something rattled in the background and I heard paper shuffling before Noah came back on the line. "I don't know if they'll go for that, Mason. But I don't know anyone better than you with cryptids. Except maybe Larry."

"You kind of burned that bridge today."

Noah blew out a breath, and I could hear the frustration in his voice. "I didn't send mercenaries to Larry's orchard. You've always been paranoid, Mason, but this is beyond the pale."

"You aren't going to change my mind. Hire me on as a consultant, Emma too, or we are both out."

"Give me a day to think on it."

"No."

The door to the bathroom opened and I saw Emma gesture to me as if asking what the hell I was doing. I don't know how much she'd heard, but it was too late to stop now.

"I have an open invite to visit Momo, Noah. Is that a connection you want to give up? Another bridge you want to burn like you did with Larry?"

"For God's sake, Mason. You were supposed to be hunting that thing. Now you're telling me you have an invite to its home?" I didn't respond. I waited for the silence to break Noah, because I could wait all evening.

Finally he did curse, spat the words out. "Fine, Mason. I'll take you and Emma on as consultants. We'll have to work out an expense plan, as I'm not buying you a new car every time you drive one off a cliff. Shit, Mason."

He didn't say anything else as the line went dead. I let a small smile crawl across my lips as Emma sat down on the other side of the bed.

"What the hell was that?"

"I may have convinced Noah to take us on as his consultants."

"How in the world did you do that?" She hesitated. "You told him about the mercenaries. You called him out? Mason, are you insane? If he was in on that they could send someone here."

"I don't think they want us. They just want our information, and now they can still have it. But we'll have more freedom to do the research we need to do, and the freedom to hide from them what we don't want them to know."

Emma tilted her head to the side. "We kind of do that anyway."

I shook my head. "We lean on too many people inside their network. Think about it. What could we learn from someone like Augusta? We wouldn't have to get the Church's approval, and I seriously doubt we'd be able to, if they knew we were consulting with a witch."

Emma snorted a laugh. "And you just came up with this all on your own?"

"No. I got the idea from you. And for the record, I think it's a brilliant one."

Emma narrowed her eyes. "I don't remember telling you to do this. While I appreciate you giving me credit, which is an unusual event in itself, I really don't remember that."

"Maybe you didn't say it in those exact words, but are you telling me you haven't wanted to be a consultant a little on the outside of the rules?"

Emma paused, and a slow smile lifted the corners of her mouth.

THE END

DID YOU LOVE THIS?

If you loved this, then sign up for the author's newsletter and get access to free ebooks and exclusive stories.

Go here to get started: www.ericrasher.com

ACKNOWLEDGEMENTS

ABOUT THE AUTHOR

Eric is a former bookseller, cellist, and comic seller currently living in Saint Louis, Missouri. A lifelong enthusiast of books, music, toys, and games, he discovered a love for the written word after being dragged to the library by his parents at a young age. When he is not writing, you can usually find him reading, gaming, or buried beneath a small avalanche of Transformers. For more about Eric, see: www.eri-crasher.com

Enjoy this book? You can make a big difference.

Reviews are the most powerful tools we have when it comes to getting attention for our books. We don't have a huge marketing budget like some New York publishers, but ee have something even better.

A committed and loyal bunch of readers.

Honest reviews help bring my books to the attention of other readers.

If you've enjoyed this book, I would be very grateful if you could take a minute to leave a review. It can be as short as you like.

ALSO BY ERIC R. ASHER

The Steamborn Series:

Steamborn

Steamforged

Steamsworn

The Vesik Series:

(Recommended for Ages 17+)

Days Gone Bad

Wolves and the River of Stone

Winter's Demon

This Broken World

Destroyer Rising

Rattle the Bones

Witch Queen's War

Forgotten Ghosts

The Book of the Ghost

The Book of the Claw

The Book of the Sea

The Book of the Staff

The Book of the Rune

The Book of the Sails

The Book of the Wing

The Book of the Blade

The Book of the Fang

The Book of the Reaper

STAY IN TOUCH!

If you enjoyed this book, please leave a review on Amazon, Goodreads, or wherever you like.

If you'd like to hear more about or from the author, please join my mailing list at https://www.subscribepage.com/g8d0a9.

You can get some free short stories just for signing up, and whenever a book gets 50 reviews, the author gets a unicorn. I need another unicorn. The ones I have are getting lonely. So please leave a review and get me another unicorn!

FRIENDS OF FALSTAFF

Thank You to All our Falstaff Books Patrons, who get extra digital content each month! To be featured here and see what other great rewards we offer, go to www.patreon.com/falstaffbooks.

PATRONS

Dino Hicks
John Hooks
John Kilgallon
Larissa Lichty
Travis & Casey Schilling
Staci-Leigh Santore
Sheryl R. Hayes
Scott Norris
Samuel Montgomery-Blinn
Junkle

Made in the USA
Monee, IL
31 March 2021